GEORGE THA

Suspense

Independent Publishing Network

North Shore City

NZ

Published by Independent Publishing Network

2017

1

ISBN 978-1-78808-786-5

This book is an imprint of

Independent Publishing Network

for

Doug Harper

Bill Parkinson

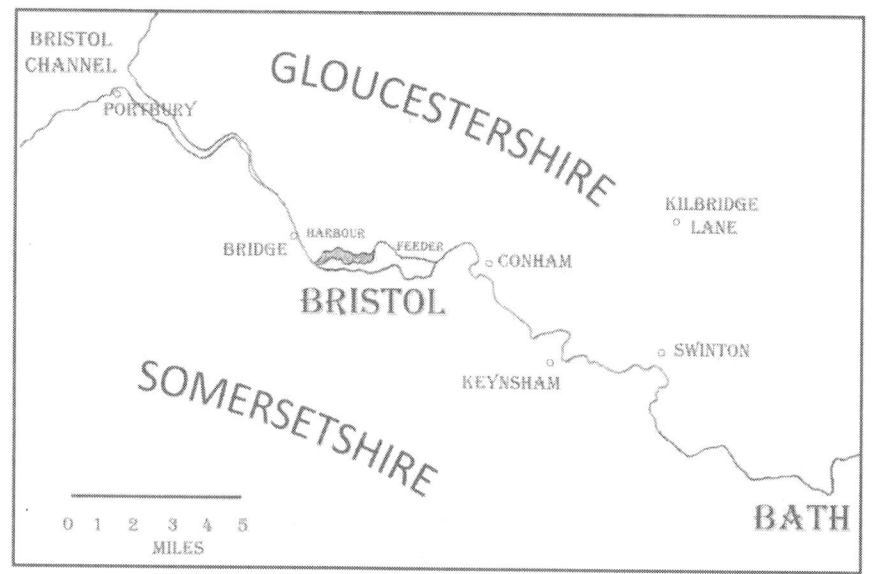

Chapter 1

Moonlight breaks fleetingly through a crack in the clouds.

Its feeble radiance falls on a flagging horseman. Wretched, alone, making heavy weather of the desolate highway. An exhausted messenger coaxing an aching body, sat in the stirrups since dawn. But for the bounty, due if he reaches his destination before daybreak, the fellow would eagerly call it a day. Relentless thirst, gnawing within him for miles. His craving for water suddenly desperate. A pewter flask dangles at his knee, drained dry an hour ago.

Until now darkness has forced him to stare, mesmerised, at the stony surface ahead of his stallion's hooves. One piece of luck there, thank the Lord. The road's been metalled, and recently. But the thoroughfare's still fearsome narrow, wide enough only for the mail coach, not a jot more.

With the moon's appearance he lifts his head. Hell, what a godforsaken wilderness he's stumbled upon. Casting around he sees nothing but barren, deserted moorland. Derelict drystone walls, ugly buckthorn hedges, boundless muddy fields stretching away endlessly on either side. Not a house or farmstead in sight. No light to be spied, in any direction. Just solitary oaks and copses of birch disturbing the monotony of a truly depressing landscape.

A shiver courses the length of his body. God knows the fellow's strong and determined and certainly not short on courage. He's travelled through more forbidding terrain than this in his time. But this awful thirst and not having stopped for victuals since late afternoon; these two preoccupations now test his endurance beyond measure. The crippling cold, creeping slowly but surely into in every limb, simply deepens his discomfort.

And the mercury's still falling. A heavy frost already rims the edges of tall blades of grass bordering the highway. Biting winds, the self-same gusts that stirred those heavy clouds, now slice through every miniscule gap in his clothing. This damnable ride, thank God, will soon be over. A couple more miles and he'll be warming before a blazing fire, making short work of a hearty meal.

Encouraged by this tantalising prospect, he spurs his grey to a canter. But with caution. He daren't risk a stumble now; that could still spell disaster. Nevertheless, the moonlight inspires a shred of confidence. Just so long as it's fickle presence persists. He offers up a silent prayer. I'm almost there Lord. See me safe to my destination.

Was it only this morning he set out from Newport, astride a strong fresh horse? God damn, it seems a lifetime ago. Riding hard to New Passage; rain lashing horizontally, stinging his eyes more ferociously with every mile. Then that infernal delay; four hours at least. Trouble with a boiler on the new steam ferry. At last the short Severn crossing. But hellish, due to the constant heavy swell. His horse bucking, kicking, frothing at the mouth with terror. Himself, heaving up over the rail, sick as a dog.

Dry land at last, back on the road. The mare, still frightened, still skittish. Bolting at Gloucester, crooking its knee in the process. More lost time coaxing the lame animal to an inn that would fix him a fresh mount. Bolting down a hasty meal and figuring the damage. With luck and determination he could still make it.

Since that break, nothing but riding, riding, riding. It's no surprise he craves comfort and rest. Red welts cover the inside of both thighs; fingers blistered to the tips, despite a fine pair of gloves. Even so, he's been making the greatest speed accordant with staying in the saddle.

Suddenly the horse puts a foot wrong. The lurch jerks its rider out of his daydream. Shit! What an idiot! Sickening realization flashes before him. Almost fallen asleep in the saddle. Adrenalin courses like quicksilver through his veins. Fright, the ache in his gut, frost laden air pricking his face; all now conspire to restore his concentration. Gritting his teeth he focuses ever more intently on the road ahead. The howling gusts persist, clouds scudding faster. The very light he relies upon waxes and wanes with capricious speed. In the distance an almost indiscernible movement registers subconsciously in the depths of his jaded senses.

Seconds later, with no chance to figure what he really glimpsed, the situation becomes shockingly apparent. His blood runs cold. That flickering movement was moonlight reflected from a vibrating rope. Stretched taut, between trees on either side of the turnpike. He's practically upon it. No chance to halt, no room to turn.

Instinct takes over. Hauling desperately on the reins, he checks his stallion's pace. But he can't avoid an impact, it's simply too late. The rope is stretched at shoulder height. In a heartbeat he figures his options. Taking a deep breath, he deliberately stands tall in the stirrups.

Decapitation was intended, there can't be a shadow of doubt. Through his courage that fate, at least, has been avoided. However, the rope arrests him cruelly, stretching and burning across arms and chest. His steed's progress continues unchecked. For a second the fellow is suspended; then falls, like a sack of potatoes, onto the rough stone highway. Pain sears through his body from nerves in every limb. What injuries he's suffered are beyond his power to reason. For now he simply lies there motionless, dazed, fighting for breath.

Two shadowy figures emerge stealthily from the hedgerows on opposite sides of the roadway. Converging on the prone figure, intent on highway robbery. Luckily his quick thinking in the saddle has robbed them of the advantage they'd counted upon. Head still reeling, the horseman drags himself to one knee. Unaware of the approaching assailants but intuitively anticipating the attack. On instinct he pulls a percussion pistol from his belt. By the time he's cocked the hammer, one villain's already upon him. With no trace of compunction, the scoundrel fells his injured victim for a second time, with a rough wooden cudgel.

Snatching the firearm from unresisting fingers, the two attackers fall on his slumped body, rummaging skilfully through his pockets for valuables. Their search yields little and they bandy wicked oaths of disgust. As he stands to leave, the shorter one wrenches free a shoulder bag that's been concealed by the traveller's limp form. He runs forward to catch the riderless horse whilst his companion retrieves their rope. Barely two minutes have elapsed since the ambush was sprung but the deed is now complete. Within seconds the pair have vanished into a copse beside the road.

Hours pass. Dawn breaks. The first travellers of the day are abroad, elsewhere along the road. Birds chirrup in the trees as if nothing untoward has taken place. The inert figure on the highway stirs as consciousness begins its halting return. Befuddled, the man tries desperately to understand. Where the hell is he? How has he come to be here? Why, O God, is his head throbbing like this? No immediate answers appear. But then slowly, one by one, the events of the previous night seep back into his mind. The rope. The fear. The fall. The excruciating pain. Within minutes a sketchy picture of the awful episode has fallen into place.

Painfully he drags himself onto one elbow. A blasphemous cry, as the agony of every movement sears through his flesh. Far in the distance, on a hilltop, the outline of a post-chaise appears. Mercifully then, rescue will arrive before too long. He glances about him, anxious to establish the consequences of his horrible adventure. There's a goodly quantity of blood, splattered all over his clothing. A long, ragged abrasion to one forearm, fragments of grit lodged deep in the rapidly congealing scab. But as far as he can tell, no broken bones. Unsurprisingly, the horse is nowhere to be seen. Likewise his shoulder-bag and pistol.

As he counts the cost, his face assumes a wry expression. Setting aside the pain and injuries, which will surely mend in time, his personal loss is slight. The plundered items were not his own, they'd all been supplied by his employer. A master whom, whilst he might well rant over the loss of a horse and pistol, will in truth lose little sleep on their account.

But the contents of the shoulder bag? The messenger was never privy to what they were. However it was the urgency of their delivery that occasioned that desperate ride through the night. The bloody bounty, damn it, well that will now be forfeit. But his master's reaction to the loss of whatever was in that satchel? That, he muses, might well be a different matter altogether.

Chapter 2

Thomas Maynard silently slips his sharp steel chisels, one by one, into a time-weathered buckskin roll. Slowly and deliberately, half-turning, he hangs up his worn leather apron. Dust bursts out, sparkling in a bright shaft of sunlight, as the garment drops noiselessly onto its hook.

It seems the mason's determined to avoid attention. Attention to the methodical preparations he's making for leaving his yard. His day started hours ago, well before dawn, head brim-full of tasks to be accomplished. Since then he's struggled fruitlessly to keep himself focussed. His preoccupied mind immediately drifting away from every job at hand. Thoughts wandering uncontrollably, agonising over the many possible outcomes of the day ahead.

The result's been inevitable. Instead of completing the jobs, he's merely chipped away listlessly at an unfinished transom atop his bench. The time to depart has come and nothing of any consequence has been accomplished.

It's mid-morning. Early January. Fresh, bright and chilly. The kind of day to fool you that winter's over. A piercing sun, low in the clear blue sky, hangs over the facing bank of the Avon. Taking a final glance across rolling green pastures, stretching into the distance, Maynard has to screw his eyes up against its glare. This placid stretch of river, flowing past his stone-yard, usually bristles with barges and other small vessels. But for now it's deserted, as is the tow-path skirting the wall bounding his premises. Not a living creature in sight, bar a flock of sheep grazing the pasture opposite his makeshift landing stage. All is sublime, relaxed, at peace. In stark contrast to the mason, stomach knotted with apprehension concerning the ordeal ahead.

But there is no way out. He's committed to that appointment in Bristol. He'll not risk turning up late and so, within a quarter hour, he must be away from here. As he contemplates the ride and the weather he wonders if he can be back before daylight fades.

His gaze falls on his three fellow masons. Each at his own bench, bent to his particular task. Confident none are paying attention, Maynard slips through the back door of the workshop. By the time they realize he's left, he will be well on the road. He has no inclination to advertise the reasons for his absence. Ironically he trusts all three of them implicitly, even the improver. But slipping quietly away will avoid questions. Thus avoiding the need for answers and any loose talk that might easily ensue.

The secrecy he's striving so desperately to achieve is, more than likely, unnecessary. Deep down Maynard knows it, but that doesn't change a thing. He's naturally cautious. He can't help it. And there's a real conviction in his bones about today. It could change the course of his life. So it's vital that nothing be permitted to jeopardise the outcome. A word or two in the wrong company might jinx everything.

And so he passes noiselessly through the wicker gate, tapping mallets and ringing chisels echoing ever fainter in his ears as he strides purposefully away.

Soon the cluster of buildings that comprise Maynard's yard are well behind him. He climbs the gently sloping pasture to the farmhouse, heart of his father's modest smallholding. A movement draws his eye to a dray, over on the far side of the dwelling. He instantly recognises the weather-beaten cart and the restless colt between its shafts. And there indeed is John Carey, who must have turned up much earlier, to clear out the privy pit.

Instinctively the mason bellows out a greeting. He and John have been comrades since they were lads. Since then their stations in life have drifted apart, but the age-old friendship obstinately survives. Now and again they'll meet up at the Boar and put the world to rights over a jar of ale. But just now John

7

is wielding a filthy, brimming shovel. The thought of the stench he'll be stirring up deters Maynard from rushing to join him. However, on hearing his name, the gong farmer thrusts his spade deep into the reeking pile and strides purposefully in the mason's direction.

Determination is written on his face. Leaving Maynard in no doubt his friend has something he's anxious to chew over. It's been this way since they were boys. Once an idea's lodged in the man's mind, he won't rest 'til he's shared it with some poor body. The wisest course of action, Maynard figured years ago, is simply to hear the fellow out.

'Marnin' Thomas', grunts John, his expression uncommonly serious, 'Raw morning ain't it? I'm fair chilled to me bones. And you, my fine friend? Thriving, are ya?'

Maynard draws breath to reply, but never gets the chance. John has already launched into the tirade of which he's plainly desperate to unburden himself.

'Well, what about the events on the highway last night? You must have heard about the gory attack? The traveller? Why, it can't be a mile from this very spot the dastardly outrage was perpetrated.'

Maynard shakes his head, well confused. He's seen no-one but family since supper yesterday, save his three masons as they turned in for work. But not one has breathed a word about any trouble in the neighbourhood.

That said, he's not the least surprised his friend's already familiar with the latest nuggets of news. For as long as he can remember the fellow's been blessed with an unrivalled nose for rooting out information. Occasionally his accounts turn out to be mere scuttlebutt. But more often they're close enough to the truth. Maynard ruefully admits to himself, on a walk home from the Boar, that he comes back immeasurably better informed than when he arrived. If it weren't for John the self-absorbed mason would be ignorant of scandals that happen, from time to time, in the village.

It should be the other way about. Maynard's education is unquestionably superior to Carey's. If either read newspapers, it should by rights be the mason. But all his time and effort, every minute, every ounce of energy, are totally consumed by his precious business. Riding into Bitton for pamphlets is a pointless luxury, one he'd certainly never countenance.

'No John, that's news to me friend. I've heard not a whisper. But you're our first visitor this morning so maybe that's to be expected. You sound proper rattled though, not like you at all. Whatever is this atrocity you're so hot and bothered about? What's happened?'

'Got it from that Ercott fellow, down at the wheelwrights, Tom. Turns out yet another robbery's happened, on the Bath Road' replies Carey. 'A great deal more violent than any of recent. Solitary messenger, that's what they're saying. God knows why, the silly fool must have been making his way in the dark. Whatever, he was set upon; sometime in the small hours. Goes without saying he lost his horse. Took a cruel beating into the bargain, apparently. They reckon he's lucky to be still of this world.'

'Damn it to hell John', replies Maynard, frustration rising in his voice. 'I'd counted on these attacks coming to an end. Why, it must be four months since the last one. With the new stage runs more frequent I figured those ruffians would shun the highway, for fear of discovery. But it's getting worse. And it seems there've been other nefarious going-ons round here recently. The lads tell me about pilfering, from houses on the outskirts of the village. Felony's becoming run of the mill around these parts, yet again.'

Long ago the two realised their neighbourhood is as lawless a shire as can be found in the land. Every sort of wrongdoing prevails; be it highway robbery, burglary, rustling livestock or simply wanton violence. Crimes like this have been

9

commonplace for years in the rolling countryside between Bristol and Bath. An attack on a traveller is a misfortune that could befall anyone; indeed that's the principal reason Maynard's so eager to get back from Bristol before dusk falls. The constant flow of folk between the two cities, a dozen wealthy estates within half an hour's ride, the easy pickings afforded by this sparsely populated stretch of countryside; all make this area a favourite stamping ground for thieves and vagabonds alike.

There's no discernible pattern to the litany of crime. For generations its severity has waxed and waned. Occasionally some local constable redoubles his optimistic efforts to bring it to an end. But that never has any lasting effect. It's become obvious, lately, that hardened criminals are now working the border between Somersetshire and Gloucestershire. But this situation should be of no surprise to either the constables or the local inhabitants. After all, in 1831, what county in England is free of such afflictions?

A stranger would figure the felonies to be random acts, simply crimes of opportunity or convenience. Leaping to this conclusion would be rash. The locals round here know better, or certainly think they do. They harbour a well-founded suspicion at least. Which is that all this trouble is down to just one group of lawless ruffians. Known hereabouts as the Kilbridge Lane Gang. A fanciful name that's stuck, over the years. Because the villains are said to gather in a village of that name, up in the hills, some three miles north of Swinton.

There is no other law out here, aside from the village constables. The authority of each being limited to his own parish. Co-operation between them is unheard of. Most are retired soldiers, well past the age for adventure. They consider their occupation more a pension than a mission. Currently not a man jack amongst them is inspired to tackle this problem with any vigour. No, they turn a blind eye, persecuting instead the drunks and vagrants who wander aimlessly through their bailiwicks.

But there's another facet to the activities of this ruthless gang, more insidious than mere robbery and rustling. One that's left a deep mark on the mason himself.

As a youngster he'd heard rumours of a practice that sprang up around ten years previously. Initially the targets had been wealthy landowners and farmers. A few animals would turn up dead in the fields, throats savagely slit. The identity of the perpetrators ever remained a mystery. Days later the unlucky landowner would receive an anonymous message. Informing him of nameless men, happy to keep an eye on his stock. Preventing such unnecessary accidents ever occurring again. For a reasonable and regular fee, naturally.

From time to time the ransoms required collection. The extortionists then running a real risk of being caught in a trap. But a solution soon emerged, taking advantage of the regular Brislington and Lansdown livestock fairs. With hundreds of people milling around, it was child's play for a body to vanish into the crowd. To distance themselves yet further from their villainy the extortionists enlisted anonymous intermediaries. Gormless, unwitting farm lads, employed simply to collect the cash. For a few pennies the real crooks ensured that if anyone was apprehended, it wouldn't be them.

The task of intimidation was not, of course, entrusted to hayseeds. Every mark received a regular reminder of the consequences of failing to furnish his instalment. In the weeks leading up to a fair, strangers, on one pretext or another, would turn up at a victim's property. There they'd spit out thinly veiled ultimatums, face to face. On no account must the payment be missed. Soon after the scoundrels would mysteriously disappear; melting into the countryside. Count on it, the same face would never turn up a second time.

Naturally some victims shared their information. Suspicion grew about the identity of the ringleaders. But solid evidence simply couldn't be found. And people knew, deep down, that the repercussions of botched accusations would be shocking and bloody. For all these reasons the same despicable chantage carries on to this very day. Continuing with impunity, no effort being made to track down the perpetrators.

Maynard grew up vaguely conscious of this extortion. However, it was nothing to concern him. It beleaguered rich landowners, not his parents and their modest farm. But the memory of a Sunday morning with his dad, years ago, still stirs up a sickening, hollow sensation in the pit of his stomach.

Of course, it's easy to see now, how naïve he'd been. The signs were always there. Scruffy looking misfits appearing unannounced in the yard. His dad muttering with them in some quiet corner. And their animals. They didn't have many, but wasn't it odd that so few went missing over the years? Neighbouring farms strangely didn't share their luck.

The worst thing had been finding the courage to confront his dad. Complicated because he'd just left home when it all fell into place. Now working in Bath, the only opportunities were during Sunday visits home. These he tried to make as often as he could, but it was a prodigious walk, even for a strong young fellow like himself.

Eventually the chance came around. He'd no intention of scaring his mother; he had to get the old man alone. A credible pretext was needed. So he suggested a barn roof might be leaking and they strolled off together to investigate. Once there, the time had come.

His mouth was dry as dust, heart pounding beneath his ribs. Was he right, or simply foolish? He had to know.

'Dad', he'd blurted, words colliding as they tumbled from his lips, 'There's something I must know, however impertinent it seems. I'm scared you're being blackmailed. That the odd balls I've seen around here are screwing money from you. Please tell me I've got it wrong.'

For an age, Edmund had said nothing. Expressionless. But it seemed some awful struggle was going on within as he wrestled with a response. At last he'd broken the painful silence.

'Damn. I prayed I'd keep this from you Thomas. But I should have known better. You're too smart not to spot what's going on under your own nose. Sadly son, it's true. Everything you fear has been going on for years. God, if only I'd had the courage to defy them, like a man. But I'm stuck out here, alone. So remote Thomas, there's none I can turn to. I've stout friends in the village, but they can't help me beat something like this. In plain terms lad I've been scared; scared of what might happen to the animals, scared what might happen to me – and you lad. I've never had the bottle to fight back.'

'But, for Christ's sake, you must have some notion of who these bastards are?'

'Not an earthly son. They're too clever for that. Every so often one turns up at the farm to intimidate me. Always a different character, faces I've never seen before. Can't tell when to expect the bastards, none hails from around here. But their part is simply to put the fear of God in me. The reckoning's at Lansdown, every quarter-day. Even then I only glimpse the urchins who snatch the coins from my hand. Two shillings and sixpence, every time. Extortion, but it's a burden I've learnt to live with, if only for the peace of mind it brings.'

'In an odd way I'm glad you've found out. It's a relief to get it off my chest. And I'm truly sorry I'd not told you before son. But now I've confessed, there's a promise you must give me. Promise you'll never breathe a word of this to a living soul. For the well-being of everyone we love, this must remain a secret we both bear in silence. Tell me son, do I have your word?'

And so, Maynard's worst fears had been confirmed. Since then, for twenty years, not a whisper of it has passed between them. The secret has just laid there, like the bones of some invisible rotting fish. A confidence which neither will ever admit. But Maynard's peace of mind had been for ever turned upside down. The casual awareness of extortion became a genuine worry, an ever present foreboding, etched into his heart.

Now, with Carey still endlessly giving voice to his thoughts about robbery and lawlessness, Maynard's thoughts flash back to that momentous morning, and the certain knowledge that this relentless persecution still dogs his father.

'You're right John, the business rattles me a good deal', Maynard interrupts, 'I reckon the whole village know what scum were responsible for your robbery last night. But there's no chance of anyone speaking out. Confidentially I believe some of our neighbours are related to these villains. Like as not they'd alibi them, despite it grating with their scruples. But while the gang carry on like this, simply pulling off the occasional robbery, no great effort will be made to stop them. It'll have to get a sight worse before the authorities in Bath or Bristol drum up the courage to act.'

Maynard pauses, lost in thought, his dark brown eyes staring vacantly into middle distance. The notion that his own business might become a target for these villains has already crossed his mind. A speculation that brings no comfort. This farm's remote location is as vexing for him as it is for his dad. John's endless prattle about the gang rekindles his latent anxiety. How he would respond if the bastards leant on him? Would he have the courage to stand up to them? Is there any more resolve in his own bones than those of his dad?

But the sudden realisation that he's got to leave snaps him out of this reverie. He switches his attention back to Carey.

'John old friend, we must talk it over. I'm anxious we do. But there's a really pressing matter to take care of. I must make tracks immediately. Nevertheless, sincere thanks for turning out so promptly to dip our pit. God knows, it's been too easy to locate recently, even in the dark!'

'Don't tarry for me', replies Carey, 'Go, if you must. But let's fix an hour together soon. The Old Boar on Thursday? There's a deal to chew over. The education of our daughters, for one, at that little village school. I want to know how Emily finds it and what Mary Ann's doing to bring her on at home.'

'Surely John you've no complaints about young Miss Eleanor King? She's making a fine fist of tutoring our girls. At no expense either, which is not to be sniffed at. She's a buxom wench into the bargain, don't you think?', Maynard responds, winking mischievously at his friend. 'Thursday's fine for me friend. Provided Mary Ann doesn't hide my boots I'll be there, at the Boar, as you propose.'

With a parting wave he strides on to the farmhouse. Bursting through the kitchen door, there's Mary Ann, back to him, busy at the range. Just the sight of her, engrossed in cooking, fills him with a warm feeling of love. He realises how grateful he is for everything. Since their move here he's become extraordinarily content. And he can't deny it's due to her.

But being in the kitchen sets his conscience nagging, yet again. She's forever busy with one chore or another, with never a chance to rest. Judged on their income they should have a live-in servant by now, not just an occasional scatty village girl to help. But he hasn't got around to fixing up the necessary accommodation. That's just another job vying for his time. In his heart he knows the answer. The sooner it gets done, the better. Why oh why is there always something else more pressing?

That oversight aside, Maynard believes he acquits himself favourably as husband and breadwinner. And it's not a delusion. Working long hours at the stone-yard, through the foulest of weathers, he's beginning to eke out a tolerable income for his family. Thank the Lord, Mary Ann takes care of just about everything else. She's a fearsomely efficient mistress, keeping the farmhouse and every other part of family life, including Maynard himself, in good order. Acquaintances declare they make a fine couple. Raised with a shared capacity for hard work and a deal of good sense. What's more the love between them is deep and enduring.

15

In all other respects these two are poles apart. Thomas being a tall solid fellow, with dark eyes, strong features and a muscular frame. A well weathered face and powerful hands, calloused by a lifetime of manual work. Easy going, unless he's allowed some silly worry to gnaw away at his mind. When that happens he's preoccupied and it's impossible for anyone to get his full attention. Since boyhood he's been ambitious, always pushing himself onto greater responsibilities. These contrary sides to his character don't make comfortable bedfellows. A dilemma that Mary Ann has, after years and countless heartaches, just about learned to cope with.

In contrast, she is confident and unshakeable. Just five feet tall, a good ten inches short of her husband. But lack of height is more than compensated for by an irrepressible spirit. Bright-eyed and vivacious, a smile permanently hovering on her lips, she always looks for the best in every situation. Graceful and comely, fair hair falling in long curls between the ribbons of her cap and over her shoulders. She simply never stops. Forever embarking on some new endeavour, often several at the same time. Visitors to her kitchen swear an invisible energy exudes from her very presence.

Such is the contrast between them. Mary Ann confident, impulsive, fizzing with enthusiasm; Thomas, reserved, pensive, weighing everything carefully before making a decision. She sometimes taunts him for being lost in a world of his own, but secretly admires his good sense. The obstacles he's overcome to ensure their little family's future can't be discounted. For him, she's an anchor, giving unconditional support and encouragement; the confidante who listens to his hopes and fears. He knows his own strengths, but that doesn't shelter him from his doubts. Talking these over with Mary Ann gives him perspective.

These confidences mean she's the only person in the family with even a notion about his appointment in Bristol. So she's not surprised when he merely kisses her on the nape of her neck and then rushes to fetch riding boots, coat and gloves from the scullery. Returning, he throws himself into the nearest chair.

'How's our invalid today?', he asks her, busily lacing his boots, 'Any change?'

Emily, their seven year old daughter, has been unwell since the weekend. All Monday they'd watched her cheeks growing redder and felt her brow burning with fever. A hacking cough developed and she slept fitfully. By morning they were really concerned. Yesterday Mary Ann had campaigned earnestly to call in Doctor Barnes but Thomas wouldn't hear of it. Physics, in his view, do harm than good. He's confident he'll know when it's necessary to summon help. But, having prevailed, a sliver of doubt remains into his mind. He's anxious for reassuring news.

'She's perked up Thomas, thank the Lord. She won't quit her bed yet, but she has supped some bread and milk. There's a bit more spirit in her, so God willing she's on the mend. I'll bring her down here to the kitchen, once you're gone. With luck we might get her back into school next week.'

Contemplating the husband sitting before her, knowing what he's so desperate to achieve today, pride swells in her breast. But at the same time she's worried, as always when he leaves to make a long journey. So far what he's told her is sketchy; if he was more fulsome she might help quell his apprehensions. But these are matters of business and she understands him only too well. Until things are clearer in his head he'll keep the details to himself. And so he must confront these worries alone. Later, probably this evening, he'll tell all; only then will he look for advice. God, she thinks, if only he was less secretive, I could share his anguish more readily. But it's been this way since they met. She'll never change him, she knows that full well.

'You've not forgotten the new curate called yesterday Thomas?', she asks, a reproving note in her voice. 'He's anxious you visit him as soon as you're able. Mark you, this is the second time he's asked. Remember a week back he caught you at the church door? I was embarrassed I couldn't promise when you'll call on him.'

Inwardly, the mason groans.

The reverend Arnold Betts only recently succeeded the previous incumbent of St Wilfreds. He's made no efforts to disguise his determination to make the mason's acquaintance. The church he's inherited is beautiful but extremely old. Maintenance has been neglected for years and rainwater has found its way into the fabric. Doubtless he hopes his capable parishioner will undertake any necessary repairs at cost.

In other circumstances Thomas would welcome the opportunity to oblige. But just now there are a host of other tasks demanding for his attention. He senses, however, it will be impossible to forestall this entreaty much longer, especially with Mary Ann campaigning on the clergyman's behalf. Notwithstanding he pushes it to the back of his mind. There's no profit in fretting over problems he can't tackle immediately.

At last he's ready. He retrieves a small leather case from his writing-desk in the parlour. Buttoning the heavy coat, pulling on his riding gloves and, smiling just a little too broadly to conceal his growing apprehension, he bids a cheery farewell.

'Wish me luck my darling', he implores, kissing her warmly on the lips, 'you know the right outcome today could make a huge difference to us. Have you asked Dad to saddle Hermes for me?'

For nearly two years Maynard's small family have been living with Edmund on his thirty acre smallholding. It's been in the old man's hands for as long as Maynard can remember. He still husbands a few sheep and cattle, but the number's diminishing steadily. The lion's share of their household income is now coming from his son's masonry business. An enterprise that's thrived since the young couple moved here to set it up. Edmund's not sorry to be taking life at a slower pace; equally he's delighted to do his bit in the stone yard whenever Thomas asks.

Mary Ann yells back her goodbyes, but Maynard doesn't notice. He's already away through the door and into the farmyard. Sure enough there's Hermes, in his loose box, saddled, brushed and ready for the journey. He leads the chestnut stallion clacking noisily out onto the cobbles of the yard, alongside the worn old mounting block that doubles as a stand for Edmund's milk churns. The mason is thirty two years of age, agile and strong. From the block he swings one leg effortlessly across the horse's back and gripping the reins he sets off at a trot, up the muddy farm track to meet with the Bath Road.

Out on the highway he consults his pocket watch, anxious to reassure himself he'll not be late. It's just ten-fifteen. The destination's a full ten miles distant but he's confident of setting a respectable pace. Fortunately most of the roads he'll take are well maintained. The meeting place is close to College Green in the heart of the city, just a stone's throw from the docks. With any luck he'll arrive there just gone noon. And, providing a speedy conclusion to the business is achieved, there's every chance he'll be riding homeward again by about three o'clock. Meaning he'll be back in Swinton as darkness falls. Such, at least, is his plan.

~

'What in God's name brings you back here John Carey? Rubbing that filthy smock of yourn against my nice clean walls. Curse you husband, you've not taken your boots off neither. How often do I have to tell you, you great lummock? There's a rule - on wash days this house is strictly out of bounds. Good Lord man, you only left here an hour ago; what excuse can you have for coming back so soon?'

Betty Carey stands at the centre of her small scullery, vaporous bubbling tubs of washing surrounding her on every side. A wooden ponch in her right hand drips a steady stream of white suds onto the tiled floor. Foggy air, moist and humid, swirls around her ample frame. Steam hisses to escape from a gurgling copper, billowing into the room, bringing with it a pungent aroma of coal-tar. Outside, beyond grimy window panes, sheets and garments flap in the breeze, stretched to dry across the hedges of the tiny cottage garden.

Monday is Betty's busiest day, the toughest of the week. She's a grafter because she has no choice. The accident saw to that. A year back John was labouring on the estate. Not much of a living, but sufficient. Without warning, the horse he was leading fell into a fit. Rolled over, trapping the poor fellow's leg between its own heavy bulk and the blade of a plough share. To this day she can't forget the sight of the blood and the ripped flesh as they'd bound the wound, as best they could, before some kind workmates carried him home.

Thank God, John didn't lose his limb. But he's not been good for heavy work since then. They weren't thrown out of the cottage, which is a blessing, but the whole family's had to turn-to to make ends meet. Between them they can just keep their heads above water.

Once he could walk again, John scratched around for easier work. Odd jobs in the main. Clearing middens, repairing fences, fixing broken windows and the like. Betty started to take in washing from more well-to-do neighbours. Even the children came up with schemes to scratch a few pennies. And it's John's exclusively grimy occupations that resulted in him being banned from home on Mondays. Giving rise to Betty's furious outburst, when he suddenly appeared at the door.

'I'm sorry my love. I was stupid. As I finished up at the Maynards I realized I'd left me lunch pail in our front room. Me next job's out Lansdown way so there was nowt for it but to come back. You wouldn't have me starve would you? But now that I'm here my love, how about making us a cup of tea? Blimey, we could enjoy it together! How often do we ever get a few minutes to ourselves during the day?'

'Do you give me a choice man? No. You'll only stand there pestering, until I give way. Alright John, but get yourself out of here. Park your filthy backside on that bench in the garden, you obstinate lummock, while I brew up. But don't go near the sheets. God, I'll do anything, just to get you away from my clean scullery.'

'And if you've very lucky, I might spare you a minute, she shouts through the open door, 'Provided I can keep my distance from your disgusting clothes and that you promise to leave me in peace then. Young Susannah Creswicke from the big house will be over in half an hour to collect their sheets. She mustn't see you hanging around or I'll lose their work. You'll have to sup up real fast and get back on that dray.'

'Will you be vexed if I meet up with Thomas on Thursday Betty?' he asks on her return. 'I bumped into him when I was over there. But he was in an almighty rush. We hardly spoke. I promised we'd catch up on his news. That's alright isn't it?'

'Oh! Of course that's fine John, fine. Don't let the fact you'll be drinking away the housekeeping bother you', she replies sarcastically, but her eyes betray a genuine concern, 'Spend all evening with Thomas Maynard if you really must. That'll be simply fine with me, as I say'.

But it's not the expense that irks her. A hard life has put a wise head on her shoulders. The ongoing friendship between her husband and Thomas is starting to make her feel uncomfortable. The stark difference in their fortunes seems to be increasing by the month. And the two men's continuing closeness simply rubs it in.

It's bad enough she's had to turn to doing other people's washing. And still it feels like they're becoming steadily poorer. Meanwhile the Maynards prosper, and it's all too obvious. Thomas's new enterprise seems to go from strength to strength. Her other friends must have noticed the disparity. Like as not they're talking about it amongst themselves at the moment. It's

21

just embarrassing. How long can this silly friendship go on before it becomes a charade?

'No. Something's clearly not fine with you Betty, I can tell. You're fretting about something you've not confided to me yet. Come on lass, spit it out. What's it all about?'

'It's nothing John, honestly. It's just me. I know I'm being touchy. But is it really sensible to maintain our acquaintance with the Maynards? They're doing so famously and, let's face it, we're not. How much longer can we be worthy to call them our friends?'

'God woman! For ever and a day I'll wager. What's brought all this about girl? Has Mary Ann said something to make you feel uncomfortable? I'd never expect that of her.'

'No, not at all, she's always kindness itself. She hasn't any airs or graces and she's just as pleasant to me as ever. But her clothes put mine into the shade. When I call at the farmhouse there's always cake with caraway seeds and the like. What do we live on John? I'll tell you. Bread in the main. Cheese if we're lucky. Crannings, when times are really tough.'

'Sides, she's got a girl from the village comes in three days a week to help with the housework. It makes me feel so awkward. When she comes here I've only crumbs to offer John. And she's become, I don't know, so confident, so assured. I can't help feeling like a second-hand Sally in her company.'

'Well, all you say is certainly true my love. Thomas must be raking in a lot more money than us', replies Carey, 'Since he left his uncle to set up that business, things have taken off for him. But he's no different with me. I'll swear our friendship is solid as ever it's been for the last twenty five years. Heavens, as nippers we'd spend every day in one another's pockets. It takes more than a measly bit of money to rub away a bond like that.'

'Well, I hope you're not mistaken John Carey. In my experience money bends the strongest wills. Now, for the love of

22

God, get out of my house. I've still got more washing here than I know what to do with.'

Chapter 3

The metallic clink of von Winneburg's riding boots echo noisily down the endless marble-tiled corridor. The footwear of the uniformed flunkey, detailed to escort him, makes no sound whatsoever. Buckskin soles he guesses, chosen carefully to guarantee the servant's obsequious transparency.

To his left clear windows rise up over three times his own height. To his right ebony busts of Roman Emperors occupy niches between each pair of marble pillars they pass. Above him, for as far as he can see, hang huge candelabra covered in gold leaf, their magnificent opulence in stark contrast to the simple white walls and ceilings. Ornate tables are situated at intervals in front of the windows, decked with bowls of freshly cut roses reflected in the highly polished surfaces.

Von Winneburg is not a man to be easily impressed by wealth. Head of a noble family himself, he has two magnificent estates and other grand residences of his own. His elevated position has taught him to take his own absolute authority for granted and expect the obedience or tactful compliance of almost everyone with whom he comes into contact.

Yet here in Charlottenburg, having been unexpectedly summoned by a royal writ, Count von Winneburg's natural self-confidence wilts as quickly as feverfew plucked from the field. Once admitted he's become unsettled, intimidated by the sheer grandeur of this vast palace, and more than a little agitated about what reason might account for the urgent summons he's received.

Helga, his dear wife, is of course distantly related to Friedrich's own morganatic spouse, the Princess of Leignitz. Could that be it? But no, in over six years that's never been cause for an audience with the monarch. However, suddenly here he is, completely unprepared, within seconds of coming face to face with the Elector of Brandenburg, King of all Prussia.

The silent flunkey stops abruptly beside a pair of huge polished double doors. Silently opening one he bows discretely; indicating, with barely more than a whisper, that von Winneburg should enter.

Following him closely through the portal the servant stops again, draws himself to his full height and announces, "Your royal highness, the Count of Graudenz." Within the blink of an eye he has silently withdrawn, pulling the door to with a click as he does so.

The nervous nobleman finds himself in an enormous hall, outrageously picked out in gold, decorated as if to make the rest of the palace look quite simply ordinary. At the far end is a grand dais, seven wide steps carpeted in a deep venetian red, leading to it. Upon this stands a huge cushioned throne with golden canopy above, upholstered in the same rich red velvet, a royal coat of arms embroidered in each corner.

But the imposing throne is empty. The man entitled to occupy it sits instead at a mahogany writing desk, carefully positioned to get the best light from huge windows overlooking the park. No robes, no insignia. Just moleskin breeches, a grey silk shirt and a velvet smoking jacket. Surrounded by papers, he's scribbling intently and doesn't deign to turn his head when his guest approaches. Still writing, he speaks; in perfect French, of course.

'Winneburg, you're considered something of a diplomat here at court, so they tell me.'

'I'm honoured you should say so your majesty,' the Count rejoins, trying his hardest to match the king's effortless command of the French tongue.

'A man blessed with astute thinking and sound judgement is what I hear.'

Von Winneburg is at a loss for reply. Can the King really know anything about him at all? Why has he suddenly taken

25

an interest? Are these remarks a prelude to some subtle trap? Fortunately for him Friedrich Wilhelm, monarch of all Prussia, doesn't wait on an answer.

'So. I'm interested in your opinion man. The Deutscher Bund.'

'The Confederation majesty?'

'What's your view Winneburg? What does it mean to Prussia? How much of our treasure, how much of our effort, should we invest in making this venture a success?'

Oh God, this must be a trap. What else can it be? Why, in Heaven's name, is he asking me such questions? I know no more than the next man about all this. What, in God's name, is prudent but might also sound like be an intelligent answer?

'Well sire, in my view a single united German nation does hold certain advantages for Prussia in the future. But as it stands today the Confederation is surely little more than a talking shop. I mean to say, many distinguished and noble persons attend the Confederal Assembly in Frankfurth, but it has yet to deliver any laws that bind Prussia, or Bavaria, or indeed any of the sovereign states. Nor has it produced any resolutions that actually benefit us, to any meaningful extent. And it won't do for some years to come, as far as I can see. The powers of all sovereign princes, such as your majesty, remain supreme. Whilst that's the case, the influence of the Assembly must surely be subjugate. '

'Just what most of my advisers are telling me every day', retorts the king, 'But let me open your eyes. Your answer, and theirs, may be long on reason. But equally short on courage. In less time than you credit the Confederation will become a unifying force with real teeth. This must come to pass or our future as Germans, indeed as Prussians, will be fatally blighted. Don't forget, it's only twenty five years since we surrendered almost everything to that barbarian Napoleon at Jena. The

26

German peoples must never allow themselves to be placed in such a position of peril again.'

'That's why, Winneburg, it's crucial that the Confederation succeeds, why it must bind us all as one, to ensure the greatest advantage is gained from of our overwhelming strength. And when this happens, it must be we, the Prussians, who are at the helm. We alone possess the necessary qualities of leadership and have the undeniable right to take up the reins of this new confederation.'

'But surely the Austrian delegation presides over the assembly, doesn't it?' asks von Winnenburg, 'Weren't they handed the responsibility of leading the Bund under the treaty?'

'The treaty eh? Pah. Of course you're correct. But we can't let it remain that way. Between you and me, Austria isn't fit to shoulder that standard, nor is it capable of doing so for long. You realise Metternich practically governs the country? He's got no time whatever for a unified Germany. He's no interest in joining the Zollverein either. That will make trade with his country very difficult in the future. No, Metternich's sole interest seems to be gaining power for Ferdinand, and in that way holding on to it himself.'

'But majesty, in that case, won't he do anything to prevent Prussia taking it from him.'

'If he didn't have other problems on his plate, that might be so. But fortunately he does. The Habsburgs once more have Lombardy in their domain, but our agents tell us the Italians are preparing to take on Franz and win it back. Venetia too. If what we've heard is correct, Metternich will soon have his hands full. Especially if Napoleon comes to the aid of the Italians, which I think he must.'

'It's an irony when you come to think about it. Why it was we Prussians who freed the world from the despicable French despot. It was Blucher and his brave cavalry, at La Belle Alliance, who actually thrashed those cheesemongers. The very same battle that pompous Englishman Wellington likes to call Waterloo. Ha! He shouts to all the world about his victory, but without us it would have been a total disaster. Where were the Austrians then, eh? They were part of the Seventh Coalition, weren't they? Nowhere to be seen, that's where.'

'I trust you follow me Winneburg? Austria has no claim to rule a united Germany; but we do. We surely, surely do. We must make certain of it by all means possible. Through political skill, clever negotiation, guile and by strength of arms if necessary, we must craft the future as we intend it to turn out.'

'Quite so majesty; but how can we achieve this without starting some terrible conflict with our Austrian neighbours?'

'I don't suggest we nakedly attempt to seize control von Winneburg. Oh no. We're facing a long game and we must play it extremely carefully. We'll prevail by defending what is ours and then through taking territory at the expense of nations outside the Confederation – the French, the Russians and others. Such victories will demonstrate to the world our superiority in both force and diplomacy. In this way we'll gain the allegiance and support of the other German states in the confederation. The Deutscher Bund itself will bring an end to the Austrian leadership.'

He rises and turns to look full-face at von Winneburg for the first time. With his stern countenance, strong nose, brown eyes and wispy moustache, he could be none other than the King of Prussia. The searching eyes bore hard into those of his visitor.

'And that is why I've called you here Winneburg. We must be vigilant, we must be ready to take advantage whenever it presents itself. I'm relying upon you to help me carry out one small but vital part of my plan.'

'Majesty, any resources I command are at your immediate disposal.'

The king breaks into a derisory laugh. 'No, you misunderstand me completely Winneburg. I'm not looking for armies, still not yet for fortunes. The assistance I require will come from you, and you alone. But let me explain, as there are intricacies here of which you will know nothing.'

'Hanover, Winneburg. It's a Confederation state, is it not?'

'Indeed it is majesty.'

'Yes. Indeed it is sir. But it's the one Confederation state that's not governed solely by our German brothers. You'll know of course Winneburg, that the English King still has significant influence over that realm? That the Elector of Hanover is still the King of Great Britain.'

'Now you remind me majesty, yes, I'm aware that is the case.'

'Well, believe me, the British involvement is far from superficial. Their sway is so enshrined there's even a Hanovarian Chancery located in London. The envoy based there is responsible for keeping his British and Hanovarian masters fully briefed on political developments on both sides of the English Channel. I think we can assume that this man, who goes by the name of Ernst Friedrich Herbert incidentally, is likely to be privy to more British secrets than you or I could hope to discover in a lifetime. Now, our friend von Steinard informs me you have some sort of distant family connections with the fellow. Is that so?'

Damnation. Wrong footed. Von Winneburg's not sure at all. He vaguely recalls his grandmother's sister did marry a Baron in the Herbert line. Perhaps that's what the King's referring to. The best he can muster is a non-committed mumble.

'So, von Winneburg, I shall be relying upon you to foster an understanding with this diplomat. Build a closer relationship through letters, meetings, personal favours; whatever you judge necessary. Give him anything that will help us. Women, money, I don't want to know. Spare no expense. It's essential that you

29

become his confidant. Through him we shall eventually discover what the British are thinking, what they're planning, what they're most likely to do next. Be in no doubt, they play a critical part in my plan. They are able to negotiate with the French in a way we cannot. They've insight into parts of the world where we walk blindfold. Moreover there's talk of revolution in other corners of Europe, besides Italy. Countries where we have an interest and the English have all the intelligence.'

'At the moment, I need to understand the progress of a conference being held in London to decide the future of Belgium. The country recently declared its independence from the Dutch. Naturally we have offered to restore it to Dutch rule, which would be an easy task for us, and the French have pledged support for the Belgians. Metternich – the meddlesome fool – is so anxious to avoid confrontation that he's agreed to a conference with the British. It's been in session since November but it's likely to last a good few months yet. If we're to demonstrate our superiority whilst the Austrians fail, I must know what direction it's taking.'

'I'm sure Herbert will trust you in time. He may be an envoy, he may be a diplomat, but in the end he's still a German. You and he speak the same language, you come from a similar background, you share a family allegiance. It's now your first priority to make this man your friend.'

'But majesty, surely we have a department for foreign matters that are more specialist in this sort of work?'

'Spies you mean Winneburg? Yes, of course. But our enemies know who they are. Any intelligence they gather is likely to be disclosed to others before it ever reaches me. No, I want you precisely because nobody will suspect you might be gathering information. If you employ tact and delicacy even Herbert himself won't suspect he's revealing information of value, at least nothing that's likely to be passed back to Prussia. Your mission, Winneburg, is to make this come about gently, subtly, tactfully. Take your time. Persevere, with patience, until you have a firm understanding with the man. One that you will finally exploit to our advantage. Now I'm told you've received an invitation from the English court to attend a royal reception later in the year?'

'Why yes and I have provisionally accepted, your majesty. In fact I've just written to the palace to check there will be no objections to making the visit to Great Britain.'

'Reassure yourself, no obstacles will be placed in your way. I had a hand in ensuring that invitation was extended to yourself and Lady Helga. If you cannot find an earlier excuse to visit England, this could be the natural pretext for a personal meeting with Herbert. Make sure you arrange to visit the Chancery whilst you're there. It's located within the Palace of St James. Very convenient for your reception!'

'Thank you sire. I'm most honoured by your confidence in my abilities. I'll write to Herbert immediately.'

'You'll do no such thing von Winneburg. You must be far more careful than that. Discovery would be disastrous for me and might put your life in danger. What you'll do now is attend here at the Schloss every day for the next two weeks. I've assembled a number of trusted nobles and ministers who will give you a comprehensive briefing regarding the political situation across Europe. Some of them also have a wide range of personal contacts and they'll find a way for you to come to Herbert's attention, to all appearances by accident. Now, the footman will accompany you to my equerry and he will furnish you with more details.'

Somehow, unseen, the king must have silently summoned the flunkey for, no sooner has he spoken, than the door opens and the obsequious skin-shod fellow is there yet again.

Von Winneburg wisely and correctly assumes that the audience is at an end.

Chapter 4

Boffy's water-meadow lies between the river and Four Cross wood. It's at the farthest extent of Edmund's small estate; fine pasture during dry summer months but frequently boggy through winter. Lush grass thrives right down to the water's edge; chickweed and clover cover the gentle slope that climbs up to an isolated copse of willow. Deserted, quiet, sheltered by the wood from winds, it must have been this way for a hundred years at least.

Edmund stumbled across it the day he was handed the keys to the smallholding. Since then it's been his sanctuary. A reliable retreat when there's a need for contemplation. A refuge where he's certain to find peace, where no-one will ever disturb him.

And this morning the urge to do that filled his head when he awoke. So he'd rushed through his tasks as quickly as possible – the milking, then saddling the horse for Thomas. Finally he'd driven his few remaining cows this way, towards the meadow. Now, picking his steps with care over the soft ground he finally reaches the copse. There's a smooth flat rock just a stride within its margin. Throwing across it a hessian sack he's brought along for comfort, he settles himself down and gazes thoughtfully across the water. Stands of bull-rushes rise optimistically from the shallows, holding firm in the gentle breeze. A solitary moor hen fishes half-heartedly between the stalks, its head darting up and down below the surface. In a month or so there'll be celandines, ready to welcome the spring.

Who – ponders the old farmer, and not for the first time – who on earth was Boffy? Nobody has ever answered that question. There are men in the village nearly ninety years old and God knows he must have asked every one. Almost certainly the fellow was a previous tenant, or maybe a previous landowner. Either way a farmer just like himself, who husbanded the smallholding now in his own care. Is it really of any consequence?

To most, possibly not. But for the old man it has significance. Going right to the heart of a concern half admitted to himself, something that's been niggling him for a while. This land's been farmed for centuries, not just by him, but by countless others before. Men who've devoted every ounce of their blood and sweat to make it work. And what did they have to show for it, after all that toil? Nothing. All of them, just like Boffy, are long since forgotten.

He twists around to reach inside his coat for his pipe and pouch of baccy, wincing sharply as a searing pain catches him yet again beneath the ribs. Just another indignity to be tolerated, he reckons, for daring to grow old. And it's not the only one. Luckily, he can still put in a hard day's work, just like he did when he was half this age. But by early evening he's all in. Around nine o'clock a wave of tiredness comes upon him like mist rolling across the fields. He tries to conceal it from Mary Ann and Thomas, but it's getting steadily more difficult to deceive them.

Involuntarily this stitch, or whatever it is, forces him to draw air in sharply, between tightly clenched teeth. He holds himself tense and motionless until the pain subsides. And then, just as before, the discomfort melts slowly away.

How much longer can he continue to run this farm? After all, it imposes a routine from which there's never any escape. Whatever the weather he must be up at five for milking. Whether it's snowing or raining there are always jobs, like fixing fences, that just can't be put off. The same old things he's been doing, day in, day out, for forty years or more. He's hardly given them a thought up to now.

But how long can it go on? Five years? Maybe. Seven or eight if he's fortunate, provided these awful pains disappear. Maybe only one or two if they don't stop. Whatever, he knows in his heart that he must start to make some plans. His son's a

33

fine boy. Edmund's proud of him; what a credit he's turned out to be. But he's no farmer and never will be. He won't want to take this on. Not in addition to running his own business.

There's Hannah of course. He might talk to her. But with two young daughters to look after, and the farrier she married being forever busy, is there really any chance? Somewhere deep inside him is an unspoken prayer. A yearning that everything he's worked for over a lifetime isn't going to fritter away before his very eyes. What a relief it would be to know that someone was picking it up the traces, carrying on, making it even better for the future.

God, how long has it been now? Difficult to recall. He and Ada had got wed years before of course. Both poor as church mice, children of impoverished labourers on the estate. Their families literally scratching an existence, always short of food, living in penury. Come his own time to find work there was, of course, no choice. As the father, so the son. He too was taken on at Roundwick Hall. At fourteen years of age he'd been certain it would be his lot for ever. Labouring on the land, gaining no skills to speak of, coming home each week exhausted, hungry and with a pittance in his hand.

At eighteen he'd found a girl. Love changed everything. With Ada by his side the future took on a more optimistic hue. They had to move in with her widowed mother, naturally. All squeezed into a tiny cottage with four draughty rooms, close by the Bath Road. Every day he'd rise at five-thirty and trudge the mile to work. Every day at six he'd return by the same road. And every day he passed a dilapidated, deserted smallholding, a dwelling that seemed to have been empty for years. What would life be like if he had a place like that of his own? He couldn't help but dream.

At the time he was taken on, the master at the big house had been an irascible old devil with a shocking reputation. Edmund's own father lived in terror of the bully and often came home with tales of his cruelty. The youngster, thankfully, never came across him. The old man had been taken unwell, confined to his bed, just before the lad's first day. Within three months

34

he'd passed away and his nephew, Sir James Whitefield, arrived to take up the reins. At twenty one the new incumbent badly lacked experience. People tittered behind their hands at some of his mistakes, but the majority eventually came to respect him. In contrast to his uncle he was a fair, sensible master with a disposition that bordered on the benevolent.

Before a year was out, Ada fell pregnant. Despite the hardship, the lack of space and the scarcity of nourishing food, the pair couldn't have been happier. Her mother bustled about making preparations, borrowing and begging clothes and blankets that would be needed when the baby arrived. Eventually it came to pass. Their firstborn was a boy. A difficult delivery. A neighbour had to stand in as midwife and it left poor Ada exhausted. At first the child appeared healthy but obstinately refused to take the breast and became steadily weaker as day succeeded day. In the end they begged the priest to come to their cottage. He christened the fading infant after his father. By nightfall their precious baby was with the angels.

This had been Edmund's first experience of tragedy and it hit him like a sledgehammer. Ada cried for weeks; nothing her mother or husband said would console her. Overnight their joy had been transformed into sadness, bitterness and self-recrimination. Months passed before there was any sense of life returning to normal.

The circumstance had changed them both. For the first time they'd realized that there were emotions even more heart-wrenching than the day to day tribulations of their wretched poverty. In some ways it strengthened them. Edmund, on the day of the funeral, made a silent vow to himself. Somehow he would free them from the helplessness of being poor. He didn't know how and he didn't know when, but he was not going to rest until he found a way.

It hadn't been long before Ada was pregnant yet again. Six months of apprehension and worry followed. For Edmund it was torture. He'd done nothing to improve their lot and yet again they faced the possibility of troublesome birth. In the end his fears were groundless. The baby came easily. Again a boy, but

35

this time strong and boisterous. He suckled well and every day seemed heavier in their arms. They breathed, as one, a sigh of relief. How to name him though? Superstition seized Ada, she wouldn't countenance Edmund again. Even now that might just put a curse on the little lad. So he became Thomas, after her own late father.

Hannah arrived a year later. Her birth was a struggle and Ada contracted an infection which lingered for several months. After that there were no more children.

The responsibilities of fatherhood put new energy into Edmund, his spirit and purpose refreshed, even in his work, which was almost always numbingly mundane. The other labourers resented, to a man, the harsh conditions, the ceaseless effort and the tedium of their employment. They did what was asked of them and no more. At six o'clock they'd be away to their homes as fast as possible.

Late afternoon, on one particular winter's day, the foreman had come around asking for a man to stay on late. Without quite knowing why, Edmund put himself forward, to the silent sneers of those around him. It turned out there'd been an accident earlier on; the cowman had been injured and help was needed with the herd. When Edmund got amongst them things were already out of hand and several of the beasts were clearly distressed.

No one was more surprised than himself at what happened next. By talking quietly and soothing them he calmed each one. It seemed he possessed a natural talent for dealing with animals. From a situation that had gone badly awry, order was restored. The foreman said little, but he'd taken note. From then on, whenever an extra pair of hands was needed, it would be Edmund who was called in from the fields. During one exceptionally busy lambing he managed to revive a new-born where even the shepherd had given up hope. An unusual and disjointed apprenticeship, but Edmund was turning into a first-rate stockman.

Unknown to him, even the master had come to hear about it.

Thomas and Hannah proved to be a blessing in more ways than one. Sir James had brought in a policy of providing tied cottages, whenever possible, to those estate workers who had young families. The Maynards were among the first to benefit. In due course they took the tenancy of a terraced dwelling on the edge of the estate, neighbouring Walter Carey, a fellow Edmund often worked alongside in the fields.

But for a curious twist of fate, that might have set the pattern of their life for ever. Labouring, living on a pittance, very occasionally being allowed to work at something he found rewarding. But never managing to honour that wordless promise he'd made to himself. He'd no suspicion that anything might happen to break this mould when, out of the blue, his brother turned up.

It caused quite a stir amongst their neighbours, as Sam rode up one evening astride a handsome chestnut mare. He'd never visited their cottage before and had to ask for directions several times. The two brothers were not estranged; they simply didn't see one another from one year to the next. Edmund being too impoverished, Sam far too busy.

Sam had left home at thirteen, with nothing in his pocket, off to find his fortune. Somehow, against all odds, he had done just that. Eventually getting himself apprenticed to a mason, and later setting up on his own, discovering plenty of opportunity for a reliable craftsman in Bath. In fact so much work that he could rarely tear himself away.

'I've come with sad news Edmund', he'd said quietly, as soon as the family had ushered him into their little parlour. 'Father passed away the night before last. I was at his side to the end. He didn't suffer. But I knew I must straightway ride down to give you the news. You've not seen him for an age now but I know you loved the old man, as did I. You shouldn't hear this from anybody else.'

37

Their invalid father had moved close to Samuel after losing his wife. Sam did his level best to look after him. Edmund, by contrast, had rarely seen the old fellow since he was around eighteen years old. Nevertheless, the news touched him deeply. He bitterly regretted selfishness, failing to visit him whilst he was still alive. Yes, he'd always intended ... one day ... but somehow, like so many other things, it just never happened.

An awkward silence. Then everybody talking at once. Remembering the old man. Their childhood, adventures they'd had together. Suddenly Sam became serious once more.

'This might come as a surprise to you Edmund, it certainly did to me. I'd always thought the old man penniless. But blow me he's left a half-reasonable estate. In total, around two hundred pounds. He's bequeathed it between us.'

Ada and Edmund gasped. The thought of what a sum like this could mean – several years' wages for Edmund – left them speechless.

'Brother, I've come to a decision', Samuel continued, 'You'll gainsay me, but I beseech you not to. I've done pretty well enough for myself already. By accident or design - I'm truly not sure which – I've got no offspring, nor am I ever likely to. But for you Edmund, the picture's different. I imagine the needs of your brood are greater than you've got the means to satisfy?'

'Take the whole inheritance brother. You can consider my half a loan, if you must. But I doubt I'll ever be press you to repay me.'

This was the start of it all. He can see the moment in perfect detail, so clearly it might have been yesterday. Generosity that gave him the means to honour his promise.

In the days that followed his head was a maelstrom. Nine year old Thomas kept pestering him with questions. The boy was old enough to understand what had passed and he now idolised his uncle. Edmund tried to make sense of what he should do. The dilapidated smallholding was still vacant. His foolish dream of owning it persisted. With his newly acquired skills in husbandry he was confident he'd be able to run a small farm. But could he actually make this daydream a reality?

He screwed up his courage and approached the estate's land agent. Who unsurprisingly knew all the property's particulars. It seemed that Sir James held a lien upon the land which only he could lift. Not only would Edmund have to negotiate a good price for his intended purchase, he'd also have to persuade the same man to let him to quit his position. It seemed like an impossible task.

But Edmund's hopes were sky high and nothing could discourage him. Heavens knows how long it took him to secure a personal audience with Sir James. But when he did, he must have made his case well. He could sense that his arguments were being heard. However, it was abundantly clear he wasn't going to come out of it without an obligation.

'Maynard', Whitefield observed, during the course of this negotiation, 'Your petition's extraordinary, you must realize that. I've never come across anything like it before. I image your audacity has been encouraged by my own fair-mindedness. That said, your ambition impresses me. I'd like to help you, but there's an obstacle.'

'On the strength of your value to me as a labourer, I'd let you go. But your talents with the animals here makes you somewhat indispensable. Can't see how it can be done. '

Anger swelled in the young man's chest, tears formed in his eyes. This was so unjust. He was never paid for extra duties, yet here he was, being shackled by them. To his credit he had remained calm and suggested a resolution.

'What if I give a solemn promise always to return if you need me?', pleaded Edmund, 'Take an oath to help out if there's ever a crisis?'

'A good start lad', replied Whitefield, 'But I need more than a promise, I'll require a contract.' Edmund's face broke into a wide grin. Instinctively he put out his hand, but his employer took no offence. Instead Whitefield grasped it firmly in his own. A few days later a document had been drawn up by the estate manager, Edmund put his mark on it and the deal was struck.

Edmund shifts his bottom on the unforgiving stone. The overnight frost has done its work well and a biting chill is creeping through the thick jute sacking. Just a small adjustment makes it considerably more bearable. He knows there are tasks back at the farm, that by rights he should return. But he makes no move. He's determined to reason this conundrum through. Soon, very soon, he must have it all out with Thomas and Mary Ann. He'd like it to be crystal clear in his own head first. The pipe has long since gone out. He repacks it methodically as he continues to muse on how things have turned out.

His venture as a smallholder started out better than expected. The bequest ran to purchasing the property and a few animals besides. Whitfield never took unfair advantage of their contract. Certainly he called on Edmund once or twice, but it didn't tax him severely. Rather there was good reason to wonder if his old master wasn't secretly giving him a helping hand

Sometimes, when the weather was foul, he'd discover sacks of feed in one of the barns; sacks he knew he'd never put there himself. At harvest time two or three estate workers might turn up on some spurious mission and ended up helping him for the rest of the day. It all served to bolster his spirits, he worked hard and the smallholding prospered. In time he saved sufficient to purchase a few more animals, eventually build a small stable, a second barn and some outbuildings down by the river. Ada was happy, the children were happier still. Particularly Thomas who would rush off to spend time with his best friend John, even though they now lived a good distance away.

They'd been in their new home just three years when the lad disappeared.

One Saturday morning he failed to appear for breakfast. Hannah didn't find him in his bedroom so they assumed he gone to the Careys' without telling anybody. By lunchtime he'd not returned so Edmund grudgingly made the mile walk to bring him back. When it turned out the boy hadn't been there at all, the first shoots of concern started to appear.

On getting back to the farm the situation hadn't changed. Again he went out, looking in the barns and outbuildings, racking his brains as to hides and haunts the lads used in their play. Still no Thomas and as the afternoon wore on the whole family was becoming really worried.

Eventually they'd raised every neighbour they could find to help them in the search. People were combing ditches and woodland, others walking the bank of the river, fearful lest they might discover a body floating amongst the reeds.

By six in the evening, panic had set in. Ada was beside herself. It struck her that her eleven year old son, who they'd thought old enough to look after himself, was really just a child. And now he was gone, lost or maybe abducted, never to be seen again.

Just as they'd given up hope, a horse trotted into the yard. It was Samuel, astride his bay. And wedged between himself and the pommel was the missing lad. Ada had run out first, at the sound of hooves on flags. She was so overcome with relief that she collapsed sobbing on the ground. Edmund and Hannah appeared and soon the farmyard was a madhouse of tears and joy.

The mystery soon became clear. Ever since Sam's previous visit, Thomas had set his mind on becoming a mason. He'd no real idea of what this entailed, but his uncle had long been the boy's hero. Only one ambition filled Thomas' mind - to follow in his footsteps. The determination became so strong he eventually decided to act. Rising at the crack of dawn he set out to walk the three miles into Bath. Having no idea where Samuel's business was situated, he had to ask many times for help and directions. But eventually, through sheer persistence, he found his uncle's stone yard.

Samuel was busy and working alone that morning; his nephew's appearance threw him completely. All he could do was settle him down with a mallet, a blunt chisel and a piece of scrap limestone. All afternoon, the boy chipped away until Samuel was free to saddle up and ride him back home.

That night, for the first and only time, Edmund had taken the belt to his son. His anger was genuine, but so was his sense of relief. Above all he was confounded by a suggestion his brother had made before riding off. In a year's time, Samuel declared, he'd be prepared to take Thomas on as an apprentice. It would entail Thomas permanently living away from home, but lodgings could be provided in his own house.

Had he made the right decision? God, it gave him enough grief and uncertainty at the time. The boy was desperate for it, he'd never see another opportunity as generous as this. Once he left, of course, the chances of him eventually taking on the farm would go with him.

He and Ada had chewed it over endlessly but eventually they agreed. It would be the making of the lad. His resolve should be rewarded by the chance to make good.

And indeed he did. A year later Samuel collected his nephew and took him under his wing. The youth was a quick learner, rapidly acquiring the skills of dressing, carving and fixing stone. At seventeen he became a regular member of Samuel's team, respected by his workmates. New strengths showed through as he started to take charge of small jobs and organise the others' work.

Samuel eventually made him his overseer, discovering the lad was a competent leader who had an easy way with clients. More and more responsibility came his way. By the time he'd reached twenty one he'd built up some savings of his own and was a senior figure in Samuel's firm.

Around that time Mary Ann came into his life. One of his workmates asked him along to a picnic party in Victoria Park. And there she was. He fell for her immediately, paying her as much attention as convention permitted in the following weeks. She was a spirited, intelligent lass and worked as a seamstress, living with her parents on Bathwick Hill. It wasn't long before they were spending every minute of their free time together. Thomas had taken a small apartment in the city and saw no obstacle to asking Mary Ann's father for her hand.

The wedding had taken place a month later and, by the end of the following year, Edmund was a grandfather. Tears fill his eyes at the memory. He can recall, as if it were yesterday, being collected from Swinton and driven to Emily's christening service in Bath. Ada should have been alongside him, in the gig, but he'd had to leave her behind. Poorly for days, she'd felt too ill to make the journey. He'd known she must be in great pain, wild horses couldn't have kept her away otherwise. And he was right. A few weeks later another family church service was held. But this time he'd had to walk behind his precious wife's coffin.

Wiping his eyes he draws deeply on his pipe. What can he do now to prepare for the future? Thomas is here now, living with him. But the man's a mason, never likely to become a farmer, nor even wish to be one. It's too early to be certain how well his business will do. Can they all survive on the profits he'll turn? If not, what could be done to keep the farm going?

The old man is no nearer finding answers when he hears the clock on the parish church striking twelve.

Chapter 5

'Pipe down man, for God's sake. 'D'ye wanna get us flogged?' The hoarse whisper, coming from the neighbouring cell, is barely audible. Doggart, sitting awkwardly, with his back against the wet stone wall, can just about make it out.

'Courage me 'andsome', he retorts, his words betraying a hint of derision, 'No need to get jumpy. Just trying to pass the time. You don't usually whimper like this big man. I'd credited you with more guts."

'If yo' value your miserable life Doggart', comes back the indignant, still hushed reply, 'You'll watch that lip o' yours. Yo' might not care if they keep you another few days in this stinkin' hole, but ahm due for release on the morrow man. Half a year locked up in this cesspit is all ah can take. I canna afford for the gaolers to find me gossiping with the likes o' yow.'

The prisoner in the next cell to Doggart is nervy and exhausted. Today he's been one of a dozen forced into eight hours straight on the treadmill. Raising rancid well water used for drinking and washing within the prison. Rank and foul-tasting on account of the nearby river which leeches filthy effluent into the soil below.

'Take it easy lad. No turnkeys will be patrolling the landings tonight. They've got other things on their minds. Or have you forgotten it's Thursday. A hanging day tomorrow.'

In the distance, as if to confirm to Doggart's assertion, the dull thud of mallets can be heard, resounding on stout timbers. The gallows are being erected yet again, atop the main gate. Affording a splendid view to the crowd that will doubtless assemble early on the coming morning.

'You're probably right there son. But for God's sakes stay alert, and keep tha' ruddy voice of yows down. Ah meant what ah said. Ah've done ma one hundred and eighty days now. Every one marked up here on me wall. Six months banged up in a hovel stinking of a hundred cretin's excrement. Stuck in a cell six by nine with nowt but a stone bed and a slop pail for company. Ah canna take any more of it man.'

'You think that's rough eh? You and me, we've got it easy here fellah, trust me. I've been confined in Lawford's Gate. This is a palace compared. God, at least we get fed in here. At the Gate you find your own victuals or starve. And you say this place stinks? Smells like a summer rose to me. Moan if you must, but you'll still get your oatmeal tomorrow along with near on a pint o' milk.'

'True enough man, I'm grateful for the slop in me bowl. And you're right, there's others worse off than us, for sure. We'll get more nourishment than those poor sods waiting to face the rope in the morning. They'll have been on bread and water for three days since.'

Somewhere along the corridor, a slow, steady drip marks the monotonous passage of time. The air hangs heavy and motionless, permeated by a putrid stench. Now and then distant moans and shouts can be heard from the condemned men. Their cells are at the very end of the block which is home to these two jailbirds. Four three-storeyed wings make up this establishment, spreading out like the fingers of a hand. At the centre is an administration building, just behind the prison's main gate. Its imposing stone portal has been designed to resemble a small Norman castle. From either side of this a twenty foot high marble wall traces the shape of a lozenge around the perimeter.

'Poor bleeders, they'll be in tight irons for sure, wrists and ankles. No easement for them, whatever they might offer the gaolers. Any notion who they are?'

The New Gaol has been up for around ten years now. It's radically managed and runs on the Separate system. Which means inmates are banged up in their cells for most of the day and night. Peaked caps mandatory whenever they're out, so they can't catch sight of one another's faces. Names never used to address the prisoners, just numbers, given them when they first pass through the gates. All forms of communication strictly prohibited. Punishments for transgressing this rule are punitive. Despite this, news somehow gets around from one inmate to another. And Doggart is one of those convicts who comes by more news than most. If anybody knows, he will.

'Oh aye, lad. There's two brothers from Bedminster, nabbed for highway robbery and horse stealing. A farrier, found guilty of uttering forged notes. And four young lads, fresh out of Cardiff, here in the city for legitimate work. But they kicked up a disturbance at the inn where they were lodging and the landlord tried to put them out. Knifed him, according to my mate on the treadmill yesterday. Big news apparently; desperate attempts to get the youngest reprieved. Not that we'd know any of that, locked up in here.'

'Blimey, a proper show. There'll be a big crowd for sure.'

'Aye. We'll hear 'em. About six o'clock I shouldn't be surprised. All clamouring for their entertainment. The Broadsides will do a roaring trade. Full confessions, last words, all that bloody nonsense. Seems William Calcraft's been summoned down from Newgate to 'ang 'em. Special like, on account of the four young lads.'

'Sweet Jesus, it'll be a spectacle then. Now, Doggart, put a cork in that mouth of yours. Ah can see the turnkeys. They'll be coming to check we're tucked up snug and cosy for the night.'

This prison is the pride and joy of Bristol's penal establishment. Two hundred inmates, men and women, are incarcerated within its walls. It stands proud, alongside the cut, itself an innovation of the new century. A muddy, cheerless channel, dug to divert the river Avon since its flow was dammed by the construction of the floating harbour. Its situation gives the gaol a menacing appearance, bleak and foreboding, designed to put the fear of God into the minds of aspiring criminals.

Far across the city, as night follows day, fresh paper runs through hot printing presses, committing to ink the speculative confessions of the condemned men. Gallows Broadsides. Sheer fancy and invention. But who will be around to contradict?

Almost dawn and a crowd's already mingling at the gate. Early arrivals, laying claim to a spot with an unobstructed view. Boys running between them selling gin, touting chocolate confections, others with hot chestnuts and copies of the infamous Broadsides. Above them the wooden gallows, now complete, gaunt and threatening. These early birds will get to see it all. But there's little space, just a narrow road in truth, between the gate and the cut. People reduced to standing on the other side of the river will struggle to relish the full agony of the condemned men. And so, as the dawn chorus swells, this frontage crams full with bodies, shoulder to shoulder, jostling one another, all eager for the entertainment to commence. Traffic on the road grinds to a standstill, blocked by the sheer press of numbers.

Within the administration building Calcraft is calmly making his preparations. The first hangman attempting to apply science to his craft he has, during the night, ascertained the weight of each victim. They should drop about eighteen inches; ideally thrashing wildly as they go to meet their maker. But never, as sometimes happens, should they be sliced through at the neck. With this in mind he measures his ropes and forms the nooses.

One floor below the Ordinary draws deeply from a flask secretly carried in a pocket of his surplice. This part of the job he truly abhors. It makes him sweat profusely, he can't sleep for days, before or after. Usually it fills him with such vicarious fear it's all he can do not to throw up.

47

As prison chaplain he's obliged to lead the prayers and to stay with the men until the ropes are placed round their necks. The others see them as beyond contempt, rightfully getting their just deserts. But the Ordinary is a man apart; his duty is to show compassion, he must share their anguish. And so he does. God knows, he's not without fault. He left his last parish after a misunderstanding over a young lady in his congregation. Deep down though, he's a good man. He will do his duty, at whatever cost to himself. He snatches up bible and prayer book and hurries from the room. He's expected. He must not be late.

For those lucky souls who'll get some breakfast today, it will be late. Milk and porridge are normally be dished out at seven-thirty, but that's the exact time the execution party will gather in the prison yard. To ensure other prisoners don't disrupt this process they'll be locked in their cells until after eight o'clock, the time appointed for the drop.

Strickland wakes from a deep sleep, shaking his head to clear his mind. It's eerily silent. You could hear a pin drop. The condemned men have, for an hour now, ceased their intermittent wails. The faint light of dawn is creeping through the filthy window of his cell. Again, the jangle of keys. All necks craned to catch a glimpse of the gaolers who've arrived to collect their charges. More clatter as cell doors swing open and the unfortunate men are unshackled from chains and rings on the cell walls. Muted mumblings from both turnkey and chaplain, who starts to pray as the men are gathered into a group.

Suddenly the silence is shattered. A zinc bowl beaten hard against steel bars. Picked up on immediately and joined by fifty more. Oaths and cheers swell the cacophony to a thunderous roar. The other three blocks, though distant, join in the outburst and within seconds the whole prison resounds to a crude salute for the men about to die.

The party shuffles slowly out into the prison yard. The priest continues his intonation, reciting psalms he hopes the men will recognise. His mind's a torment. His mouth dry as desert sand. He feels for the flask, but he knows it's forbidden. Just like a cortege, they inch forwards.

'Halt!' The turnkey, stops the group on a square of cobbles, in the centre of the yard. Gaolers push the prisoners apart and stand ready beside each man. At the turnkey's signal their chains are removed and wrists bound tightly behind them with strong cord. Another cord is dropped over the shoulders of each and secured just above the elbows. The men's legs are still free, but their arms are tightly pinioned.

The chaplain moves down the row of men. Seven in all. Standing before each individually, he recites the Lord's Prayer. Some mumble incomprehensibly, others stay stonily silent. Can they not remember the words? Or have they passed the point where they care? Not one speaks out loud and clear.

A further signal and white nightcaps are pulled down over the heads of the doomed men. The city's under-sheriff joins the group as the turnkey calls 'Proceed'. The convicts are now sightless, nightcaps obscuring all vision, so they're half led, half jostled, to the tower doorway beside the huge wooden gates. Here they clumsily negotiate a flight of spiral steps, eventually reaching a stone platform spanning the two turrets.

With much tripping and fumbling the upper doorway is reached and they stumble out into the tepid light of dawn. The crowd, by now, has swelled to a multitudinous number. As one, they let out a deafening roar on seeing the party appears and moving towards the gallows. They're now part of a spectacle that's been designed to impress. The architect of this impressive structure had trapdoors built into the stone platform. When the temporary gallows are erected, its hooks are arranged directly above. Calcraft stands calm and motionless in patient attendance. His ropes already rigged.

The condemned men are pushed roughly and blindly to their places. Their ankles are bound with straps. Calcraft and the turnkey confer before each, the executioner determined to ensure men and ropes are correctly matched. Satisfied all is in order he places a noose around each man's neck and pulls it tight. Professional beyond measure, he adjusts them so that the knot sits just behind the left ear, or where he figures that is, under the white hood. This precaution might, with luck, ensure the man's neck snaps at the drop, saving him the agony of choking to death in the strangling ligature.

Calcraft steps back to the lever, cunningly obscured, beside the tower door. Another roar from the crowd, "Hats off!" A respectful salute to the men about to die? No. The mob is simply demanding a clear view of proceedings.

The Ordinary, almost in a swoon himself, offers a last blessing on the souls of the poor wretches waiting for death. He retires rapidly, vomit rising into his mouth. In his place the under-sheriff steps forward. The crowd, uncontrollably raucous until now, falls into a deathly silence. The sheriff raises his arm. A puff of wind ruffles the white handkerchief in his hand. The clock of nearby St Mary Redcliffe chimes the first knell of eight.

The sheriff's arm falls.

In a narrow passage beneath the platform, three gaolers are stationed. There are no windows and they can't be seen from outside. They have just one job. As the trap doors open, the feet and ankles of the prisoners suddenly burst into view before them. They sense the roar of the crowd and a profusion of legs thrashing in front of them. Without delay each grabs a pair of ankles and allow his full weight to come to bear, until his own feet leave the floor. In less than a minute, all movement has ceased.

It's done.

The roaring of the crowd outside gives Doggart a further chance to talk freely with his neighbour. 'So, what time do they throw you out my 'andsome?' he enquires.

'Twelve ah reckon. When that lot out there have dispersed. God Doggart, this hanging has given me cause to ponder. Ah could so easily have been amongst that sad bunch that took their last walk just now. Ah've simply never been nabbed for the right crimes.'

'Well, it's obvious you don't hail from this part of the world', replies Doggart, 'What dreadful misdeeds have you perpetrated elsewhere my friend? And what will you do once you're out of here?'

'Reckon it's too risky to declare such things even to you Doggart. Rest content in knowing ah've done some terrible things in me time. But narry prospered as a result. And ah canna venture home to Durham anymore, me face is far too well known there now. So, reckon ah shall linger in this city for a while, aiming to fall in with some like-minded fellows, serious about improving their position, if yow take ma meaning. Every man must eat.'

'Oh yes friend. I follow your drift perfectly. Better still, I'm pretty sure I can help you. Do something for me Strickland and I'll make it worth your while. Get a message to my wife for me; on pain of death. In return I'll direct you to precisely the sort of cove you're hoping to meet.'

Chapter 6

As Strickland places his foot outside the prison gates Maynard is ten miles distant, making good progress on his ride to Bristol. The road through Swinton and Bitton is busy with folk and he passes several acquaintances. But slowing Hermes just sufficient to raise his hat and call out a greeting. He's no intention of stopping to converse, because that's sure to make him late.

Before long he's surrounded by open countryside, on the steady climb out of Bitton. With the bustle of the village at his back, he's free from distractions. A chance to mentally prepare himself. He tries to envisage the challenge that awaits, but with so little to go on it's tough to reason it through.

For certain there'll be some searching questions during the course of this afternoon. Whatever this enterprise is, no-one will engage him without diligent examination of his credentials. All he knows is that the work concerned is substantial. Where and what it involves remains a mystery.

So, his expertise and his experience will surely be called to account. Doubtless he'll be asked about projects he's worked on in the past and how he's tackled them. He mustn't waste the chance to get this right in his mind. No tripping over words when he's at last given the chance to speak. He must appear confident, knowledgeable, a man of the world. What sketch of his business can he conjure up that puts it in the best possible light? What are the most impressive things he's achieved in the years since his apprenticeship? The long, empty road affords him the opportunity to reflect and figure out these answers, and decide on ways to impress the nameless individual he's agreed to meet.

The rate at which he's advanced himself, from being a mere novice, is something he must stress. How quickly he was given responsibility to deal with the clients. And his success with those clients, getting their agreement, keeping them happy whilst the work was underway, dealing with problems whenever things went wrong. Perhaps this person will know some of the clients he'd worked with? Maybe he'd consider approaching them as a reference? Anyway, being often charge of the business at just twenty-one; that is a real achievement, even if the proprietor was his own uncle.

Might the fact he'd then left to set up his own business seem suspicious? Why did he quit such lucrative employment to try his hand alone? Can he explain that without giving the impression Samuel had some reason to dispense with his services?

Because nothing was further from the truth. Samuel had been delighted with Thomas' rapid progress. When the youngster suggested he'd like to start up on his own, he gave all the support he could muster. It would be a brave venture, but one that might see him master mason far sooner than staying where he was. And Samuel, with his years of experience, had the insight and contacts to find Thomas the first thing he'd need – a sizeable job he could take on alone. He put the word about and kept his own ears and eyes alert.

It wasn't long before a clergyman he knew suggested he contact a certain Mr John Hare. Annoyingly this entailed a ride into Bristol, but Samuel was happy to put himself out for his nephew. Hare turned out to be a wealthy industrialist with an intriguing story.

'I thank the Lord every day', he'd said, 'I arrived in this city with nothing in my pocket. As a youth I'd walked here from Crowcombe, determined to make my fortune. And somehow that's come to pass. I can hardly credit it myself. But I worked and saved until eventually I managed to start my own business. It's still there, down at Temple Gate, the big linoleum floor cloth factory. People tell me it was the first such manufactory in the world.'

'Fifty years I've been in Bristol now', he continued, 'I reckon it's high time I gave something back to the city. I come from proud Jewish stock, so I've decided to erect a Zion chapel. And that's why I'm casting my net Mr Maynard. To sniff out builders and masons whom I could trust to make a first rate job of the construction.'

'I'm sure I can help you there', replied Samuel, 'Where will it stand?'

'Oh, that's easy. You see Maynard, when I finally reached this city, all those years ago, I'd been walking all day. I was exhausted. I simply sank down where I was standing, my back against the parapet of Bedminster bridge. I was there for hours, just staring at all the huge buildings, taking in the smells and the noises, feeling the sun on my face and the dust in the air. I'd made it. I was here. It feels like my success in life started then. So, that's where the chapel must be, right next to the bridge. I've already found a piece of land and purchased it. Now I just need to get the work underway.'

The following day, with considerable satisfaction, Samuel related this to Thomas.

'Of course, if you're still serious, it will mean some big changes', he warned, 'I can help you to put a quotation together, I can help you secure the contract, but I've neither men nor tools nor materials spare to help you carry it though. Especially as the job's in Bristol.'

'If you're to make this work, you'll have to find a yard for yourself and, I reckon, a couple of other lads to help you. You'll need to quit my employ of course. But it's the right job for you if you can clinch it. Hare says it'll be a brick construction. That means he'll be engaging a builder to put up the shell. He wants a mason for the ornamental facades, the doorways, the windows, the corbels and the like. They're the very things you know best Thomas and you wouldn't have to trouble yourself with the other aspects of the construction.'

'You must make your own decision lad, but to my mind this is ideal for you. Give it some thought. I've promised Hare I'll have an answer for him on Tuesday. Consider whether you're really determined to do this. Let me know first thing next week.'

Maynard went home that evening with his mind in a torment. This was his first truly momentous decision and it had to be taken soon. Lately living had become very comfortable. Working for his uncle provided real security and some of the good things of life. It had changed so much to the way things were before his apprenticeship. Were he and Mary Ann really prepared to put this all at risk?

Of course she knew in her heart what the right answer was. If they let this chance slip by they'd both regret it time and again. It had to be his decision but she encouraged him fiercely. He agonised and vacillated, one minute full of enthusiasm, the next plagued by doubts. In the end she lost patience.

'If you're that confused, why don't you go ask your father for advice?'

So he followed her suggestion and it turned out to be the best thing he could have done. The very next day he rode to Swinton, surprising Edmund greatly. The proposition came as a shock to the old man who took some time to grasp the details. But his advice was definite.

'It's a golden opportunity son', he said, 'You might wait for ever to find anything nearly as right for you. Why aren't you jumping at it?'

'The job's in Bedminster dad. I'd have to rent a yard there. We'd need accommodation. I'll have to take on men. It will involve laying out a deal of money. I have some savings, but this would leave us with next to nothing, maybe even in debt.'

'Well, we can't have you in the debtor's prison Thomas, but don't turn it down unless it's truly impossible. Why, when I finally got this farm it was like holding a hand of cards. It could all have gone horribly wrong. If there'd been disease amongst the herd or the like, our father's legacy might easily have run

55

out. But I'm so pleased now that I did take that risk, because it made an amazing difference to my life – and yours - come to that.'

'I know dad', Maynard replied, 'But this scares me. Once it's started, I've burnt my bridges. There's no way back.'

'Well, here's an idea to mull on', his father countered, 'Why not set up your business here at the farm? You could easily improve those outbuildings down by the river. It would be no trouble to move your stone to and fro by boat. That's how it's usually transported anyway, isn't it? Why don't the three of you come and live alongside me here, in the farmhouse. It would take a big slice out of the capital you'll need to start son and give you an easy way out if the venture did turn sour.'

His offer was came out of the blue. But it was a godsend, manna from heaven. Maynard realised the sense of it in an instant. The rough stone he'd need was mostly quarried along the banks of the Avon. Wherever it might end up, the first leg of its journey was nearly always by barge. And Swinton sat smack between the two cities where he was most likely to find his future work. Admittedly it would be a bit of a squeeze in the farmhouse, since Edmund had become accustomed to living alone. But it could be done.

'Say you'll come', his father encouraged, 'I've felt like a pea in a drum since your mother passed away and young Hannah got wed. She calls once a fortnight, but she's awful busy with that blacksmith of hers and the two babes. It would be wonderful to have a family around the place again. It would take years off me. There'll be a big room for you and Mary Ann if I clear out my clutter, and that little place under the eaves could be spruced up for Emily. I think we'd rub along just fine.'

'In that case it's done', his son had replied, ' I'll gladly accept your offer dad, before you think better of it! I'm going straight back to Bath now to tell Mary Ann. Then I'll draw up a keen quotation for Hare. With your help keeping my costs down, there's no reason why I can't win this job.'

And that's the way it had turned out. Within a month, work on the new stone-yard started. A rough landing stage was formed using stout tree-trunks driven deep into the riverbank. A low wall built to provide some security for the perimeter. It encircled the existing outbuilding and a new one with two small rooms that could be locked to secure the tools. Finally a tiled canopy, spanning the yard, was erected against the walls of the two outbuildings. This area beneath would become the dressing shop, where most of the masons' work would take place. Chiselling is a dusty business, best done in the open air. But bad weather interrupts progress unless there's a way to ward off the worst of it. So, much of the mens' time would be spent here, slogging through the banker-work and pointing up fine details; a solid roof would be indispensable.

The contract with Hare was indeed soon secured. On the strength of that, Thomas cajoled two journeymen masons, previous acquaintances from jobs done in Bath, to join him. The customary deal was agreed. They'd remain self-employed, but rewards from the job would be split between them, Thomas getting a larger share for securing the work. The new men, Lionel Emden and Ben Gurney, found lodgings in the village without much difficulty. They were happy to risk an exploratory move from Bath, but refused to make any real commitment until they could see how the venture shaped up.

It was all very timely since Hare was not a man to let the grass grow under his feet. He'd already engaged an architect and soon got permission from the Corporation to start work. Thomas was told that a master builder called Elijah Locke had been engaged alongside him. A Bristol man it seemed, but not somebody he or Samuel had ever come across in the past.

Maynard was contracted to create pieces that would give the building character. The cornerstones, the quoins, the window and door cills, jambs, lintels, mullions and transoms and also two large circular ornamental panels for the gables at each end of the building. These would elevate the chapel from an otherwise ordinary brick-built structure. Doubtless many additional pieces, both external and internal would be required

57

before the job was complete. Locke's task was to put up the walls and the roof. And he'd convinced Hare that he should be in overall control of what was done and when. But of course, he'd added, the two teams would have to work closely together.

After several meetings involving everybody concerned, the trenches for the foundations were cut. That was in June of 1828. At some point after that, nobody could remember exactly when, Hare brought in an overseer from the floor-cloth factory as his clerk of works. Which surprised them greatly since the new man, Jeremiah Baker, was reserved and seemed more than a little overawed by the sudden responsibility.

As the footings grew from the ground Thomas came into frequent contact with Locke. Hare's visits to the site dwindled and Baker, whilst ever present, was reluctant to get involved with the endless string of issues requiring resolution. With or without his help, the builders and masons had to work together like clockwork. Every section of ornamental stonework had to be keyed into the walls at just the right time to allow the next courses of bricklaying to be laid. Dimensions had to be double checked and agreed, bosses and tongues carved to make the joints as tight as possible. The two ornamental panels, depicting bible scenes, were a particular challenge. These heavy pieces would have to be hoisted to roof height carefully and fixed so firmly there would be never be a risk of them falling. In no time the two gangs of men were working as one.

Baker turned out more a hindrance than a help. It was almost impossible to get him to make a decision. Maynard chuckled inwardly at the contrast between the overseer and Locke. Once he'd weighed up a situation he'd fix his course of action; no second thoughts, his mind was made up. The mason guessed the builder must be around forty years of age, perhaps a little more. Not tall, but robustly built, with a friendly face and a fine showing of red hair. Every challenge was taken in his stride and he drew others in with his easy manner and evident confidence. Somewhere, jumbled up with his broad west-country drawl Maynard detected the occasional hint of some Irish ancestry.

His good nature and humour would put strangers at their ease and Maynard envied him for this. But he wasn't always benevolent. Behind this affable exterior was a determined, hard-nosed businessman who cajoled his workers – and Thomas - relentlessly to meet their commitments. But even that didn't stop Maynard from liking the man. He blessed his good fortune; God knows he might have been lumbered with a far more difficult character.

The builder employed a small team of workers, but they were well organised and efficient. Maynard guessed, correctly as it later turned out, that Locke had exaggerated the size of his outfit when negotiating with Hare and had also offered an attractive price to ensure he won the job.

With problems being quickly resolved by Locke, rapid progress was made. Locke's confidence and optimism was justified. The surveying work had been thorough and no complications or major surprises arose. Maynard's clear-thinking and disciplined approach encouraged his fellow masons to meet the challenging schedules they were set. Consequently the builders and masons worked efficiently alongside one another with remarkably few occasions when Maynard and Locke had disagreements about how to proceed. Hare was delighted with the way things were unfolding and there was little doubt the chapel would be completed on time. The two governors could feel relaxed, but for one cloud looming on the horizon.

This job had required both of them to stretch their little enterprises. True they'd be handsomely rewarded for this commission, but to keep their men gainfully employed they'd need new contracts, and quickly. Something the mason had joked about when they were hoisting the roof trusses. Some days later Locke proposed to Maynard that they should share a bite of lunch at the New Inn on the Causeway.

'So, have you got anything lined up when the chapel is complete Thomas?' Locke enquired once they were seated in front of ale and pie, 'In two months we'll be done here. Finished.

I don't know about you, but I've got nothing else secured for me or my men.'

'That's been worrying me too, Elijah' replied Thomas 'I took the journeymen under my wing when I started this; Emden and Gurney. I knew them only casually I was working for my uncle in Bath. But now I count them as friends. It would pain me to lose them because I can't find them employment. And then there's the improver. He's turning out to have a useful pair of hands too. So, I've now four mouths to feed. When this job winds up I've no idea where to look for the next.'

'What about your uncle? He must have ideas. Didn't he secure your contract with Hare?'

'True enough Elijah. I've talked to him about it, particularly opportunities in Bath. But business has gone a bit slack there and he hasn't any encouraging suggestions. My yard in Swinton is excellently placed, provided as I get work either here or in Bath. But there's no call for masons around the villages. Unless I turn up another Zion chapel sharpish my men will return to Bath and I'll end up carving gravestones for the deceased people of Bitton!'

'The deuce Thomas, surely your ambition is fiercer than that!', Locke exploded, 'You may count upon it mine is. But don't lose heart lad, all may not yet be lost. I've heard whispers of something that might just be the answer to our dilemma. I promise nothing. And I daren't share any details yet, only mention it concerns a major project under contemplation by the City of Bristol authorities.'

'There's a slim possibility we might find a way in. Together. If the rumours I've heard turn out true, it's exactly what we're looking for. But we haven't any reputation. There's bound to be stiff competition. We might have to resort to smart footwork if we're to succeed. By chance I know a man who might help. To explain what it's about, at least. But I need assurance that you're with me. I'd have to take overall charge of whatever's to be done. Which means you'd be working for me.'

'We've knocked along pretty well together over the last few months Thomas. I know I can count on your reliability and your discretion. And we get the job done. If there's a play to be made for this, I need a sound partner. You ought to be the very man for the job. So, what do you say? Are you game?'

For Maynard only one answer was possible. But truthfully the noises Locke had made about unusual approaches unsettled him. He'd already noticed that Locke treated regulations, occasionally the law, with a pinch of salt. But all this was swept aside by his eagerness to get the future sorted out. It wasn't just his men, he longed to repay something to his uncle for everything he'd done. Eagerly he seized on Locke's proposition, ignoring his misgivings.

'You can count on me Elijah' he replied, 'Just tell me what to do.'

'I've already arranged a private meeting with this fellow I mentioned, who works for the city administration department, two weeks from now', said Locke, 'it would go better for both of us if you're there, alongside me. It won't take place at the Mansion House, or anywhere else you might naturally assume it might. We've deliberately chosen a venue where prying eyes are unlikely to notice. It will be just the three of us; we'll convene at Gaunt's Hospital near College Green. I'll meet you at the rear entrance at precisely thirty minutes past noon, Friday after next. Wait for me outside. There's a trough where we can leave our horses tethered whilst we're in conference.'

It's this arrangement that's led to Maynard to be riding into the city, bound for the Green. He's not complacent, knowing full well from his uncle that negotiating with any corporation is usually fraught with pitfalls. God willing his own lack of experience here won't count against him, or lead him to make foolish decisions. One thing that gives him hope is Locke's bravado and confidence. Despite his misgivings, now flitting like moths somewhere deep in the pit of his stomach, he's determined to stay the course. After all, this meeting does hold out the tantalizing hope of a small fortune. If it goes badly awry, so be it. In the end, what does he have to lose?

In this somewhat ambiguous frame of mind he reaches the hospital, hitches Hermes near the trough, perches himself on a nearby bench and awaits the arrival of Locke.

Chapter 7

'I cannot stress this strongly enough', Gabriel Hartnoll intones gravely and with a steely emphasis, 'The matter we are about to discuss is held by the City of Bristol in the utmost confidence. I have convened this meeting solely to explore possibilities. Should questions ever arise on this matter - from any persons whomsoever, even should they be city officials - you must never admit this meeting has even taken place. I shall certainly never own to it myself. Are you both quite clear and definite on this gentlemen?'

The man utters his words ponderously and with gravitas. He gives every impression of being a person to whom others listen obediently when he chooses to speak. His dark eyes seem to penetrate the very thoughts of the others as he favours each in turn with an unblinking gaze.

Hartnoll, Maynard and Locke are seated around a square oak table in the middle of a bare room having neither carpet on the floor nor paper on the walls. For Maynard, events have taken a somewhat curious course since he reached the hospital yard. Locke, appearing suddenly from nowhere offered a perfunctory greeting. Where the builder had left his own horse was a mystery. Losing no time, he ushered, indeed bundled Maynard not into the hospital, as he'd expected, but towards a side door of the neighbouring building. This has to be St Mark's Church, he thought, sometimes called the Lord Mayors' Chapel. Behind its door they'd found the spartan chamber in which they are now seated.

The intended purpose of this room is unclear. A musty odour hangs in the air. Patches of damp and mould spread over the plaster. If used at all, it's probably as a robing room or for storing unwanted bric-a-brac. Tall wooden lockers are ranged along one wall. A small stained glass window, set high in the gable end, admits a derisory scrap of light. Maynard took all this in at a glance as Locke practically pushed him through the entry. The furnishings, equally austere. Simply the battered table and four upright cane-backed chairs. Seated on one was a

63

man who appeared perversely at ease, given these curious surroundings. Portly, between forty and fifty years of age, dressed in expensive clothes and having a florid complexion and greying hair, he cuts a striking figure in stark contrast with drab and gloomy room.

Locke introduced him as Mr Hartnoll. He referred to the gentleman's position, working for the city administration, directly responsible to Sir Charles Wetherell, a dignitary with much influence over public works in the city. Maynard easily credits this, for Hartnoll is immaculately manicured, serenely composed and evidently accustomed to his own importance. His curious manner of speaking is direct and painfully formal. As the words issue from him, Maynard fancies he might be in a courtroom, listening to the contents of some dusty legal document being read out aloud.

The courtesies of introduction over, they'd quickly proceed to the matter at hand. It's at this point that Hartnoll summarily, and without apology, makes the first of many pointed warnings regarding the shroud of secrecy that overshadows their discussions. Surprised and taken aback, Maynard grudgingly offers a solemn commitment to keep confidential the matters they're about to consider. Only when completely satisfied on this point does Hartnoll, with further unnecessary solemnity, proceed to sketch out the background to their business.

'You may be aware Mr Maynard' he begins 'that there has long been an aspiration to erect a bridge between Clifton Down and Leigh Woods, which lie on the Somerset side of the Avon Gorge. The city authorities have been convinced for years that such a bridge would be advantageous for commerce in the city. Already some of our prized shipping trade is moving to Liverpool and it is vital that we arrest this trend. Believe it or not, the intention to build this bridge has existed since 1753. In that year a wealthy merchant, Mr William Vick, bequeathed £1,000 to an investment fund with the sole purpose of financing its construction.'

'His bequest stated that once, through accumulating interest, the endowment had grown to £10,000, construction should commence immediately. The responsibility for carrying out his wish was put in the hands of our Society of Merchant Venturers. But many years have passed and the cost of materials has increased. As have the remunerations of craftsmen and labourers. If such a project was put in hand today the total needed would be nearer £50,000. Thus, whilst the Corporation ardently desires to proceed with Vick's original intent, it has found itself considerably short of the necessary funds.'

'The Corporation sent a petition to our government, convincing them such a bridge will be a sound investment. Some of the monies are therefore coming from central funds. The remaining capital is being raised from private investors, here in Bristol. All on the proviso that we impose a schedule of tolls for traffic over the bridge once complete. The revenue generated will be used initially to repay these many loans; subsequently it will provide the city with a valuable annual income.'

'A parliamentary Act to authorise this, and set down the terms of the government's financing, was passed nine months ago. Stating the construction must be a suspension bridge made of wrought iron; it is quite specific on such details. In consequence we established a competition to seek the most elegant, cost effective design. I imagine you have read about this?'

Anxious not to appear ill informed, even though he surely is, Maynard nods. He's sure he has heard something about this, probably from John. But probably wasn't paying attention at the time, his mind otherwise distracted by some pressing work problem. So now he's on the wrong foot, hoping he'll not be made to look a fool.

'Sad to say, when the Corporation established this contest, it made a somewhat elementary mistake. Although believe me Mr Maynard, I would never admit having confessed this to you. That error has already delayed construction by a year, with the consequent loss of revenues that we could, by now, have been collecting from the tolls.'

'And can you take us into your confidence - to let us know the nature of this error?' asks Maynard, lapsing unconsciously into the overly formal pattern of Hartnoll's speech.

'Indeed Mr Maynard, indeed' Hartnoll replies, 'The Corporation decided the competition should be judged by an expert unquestionable in such matters. A man in whom they, and all Bristol's citizens, could place absolute confidence. To pick out the design that delivered the strongest, most pleasing structure and, not least, generate the most profitable return. With that aim in mind they appointed Mr Thomas Telford.'

'How fortunate to secure his help. Undoubtedly he would be an excellent choice', interjects Maynard who, perhaps understandably, is in awe of this famous engineer. He knows that Telford himself started his career as a stonemason, a fact that unconsciously endears him to Thomas.

'He's got an outstanding reputation. Why, there's that huge aqueduct in Wales and the bridge over the Menai Straits at Anglesea. Isn't that similar to the one you plan to build?'

'Your enthusiasm is understandable Mr Maynard and I wish it had been borne out by events', continues Hartnoll. 'Sadly, it was not. Mr Telford took several weeks to review all the designs submitted by our twenty two competitors. In the end he determined not a single one was satisfactory. The conclusion he reached was that only he, himself, possessed the necessary skills and experience to design the structure we need. Consequently, instead of presenting us with a winner, he presented us instead with his own proposition.'

'Of course this threw the city authorities into confusion. Under no circumstances could it accept the winning entry from the judge - that would have made us a laughing stock. Bristol would have been subject to ridicule and derision throughout the country. Why, the government might even have rescinded their endorsement. And so no progress had been made, worse still we had lost the best part of a year.'

'But I've heard Mr Telford is a fair and honest man. That certainly seems to be his reputation', counters Maynard, 'It's difficult to believe that he would have exploited his position as judge purely to profit from it by awarding the work to himself.'

'Oh no, Mr Maynard, you completely misconstrue his intent', replies Hartnoll, 'Most certainly Telford is fair, very fair indeed. Almost altruistic in fact. Previously, when he's worked on our behalf, it's been difficult getting invoices from him for the services he's rendered. But he's also doggedly single-minded and supremely assured of his own infallibility. Some people consider him to be an awkward and arrogant man.'

At this point Hartnoll leans forward with a grunt and pulls a long cardboard tube from the leather document case that's been resting against one leg of his chair. With a dramatic flourish he extracts a long rolled document. Untying the blue ribbon that secures it, he spreads it out across the surface of the table. Locke and Maynard feel obliged to hold down the corners of this lively coil of cartridge paper, clearly determined to return to its original form as soon as it possibly can. An intricate engineering drawing stares up at them from its face.

'There gentlemen, observe with your own eyes. This is Telford's design. Just look at these vast gothic towers, rising from the level of the river to well above the sides of the gorge', Hartnoll waves his hands dramatically by way of demonstration, 'Ornamented just like a palace or a cathedral. I'm sure you can estimate for yourself Mr Maynard the likely cost of such a structure, if it were to be crafted by skilled men like you. Why, even if Telford had been a legitimate entrant, there is no way the city could afford such an elaborate design.'

'But he was adamant that the gorge is too wide, at four hundred and fifty feet, to be crossed by a single span. He insisted that we must have three spans supported by the two massive towers you see here. I understand you have respect for this man Mr Maynard, but I can assure you his involvement has resulted in nothing but frustration.'

'So, how does the matter stand now?' Maynard asks. 'I assume you're sharing this information with Locke and myself because we can help in some way. But how exactly?'

'We initially kept this ridiculous outcome confidential' replies Hartnoll, quietly ignoring the mason's question, 'letting the individual contestants know that there was no winner; otherwise limiting public statements as to what had transpired. We foolishly believed we might keep it quiet. That was extremely short-sighted. The newspapers and the pamphleteers have prodigiously sharp noses. Reports of what occurred soon got abroad, eventually into the journals, and a considerable degree of public outrage ensued.'

'To regain the confidence of our citizens we quickly announced a second competition which is now in train. But the Corporation has learned its lesson. This time it will be judged by a committee selected from the city administration – of course it includes some venerable architects and engineers - but none with the arrogance of Mr Telford. The committee is due to reach its decision soon and the result will be announced on the sixteenth of March this year.'

'I'm truly surprised', Maynard exclaims, 'If I'd not heard it from your own lips Mr Hartnoll, I'd never have credited Mr Telford with being so foolish and obstinate. Nor guessed that an important project like this could get into such a tangle. I've been under the impression they always run like clockwork. But I want to ask you again, Sir, what can we do to help?'

'It's remarkably straightforward Mr Maynard' explains Hartnoll, 'The city simply cannot afford any further delay. There are too many risks involved. The longer we procrastinate, the greater the loss of income from tolls. And there are other risks of potentially greater consequence.'

'As you know, this country is currently living through a period of political unrest. There is widespread public agitation for reform and it's almost certain that a bill will be brought before Parliament in the near future. Several members of the Council believe, should such reforms come to fruition, they will radically change the representation of cities like Bristol in the House of Commons. It's also conceivable that the wranglings over reform could precipitate a change of government and maybe a repeal of the Act that underwrites this project.'

'The phrase "strike whilst the iron is hot" is now uttered often by our leaders in the council chamber. In short, it's considered vital that construction commences as quickly as possible, and then advances rapidly to a point where it would be patently irresponsible for any government to curtail its progress. We have no time to lose.'

'Under normal circumstances' he continues, 'the committee would select the winning entry after which the Corporation would embark upon the tender process for construction. And then there would be a further contest between all those parties bidding for the works. It is a sensible process, but one that takes several months to complete. We cannot now tolerate the delays that such bureaucracy entails. We are determined to make a start on the building work as soon as we can – hopefully within a few weeks - certainly before the date when the competition's outcome will be announced.'

'Forgive me', interrupts Locke, 'I don't understand. How can building commence before it's known exactly what should be constructed?'

'Well gentlemen, this is where a degree of privileged insight will allow us to make a confident prediction. Supported by influence in the right quarters, we can nudge the decision in the right direction. The first time around we saw some promising designs from a young man named Brunel. Perhaps you've heard of him too?'

Maynard and Locke nod. 'Of course', replies Maynard, 'The French engineer who has been working on the Thames tunnel for two or three years.'

'No. It so happens our Mr Brunel is not the person to whom you refer Mr Maynard, but his son, Isambard. Only twenty four years of age, but greatly talented nevertheless. Of course there are suspicions amongst the committee that his father may be covertly helping him with his designs. But even if that is the case, it is of no relevance. We are remarkably confident that he will prevail in this second competition, against all the other entries.'

'That being so, we are determined to prepare the ground', Hartnoll continues, 'and to quietly make a start on the construction work as soon as possible. As I say, we are counting on Mr Brunel emerging as the victor. Anticipating this we intend to appoint contractors who will start work very, very soon. The formal tendering policy will be suspended due to the extraordinary circumstances. That said the Corporation cannot, under any circumstances, be seen flouting its own governance. Eventually proper contracts will be established and it will appear that they were awarded in the normal way. Only a small number of people will ever be aware that we have deviated from the prescribed processes.'

'But if you don't encourage competition for the construction work, how will you achieve a good price?' asks Maynard

'Simple Mr Maynard' replies Hartnoll, 'Each party approached will be asked to name a price for the work involved. These will be reviewed by experienced men selected from the Chamber of Commerce. They will advise us as to the value being offered. Moreover, we shall insist that any work performed during the first three months is entirely at the contractor's own risk and expense.'

'If any party appointed disputes this arrangement, they will never see a formal contract and will lose every penny of the investment they make. For this reason we shall not to involve the bigger building enterprises; they're unlikely to play along and the risk of word leaking out is considerable. Instead we are approaching small outfits like yours gentlemen. We cannot see any problem with this since the overall construction will be broken down into several smaller undertakings. Each be assigned to a different company, possibly a company such as your own.'

'Lastly contracts will be awarded progressively. For instance, you might be initially engaged to construct an abutment, simply that. Only after successful completion might you be engaged to build the tower above it. By taking these precautions Mr Maynard, we are confident of ensuring fair and equitable costs despite our unusual method of engagement.'

'I don't doubt it', observes Maynard, 'You've thought this out very thoroughly. All your scheme needs is companies that are prepared to work at risk. It's a singular approach but I'll concede it has a chance of success.'

As he says this, Maynard's mind is churning furiously. The nub of the meeting has turned in a minute or so. Usually, at this point, he'd be asked to name a price. His challenge being how to make profit whilst winning the business. But instead he was being asked to risk his savings, just to get the job. Heavens, did Locke know things might turn out in this way?

As if sensing his partner's discomfort Lock breaks in, steering the conversation on a different path altogether.

'Gabriel. You and I have already had some preliminary discussions. We're grateful to you for clarifying the position. But I'd understood your object today was to affirm Maynard's fitness and capability to your own satisfaction. I'm confident that his men and my own are more than competent to construct the abutment you mentioned and many other parts besides. What more do you need to hear from Maynard, that will set your mind at rest regarding his suitability?'

Hartnoll nods in agreement, carefully rolling up Telford's drawing. For the next forty-five minutes he subjects Maynard to an endless barrage of questions. Concerning his family, his apprenticeship, the works he's undertaken since, and then details of his collaboration with Locke on the Zion Chapel. He interrogates the mason about experience of his fellow workers,

71

the transport he uses for carrying his raw materials and finished work. By the end of this Maynard is mentally exhausted. It seems there is no topic about which he could possibly provide more information. Nevertheless he judges that Hartnoll's confidence in him has grown along with his answers. After pouring for an agonising period over his notes, Hartnoll summarises his position.

'Gentlemen', he says, 'You are now fully aware of the situation. I have shared with you the city's difficult position our plan to make the best of a bad job. Yet again I must warn you never to repeat a word. Should that happen the Corporation will ensure you never get work around here again.'

'I do believe, between the two of you, you have a strong proposition. Understand that I cannot sanction your involvement on my own authority and be aware there are other firms, like yours, with whom we are also in discussion. These may offer more compelling options. However, be assured, I shall be making my own recommendations to the committee very shortly. The details of work required for the initial phase are outlined in this document', Locke reaches yet again to his case, retrieving two further bundles of paper, 'as are the conditions to which you must agree. Here is a copy for each of you. If you are still interested I expect you to submit details of your costings to me within the week. I shall make any decision on this known to Mr Locke in due course.'

'If successful you would start work almost immediately at your own risk. Formal contracts will not be drawn up until two or three months from now. But if you are involved gentlemen, I can assure you the speculation will be well rewarded. There is considerable scope for further work here. If you are as capable as you say, this should be well within your reach. I would be surprised if you didn't eventually profit to the tune of £5,000 apiece.'

'Now' he says, rising, 'There's another appointment to which I must go with some haste. If you will excuse me, I'll take my leave.'

So saying he picks up his case, slipping its straps through the brass buckles. Pushing back his chair he rises and makes for the door. Here he turns to deliver a parting remark.

'Just one more thing. I must insist that you both remain here for ten minutes at least after I've gone. Then you are free to make your own exit. Leave the door. The caretaker will see to it later in the day.'

The latch falls with a click as the door closes behind him. Locke and Maynard remain seated. Neither speaks, as they ponder over the encounter with equal astonishment. Eventually Maynard breaks the silence.

'Well, I'll be damned', he says, 'I've never come across anything quite like this before. I think you know this fellow a lot better than me Elijah. I noticed you called him Gabriel and he didn't object. Tell me what he's like. Is he honourable? Can he be trusted? Was all this a figment of the man's imagination or is it fact?'

'Oh, he's not deluded Thomas', Locke replies, 'He's quite a senior man in the city council; he has the ear of several aldermen. That's how he comes to know all this. And it seems he's been instructed to engage firms that can extract them from the mire they've found themselves in. We're lucky to have met with him. I'm sure his opinion will count for a deal and you clearly made an impression. Trust me, you won't have wasted the day away from Swinton. But Hartnoll will look to me for guarantees and so Thomas all directions must come from me if this is to work. Can I count on your agreement?'

The mason's secretly bristling at Locke's assuming manner. But he doesn't show it. To have a hope of this job it seems he'll have to play second fiddle to the builder. Who hasn't even consulted him about his willingness to work at risk of no payment. It just doesn't seem right. But on the other hand, what an opportunity. A real chance to be engaged with this project for months and to make a handsome profit. If he backs away, offends the builder, what then?

73

'Is there no way we can avoid his demand that we risk out own money Elijah?.'

'Be sensible Thomas', Locke's reply sounds conciliatory, but a harder edge is creeping into his voice, 'Look at the thing practically man – what other choice do we have? Are you going to find work that will make us ten thousand pounds? Not on your life. Don't misjudge Hartnoll either, he's a cautious man. He'd never have set up this meeting if he wasn't confident of making things happen. He talks of other contractors but I'm convinced he wants us to have this. All he needed was to establish confidence in you and that's been done. So, think hard. If you walk away now, you'll be laying your men off inside a month. Once they're back in Bath your little business is as good as finished. Is that what you want Thomas? Carving epitaphs on headstones until you require one yourself?'

Resentment churns in Maynard's breast. He is trapped. But he knows Locke's right.

'Very well. I'm not comfortable, but I'll do it. I'll work with you to deliver Hartnoll his quotations. Let's see what happens then. And yes, I'll take direction from you, but promise me your demands will be legitimate and reasonable.'

'Thomas, of course they'll be reasonable, you have my word. I've no intention for this to be a burden. But heed my advice. Don't ask too many questions; that will do us no good. Hartnoll has told us much today that we shouldn't rightly know, but there will be other things it's better you never understand. For one, how we got to meet him here in the first place.'

'Trust me Thomas. Just accept that not everything will be neatly recorded and documented. We're into a more exciting game than our little Zion chapel. It's going to require courage and trust.'

'Are you suggesting Hartoll's not entirely honest Elijah? That would worry me considerably.'

74

'For God's sake man, stop looking for guarantees at every step', Locke's palm thunders down hard on the table in frustration, 'Be realistic man. This fellow works at the Mansion House. He's surrounded by politicians every day of his life. They're all charlatans of one shade or another. It would be a miracle if a little of that hasn't rubbed off on him.'

'What do you mean?'

'He'll not be as white of the driven snow Thomas. But I'm sure he's being straight with us as far as this is concerned. I believe every word he's told us about the political risks, I really do. Just look about you. The country's in ferment. It may be quiet in your little backwater Thomas but there's trouble all across England for months now. If it's not rick burning or machine wrecking, it's folks getting violent about this parliamentary reform. '

'The newspapers are full of it. Theatres closing in London, shopkeepers boarding up their windows at night. All because they're scared of mobs running wild. The business over Catholic emancipation nearly tore the Tory party apart. Believe it Thomas, there's unrest and trouble everywhere. Only a fool would rely on a stable government over the next twelve months. Just about anything is possible. You and I must seize this opportunity now, before something upsets the apple cart. Say, my friend, are you with me or is this too scary for you to stomach'

'Count me in Elijah. You've convinced me. I'll do everything I can to make it work. A year from now we'll be celebrating our fortune and laughing at my misgivings.'

'Well done Thomas, you've proved yourself a businessman after all', Locke booms, 'Here, take my hand, friend. Now, we'll need to get those figures to Hartnoll quickly, so be sure to bring your estimates to the chapel with you on Wednesday.'

'What's more, our ten minutes is up. We need tarry here no longer. Time we set out for home. Take good care on the road my friend, I'll see you the day after tomorrow.'

Chapter 8

The first few hours after Thomas left had flown by for Mary Ann. She'd made Emily comfortable in the parlour, swathed in blankets, propped up in Thomas' armchair. She searched out a wooden solitaire board, purchased years ago in the market at Bath. Together with slate and chalk, this would keep the invalid amused for ages. Happy the little girl was looking decidedly less pallid, so Mary Ann had returned to her baking.

Despite longing for help around the house, cooking was the one aspect of her wifely duties that gave her real pleasure. As she rolled out pastry and raked the fire in the range she contemplated what improvements they could make to the farmhouse. Assuming Thomas really had got on well in Bristol today.

In fairness, their dwelling is not in bad repair, but it that doesn't stop Mary Ann from making plans. Chiefly the construction of another room somewhere, where a live-in housemaid might be accommodated. That's the first priority in Mary Ann's mind.

When they moved here, two years ago, the house had hardly changed since Edmund purchased it in 1809. True, he'd put up some new outbuildings and improved the farm a good deal, but he'd made no efforts to modernise the family home itself. The paint had mostly worn off the exterior and what little there was inside they'd found chipped and discoloured.

So, once the alterations to the stone-yard were complete, she and Thomas had set about the farmhouse with a will. If they were to live there happily with his father it would have to be more convenient for Mary Ann to manage. They'd fitted a pump in the kitchen, drawing from the well outside which, until then, was Edmund's only source of fresh water. A wooden sink was installed alongside the pump and a new iron range complete with oven was squeezed into the chimney breast. They hung new paper in the parlour and bedrooms and they paid John Carey to paint every inch of the building that required his efforts.

The house has only two floors but upstairs are three good-sized rooms. One bedroom for Edmund, another for Emily and the largest, overlooking the river, for her parents. Every other room in the house is shared, so Mary Ann had been delighted to find she and Edmund were rubbing along like father and daughter. Unsurprisingly she became partly responsible for the old man's wellbeing. Providing his food, doing his washing, making his bed; all these little extra tasks had increased her work as mistress of the house. It became clear in no time that proper housemaid was needed, but whilst there's no place for a girl to lay her head, that's just not possible. Until then she must make do with Amy Pollard, who walks up from the village three days a week and stays for a few hours each time.

If truth is told, Mary Ann can't make up her mind about Amy. It's only a couple of months since the fourteen year old was engaged. She was willing enough from the start, if a little slow on the uptake. But it's her behaviour when she's not working that concerns her mistress. Only after taking her on did Mary Ann hear gossip about Amy's liaisons with lads in the village. Never fond of tales, certainly never accepting them to be true without question, she was unwilling to finish the girl's employment on the basis of mere tittle-tattle. On the other hand she musn't be allowed to become a bad influence on Emily. The sooner Edmund fixes up a room, the better.

Later in the day, shortly after lunch, just after she'd put Emily back to bed, something happened that's been preying on her mind ever since. Edmund, who had been working in the fields since milking, had joined them for lunch. She subsequently found him, and not for the first time, dozing in the kitchen. This was a recent development, but something he was doing with increasing frequency. Whilst he still gave every impression of being a strong and active farmer, old age seems to be gradually creeping up on him.

Her train of thought was interrupted by a knock at the door. She didn't expect any visitors that afternoon so she was intrigued to find a short, grubby-looking lad of around twelve years old standing on the doorstep. Not only was the boy decidedly out of breath, he also seemed to be tongue-tied by the momentous responsibility of his errand. A little gentle coaxing from Mary Ann established that he'd been dispatched from the Whitefield estate.

'Masser's sent me wi' a message for ol' man Maynard', he spluttered when Mary Ann's prompting had finally persuaded him to utter more than two words together, 'instructed o' me that I should give it 'im direc' like.'

'You'ld better step inside then ', she replied, 'You can see for yourself that he's asleep, but if you sit down there quietly I'll see if I can wake him for you.'

Something about this odd turn of events had already created consternation in her mind. When she'd roused Edmund, she busied herself again at the range. But made certain she was able to overhear every word of his conversation with the boy.

'Tis Sir James his self that sent me to find ee', the lad started, 'He asked that you come back wi' me now to lend a hand with them ewes. There's a sticky problem wi um and he reckons 'tis only you has the gumption to fix it.'

'I'll gladly come and help lad', said Edmund, 'but tell me what's amiss. What is it that can't be resolved without my assistance.'

'I told ee', it's the ewes, sir. They're in lamb, around a dozen of 'em. Started last night it did and the first two out have already been lost. The guvnor declares if you're there the rest will be born healthy.'

'Surely the sheep aren't lambing now son, it's January.'

'That's so, but they are, for a fact. On account of a stupid oversight. Last August 'twas. No one admits how it came about, but a ram got loose in top field with twenty or so of the Cotswolds. An hour he was there, by the time he were spotted. They tipped him out sharpish but the damage were done. Course, he wasn't supposed to be anywhere near em, so there was no reddle bag tied on nor nowt. They just had to bide their time to find out the damage. Turned out he'd covered twelve of 'em. Course then they had to be moved to a barn, on account of the weather and that. Them animals have been there all over Christmas and now their time's arrived. Caused plenty of inconvenience all round I d' reckon.'

'It can't be that difficult to deliver a few lambs though son, even at this time of year', replied Edmund, 'What does the shepherd say for himself?'

'Gone sir. Left in November. Reckon the guvnor gave him notice, meself. Probably his fault the ram got loose, to my way of thinkin'. That's what the others believes anyways. Masser says he's going to find another, but I reckon he'll wait for spring. Meanwhile we've got a couple of stockmen looking after them. They're confounded, they ain't no idea between um. Reckon that's why ee' sent me to get you.'

As Mary Ann eaves-dropped, a worry began, one that's been growing ever since. She could understand why the estate wanted Edmund but, damn it, there were still ten ewes to be delivered. Why, that could end in her father-in-law spending the entire night is a freezing barn. Something he shouldn't be doing at his age. If Sir James had really thought this through, surely he'd not be calling in that long-standing obligation he'd squeezed out of Edmund?

But she'd forgotten Sir James was himself getting older; he and Edmund must be a similar age. He probably hadn't realized the full implications of his summons. Tongues were wagging in the village anyway, about him and the state of his mind. Three years ago he'd been widowed. But, lo and behold, within twelve months he'd taken another wife. This one was less than half his age and that simple fact set off an avalanche of gossip.

'Rest here for five minutes son', Edmund said to the lad, 'I'll need to collect me farrowing hook from the barn and lay me hands on coat and blanket. Then we'll walk back up to the estate together and you'll have done your duty. Mary Ann', he called over 'It seems the estate needs my help with the husbandry. Reckon I'll be gone for the rest of the day but I should be back for supper.'

'I sincerely doubt that Edmund. This will exhaust you', she'd answered, 'Is it essential you go? Is there no one else in the village who might help them out?'

'I made a promise years ago Mary Ann', he replied, 'and I shan't go back on my word, not whilst Sir James is alive. He's a gentleman; always a good master to me and, dare I say it, maybe even a friend into the bargain. I'll be fine. Don't worry about me girl, I'll look after myself.'

Nevertheless, as she watched them both walking away up the farm track, Mary Ann was far from reassured. Even if the lambing was finished by the end of the day, there was still the mile or so to be walked back to the smallholding. She knew in her heart that nothing could have been done to stop Edmund going, but resolved he'd not spend all night alone in a draughty barn, nor yet make the homeward journey on foot. However, with Thomas away in Bristol, Hermes with him, there was nothing she could do by herself. Consequently, in a state of increasing agitation, she impatiently waited on her husband's return.

The bright sun held out until early afternoon, but then the sky started to fill with ever darker grey clouds. Now, at half past four, the heavens are leaden and a cold wind is driving through the gaps in the doorframes. As she contemplates this through her kitchen window, Mary Ann's agitation increases by the minute.

In a vain attempt to divert her mind she's rearranged her cupboards for a third time when suddenly there's the sound of hooves ringing on the cobbles outside. In seconds she's through the door and out the yard. Thank heavens, it is Thomas at last. A powerful feeling of relief swells within her. Giving the man no chance to dismount she yells out her request above the howl of the wind.

'Edmund's up at to the estate Thomas. I'm really worried he'll try to walk back alone. Can you drive straight up now, to collect him?'

'Have a heart woman. Let me at least get out of the saddle,' he replies, 'But if you're certain it's necessary, of course I'll go, just as soon as I get the trap hitched up. Looks like there'll be a full moon tonight; provided this cloud holds off there'll be light enough to guide me. Even so, run inside and fetch me the bull's eye, just in case. While you're about that I'll water Hermes and get him between the traces. And bring me back a sip of something, I could do with a drink myself.'

Mary Ann's face lights up as the weight that's been on her conscience is shouldered by her husband. In the kitchen she lights a taper and searches for the lantern, discovering it at last in a box under the sink. Filling a mug with porter she carries both items back to the yard. On hearing her account of the afternoon's events, Thomas begins to share her concerns.

'You can stop fretting now my love', he reassures her, 'I'll find the old fellow and I'll stay alongside him if it comes to that. But I'm sure he'll have done sufficient by now to justify an honourable retreat. We'll have him back here in no time. I'm all in, but I'm more than happy to do this for the old man. I owe him so much, it'll be a joy to be able to render him a service.'

And so, just when he envisaged mulling over the day's excitement with Mary Ann, Maynard finds himself yet again back on the road, with only himself for company. All the way back from Bristol his mind had churned incessantly over everything that had happened, all the words that had been said. Now, as he coaxes Hermes reluctantly along the lane in the dusk, the very same questions pour back into his mind. Why all the secrecy? What exactly has he agreed to? Why is he left with this niggling sense of unease? Isn't there anything he can do to rid himself of the mystery, the uncertainty?

All this thinking doesn't help. What are the alternatives? If he backs out now, he'll look a perfect fool in front of Locke. He'll also lose the only possibility he knows of the work that's so badly needed. But if he does nothing he'll be committed deeper and deeper, until there's no way out. God, what a fix. At the start he'd been confident to put his trust in Locke. But thinking back to some of the remarks the man's made, he wonders if that trust is fully deserved.

And hadn't Hartnoll's behaviour also been distinctly odd? Why had he been so determined not to be seen with the two of them? Is it really likely that anybody would have been spying on them? When he'd reached home, just half an hour ago, he'd been ready to share all these concerns with Mary Ann. But he realizes now that he can't. What good would it do? He can only present her with unanswerable questions and the ramblings of his own fretting. There's no point in taxing her with such quandaries when she's deeply worried about Edmund's health. No, he must face the fact he's made his decision and stick by it, not allow his unruly mind to debate it any further. These dancing demons must be firmly banished from his head.

Nearing the big house, Maynard steers Hermes towards the stable block, situated at some distance from the main building. He figures there'll be a good wait before Edmund's ready to return, so it seems an impertinence to take the trap further along the sweeping drive. It's now so dark he must strain his eyes to make out the surroundings. The expansive yard appears deserted, save for one lugubrious stable-hand ponderously stacking pails. He pays no attention to the trap as it clatters in between the gateposts.

'Hi lad', yells Maynard, from the bench seat of his conveyance, 'I'm here on business with Sir James. Where can I tether my horse?' The unhelpful fellow just shrugs his shoulders and points to an iron ring set on an outer wall, continuing vacantly about his own business. Maynard takes the fellow at his word, or rather his shrug, and ties Hermes where he'd indicated. Then, since the hard-worked animal has only paused since the ride home from Bristol, he picks up one of the buckets not yet collected by the lad, fills it at the trough and bends to place it within reach of the horse.

A sixth sense tells him that's he not alone and the words 'Good evening sir', uttered in a soft but confident female voice, seem to be addressed to him. 'You must be the mason from Swinton village'.

He's taken completely unawares. His mind, still mulling over the day's events, hasn't properly registered the presence of this other person. Surprised, he stands up, turning towards the voice as he does so. Hermes, shying at the sudden movement, nudges hard into his back. Maynard's foot strikes the bucket which slops water all over the flags. Within seconds the poor fellow is covered in confusion and embarrassment.

By the light of the lantern she carries Maynard sees this woman, whoever she may be, is attired in a riding habit liberally spattered with mud. Her face is aglow, hair windblown and unkempt. Despite all this it's obvious she must be a lady of some rank. Is it simply the way she carries herself or maybe the manner of speaking? He can't tell but whatever he knows that her station in life is some way above his own.

The knowledge increases his chagrin. Here, of all places, he'd hope to make a good impression. To be recognised as a man who is making progress in life. Instead he must now seem like a country bumpkin, clumsy and lost for words when coming anywhere near the gentry.

Luckily the lantern isn't bright enough to expose his flush of embarrassment and the sound of her pleasant laugh starts to dispel his fears. There's no derision or superiority in her manner at all. The notion that he's made a fool of himself dissolves and his natural confidence returns.

'Madam, please forgive me, I'd no idea I was not alone. I'm honoured to make your acquaintance. But how do you know anything of me? I rarely visit the estate and we've not met previously as far as I'm aware.'

'Indeed not Mr Maynard, you are correct. But it's impossible for me not to see, in your face, a striking resemblance to your father. He's been here with us most of the day, as I'm sure you know, helping with the lambing. For my sins, I have taken a keen interest in the livestock on this estate, especially the Cotswolds. So, I have spent some time in the barn this afternoon, watching him at work. It has been an education for me. He has such a natural and easy way with the animals, nearly always succeeding where the others struggle. We really are most grateful that he came to assist us.'

'But do forgive me Sir' she continues 'It's not fair take advantage of you; I should introduce myself properly. My name is Sophia Whitefield; I do believe you have met my husband, Sir James, in the past.'

Of course, what a fool he must be. Her riding clothes are filthy but they fit immaculately and she carries herself proudly, erect and elegant. So, of course, this is squire's new wife, about which there's been so much tittering. Even he has caught up with the gossip. Well, to him she seems like a very composed, down to earth lady; must be that, he guesses, she's only just returned from a ride.

He's correct. Unknown to him, it's only riding and caring for horses that's keeping this young woman sane. A secret she keeps from the world because there's no one with whom to share her angst. As the new lady of the manor she's envied by all; whatever she desires is hers. And that's exactly how it seemed for the first few months. Her husband puts no constraints on what she may spend or where she can go. But oh so slowly it's dawned that she's trapped, albeit in a palace, miles from the life she's known and her friends for many years.

She's visits Bath regularly, trying to join in with society, but it's not something she can do every day. Left to herself in the house, she quickly becomes bored beyond measure. Other women turn to petit-point and embroidery; such things don't interest her one whit.

So she's taken to riding alone, exploring the many acres of Whitefield estate. Not just riding, but rubbing down and stabling her horse when she returns. In this way, she can legitimately be absent from the house for most of the day and nobody finds it odd.

Elsewhere, eyebrows might be raised. But here only the servants take any notice and they just consider her slightly eccentric. If they'd only known her before she married the master. Then they might understand.

Sophia Durrant, as she was then, was raised in London. Her father was an equerry; in consequence the family spent much of each year in the capital. A country residence in Norfolk served as a retreat when duties permitted and occasionally when his wife tired of life at court. At such times she'd feign some imaginary ailment and, taking Sophia with her, retire to the provincial estate to recuperate.

Cosseted, comfortable and principally a city girl, Sophia happily passed the first seventeen years of her life.

The affluent circles in which the family moved ensured a predictable rhythm to her existence. There was a wide circle of friends, mostly of a similar age, on whom she would call during the day. In the evenings, a constant round of balls and dances, theatre visits and dinner engagements. An exciting life with hardly a minute spent alone. So many diversions, she was never bored.

Sir Vernon Durrant and Lady Elizabeth were anxious to see their daughter make a good marriage. Conscious of their elevated position, as functionaries of the royal household, it was essential she be well provided for and do honour to their own rank and standing. But they'd deliberately not rushed her in the matter, despite several, to their eyes, suitable proposals. Their indulgence dictated that she end up happy, not just well-matched. So they let her set the pace.

For some unfathomable reason that pace was slow and Sophia was twenty one by time she met Wigmore, a young Major in the 52nd Regiment of Foot. But from the first it was obvious that Edgar was an ideal suitor. Already recognised for bravery, son of a baronet, charming and handsome, in every respect he was a perfect match.

Within six months the young officer had asked Sir Vernon if he might offer his hand and the equerry was overjoyed. It would be a union smiled upon by both families, morcover the two were deeply in love. With unrestrained pride the Vernons issued their invitations and made preparations for a lavish ceremony.

But a week before the anticipated event Wigmore was summarily recalled to barracks. For two years the army had been beleaguered across Burma. Engaged in sporadic skirmishes against an enemy that would suddenly appear from the hills and just as quickly retreat back into them. It had been said the troops deployed there could quell any uprising; but this was turning out to be a fallacy. Things were going awry and worsening. New blood, fresh ideas, more effective tactics; all were desperately necessary if the situation were to be reversed.

Wigmore's reputation in the field picked him out as having these capabilities. Once recalled he was sent by ship to take up a senior command. His orders unambiguous. Retake control, without delay and at any cost. The fellow always led his men from the front. Within a month of setting foot in Yangon he was seriously injured in the battle at Danubyu. Before he could be transported home his wounds became gangrenous and he died.

Desperate with grief Sophia was suddenly faced with a funeral instead of the grand wedding she'd planned. Her whole life shattered, nothing would to console her. She withdrew from the world, staying to her room, avoiding visitors with any possible excuse. Two years passed. Yet again her parents fretted, at first for her state of mind and then because she risked becoming too old ever to find a suitable husband.

It was time for Sir Vernon to take matters into his own hands. As the weeks wore on she betrayed just a spark of interest in life. What she needed was someone to cherish her, a man who could provide for her. And there was one he knew might relish this. Whitefield, an old associate of his from long ago. He'd been widowed recently. But he was also a wealthy landowner, a baronet and, to Vernon's certain knowledge, the perfect gentleman.

With all the tact he could muster Sir Vernon brought the two of them together. He lobbied each enthusiastically, in different ways. With Sir James it was simply just gentle encouragement, sowing the seeds that a wife such as Sophia would bring joy back into life after his loss. With his daughter he was kindly but practical; a marriage of convenience was not the worst thing in the world and he talked up the advantages she'd gain from such an arrangement.

Whitefield was easily convinced. Sophia, too weak to resist from the grief still eating at her heart, capitulated under the onslaught of her father's persuasion. He prompted Whitefield to propose, his daughter graciously accepted. Though much older, he was a handsome and amusing man; she reasoned he'd make as good a husband as any. Whatever, of her own free will, she embarked on a life dramatically different to the one she'd envisaged a couple of years earlier.

Once married and installed at Roundwick Hall her zest for life recovered. Everything was new, exciting. The countryside, practically a mystery to her, following a life spent mostly in the drawing rooms of stately town houses. There was much to learn as she assumed her duties as lady of the house. Her new husband was a fascinating man but much consumed with the running of his estate. For six months or more the new life occupied her completely and she was generally content.

But as the novelty faded away as the isolation of her new situation became all too apparent. Whereas friends used to call on her two or three times a week, now there was no one. No companions to share confidences or a convivial afternoon. Sir James, caring and interesting though he might be, was always tied up looking after his crops, his animals or his tenants. They'd meet at breakfast and then again at dinner, but that might well comprise the entirety of their day's intercourse. Otherwise she was left in the company of servants, friendly enough, but no substitute for the companionship she craved.

She realized how much she missed the social engagements and she wasn't one to sit and read. The management of the house lost its fascination. James was always engaged in some business in which she couldn't share. The difference in their age became a barrier to any meaningful understanding between them. To dispel the boredom she'd turned to riding and taking an interest in the animals. In her current state of mind any diversion was welcomed with open arms.

'I apologise we'd sent no one to meet you Mr Maynard' she continues, 'Walk up to the house with me. I'm sure we can find you a glass of Madeira wine whilst you wait for your father. He must be nearing the end of his work by now. When I left him late afternoon there were only three ewes left. I'll summon a lad to run over and ascertain the situation.'

So saying she leads Maynard across the stable yard, between an avenue of beech trees, up a flagged path to a side door of the main building. He can observe her more closely in the light of her swinging lantern. She's certainly handsome and holds herself with a confident poise, elegant despite heavy riding boots and the uneven flags. No words are exchanged but he's acutely conscious of her presence beside him. Why does he suddenly feel self-conscious and foolish? Perhaps because he's never found himself in such a situation before. Is she expecting him to make conversation? If so he's at a loss.

They enter the house through a well-lit vestibule. On one side there's a small private withdrawing room, on the other a long passage stretching into the distance. He guesses this part of the house to be where business is conducted with tradesmen and messengers. Ushering him into the snug, Sophia suggests he take a seat. The furniture is elegant; he perches uncertainly on an ornate sofa with scrolled arms and clawed feet. The walls are covered in a light buff paper, hand-drawn cartoons pasted over them at random. She pulls a sash by the fireplace, a bell tinkles somewhere in the distance. It's answered shortly by a maid appearing noiselessly from the corridor. Sophia instructs her to fetch Maynard a glass of wine and some periodicals from her husband's office.

'I trust you'll find this comfortable enough until your father joins you', she says, standing beside the doorway. In the light of gas mantles, burning around the room, Thomas notes her comely figure and a spirited light in her eyes. She looks at him studiously for a second or two and then smiles enigmatically before turning on her heel.

'I doubt I shall we'll meet again tonight Mr Maynard, but I'll do my best to see that your father is relieved of his duties as soon as possible. Take care as you return. I wish you both a safe journey home.'

Maynard find's he's breathing fast and can feel his heart beating. As she disappears along the passageway his mind races. She's a very beautiful woman. And their encounter sparked something within him, a desire that he doesn't want to admit to himself. Never, since first meeting Mary Ann has he felt quite like this. It's ridiculous. Why, they hardly exchanged more than a dozen words. He's ashamed and can't figure it out. Happily it won't be a problem since he'll not meet her again.

Seated alone, Maynard thumbs through the magazines he's been brought. An article takes his interest and the lustful feelings aroused by her presence are forgotten. Now she's gone he can't understand how he surrendered to such a weakness of his own character. Luckily it's been exposed to no one; it'll stay a secret never to be divulged. No more than a quarter of an hour passes before his father appears in the doorway, along with the morose lad from the stables who had been sent to fetch him.

'Thomas, my boy, what a surprise! I didn't expect to see you here son, especially after your long journey. I could have walked back to the farm myself, no trouble. However it's kind of you to collect me and I thank you for it. I assume Mary Ann put you up to this? I sensed she was fretting when I left the house.'

'I won't lie father, it was she who insisted, the very moment I returned from Bristol. But if not I'd have done it in any case. It's too late and too cold for you to be walking such a distance tonight.'

'Well, a ride home and a bite to eat will do me proud Thomas. It's been a hard day in that barn I can tell you, but I'm very pleased I was here to help. It's only right to honour a promise. The gormless lad was muttering something on the way over, but I couldn't understand a word. Something about Lady Sophia I think? Are you expecting she'll return before we depart?'

'Father, from her manner, I doubt it. You know as much as me. I've no idea if anybody will come to see us off, she just didn't say. But for sure there's no one here and it's getting late. I think we should take our leave.'

As they amble back to the stable block Maynard is heartened to see the clouds clearing and a bright moon bathing the countryside. The journey home will be slow since there are countless places where the track has ruts and potholes. But he reckons half an hour might see them back at the smallholding.

Taking the reins he walks Hermes slowly forward, every fibre concentrating on the track ahead. Edmund, perched on the bench seat beside him, enthusiastically recounts the adventures of his day which he's thoroughly enjoyed. It seems he succeeded in delivering every lamb without losing a single one. Moreover Sir James himself had walked across to the barn to thank him personally. The highlight seemed to be Lady Sophia, who had spent a long time discussing the process with him, a conversation that caused him no small embarrassment but also, evidently, some delight. She'd apparently been very matter of fact and had gone on to ask him about his time on the estate and his fortunes since then. Like his son he'd been animated by her visit though, thought Maynard, probably not in quite the same way. As he eases Hermes between ruts and boulders

Maynard can only lend half an ear to these ramblings, since his mind is focussed on avoiding trouble.

Edmund is now in full flow. By the time he's reached an account of a conversation he had with one of the under-stockmen, Maynard has eased the trap out of the drive and onto the narrow track leading to Swinton. The way is bordered by low drystone walls; trees in the fields behind them appear like ghostly shadows in the moonlight. Suddenly Maynard feels the trap jolt as if a heavy sack had been thrown aboard.

In a split second an arm encircles his shoulders and a rough hand covers his face. He's dragged bodily from the seat; in no time he's lying on his back, on the track, with a ruffian sitting forcefully astride his chest. Wrenching his head to one side he realises his father's suffered a similar fate. A long black cloth is wound around his assailant's mouth, a tightly fitting woollen hat is pulled down so that only the eyes are discernible. The mason's attempts to struggle prove useless, he quickly realises he's firmly pinned to the ground. The attacker rips away Maynard's scarf, so that he can identify, in the moonlight, the man whom he has brought down.

'Drat. 'Tis just that wretched mason fellow' he says aloud to his companion, 'The one from up river near Swinton. The bastard u'll be bugger-all use to us. Won't have owt on him. Probably nothing but gravel in these pockets'.

Despite this the highwayman is skilfully riffling through all his victim's clothing searching for anything of value. A whiff of stale acrid pipe tobacco, ingrained in the fibres of the man's clothing, reaches Maynard's nose as the assailant leans forward to rummage in his shirt.

'Bollocks', the assailant concludes, 'these two are just a waste of time. What say we cut their throats and have done with it?' With a flourish he produces a long silver blade that glints in the moonlight, pressing it firm against Maynard's neck. His associate, who's been completely silent up to now, becomes agitated. 'Stay your hand, you mindless fool' he mutters in a low voice that Maynard can only partly make out, 'The cap'n ud have yer balls for breakfast, yer know that fer a cert'nty'. At least, that's what Maynard reckons he's heard, but he can't be sure.

'Right then' said the first, 'Well, they're not coming after us, I'll damn well make sure of that. We'll relieve the buggers of their boots. And, so saying, he and his compatriot wrench the footwear off both Maynard and his father and leap over the wall on the near side of the track. Within seconds a thud of hooves, galloping over grass, fades quickly as the now invisible miscreants flee the scene.

For some moments father and son lay silent and inert, too shocked to move. The entire episode has happened so quickly, it's completely confounded them both. Winded by the assault they struggle to come to terms with the danger that's passed. The mason is first to regain his composure. Pulling himself to his feet, he heaves his father up from the ground and helps him back onto the trap.

'Lord have mercy on us! Reckon I know where that pair hail from', he says, 'John Carey warned me this had started up again. But I was still taken cold when it happened. Had no clue there was anything amiss until that villain tumbled me off the trap. What about you father, are you injured or just shaken like me?'

'Just shaken, son. I'll be right as ninepence once I've got me breath back. But this is a warning for us lad. We'll have to be more alert to danger in the future. These would-be highwaymen have become audacious beyond a joke. Carey's right. That old friend of mine, the stockman, was telling me about it this afternoon. He says there's a deal of theft now from the bigger houses hereabouts, though word don't always seem to get out.

These buggers have been a plague for years, but lately they seem to be much better organised and determined.'

'Well father, we're still alive. And we're not badly hurt. Thank God it hasn't cost us much more than our dignity and our boots. I'll wager our assailants probably didn't ride off with those either. I reckon they pinched them simply to prevent pursuit.'

At this he struggles, in his stockinged feet, through the long damp grass of the bank and over the wall following, to the best of his recollection, the track of their assailants. Sure enough, having stepped in one large liquid cow pat, he spies two pairs of boots. Recovering them, he finds it's nowhere near as easy to clamber back over the wall from the field as it had been from the other side. In fact it's uncommonly painful and he realises his ribs have been badly bruised in the fracas.

All in all though he knows they should be grateful for coming off so lightly. The outcome could have been far worse. Hermes, not easily perturbed, stands calmly on the track nearby, casually dragging up mouthfuls of lush grass at the side of the road. Flourishing the boots Maynard clambers once more onto the trap, seizes the reins and sets out for the safety, rest and refreshment that they will undoubtedly find at home in Swinton.

Chapter 9

Relentless driving rain lashes the windows of the private coach conveying Sir Charles Wetherell, King's Counsel, Member of Parliament for Boroughbridge and Recorder for the City of Bristol, from a sitting of the House of Commons to his official chambers in Bristol. For here, where he presides over the administration of justice, a number of local problems demand his immediate return. Every day this week, whilst he has been on business in the capital, a swathe of dispatches arrived outlining issues only susceptible to his personal intervention.

The skies are grey, the roads awash, mud flying in gobs from the iron tyres. The coachman's bent forwards, practically horizontal, in a futile attempt to avoid the lashing of the storm. Wind howls ominously around the speeding vehicle. Despite its fine quality and expert workmanship, Wetherell's painfully conscious of chilling draughts seeping in through invisible cracks. The penetrating cold, exacerbated by four hours already, spent in this confounded conveyance, has started to gnaw deep into his bones.

For an age now every week has involved at least one journey of a hundred miles or more. Pleasant enough during summer; more like a punishment at this time of year. The travel is an inevitable consequence of the many responsibilities with which he's continually forced to juggle. He couldn't maintain his position on the opposition benches without showing up regularly in Westminster. His wife gets bitter, yes really bitter, if he doesn't spend some time at home. And these judicial responsibilities in Bristol mean he has to journey down at least twice a month.

He never planned this. For better or worse it's become his expected way of life. And, if anything, these arduous and time consuming trips seem to be happening more frequently, not less. Damned inconvenience, he could do without it. Let's face it, he's a good deal less tolerant now of this moving around than ever he was in the past. Probably all down to his advancing years. Nearing sixty, still fools people that he's every bit as energetic as ever he was. But the aging body won't be fooled. It's not nearly as forgiving of the discomforts that come with heavy responsibility. Oh well. If nothing else these ghastly interminable trips give him ample opportunity to reflect on life.

If things were fairer, if the rewards reflected his dedication, then he'd be travelling in considerably greater comfort. Hasn't he proven, over many years, that he can hold down these important appointments at the same time and excel at every one? Here he is, both a judge and Member of Parliament with responsibilities that are greater than ever. And the issues heaped on his shoulders in both Bristol and Westminster are just endless. No Sir. His status and his experience mean he's worthy of better than this.

To some extent the recorder's self-satisfied reasoning is justified. But a more perceptive, less partial observer might look at matters through a different lens. Many of these demands on Wetherell's time, he'd likely figure, are really of the fellow's own making, the product of frustrated ambition or a determination to advance his own personal and political agendas.

The judge has indeed established himself as a fearless and dogmatic parliamentarian. Representing a Tory party still licking its wounds from its recent defeat. He's a frequent and articulate speaker. But all too often his dogged campaigns are considered rebellious, neither endearing himself to his party, nor advancing his career.

As a lawyer, his professional prowess has never been in dispute. Why, the man was appointed King's Counsel at just forty six. But he continued to push hard for advancement and was passed over on every occasion. An idea entered his head that the recognition he deserved was being unfairly withheld.

The hankering to protest swelled within him. What astounded his colleagues was the way he chose to vent his anger.

It was all, of course, legitimate and proper. But not the conduct expected from a man in his position. He elected to defend a group of prisoners arraigned on charges of treason. Not just any prisoners, of course, but notorious revolutionaries, almost certainly guilty of the offences alleged. But Wetherell, brilliant lawyer that he was, stretching the statute book until it creaked, secured their acquittal.

His motives were transparent to both the Lord Chancellor and the Temple Bar. It was seen for exactly what it was. A treacherous act. A thinly-veiled defiance against the institution that had nurtured him kindly in the past. An institution that, whilst ponderous, still had the power to honour him further or quietly put him out to grass.

In proving his prowess at the bar he'd triumphed. But his success turned out to be a curate's egg. He was subsequently offered respectable legal offices, but they never figured among the highest ranks. At one time in the past he'd held the position of Solicitor General, but it was never to be offered again. It seems these events have made Wetherell what he is today; a middle ranking legal officer and a campaigning politician considered by many, including his closest compatriots, to be pedantic and bigoted.

And now, with many miles having passed under its wheels, the grime covered coach clatters into Queen Square, coming to a halt with a jerk before the grand portico of the Mansion House. Even through the rain, now driving harder than ever, the massive fluted marble columns and the tall, elegant windows mark this out as a magnificent building. Perhaps journey's end has put Wetherell in a better frame of mind. As he descends the carriage steps, lowered by a welcoming footman, he notes the cold wet weather has at least damped down the foul smells he usually encounters at this juncture. As he mounts the marble staircase to the entrance of the building his mind is focused on the thorny issues he'll be expected to tackle during the day.

'Good mornin to 'ee Sir Charles, delighted to see you here again. Forsooth, horrible weather, ain't it? I trust your journey from London was not too difficult?' enquires Mayor Pinney, who looks up from a conversation he's having with the under-sheriff in the vast entrance hall.

'Bloody miserable man. Draughty, damp and bitter cold. Cold as hell itself I shouldn't wonder', replies Wetherell, 'and the change of horses at Malborough was slow yet again. Pleased to be back in the warm again Pinney, though peeved at the mountain of work on my plate. Suppose I shouldn't grumble though, it's the same when I'm up in London. It's tougher, now Grey's rabble are in power, than when we were running the country ourselves. We've got to trim his sails. That man's hell bent on forcing through changes and, I tell you, they'll give you no pleasure whatsoever.'

'Look Pinney old man, I really can't tarry now, I must get on. But I do need to spend some time with you alone. Can we take lunch tomorrow? There are a couple of documents we must look over together before I return to Westminster.'

A grunt and a nod from the mayor is all that's required before the Recorder strides on towards the grand spiral staircase.

From cellar to attics, the Mansion House has been appointed with no consideration to expense. The Recorder's office occupies half of the third floor of the building. Rooms of various sizes open up from either side of the wide central corridor. Each is well furnished and warmed by open log fires. Every one is paneled in finely tooled oak which covers its walls from floor to ceiling. Portraits of former city dignitaries, resplendent in ceremonial robes, hang in various places around the walls.

At the very end of the corridor, Wetherell's personal chambers. A small suite of rooms equipped with all he needs; a large wardrobe for garments, bookcases ranged around the walls, a small basin for washing and his personal mahogany partner's desk. In this sanctum he can count on privacy it's almost impossible to find elsewhere. A place to conduct meetings and to review his papers in peace.

To one side of the private suite is a huge open hall, given over to administration. Manned by thirty five industrious clerks, all being on the Recorder's staff, it looks, at first glance, like a furious paperwork factory. Gas mantles hang from the tall ceilings and brackets on the walls, filling the room with a gentle yellow light. The walls are lined by bookcases crammed with manuscripts and contracts, elaborately carved cadenzas and huge chests with brass strappings. The space they encircle is crammed with tables, portfolios, canterburies and bureaux. Condensation glistens on the upper panes of the tall windows through which the bleakness of the January day is ominously apparent. A gentle murmur of muted conversation fills the room.

Seated at every table and desk there's a functionary, deeply engrossed in his own appointed task. A quill pen in hand, writing carefully into a ledger or onto a document or an architectural plan. Between them this ant-hill of clerks are responsible for ensuring the city's records are maintained in good order. They also organise the minutiae of hearings and assizes, the scheduling of magistrates and judges and numerous other legal proceedings. Indeed all the clockwork of justice for the entire Bristol area appears to be carried out within this very room.

After Wetherell has been fortified by a large glass of sherry and has spent some time standing close to the roaring fire, he turns to inspect his desk. A deep pile of correspondence has built up during his absence. Silently, perhaps malevolently, lying in wait for him. It's commonplace this amounts to thirty letters a day, sometimes more. Local citizens of every rank petition him regularly on the most diverse matters that have any sort of legal connotation.

Several of the items in his tray today are simply notes from colleagues in the city administration, encouraging him to continue his strong opposition to reform in the House. A thick envelope, copperplate script, catches his eye. It's from a mercantile sea captain, based in the port. The man's received a punitive fine for trading in slaves. Imbecile. He must know it's been outlawed for years. Does he really expect the Recorder to intervene? Well, he'll be a long time awaiting any reply. Under this there must be a dozen pieces of correspondence all asking, in their own way, for the same thing. They're from local constables, titled landowners, wealthy farmers, damn it even a couple of his fellow aldermen. They're all demanding he take action to end the lawless activity of the Kilbridge Lane Gang before it's too late.

The City of Bristol is governed by a municipal corporation which operates in an independent manner, since it answers chiefly to its own constitution. Its officers are the Mayor and twelve aldermen, each of whom takes principal responsibility for one or more aspects of the city's administration. Day to day decision making and management is in the hands of thirty common councilmen - this council being a body that includes the two sheriffs. They exercise their authority with the help of constables, bailiffs, watchmen and city guards. It's no surprise that each of these bodies operates independently, and confusion often ensues. In a genuine emergency the Mayor also has a call upon the Dragoons, garrisoned close by in the city.

The laws of England are universal across the realm and administered by a judicial system that looks to Parliament for statute and the Attorney General for direction. This places Wetherell in an ambiguous position. He's allied to Bristol's Corporation but not strictly a member of it; has keen interests in the city's prosperity but does not actually represent it. His power over its citizens can be great, through sentencing them to transportation or execution; but it's unlikely they see him as impartial. No, in their eyes, whatever his formal positions, he's a city official, part of the elite. At Parliament, Bristol is not his constituency, yet his allies and enemies there all believe its views strongly influence his own. With all this as a backdrop he strives to carry out his responsibilities honourably and with painstaking diligence. For, whilst many consider his political principles misguided, Wetherell is truly a man of integrity and possesses an acute understanding of what is just and what is otherwise.

An additional complication, for him, lies in his office also having responsibility for maintaining all local records of property transactions, maps, deeds, rights of way, conditions placed on the usage of land and such associated matters. Whilst he is not directly involved in such mundane matters, the Corporation looks to him for guidance in any major endeavour involving corporate property or land. This is an unwritten duty he's been happy to accept since it increases the value he brings to his office. Informally he's become the legal adviser to, perhaps even the conscience of, the executive and as such he's usually drawn into any weighty considerations they might have.

Wetherell takes a decision on which of all the pressing matters he must attend to first. He is determined to devote some hours to preparation for his opposition speech against the long expected Reform Bill. This, if enacted, will radically widen enfranchisement and representation across the nation, but particularly in the cities. For him such a notion is untenable, unthinkable. It would simply encourage the rebels and agitators who, over the last few years, seem to be popping up everywhere. If they aren't burning crops they're breaking machines or disturbing the peace on the streets. He knows his inner conviction will equip him to speak persuasively on the issue; there's just a chance that a really convincing performance might restore his damaged reputation with the establishment he seems to have offended. But sounding authoritative on the matter will require considerable research, a good grasp of the facts and some careful planning.

Without doubt must meet Hartnoll, if only briefly, since he's quite sure he'll soon be asked to proffer advice to the executive on the proposed suspension bridge. With the announcement of a second competition the major political risk has been overcome, but regaining the time lost by the first cannot be left to chance. He is reasonably confident that things will have moved on in his absence, but nevertheless a personal review today is essential. It's critical at this stage for him to keep abreast of progress and to understand what still needs to be accomplished. Thank goodness Hartnoll is involved, since the man seems eminently capable of pushing things forward on his own initiative. He's already shown he has no need for close supervision.

One more vital task that must be started today is to review all information available about the activities and felonies of the Kilbridge Lane Gang. The sheer volume of correspondence on his desk suggests this has risen above simple rural villainy. He resolves to meet with the Sheriff as soon as possible and ask him to compile a report. He'll also raise the issue with Pinney, assuming they do meet at lunch tomorrow. The mayor is an astute and intelligent individual, someone whose opinion can be trusted. He'll be sure to have an opinion on how serious this situation really is.

But once the tedium all these various tasks draw to an end, Wetherell anticipates an enjoyable evening. The diary appointment he mentioned to the Mayor is to take dinner with his old friend, Sir Nicholas Morgan. Like himself, Morgan had trained in law and was subsequently called to the bar. But on the death of his father he inherited a large estate near Newport that now commands his full time involvement. Accordingly he resigned his profession and took up residence at the family home. Since then he's become involved in a number of significant industrial enterprises. Morgan is staying in Bristol overnight; he and Wetherell have agreed to take the opportunity to catch up on their news.

With a plan now clear in his mind, Wetherell rings a small bell on the desk in front of him and prepares to start his long day's work.

Chapter 10

None of Jed Strickland's old partners in crime would have the bottle to question his resourcefulness. The man's got many faults and a quick temper is one of them. They've all discovered that, to their cost. But the same mates know he's resilient and dependable, even in the direst of scrapes. They've shared many close shaves alongside him, carrying out robberies across the Ridings and up into Northumberland.

This morning finds the man several hundred miles from those acquaintances and the family that disowned him years ago. Now he's going to need every ounce of his resourcefulness, for he owns to no more than the clothes in which he stands. Not a farthing in his pocket and no friend to whom he can turn. The city, into which he's just been unceremoniously ejected through the prison gates, is a closed book as far as he's concerned. He's penniless, alone and in very foreign territory.

A decent meal and warmer clothes are his first priority. Some years ago he would straightway have sought out the nearest mark and used any means to get what he wanted. Whatever was easiest, just as soon as he saw a chance. But time and bitter experience have made him wiser. He's no intention of finding himself straight back inside the stinking hell-hole from which he's just been released.

In this unfamiliar city the odds of pulling off a nice clean job are heavily stacked against him. If he's forced to run, how can he figure which are the dead ends, which are clear routes to make his escape? Sadly his appearance right now will lead most decent citizens to guess he's a villain and, in any event, there are too many people milling around. He's simply going to have to put up with the hunger and chill in his ribs for an hour or so. He reasons there's little profit staying in the city so decides to set out on the journey Doggart suggested. As soon as he comes across a mark that's suitably remote, suitably safe, then he'll set about improving his lot.

Of course this plan will eventually involve asking for directions; Doggart couldn't explain every twist and turn all the way to Kilbridge. But Strickland's confident he can get within five miles of the village without talking to another soul. Simply follow the river, in the direction of Bath. When you see the road run close by the river, that's the point to strike off north.

And so this becomes Strickland's game plan. Sticking to the river bank. Making as much progress as he can today in his shoddy, leaking boots. Hopefully getting far enough away from the city to come across an open door or a pair of loose shutters. Then a simple job, one that that he'll have carried off a thousand times in the past, and he'll obtain victuals at least, if not clothes and money. The river flows right past the prison gates and it doesn't take a genius to know which way to turn. In the certain knowledge that he has a long walk before him, Strickland stoically takes the first stride.

If we had sufficient time to spare, we could follow Jed Strickland on his tedious journey to the east. But we would learn little more, for the events that follow come pretty close to the scheme he thought out at the gates of the gaol. Suffice to say that he arrives a good thirty six hours later. He still smells as rank as he did when he left - he's found no opportunity to wash and might not have taken it even if one had been presented to him. But he's fed, shod in stout leather boots and wrapped in a rough blanket that might have been used by a horse before coming into his possession.

In the course of his perambulations he's quietly visited a number of properties along the way. Some of the householders will never know he called. Others might express a nagging concern over a curiously missing joint of meat or a broken pane of glass. But for Strickland this has been just another day.

Another day in which he's turned all he encountered to his own best advantage.

Chapter 11

Over a week has passed since Hartnoll met with Maynard and Locke at the Mayor's Chapel. In that interval he's been far from idle. Similar meetings occurred with four other small scale contractors, each held in a different location. None at premises that are normally used by Bristol Corporation for business.

During each one Hartnoll made copious notes in his neat, precise hand. Details of the tradesmen to whom he's talked, the number of men they employ, the resources at their disposal, the occasions where they've previously done noteworthy work. He's evaluated their strengths and weaknesses, apparently objectively and certainly with meticulous care. Finally he has committed a summary of these evaluations to paper, in a way that he's modestly inclined to admit, appears highly impartial and conclusive.

The individuals he's talked to, like Locke and Maynard, all have the capability to take on the first stages of the eagerly awaited suspension bridge. And Hartnoll's genuinely keen that the bridge project should be a success. For the good of Bristol and its citizens of course, but more importantly to establish his own reputation, through the small but essential part he's intending to play.

In parallel with the meetings and preparing his report, Hartnoll's continued to push forward with a subtle campaign he'd quietly set in train as soon as the second competition was announced. For it was then inspiration had sprung into his mind. What appeared to be a complete fiasco might well be turned to his own advantage.

Public contracts were always managed in a strictly procedural manner, subject to audits that protect them from any misfeasance. Presented in the right way, the very real danger of this project failing to advance quickly enough might persuade the authorities to relax this rigorous governance. Of course it would mean that any alternative proposed must recover their reputation speedily from the debacle Telford's intervention had brought.

Convincing the aldermen to abandon these processes was not something to be achieved by merely presenting the proposition as a good idea. No, Hartnoll has been astute enough to recognise that this notion must in no way be directly associated with himself, a mere functionary - if a senior functionary - of Wetherell's office. If it was not to be discounted out of hand, it would have to be seen to come from aldermen and councilmen far better recognised and respected than himself. He'd need to engineer things such that those individuals would turn to him to put any plan they agreed into action.

Fortunately Hartnoll's long service with the Corporation, and his involvement in many previous construction projects, has resulted in strong relationships with several of the councillors co-opted to the committee adjudging the second competition.

It was with these august men that he started a campaign of subtle lobbying many weeks ago. Often during a legitimate meeting on some entirely unconnected subject, perhaps at a recess, he would raise the dilemma of the bridge. On other occasions, through pure coincidence it seemed, he had just happened to find himself in the same tavern as one or two of the burgesses he was determined to influence.

Through these casual conversations he learned of others who might either support or perhaps violently oppose the radical approach that was in his mind. This led to yet another set of apparently chance encounters. The latter became progressively difficult to contrive; they involved him approaching near strangers and required real audacity. But Hartnoll is resourceful, an intelligent man with a sound knowledge of the

Corporation and a good deal of nerve. In the event he succeeded remarkably well in sowing the seeds of his proposition.

In the process of this campaign he discovered that two major factors were key. The first being the predilections of the men he was influencing. Bristol Corporation is not unusual. Its governing body stinks of the political, reflecting the government of the nation. There are Whigs and there are Tories. Moreover there are factions within each group - the Tories with their Steadfast Society and White Lion Club, the Whigs with the Independent Club. Unsurprisingly, within all these groups, there's a certain amount of dissention. But the people who make them up are from the same mould – they're all mercantile traders or bankers or ship-owners or similarly employed. In short, prosperous men. They understand business and they know that often profit is only accomplished at the expense of a little risk. So Hartnoll had sometimes embarked on his crusade anticipating stiff resistance, only to discover the idea was almost torn from his hands by an enthusiastic audience.

His second trump card lay in the office he held, together with his superior's frequent absence. Without ever actually stating such, Hartnoll allowed his listeners to assume that the views he expressed, the ideas he fervently advocated, were actually those of the City Recorder rather than his own. He inferred that the propositions were the only viable way forward that they'd comply with both the laws of the land and the Corporation's own regulations and that this was Wetherell's decided conviction.

What Hartnoll was outlining to his audience made enormous good sense. Wetherell, attending the House for much of that time, was not there to comprehend closely, nor gainsay the story being put about by his employee. Hartnoll advocated a pre-emptive start to construction, commencing immediately the winning design had been announced, thus giving the city the speediest return on tolls and forestalling any future attempt to cancel the project. Since this clearly could never be

110

accomplished by working to the normal commercial process, he suggested there might be an alternative and alluded to a forthcoming report that would detail a way to resolve this conundrum.

As he inferred then and continues to infer now, this report will be issued by Sir Charles Wetherell's office rather than by a certain Gabriel Hartnoll. For Hartnoll is determined to distance himself as much as he is able from the proposition, and most especially from any association with parties such as Maynard and Locke.

So, today finds the clerk at his own desk in the Mansion House. He's turned his attention, finally, to completing the report he's promised to deliver. The details of this report have been thought through time after time in his mind; all that remains is to commit its substance to paper. And this is the essence of his plan:

The overall work will be divided into several parts, the first of these being the erection of towers at either end, with subsequent endeavours being the construction of the deck and the manufacture and installation of the cables. The initial phase need only concern preparation for the towers. The Corporation, he will say, has identified five building firms, each medium in size, all of whom are eager to have a part in such a prestigious undertaking.

A choice of two builders will be made to construct the abutments, these being necessary to support the towers and minimise the span of the deck. Work on these should start immediately. He will include an appendix to the report comparing the merits of all the builders considered, including their willingness to commence work at their own risk.

There is minimal risk since specialist skills are not required for such relatively simple structures. In the unlikely event of a problem occurring it would be straightforward for another builder to continue. It simply is not possible, in the time available, to establish proper contracts before the work commences; the normal tendering process is far too lengthy. Thus the committee is strongly advised to select the two builders required on the basis of evidence carefully gathered and presented in the appendix to the report. The names of those who seem most suitable appear on the final page.

Strictly speaking, no commercial policies will be breached, since the builders will not be contracted for reward. If their performance turns out to be satisfactory, and if they later happen to be successful in a formal tender process, their services might then be retained. Meanwhile vital progress will have been made without any abuse of statutory process.

Hartnoll spends several days in the production of this report, during which he is often still at his desk at midnight. It is written, rewritten, corrected and improved. Finally he is satisfied and delegates clerks to make a dozen copies. The document is presented to the selection committee in early February.

~

It is Tuesday morning and nothing has been heard from the committee. More than a week has passed following the meeting convened to consider Hartnoll's plan. During those long days he has sat at his desk, apparently engrossed in his work. But in truth he's been unable to keep his mind on his assignments. He has played his hand. If Wetherell were to get wind of his misrepresentation he knows he couldn't explain it away.

Did he but know it, his concerns are groundless. Through pure inspiration he has conceived a simple but irresistible strategy. His meticulous execution has given it a momentum of its own. His artifice has succeeded to a greater extent than even he had dared hope.

The councilmen he's lobbied have been eager to promote his plan as if it was of their own devising. Why shouldn't they take the credit after all? It's a scheme with some merit, resolving the impossible fix in which the administration has found itself. Their wholehearted endorsement has persuaded the committee that there's minimal risk in passing the plan.

The attention of everybody who had a serious interest is currently focussed on the outcome of the competition. Small scale activity in the Avon gorge at this stage is unlikely to attract scrutiny. Building preparations might be obvious to anyone who looks closely, but some sort of activity there would surely be expected. It will likely be assumed to be a ground survey or suchlike. As long as nothing major started until a few days after the announcement it's highly unlikely suspicion will be aroused.

Thus it was that his scheme, unknown to Hartnoll, had already secured the Corporation's agreement. It was quite deliberate that no formal announcement was made, and that the minutes of the meeting were highly ambiguous in their wording.

The only risk to his plan had been that the committee might choose contractors other than Locke and Maynard. But Hartnoll had done his work far too thoroughly for that to happen.

The following day he finds himself summoned to a meeting with the chairman of the committee. He's instructed to put his proposal into action immediately. He is also informed that some sort of stipend will be arranged, in advance of contracts, for each of the firms selected, since the Corporation does not want to risk possible interruption if either contractor were to go out of business. This will be accounted for as payment of ex gratia expenses which he must personally manage. On no account must the council's books reveal deviation from the statutory process. Hartnoll struggles to suppress a triumphant grin and returns to his desk to carry out this heavy responsibility.

~

That very evening Hartnoll can be found strolling along a broad tree-lined street on the outskirts of Clifton Down. Before long dusk will descend; an army of starlings are making a furious noise as they prepare to roost. The buildings in this part of the city are terraced, nevertheless they're large and well maintained. The area boasts a genteel air, suggesting its residents are men of significant status. Hartnoll seems to know well which house he intends to visit, turning aside quickly and climbing the three wide stone steps to knock upon its front door.

A nervous young servant girl admits him without introduction and takes his coat. She shows him immediately into the study where the householder, seated at his writing desk, transpires to be someone he already knows.

'Welcome Gabriel', Locke calls out warmly, 'Tilly - fetch my visitor a glass of brandy will you?'. Rising he shakes his visitor by the hand, ' I'm sure you need something to fortify you after your journey.'

'Come in man and join me by the fire. God, it's been a trying few weeks whilst the wheels have been grinding in that Mansion House of yours. A strain on me and that's for sure. I dare say a few hairs have gone grey in the process. Now, tell me you have some news - whether it's good or bad.'

'Indeed I have, brother-in-law' replies Hartnoll, 'And I'm delighted to say things have turned out better than we planned.'

114

Is it conceivable that either Locke or Hartnoll are this foolish? Related by marriage and yet still planning to conspire so blatantly? Not in the least, since they're absolutely confident of never being exposed. Through a curious train of circumstances their relationship is concealed from all but a handful of individuals.

Indeed, they were oblivious to it themselves until around four years ago and it only came to light in the aftermath of a death. Locke's wife, Rachel, had elderly parents living close to the city. Her father Septimus had been rector at St Augustines' until he became too frail to carry on. The parish was generous, he had to quit the rectory but he and Harriet were given the tenure of a small cottage nearby.

There they lived for some months, Septimus now aging faster than the passage of time itself. It was not long before he passed away, leaving a widow almost as frail as himself. She was terrified at the prospect of living alone so Rachel reorganised her own home to provide her a room. They could tell the death had affected Harriet deeply. She became very confused and ate almost nothing, no matter how appetising the food placed in front of her. Weeks before she was bright and coherent, now she'd ramble for hours.

Usually the maid took meals up to the old lady, by now mostly confined to her bed. One day, feeling daughterly, Rachel carried up the bowl of broth herself. When she entered the bedroom the old lady appeared to be asleep. But as she placed the bowl on the bedside cabinet her mother's scrawny hand emerged from under the sheets and seized her by the wrist.

'Daughter', she croaked, 'I know I'm not long for the world now and there is something I must tell you before I pass on.'

Rachel realized with a shock that the old woman was, for once, entirely lucid.

'Rachel, you always were our little girl - Septimus and mine, I mean. That's how we thought of you and that's what we've always let you believe yourself. But the truth is daughter that you're not. We were not your parents, though we would dearly loved to have been so. No girl. You were born to a vagrant, a destitute young woman who lived on the streets, was always in drink and who sold her body whenever she was sober enough to do so. You were born on the streets and your birth almost sapped the life from her. She lost the energy to get food and hadn't the strength to care for you.

A friend of Septimus had care of her parish. He learned of this and petitioned us to look after you. He knew we were childless even though we desperately yearned for a family. We needed little persuasion. We took you into our home the next day. The other little one, she went elsewhere.'

'What do you mean mother, the other little one?' Rachel had asked, but the effort of making such a long speech had exhausted Harriet and her head fell vacant and expressionless on the pillow.

Intrigued, Rachael immediately set out on an investigation of her own. Searching through her father's letters she eventually tracked down the minister who had arranged her fostering. The old man was infirm, but clear headed and his memory still intact. He confirmed what Harriet had related. Her real mother, an alcoholic and a prostitute, had given birth to twin baby girls. He had taken pity upon them, born on the streets, unlikely to survive above a week. Realising he would never save the mother, he had convinced her that the babies should be placed with people who would care for them properly.

Since then the two sisters had been raised by families separated by just a couple of miles but in complete ignorance of one another's existence. After much coaxing, the minister finally recalled where her sister had been placed. And the very next day she was reunited with her twin.

116

Rachael was unable to contain her delight. She insisted Locke accompany her to meet Abigail, her newly discovered sister, and on that day he first encountered Hartnoll. The two men discovered common interests and were easy in one another's company. Within weeks they were not only brothers in law but also potential partners in crime.

It wasn't long at all before Hartnoll came up with small ways in which their relationship could be put to mutual advantage. The council had small building projects to execute on a regular basis. He didn't have control over awarding these jobs to builders, but he worked side by side with the men who did and steered them skilfully in Locke's direction. However, he always distanced himself entirely from Locke's business. His lobbying for the builder was never too fervent, or too obvious. And it was only in the past couple of months that a major opportunity, with potential to make them both extremely wealthy, had become apparent to him. And now, as a result of his ingenuity and his nerve, this more ambitious scheme had delivered its first fruits.

'Congratulations Gabriel, you've made a truly excellent fist of this shenanigan. May Heaven, the angels, and of course the good Corporation of Bristol, reward you handsomely!' cries Locke, exuberant with relief and delight, 'There's no cause for delay now. We must make ready to start. When will the winner of the second competition be announced?'

'In just under three weeks' time, Elijah. On 16th March. It's a Wednesday. You're absolutely right. We need to start our preparations. Immediate action is called for. Once our plan is underway, there won't be a living body with sufficient confidence or courage to put a stop to it.'

'Believe me Gabriel, I've taken all the necessary steps. I think we just need to ensure now that our friend Maynard is equally ready for the fray. Which reminds me, Gabriel, I wanted to get some reassurance on his behalf. I must admit I've grown quite protective of that young man whilst I've been working alongside

117

him. I'd appreciate your word on it that our little plan isn't going to put him at any serious disadvantage. I sense the fellow's still mighty nervous about the whole thing.'

'Relax, Elijah. I omitted to mention, neither he nor you will now be working completely at risk. The committee have undertaken to advance some sort of consideration for expense. Maynard will be looked after. We are in much greater danger than he - should we ever be exposed. Please don't be insulted when I remind you to be exceptionally careful when we're with him. It's critical that we don't hint of the true nature of our relationship to him, or anybody else. In fact, to avoid anybody suspecting our collaboration in this business, it might be best if we only meet in future at his premises. That will give us both a good excuse for being together and his presence contradicts any notion of a conspiracy between us.'

'I take my hat off to you Gabriel,' replies Locke, 'You are the sharpest fellow I've ever met. For every obstacle, every predicament, you come up with a truly ingenious solution. My friend, I'm full of admiration, I feel honoured to be your brother-in-law. Why don't we travel down together to Maynard's stone-yard on the morrow, take him the good news and ensure his part of the plan is ready to commence.'

Full of cheer Locke calls out to his maidservant for more brandy and the two men spend a further hour engrossed in conversation about their families. Finally Hartnoll takes a hired cab to his own home to prepare for the following day.

~

The early morning of Friday 25th February started out bitterly cold, but now the sun is burning away the mist as it rises slowly over the horizon. The air is clear, birds are singing, without a doubt a hint of spring is in the air. However, an overnight frost has chilled everything in Maynard's yard - stones, blocks and tackle, chisels, hammers - making the first hour of work difficult and painful on the masons' fingers and thumbs. But using mittens, together with a good deal of blowing on hands, has enabled Maynard, Lionel Emden and Benjamin Gurney, together with the young improver Peter Austin, to make good progress carving the remaining finials destined for the Zion chapel.

Over the past few weeks, Maynard has sensed a growing air of restlessness and uncertainty amongst his colleagues. Their concern has never been directly shared with him, but he's seen them huddled together in hushed conversations and the atmosphere is more strained and reserved than ever it has been in the past.

They have occasionally asked him about what will happen to their partnership, once the chapel work is complete. He's only been able to reassure them in the vaguest possible terms.

'I'm giving some thought to another job that might come our way', he has blustered when challenged, but this assurance is so vague he's certain none of the men is convinced. He's not dared broach the possibility that this 'other job' might involve working for a goodly period with no reward. He knows such a detail would convince them the opportunity is real but the prospect could equally scare them into looking for alternative employment.

As they continue, with rifflers and glass paper, to put the finishing touches to the delicate stonework pieces, Maynard knows his time is fast running out. If this plan for the bridge doesn't come to fruition shortly, Lionel, Ben and Peter will surely start to make their own decisions about the future.

With such gloomy thoughts weighing on him, hope springs up in his heart as he hears horses in the yard and, looking around the wall of the dressing shop, sees Locke and Hartnoll dismounting from a trap in the farmyard. He's so excited that, without stopping to remove his apron, he runs up the pasture to welcome them. After customary greetings have been exchanged, Maynard ushers his two visitors into the farmhouse to take some coffee.

The three are gathered in Maynard's dining room and Hartnoll has shut the door with a purpose. Mary Ann, in the kitchen, strains her ears to catch the drift of their conversation, but it's hopeless. Once refreshed, Locke briefly summarises the situation as Hartnoll had explained it to him on the previous evening.

'On my life, this is the most excellent news' says Maynard, a great weight suddenly lifted from his shoulders, 'You can't know how relieved I am to hear this. Damn! We must go and spell it out to the men at once. Reassure them there's plenty of work now to keep them busy. Their fretting has been plain as a pikestaff lately. If we're going to rise to this challenge I'll be needing their absolute support. I think it would be best, with Mr Hartnoll's agreement, if he can explain the assignment to my fellows in his own way.'

Hartnoll readily agrees, suddenly enjoying the sense of power this situation has conferred upon him. Minutes later all three have made their way to the dressing shop, and Maynard has the masons stop work and lend their full attention. He introduces Hartnoll, who is unknown to the men, and Locke who they know principally by sight from the chapel. He announces that Hartnoll is to address them on a matter of some importance.

'Gentlemen' commences Hartnoll, with the same serious manner and intonation that had impressed itself upon Maynard when they first met. 'I am privileged to be here today on behalf of the Bristol City Corporation and to acquaint you with some good news. Through the efforts of your leader, Mr Maynard, your little enterprise has been selected to work, along with Mr

Locke's firm, on a municipal construction which is still so confidential that I cannot, at this stage, tell you what it is, or where it will be located. Suffice to say that preparation for parts of this construction must be put in hand immediately. In around four or five weeks' time you will be informed where the building is taking place and doubtless some of you will need to work at the site itself.'

'Needless to say, I am imparting this information to you strictly from need. It is, of course, information having the highest degree of confidentially and you must under no circumstances mention it to anybody else until I inform you otherwise. And I do mean anybody. Not your wives, not your children, certainly not your friends. Failure to comply with this strict condition will mean you all forfeit the work. You have been awarded this assignment due to the high quality craftsmanship you have demonstrated in the construction of the Zion chapel. But I must assure you that competition for this work has been fierce. If you fail us, by breaking confidentiality, it will not be difficult to replace you.'

'Due to the timing of the first stage of the work, the Corporation is in a position to pay you only a modest stipend during the first three months. But it will be sufficient to keep you fed and cover the necessary expenses to set things in motion. Mr Maynard here will be given more details about exactly what we need you to do; he will pass onto yourselves only the information you need to know. Now gentlemen, with your permission, I will draw my remarks to a close since Locke and myself must now discuss those further details alone with Mr Maynard.'

For a moment, Emden, Gurney and Austin are rendered speechless by his short address. But they rapidly fall into furious discussions amongst themselves, speculating on the good fortune that appears to have come their way. Maynard pauses only to register the general tenor of their remarks, feeling mightily relieved that they've all taken the news well,

121

sensing their excitement and intrigue at this new secretive venture. Immensely satisfied he withdraws along with Hartnoll and Locke to learn more in the comfort of the farmhouse.

'Mr Maynard' Hartnoll begins, once they're reconvened around the dining table, 'I think it is true to say that little can prevent us now from moving forwards as we have previously discussed and planned. I trust therefore that you will now put all your energies into securing the necessary materials and make other all preparations necessary for this undertaking?'

'You have my word on it Mr Hartnoll, I'll start within the week. I'll wager the first stage isn't especially complicated. As soon as I know what materials I need I shall be in a position to order them and start work.'

'Very well. I'm sure you understand the sensitive nature of the situation and why I could not tell your men exactly what the job will entail. It is imperative, at this stage, that word is not allowed to spread too far. There are certain aspects that will remain highly secret throughout the duration of this project, such as plans and drawings and the utilisation of some specialist equipment that we've recently acquired from France. Due to the demands on these items, we'll probably leave some of them in your yard. Frankly they'll be safer here than on site. But it's vital they are secured at all times. I'm hoping you can furnish us with a robust lock up. A cellar or a small shed should do. Somewhere we can store the stuff with complete confidence.'

'That should be no problem' replies Maynard, 'By chance I built in two strong tool sheds when I set up my workshop here. I could easily move the contents of both into one and make the other available for your items.'

'Excellent. I happen to have one such document with me that I can give you a sight of now.' For the second time in their acquaintance he unrolls a sizeable drawing. 'It gives us an early view of Mr Brunel's currently favoured design. This should guide your thoughts as to the type and quantity of materials you will initially require. You see the internal structure of the abutment should be brick and rubble, but it sits on granite foundation with a local red sand stone specified for the cladding material.'

He spreads out the drawing on the table and Maynard studies it intently for some time.

'May I ask how you came by these drawings? They seem to be remarkably detailed' he enquires, but Hartnoll merely smiles benevolently at him and replies that it is better not to ask.

'I assume I should make any notes I need as presumably you can't leave these papers in my possession?' Maynard retorts.

'My dear Mr Maynard, you are at last beginning to comprehend the manner in which these things must be done. Your assumption is correct.' Hartnoll thus brings the discussion to a pre-emptory close. After giving Maynard a few minutes to extract the information he requires, Hartnoll rolls up his drawing once again and departs with Locke, leaving Maynard to ponder his next steps.

Chapter 12

Not far north of Swinton the soft contours of the Gloucestershire countryside change dramatically. The low flood plain through which the Avon flows gives way to steep hills rising up and stretching away to Bath in the east and Wick in the north. This tumbling upland region is more sparsely inhabited than the plain around Swinton. It's home to just a handful of hamlets, scattered here and there, boasting populations of no more than forty or fifty inhabitants apiece.

Typical of these tiny communities is the isolated village of Kilbridge Lane. Folklore says its name arose from the slaughterhouse which stood here, long ago, beside the small stream that still flows under its narrow thoroughfare. A clutch of run-down dwellings are huddled on each side of this dirt track, perched on a small plateau of land and barely sheltered by a grassy hilltop. Standing isolated at the summit of the hill, exposed to the elements from all directions, is a seldom frequented Methodist church, absurdly implying the presence of God in this forsaken backwater.

Alongside this worn out place of worship stands its vicarage, equally exposed and shunned by any clergy for many a long year. It is a crumbling edifice, lingering tenaciously well past its allotted time, pounded frequently by wind and rain, derelict and decaying. Although deserted by men of the cloth, the building has perversely become the home, after a fashion, to a most singular collection of individuals.

What little moldy wallpaper remains on its walls is peeling badly, loosened by rain water that frequently drips through cracked tiles in the roof. The high square windows are small and grubby, admitting a fraction of the meagre light that could be had from this overcast winter's day. A handful of tallow candles burn in saucers placed randomly around the sills and mantle-pieces. They gutter frantically, improving the visibility but slightly, casting a dull glimmer over the dusty wooden floorboards and a few sticks of chairs and tables abandoned by the minister when he at last quit this living.

Any God-fearing person who was misguided enough to stray inside would be faced with sight to daunt the stoutest heart. Small groups of men, disreputable in appearance, are scattered here and there around its dilapidated cobweb-strewn rooms. Without exception they're shabbily clothed, unwashed and unshaven. Conversation is scarce; those exchanges that can be heard are loaded with oaths and invective. At the best of times this is no place to warm the hearts of strangers. And just now the weather compounds its inhospitable atmosphere. The wind howls mournfully outside, forcing its way through the countless cracks and crevices that infest the fabric of this rotting pile.

When its last minister occupied the dwelling, he was not, by any means, a wealthy man. Nevertheless he would still have been expected to entertain his parishioners with dignity. The dining room furniture would have been of quality, selected with that responsibility in mind. And so the dining room is now the only place where anything remains that truly resembles furniture. Here too can be found the only chimney not blocked by bird nests. And in consequence this is where eight or nine of its occupants are sat, eating, drinking and playing cards.

It's no surprise that the vicarage's present occupants are all, to a man, no-goods and criminals of one persuasion or another. Not one has permanent employ; most are fathers and sons from families of Kilbridge itself and other hamlets nearby. Some take up casual work on the farms during spring and summer. But when winter sets in, especially when the weather is foul as it presently is, their days are chiefly empty and endless.

Most gather here to pass the time in company and to dream up easy ways to lay their hands on money for tobacco and drink. Practically all have a rubbing acquaintance with the local constable and have sampled the hospitality of his tiny lock-up on more than one occasion. Some have served prison terms in Bristol or Bath, mostly for robbery and assault. Probably they have been lucky, for our legal system nowadays is punitive. Sentences have become ever harsher. A man can be hanged for any number of crimes. And those that escape the rope can easily find themselves deported to the other side of the world. Even the most brazen of this band of criminals lives constantly with that knowledge and the ever-present fear of judicial retribution.

"You've had that knave up your sleeve Jacobs, you bloody cheat". These words, barely audible, nevertheless break the silence like the hiss of a snake. Suddenly tension is thick in the air, goose bumps burst out on the skin. There are four men playing Faro in the far corner of the room. For a split second time seems to stand still. In the next, one player has leapt from where he sat on the boards and dragged his accuser against the wall by his neckerchief. Without releasing this one-handed grip he bangs the man's head twice against the crumbling lath and plaster.

"Call my honour to question would you, you worthless little shit?" Jacobs spits his accusation full into the unfortunate man's face, "Must be your eyesight failing you, loser. I'll have an apology from you right now. Else blood will be spilt, and believe me Barton, it won't be mine."

Barton swallows, his breathing cut off by the cloth that Jacobs has screwed tight around his neck. His eyes dart pleadingly from face to face of his fellow players and other men now gathering around. But no-one is coming to his defence or backing up his allegation.

"Stop Jacobs, for God's sakes let me loose man. I'll own I might be mistaken about the cards you were holding. Will you accept an apology and unhand me?"

In answer Jacobs swings his victim around and flings him back on the floor, scattering cards and coins across the boards.

"Aye", he replies, "We'll bury the hatchet on this occasion, but I warn all of you to take heed. Any of you scum who call me dishonest will find my blade has his name already etched upon it."

From start to finish, this spat has been silently observed by the occupant of the broken chair placed plumb before the fire. A chair that's never moved and in which no-one ever dares to sit, other than its present incumbent. His eyes narrowed imperceptibly when the commotion erupted, otherwise he's shown precious little emotion. Not even shifted his position. He's well built, a muscular individual of forty years or thereabouts. His clothes are less threadbare that most of his companions. A full head of long black hair falls over his shoulders, wavy greasy locks. Framing a rugged face with an agreeable countenance, marred by a raw red scar running from the centre of the chin to the lobe of his right ear.

The scum using this ruin as home have no badges of rank. Even so, over time, an unspoken pecking order has emerged, every bit as strict as if this were a garrison of soldiers. And the greatest deference is always shown to the man before the fire. Benefiting chiefly from its meagre warmth. A privilege that clearly marks him out as their leader.

Perhaps it's no surprise that he's adopted the soubriquet of "Captain". Although people may have called him this before he ever turned up at Kilbridge, seven or eight years ago. Few are aware of his true identity; any that have chanced to discover his name is Hugo Wakelin would never be foolhardy enough to breathe it in his presence.

Most of these men, out of boredom, turn up at the vicarage every day. Not so the Captain. Often he's absent for a week or more at a time. It's unknown where he goes, or how, but

127

everybody suspects he has contacts spread far and wide from a previous existence. Today he has a purpose in being here. Word has reached him of a new arrival, a man who has asked to sleep here and offered to join any enterprise where his skills might count.

Wakelin hasn't become the gang's leader simply on account of his physical superiority and his frightening lack of compassion. He's also a good deal more intelligent than the others. He's can't discount that this new recruit may be on the level. On the other hand he might have been sent to infiltrate them, an agent of the authorities. Only a meeting with the fellow can set his mind at rest. But when Wakelin turned up here earlier Strickland, the newcomer, was out on the hills netting rabbits.

The man dispatched to fetch him steps through the door at this moment, with the stranger a pace behind. Wakelin wordlessly gestures the new man should sit on a three legged stool beside his chair. For a minute or more he simply stares, unblinking, into the eyes of the other, waiting for the stranger to avoid his gaze or not.

'They tell me you call yourself Strickland", the Captain challenges, "Well I've no time for fairy tales. What's your real name man?"

'God's honest truth sir it really is Strickland - Jed Strickland, to tha' I'll swear. I'm native to Durham as ye might guess ba ma accent. '

Wakelin leans forward. He pulls a long sharp knife from a sheath on his belt and flashes the blade in his companion's face. In one continuous movement he uses the same hand to pick up a dry stick from beside the hearth. Is this a blatant threat of violence intended or is he merely attending to his needs? It's impossible to tell. Sitting back he whittles the stick to fashion a toothpick.

'It's a miracle you find yourself so far from home then Mr Strickland, so mysteriously anxious to join our little group. Frankly we don't get a lot of visitors from the north. Your arrival seems a bit too convenient for me and I've got the wellbeing of my associates to account for. So, explain yourself to my satisfaction. Convince me you're not here to bring us trouble.'

'Aye man, ah can. Ah've walked here a day back from the New Gaol at Bristol. Ah've been banged up there for months with a fella who swears he knows you. Doggart is the only name I have for him. But ah can describe where his wife lives for I took a message to her at his bidding.'

'That sounds like a fair start. I'll soon know if you're lying. There's a gaoler with secrets he'd prefer me to keep quiet. He'll soon get word from Jim Doggart. But what interests me Strickland – is why did you get thrown into that gaol in the first place?'

'Well mon, it war like this, see', replies Strickland, 'I ha' a much younger brother, nineteen the lad was and a canny piece of work, like meself. Alus in trouble. I reckon 'twas down to me he ended up that way. Anyhow, the young fool ha' one brush too many with the constable. There was a hue and cry out for his blood like. Took it into his damn-fool head to set off for 'merica. Fust I hear about this he's already left for Liverpool. I'm no soft touch Cap'n but I figured the lad was ma responsibility like, so I went after him.'

'The idiot boy stows away aboard a clipper, tied up in the docks, but by this time ah've caught up with him. Nowt ah say will persuade him to leave the vessel and I canna make too much noise about it for fear of discovery. Eventually the crew cast off wi' us both still aboard and we reach Bristol undiscovered. Then the customs men come on board and start poking about. We have to make shore sharpish, by climbing down an anchor chain. We're separated an we ha' to swim for it. The water's freezing and tastes o' shit. I made it to a rope

129

hanging over the quayside, but the lad founders in the water. It makes me sick t'ma heart. There was nothing I could do to save the young fella, me own arms and legs were weak as pastry with lack of victuals and the cold. I managed to find me way out a they docks without being seen; within minutes I were inside some posh bugger's parlour getting' meself something to eat. Caught in the act by a footman, Cap'n. The bastard had a musket. That's the truth of it.'

'You spin a good yarn Strickland. Who knows, it might even be true. But just as easily it could be a fantasy you've invented for me. Doggart's reply will tell us. If he vouches for you, you'll be welcome. Until then I've a mind to keep you chained up – but don't take offence. I can't run the risk you might be working with the constables. So, that's my notion; unless there's some other way you can prove your credentials to me.'

Strickland pulls back a shirt sleeve to reveal a sinewy bicep. Halfway up is an unsightly scab.

'Look closely here Cap'n', he explains, 'When I wa' no more than a bairn meself, I helped me da' and his mates to do a jeweller's shop. They pushed me through a wee window and I opened the door for them from inside. Everyone, the whole crew, were caught the next day. Da and ma uncle, they was both hanged. But the magistrate took pity on me, on account of ma age. Transportation was ma sentence. At Newcastle they impress a tattoo on yer arm just as yer boarding the ship. Look at this scab ... you can still make out part of that tattoo. Well, on account of ma size I escaped and got ashore before the ship weighed anchor. But I've had this mark ever since. When I was arrested in Bristol ah had to mutilate meself so as the authorities would na notice it. And I've been picking away at this scab every day since to keep it disguised.'

It's true, Wakelin can see two digits roughly imprinted in blue ink beneath the man's skin. 'Strickland', he says, 'That's good enough for me. Consider yourself one of the company. And you may have turned up at a very fortuitous time.'

'You won' regret this Cap'n, Ah put my word on it. You'll find me a canny pair o' hands.'

'I don't doubt it Strickland, but I need more than that. This outfit is crying out for new blood. Look around you. The fellows here are sound in their way, but they've lost their fire, they lack any real ambition. Yes, they pull off small jobs from time to time, but they're as likely to bungle them as get them right. Just last October Tom Courtney knifed his own father when they were both creeping up on the same Romany van in the dark.'

'Deuce! Hadn't they agreed the game beforehand?'

'Agreed beforehand Strickland? That's a laugh. No, they'd not even told one another they were on a job that night. Was an almighty cock-up. The old man bled to death and we had to bury him in secret. '

'You've probably not figured out how it goes here, so let me explain. Each of these lads thinks he's God's gift to robbery, in fact to crime in general. It comes natural to them to work alone and sometimes there's bad feeling running between them. Some are here 'cos their families won't put up with them at home, others because there's a price on their heads. But they all know full well the constables won't try to take them from this place.'

'On occasion I've persuaded a few of them to work together - truly a joint enterprise. It always turns out more successful, until afterwards when they start arguing. But that's the only future for us Strickland, there's no doubt in my mind. Trouble is these boys don't have any imagination. To land a haul that'll satisfy everybody, we need to pull off some really cracking jobs. There's plenty of opportunity around here; big country mansions, miles from anywhere and chock full of valuables. But a big mark like that means complications, thought and a lot of planning. Strickland, I need someone with a brain in his head. Someone who will help me figure out the angles to jobs like that and help knock together the schemes to carry them off. A man who'll encourage the others out of their small-minded ambitions. Something tells me you might just fit the bill.'

Somewhere, in the distance, the sound of an argument building between two youngsters is making itself heard above the howling wind.

'Aye, we favoured working in groups up in Durham', replies Strickland, 'It alus helps to ha' someone watching yow back, someone holding horse if yow lucky enough to have one. Does na alus work like, as ma da' proved at the jewellers. But when It does come off, it's worth the candle.'

'Trust me Strickland, I'm thinking bigger than organising a few lags and a horse', continues Wakelin, but his explanation is curtailed by the sound of a gunshot ringing out nearby.

'Scatter lads, it's the constables'. An anonymous shout goes up from the next room accompanied by a thunder of boots as men spring to their feet. The Captain however remains calm. He knows a surprise raid is impossible as there's a lookout posted on top of the church tower. With an unrestricted view for miles around. He draws his pistol however and barks a command.

'Strickland, and you too Jackson. Whatever's afoot, it's happening out there near the porch. Look sharp; get out there and bring back whoever's responsible. I'll wager you'll find there's no real danger.'

Seconds later his prediction is confirmed as Jackson and Strickland drag in two young gang members, ashen faced, one bleeding profusely from a flesh wound above his right knee. In Strickland's hand there's a Nock percussion pistol, wrested just seconds earlier from the older lad's fingers.

'Damn. Here's a pretty turn of events to be sure. Well, Saddler, and you Young. What in tarnation are you up to? I'll wager it's lucky one of you's not dead. You'd best be able to come up with a damned good explanation.'

'Unhand me you Geordie dogsbreath', Dick Saddler hisses at Strickland, struggling to break free from the vice-like grip. But he receives, in reply, a resounding blow to the back of his head from the pistol butt and he ceases to squirm.

'You have just three seconds my boys', threatens the Captain, 'To spit out your story. If you don't I'll have you both horsewhipped till you're raw. Don't think it an idle threat.'

'All right Captain, we'll come clean. The pistol went off by accident and that's the truth. We were simply scrapping over who should own it. I know I'm bleeding like a pig, but no real harm's done.'

'Ownership?', bellows the Captain, 'Confound any bloody ownership. Neither of you is safe with it, it's not a toy. Now, where the devil did you get hold of this weapon?'

'Twas from a job we done together', Saddler breaks in to pick up the narrative from Zack Young. He's desperate to impress his leader and telling the story seems to be the best way to achieve that.

'I took young Zack along with me to give him a pointer or two. Not far from the Bath Road, we were, down south of Swinton. Mid-January I'd say. 'Twas around three in the morning. We was intending to lift a goose or two from old Masterton's place when we heard hooves in the distance. Canterin' quite smartly he was, the lone horseman. I figured he might be worth a closer look, so we stretched a rope between a couple o' saplings. Rider caught sight just in time though and steadied his self. Came off all the same but he was up for a fight, no doubt about it. That's when the pistol appeared. He had it in his breeches. But I

133

stopped him before he had a chance to bring it level. Loaded it was, but not cocked.'

'Any clues who this rider was?', asks Wakelin, 'Did he live?'

'I reckon he'll have lived all right, but we never discovered who he might be. Youngish fellow, around twenty five I should say. Quality clothes. Reckon he could have looked after himself if I hadn't introduced him to my pacifier. Went down proper the second time, he did. We didn't wait around to find out if he ever got up.'

'So, what's the score then Saddler?' You relieved him of his pistol. Anything else?'

'A leather bag full of useless paper', yells Young, the blood rising in his cheeks. 'Saddler says that should be my share of the takings while he keeps the pistol. Well, when I looked at the worthless rubbish in that bag it was plain to me the division wasn't just. I've been telling this greedy two-faced bastard that we should agree a fairer split ever since. That's how we ended up scrapping out there.'

"Why, you little shit', starts Saddler, at which the Captain steps forward and cuffs him brutally across the mouth with the back of his hand. The impact loosens a couple of teeth and blood start to trickle down his chin.

'Enough, both of you. No one rides around the country alone in the middle of the night just for their own amusement. You've looked at these papers Young; what you can recall about them.'

'There's a whole bunch of thick sheets, all the same size', replies Young who is too proud to admit he's illiterate, 'Printing on every one, all the same. All got the same big blue picture in the middle. A woman in a robe, holding a spear. And there's some sort of letter, separate like but along with them.'

134

'Tell me you've not been foolish enough to throw them away', demands the Captain

'Why no, as God's my witness. Despite they're bloody useless. I've stuffed them under me cot.'

'Then get back to your garret now', Wakelin commands, 'and bring them here as fast as you can run. Listen up, both of you. There's a rule in this place and you know you've both transgressed it. Whenever a man pulls off a job, they must inform me. Immediately. Not after a week, not after a month. Immediately d'you understand? Right Young, off you go. And Saddler, I'll take care of this pistol from now on. It's plainly not safe in your possession. Now go, get yourself under the pump, there's blood everywhere.'

The interview is over. He returns to his chair by the fire, beckons Strickland to join him again. The entire episode has been a clear demonstration of his authority over the villains sheltering beneath this roof. Strickland is fast beginning to understand the individual who is asking for his help.

It's apparent he's a man of action, but also a thinker. On occasion he'll sit in his chair for a couple of hours together, drawing on his old clay pipe. The others are oblivious, but he's no intention to stick around with this gang for ever. However, if he bides his time, there's opportunity to stash a sizeable sum before he sets off for pastures new. But not through the footling capers they're indulging in now. No, he's going to have to build them up for some spectacular exploits. The cheekier the loot, the harder it is to fence. That side of the business alone needs careful thought and some cunning arrangements. All this has been tumbling around in his mind for weeks. Strickland's arrival could be a godsend, the backbone he needs to start putting his plan into action.

Strickland sits quietly, aware of Wakelin, lost in thought. He coughs and offers the captain a cheroot from a polished wooden case he found in one of those houses alongside the Avon.

Wakelin accepts the offer and unfolds a paper wrap containing a lump of cheese and half a loaf of dry bread. The vicarage provides shelter but women won't come near the place; there's no kitchen left to speak of. So the men bring their own victuals, whenever they remember.

He sits back in his chair and takes a bite. On the surface, he's relaxed and at ease. But underneath that guise he's keen for Young's return, his mind racing with possibilities.

The leader doesn't have to wait long. The bloody example of Wakelin, breaking Saddler's lip, has made a deep impression on the lad. He's run hell for leather back to the vicarage with the shoulder-bag. Rushing in, out of breath, blood still oozing from the ball wound to his calf, he delivers it directly into Wakelin's hands.

'Is this all?' questions the Captain, 'The entirety? You're sure you've left nothing under your cot?' Young affirms this, nodding vigorously. 'It had better be the truth this time', continues Wakelin, 'Very well, you stay right here. I'm taking this to the porch, where there's still a bit of light. We'll see what we've got.'

Perched on the bench seat, door firmly shut, Wakelin examines the contents. As he slides the papers from the leather pouch it seems Saddler and Young have given a faithful account of the find. There are indeed ten sheets of rich vellum. Each adorned with a line drawing of Britannia standing before magnificent buildings. Underneath this the words 'Liverpool and Manchester Railway Company.' And a seal, printed and embossed, to the right of handwritten text certifying the issue of a single share, face value of £100. A cuss explodes from Wakelin. He's aware the documents in his hand are worth a fortune, he also knows it will be impossible for him to realize more than a few shillings for the lot.

In addition to the share certificates there's a letter. The envelope and enclosure separate. Young had clearly broken the seal and looked inside, despite illiteracy rendering this fruitless. On the envelope, just one word 'Whitefield'. The broken seal yields no enlightenment since it depicts a crest Wakelin's not seen before.

The letter is far more informative. It reads:

Mount Pleasant
Newport
January 18th

My Dear James

I trust this letter finds you well. As ever I send you my warmest greetings and hopes for further success of our mutual investments.

Enclosed with this note is my original shareholding in the Liverpool and Manchester. You will recall I promised this in exchange for your help and advance for the colliery here in Newport. James, I'm almost regretting now that we made that deal. Since the line opened it has become an outstanding success and the value of the shares you now own has increased substantially.

You probably wonder why I have sent with such haste. It is on account of another venture you might wish to join me in. Moreover a rare opportunity for you to meet one of the principals in person.

I have recently been in discussion with Mr Prothero, a fellow colliery owner down here in South Wales. He's known to run his enterprises very competently. Last summer he installed an engine to haul coal to the wharf at Pillgwenlly. It is already saving substantial time and expense. I believe we should also install a railroad, perhaps come to some agreement with him around sharing the use of his engine and trucks – a great economy for the operation of both pits.

By chance, Prothero will be with me in Bristol tomorrow throughout the day. This is a journey he seldom undertakes. I am hoping you will find it possible to come into the city tomorrow to meet us and help me convince him of the merit in this plan. The railroad would undoubtedly result in more profit for us both.

I shall be at the Custom House when business commences at ten o'clock. Please send word to me there early if you are able to join us at some time during the day.

Lastly James may I wish to beg for your help on another matter. In October my cousin from Prussia, Johann Count von Winneburg, will be visiting England with his lady. They are to be presented to the King, in London, on the 15th of that month. Following that they will journey immediately to meet me in Newport, before returning by schooner from Bristol. The Countess will bring her very best finery since she is to be presented at court. Whilst they will be well protected on their journeys, I earnestly wish to help them avoid travel through the hours of darkness. I hope you may be willing to offer them accommodation in Gloucestershire so they can break their long journey here.

I am ever grateful for you partnership, your help and guidance. I know I can count upon you as a true friend. I trust we may meet on the morrow.

Yours

Nicholas

Wakelin reads the letter once, twice, three, four times. He senses, in his very marrow, that this message, put to good use, might be of greater value than all those share certificates. It's not to be taken advantage of just now, but it fits the plan he's forming in his mind. Folding the sheet carefully, he pushes it deep into a pocket.

Re-entering the vicarage he finds Saddler and Young impatiently awaiting his return. Their fear of his temper seems to have been overcome by curiosity about the possible value of their haul. Saddler eventually manages to stammer out a question to this effect.

'Nothing in that haul for you, young Saddler', Wakelin barks, 'It's dangerous booty. For your own sakes my boys, I'm going to stash it away for you, along with the pistol. Mark my words lads, if you tried to pass off any of this loot now, you'd be hanging from a noose inside a month.'

'Whoa Juno, steady up there', cries the leading horsewoman, bringing her mount to a sudden halt on the ridge. Her grey is sweating, but she's not in the least exhausted by their gallop over the rolling parkland. She has to wait a few minutes though for her friend Adele to catch up. When she finally does, the second young lady is considerably out of breath.

'May we stand here for a few minutes?' she pleads with her hostess, 'I need to compose myself. It's so unfair Sophie, you're much fitter than me.'

'It's all a matter of practise Adele. I'm just lucky to have the opportunity. I'll wager you've not ridden properly for weeks.'

'You're right, of course you are dearest. Alfred and I seem to be entertaining in town all the time nowadays. When we're not down at Cheltenham, we're in London. It's just so exhilarating to spend a few days here with you darling; you were so kind to invite us.'

'Believe me cousin', Sophia replies, 'It's I who am indebted to you for making the visit. Most of the time I'm bored to distraction. These last days have been like a breath of fresh air to me. Fun and spontaneity just like it was before I turned into the woman you see before you now.'

'You're just saying that to make me feel welcome', Adele retorts, 'You must be so happy here Sophie. Why look.'

She sweeps her arm in a wide circle to indicate the sight below them at the foot of the ridge. The rear of the large mansion, still very grand even from this angle. A long straight drive cutting through parkland, culminating in a sweeping circle before the main entrance to the house. A stable block thirty yards to the west in a small depression, screened from the main building by a row of Cornish oak. Formal gardens, beautifully tended, to the rear; everything surrounded by a swathe of lush green parkland.

'Look at what you have Sophie', she continues, 'This most wonderful home, of which you're now the mistress. It's a palace to all intents and purposes. Why there must be five hundred acres at least for you to ride. And the house - the house is truly magnificent. I'm sure I lost count at twenty bedrooms as I walked around. You have comforts that all your friends would die for.'

'I know it must appear that way to you cousin, but things are not always as straightforward as they seem. Adele, may I take you into my confidence? If I share a secret with you, will you keep it strictly to yourself and promise me to tell no one - not even Alfred?'

'Why of course', her young relative replies, intrigued, 'What is all this about, is there something amiss?'

'Perhaps not amiss', confesses Sophia, 'But cousin, I seem to have fallen into melancholy of late, I'm constantly listless, most often I feel really sad. When James and I were married, I was so optimistic. He's such a generous and interesting man, I'd thought. And that's true, he is. But whilst he's warm, whilst he provides everything I ask him for, he doesn't love me in the way I yearn that he would. He's conscientious, works so hard and his diary is full with business. We rarely have a minute together. There's not a lot I can do to assist him in his work, he's hardly ever there to talk with me. Sadly, I've become hideously bored.'

'I know I should be more grateful for my lot', she goes on, 'and you're right. I do often ride out around this breath-taking place which brightens my spirits and lifts my heart no end. But having you here, a friend of my own age, has been so marvellous. It's reminded me of what it's like to truly live. I shall be so low again when you've returned to Cheltenham.'

'Sophie, you poor thing. You mustn't grieve like this. I imagine this is on account of poor dear Edgar? That was so very sad. Has time not yet healed the wound in your heart?'

'Oh no, I think it has cousin. In truth I think of him sometimes and the life we might have lived together. But it's not him that I miss so much as the excitement of society I enjoyed when I was younger. I do love James sincerely, but I feel imprisoned within another generation. Everybody with whom I come into contact nowadays is so much older than me - James' relatives, most of his friends, even the housekeeper and servants.'

'Well, we must do something to cheer you up and restore you to your old self', replies Adele, 'The moment we're back I shall talk to Alfred. You absolutely must come to stay with us in London, for at least a fortnight. I shall organise for all our old friends to visit us and take you to as many balls as possible. I'm sure Sir James will agree if you express your desire to come. Why, we shall have such a gay time!'

'How kind of you my love. I should like that very much', replies Sophia, 'Now, have you recovered your breath? Perhaps we should trot the horses gently back to the stables and ready ourselves for dinner?'

Adele agrees and the two canter on, side by side. Sophia falls silent again, lost in thought. Her cousin is loath to interrupt this reverie and wonders what must be going on in her mind.

Whatever it is she's contemplating now, it's obviously not something she wishes to share.

Chapter 14

'Come along Thomas', coaxes Edmund, pushing aside his empty plate, 'I've not seen you this way for a long time. There's agitation written all over you son. There's something you're itching to tell us, I'll be bound.'

He's right, of course. Maynard has never been one to show his emotions easily, but the excitement caused by the visit from Hartnoll and Locke is so great he just can't hide it from his family. Neither Mary Ann nor Edmund were in the farmhouse when the pair arrived, but somehow they've got wind and have guessed there's something afoot.

The three are sitting around the rough pine table that takes up much of their cosy parlour. Mary Ann fed Emily earlier, tucking her into bed at eight o'clock, after which they'd set about their own supper. A modest fire glows in the grate and two Argand oil lamps, perched at opposite ends of the dresser, fill the room with light. Shadows flicker around the walls as Mary Ann collects the empty dishes and carries them back to the kitchen.

'Yes, you're quite right, dad. I do have things to share with you, news you'll be really pleased to hear. A new opportunity that might be the making of my business. I thought for a moment, when I saw the stewed rabbit and potatoes, that you're both already into the secret. You know it's my favourite dish.'

'That just shows how little you know of housework husband', replies Mary Ann, 'It takes me far longer than you imagine to prepare the meals we eat. But that doesn't surprise me. You're hardly ever in the house during the day. All we know is that your friends from the chapel were here this morning and seem to have stayed around for some time. Emily said she saw you all down in the yard with the other men, having some sort of conference. Now, for goodness sakes Thomas, stop all this procrastination and tell us what it's about.'

'I'm sorry Mary Ann. I'm just so full of it I hardly know where to start. Well, one of the two fellows here today is a man called Hartnoll. He's a city official in Bristol. I first met him that day dad and I were attacked by footpads. I'm sure neither of you can have forgotten, certainly not you father? It was at that meeting in Bristol, when I learned our little stone masonry might be involved in a venture to build a bridge across the Avon. Only a small part of the work of course. But I'm sure you can imagine what that means. A project like that would mean endless work for all four of us down in the yard. For months if not years. I've not breathed a word before as there's been no certainty whether we'd win the job or not. But Locke and Hartnoll came here today to tell us we've been chosen.'

'Lord, I can't believe it', cries Edmund, his eyes alight with a fire that's not been there for years, 'This will be the making of you Thomas. Your uncle Samuel will be so proud – we must send him word immediately. And all our friends in the village will be mightily impressed. I can't wait to see their faces when I tell them.'

'Hold hard father. Please. It's much too soon for anything like that. The news is excellent, of course, but it comes with a price. None of this is yet known abroad and moreover it's vital that we don't make it public. The whole venture is extraordinarily political and under a strict cloak of secrecy. You're my own flesh and blood and so of course I'm sharing it with you. But should either of you breathe a word of it outside the family, we'd certainly lose this work altogether. Why, even my men still have no idea of what the new job entails, just that we have a fresh schedule of work to start. There will come a time when you can tell your friends, but that won't be for weeks yet. I'm hoping we can even keep this news from Emily for I dare say she'd find it harder to hold onto such a secret. So, please, will you swear to keep this information between the three of us until I tell you it may be shared?'

'You know very well we will Thomas, now you've made us aware of the consequences. But do hurry up and tell us more. When will all this start? What exactly does it entail?'

'Patience woman, I seem to have developed quite a thirst', Maynard replies, 'Before I explain everything I'm going to fetch some porter. We all deserve it. We've got something to celebrate now, after all. And I need your help to work out exactly how to go about some parts of it. So, let me get the jug and then we'll sit here until we've put a sound plan together.'

Concluding their deliberations will take some time, Mary Ann gets out bread and cheese, whilst Thomas rustles up the tankards. She's delighted that Edmund is so alert for usually, by this time, he would be nodding off. It's as though a new burst of energy is running through his veins, he's infected by Thomas' excitement and eager to hear the rest.

'So', she says once they're seated again, and after Thomas' toast to their venture, 'What exactly have you and your men have been commissioned to do?'

'Well, firstly I'll be working yet again with Locke the builder, which is a mighty comfort as we do get on well as a team. Our task is to construct a huge pillar on the south bank of the Avon gorge. Eventually one of the towers that will support the bridge deck will be erected atop it. The bridge will be some distance from the city and span the gorge from side to side. You could think of our pillar as an enormous foundation.

And this is where I need your agreement my love, for there are some aspects of this that I'm not sure yet how to manage. This work hasn't been put out to tender in the normal way. In fact that's the real reason for all this secrecy. They're keen to get off to a rapid start that they want us to commence work immediately. The catch is they can't be seen to engage us immediately. We must start off without the usual payments and guarantees.'

'Which means I must commit to the purchase of materials, tools, transport and the like without having any written contract in place. If things were to go badly wrong, there's a chance I'd end up seriously out of pocket. That's a big worry for me.

We've built up some savings from the job at the Zion chapel, as you know, so not all would be lost. But it's an enormous risk and it's not right that I should take such a decision alone. If things went wrong it could come to haunt us all. It's only fair that you both have a say in whether we go ahead or not. So, that's the question. Are you both content to gamble our security in this way? For there's truly nothing more I can tell you about the certainty of these plans for the new bridge.'

Mary Ann voices her agreement immediately. She's convinced they should take the risk. Her optimistic outlook rejects any possibility that Thomas might let them run into difficulties. But Edmund's expression betrays he's less certain and he stays silent for a moment or two, clearly thinking over the proposition.

'I can't pretend this doesn't worry me Thomas. It sounds a bit slippery, so you're right to harbour reservations. But I think back to the time I took on this farm. That was risky for me and no mistake. Whilst I was desperate to do it, the possibility of things going wrong gave me countless sleepless nights at the time. I was so anxious, some days I'd to gag for no reason. Ada would scold me for worrying and it turned out she was right in the end. She had the courage and it gave me strength. So on balance Thomas I think you should do it. We'll just put our trust in the Good Lord that everything works out well in the end.'

'Thank you father. Thank for your confidence in me, and for being prepared to support me in this venture. I'm sure no man is blessed with a finer wife or a more generous dad. Why, without you I'd never have made the progress I have so far with my business. So, I fervently hope I've figured this out correctly and truly deserve the trust you put in me.'

'There's one costly aspect that's a real worry to me at the moment', he continues, 'and that's the responsibility to transport the hewn stone from our yard here to the site of the bridge. Our worksite will be downriver, beyond the city, on the other side of the floating harbour, out towards Sea Mills.'

'Well, the only sensible way is by boat', replies Edmund, 'So we must find a haulier with vessels capable of making the journey and robust enough to carry your material.'

'Of course father, that's the obvious solution. But such transport is exceeding expensive and would quickly deplete our reserves. If things did go wrong, I could probably reuse any stone that I purchase on some other job. But a big expense on river transport is money we would never get back.'

'How much stone d'you think you are going to have to move before you have a proper contract in your hand Thomas?' asks Mary Ann.

'I'm not really sure', replies Maynard, 'To start with we just need to knock out a few dozen foundation blocks. But they'll be granite, large and very heavy. Probably fifty, I'd say, for the couple of courses to be set atop the bedrock. They'll be quite complicated, with holes bored to fix them in place, so that will take us a couple of weeks. Once those are erected we'll start shipping the cladding stones. Dozens of trips will be needed for those. The structure eventually rises up over one hundred feet.'

'Is there any chance you could hire a vessel and navigate it yourself?', suggests Mary Ann, 'That would cut down on outgoings until you're sure of the contract.'

'Hmm, that would be an excellent solution', replies Thomas, 'Certainly an idea worthy of thought. But where could I hire a vessel that would do the job?'

'Who do you know that has their own boats son?' interjects Edmund, 'Isn't there anybody you've worked with that might come up with some suggestions?'

'Well, only outfit I know are the Strachan brothers at Conham quarry. They supplied me with most of the stone for the chapel. They always deliver it here by boat. Sometimes I see their barge, the Blanche, going further upriver towards Bath. And as I recall they always have two boats moored at the quarry wharf but I've only ever seen the Blanche in use. I can't think why they should keep two, maybe it's there in case the Blanche is being repaired. It's just possible they might loan me the other one. It's certainly worth asking.'

'I'm intending to ride over there on Tuesday in any event. I need to ask them about supplies of Pennant for the core and Old Red we'll be needing to clad the abutment. By some devious means Hartnoll already has details from Brunel's design - they're very specific about a red stone being used to face all three sides of the edifice.'

'But you said it was a pillar', chimed in Mary Ann, 'Won't it have four sides?'

'At the top it will have my love', replied her husband, 'But much of the fourth side will be the face of the gorge itself. The pillar, near the bottom, will be built up against it like a chimney breast, to reduce the distance that has to be spanned.'

'But then' he adds, his mind returning to the business in hand, 'even if I can secure this boat at a reasonable fee, I shall need a shire horse too, to pull it. I don't think I'll find anyone around here with a beast that's strong enough not in full time use.'

'Yes a shire will be needed eventually Thomas. But only when you come to haul the heavy cladding stones', replies Edmund, 'The first few loads will be much lighter won't they? Surely Hermes is more than strong enough. If we put him into service, that will keep your initial expense down to a minimum. By the time the bigger loads need shifting you'll have a regular arrangement with the Corporation. Let's hope those friends of yours in Conham are prepared to lend you that boat you've seen. If so, your immediate headache is resolved.'

'You're absolutely right dad. It's a wonderful plan that would make the whole thing workable', exclaims Thomas, 'Thank you, both of you. Somehow, between you, you've swept away my worries like snow melting in the sunshine. You've come up with answers to everything. Now, thank God, I can sleep soundly. Remember though, none of us are allowed breathe a word about this to anyone. We must all be careful, vigilant regarding everything we say. '

They're all so elated it's difficult to imagine that any of them will sleep. Maynard refills their mugs with porter. Without doubt there will be a lot more conversation and laughter around this dining table before they finally retire.

Chapter 15

Since Friday of last week the squally storms and cold winds have subsided, giving way to gentle breezes and occasional snatches of sunshine. A tantalizing promise of spring hangs in the air.

When Thomas awakens on Tuesday morning, the day's already bright. A thin strip of clear blue sky can be seen in the gap between the curtains of their bedchamber. He looks across the pillows lovingly at Mary Ann, still slumbering in the bed next to him. A surge of happiness and love swells within him.

Surely no man can be more blest than he. What fortune to have married such a beautiful, tender, capable woman. True, he's not taken many years to make a pretty remarkable progress in his own career. But it's her love and support, her absolute faith in his ability that has spurred him on the success he's achieved. Whenever he's suffered from doubts, she's always redoubled his resolve. Whenever he's complained things were going wrong, she's pointed out things that were going well. And how lucky to have such beautiful daughter and be so comfortably established here at the smallholding. With a flourishing business that's growing from strength to strength. It seems too good to be true; more bounty, perhaps, than he rightly deserves.

The sight of lush fields and the sunlight glinting off the river merely bolsters this wave of well being as Maynard draws back the curtains. Those earlier years in Bath were pleasant enough and, on occasions, exciting. There was always so much going on, so many new things in which to take an interest. It would have been unnatural not to be intoxicated by the hustle and bustle of it all. But Maynard knows, deep in his heart, that he's more at home, more content, in the rolling Gloucestershire countryside, with the freedom of open fields all about and the close knit community of the village nearby. Here, he thinks, here in Swinton is where I'm surely destined to be. God, if he exists, must have put me in this place for reasons of his own. So he silently offers up thanks – to whom he's unsure - for all these blessings that are so very important.

Washing hands and face in the bowl on the nightstand, he pulls on the rough working apparel he wears in the stone-yard. Seeing the door to Edmund's room ajar, he guesses his father must already be about and is probably even now milking the six cows he has in pasture. This task isn't too arduous and Edmund, he knows, is more than willing to do it alone. Indeed sometimes he appears to relish the solitude it gives him for an hour or so. But Maynard likes to lend a hand if possible, out of affection and from a feeling that he's in debt to his father for taking in his family and his small business. Unsure how long the old man might have been at work he runs down the stairs to put on his boots. Then he hurries out to the barn to lend a hand.

Sure enough there the old man is, squatting in time honoured fashion on a small three legged stool. He's gently squeezing and tugging at the udders of one animal, mesmerized by the distinctive regular whishing sound every time a jet of steaming milk hits the side of the metal pail. Maynard calls across to him from the open doorway

'What can I do to help you father? Have you got through all of these yet?'

'No, Thomas. But only two are still waiting. You could start on Clover there and I'll move to Willow once I'm done with this one. That way we should finish at roughly the same time.'

So the mason pulls up a second stool and pail. Side by side they sit, amidst the shuffling, lowing beasts, each bent to his own task. The warmth of the cows cuts a striking contrast with the crisp air outside. After some time Edmund breaks their comfortable silence.

'That news you gave us last night' he says, 'Bucked me up no end, I can tell you. It does my heart good to see you making such a success of your life, my boy. What with you and Hannah both happily married and set-up in life, what more could I want for? You know, son, I still grieve for Ada every now and then, especially when I see both of you children so content and in love. I often feel she passed before her time was really up; if only her ailment had been better attended to, she might still be here with us today. But bless me son, I'm troubling you with the feeble wanderings of a daft old man. I should be content with my lot and indeed I am. And your good news makes things all the better. But Thomas, can I ask you something? I'll confess, I did have a nagging misgiving about what you said last night.'

'Really father? What can that be? Out with it. Let's see if I can reassure you.'

'It's not words you used Thomas. It was more to do with the look in your eye and your manner. Remember, I'm your father. I've known you since you first came into the world. I sense there's still something that troubles you in this, something you didn't own up to last night. I can almost smell it son. It's always better to share your worries, not keep them bottled up. So why don't you tell me what's giving you a cause for concern.'

'For goodness sakes dad, am I really that transparent? Nothing gets past you does it? Even when I make a real effort to conceal my feelings. In truth all is well, I promise you. There's really nothing to fear. I'm sure it's just my vivid imagination that perturbs me, rather than any actual facts of the matter. It's simply that I've been unsettled by all the secrecy surrounding this job, the unusual circumstances of our engagement and also, to be frank, by my friend Mr Locke. The man's shown me nothing but the greatest friendship - indeed he's practically been my benefactor in securing this work. But I get the

152

impression he'd be far more comfortable than me if asked to do things that verge on the dishonest or maybe even the unlawful.'

'I see. I can understand why you worry', replies Edmund, 'And from what I know you're a shrewd judge of character son. But there must be something to have put this idea in your head. What has Locke done that causes you to suspect there's a shady side to his nature?'

'Well father, that's a really good question and one I've asked myself time after time', replies Thomas, 'The truth is nothing, save for some off-hand remarks about this and that. Perhaps also the haste with which he scorns or avoids questions when it comes to regulations. When we were working on the chapel there were some things he never fully explained. I'm still in the dark about how he got to meet Hartnoll. We certainly never came across the man at Bedminster, yet somehow he knew all the details about our scheme there.'

'So in truth son, this all comes down to your gut feeling and the fellow's impatient manner', Edmund summarises, 'Well Thomas, my advice is never to discount your instinct. So I'd counsel you to keep an open mind; simply stay alert and see what transpires.'

'But it doesn't sound like this should stop you from sleeping at night. Or distract you from all the matters you need to arrange over the course of the next few days. Take heart my son. Be vigilant, but don't be discouraged. After all this is a fantastic opportunity and I'm confident it's going to bring all of us enormous good fortune. Give it your whole heart and be content. Now, which part are you going to tackle today?'

Feeling much encouraged by all this sound and confident advice, Maynard explains his plans.

'With your consent father, I mean to take Hermes off again today. I'll ride over to the quarry at Conham. That one I mentioned last night, situated alongside the river. The one run by the Strachan brothers. I'd be quite happy to buy from the pair of them again. I like them. They've always been fair in their dealings. They deliver when they've promised and what's arrived always turns out to be good quality stone.'

'Through Hartnoll I know Old Red sandstone is Brunel's choice for the cladding. It so happens the Strachans quarry that, along with Pennant. The competition entries are supposed to be secret until the adjudication's complete, but it seems Hartnoll and his colleagues have found some devious way to get information in advance. If he's correct, we'll need a huge quantity of Old Red, so I must be confident the Strachans are capable of cutting it for us at the rate Hartnoll expects. And also ensure they're prepared to transport it here by river.'

'And then there's the matter of that other barge we think they have, the one they don't ever seem to use. I'm counting on being able to rent it to us for a reasonable fee. If only I can persuade them to agree, that will take an enormous weight off my shoulders.'

'But it'll be good to see the two of them again in any event. They've always been friendly towards me and they're a terrific source of gossip about the comings and goings in the trade. Nothing much escapes their notice. They're located that much nearer Bristol, so they get to hear all the talk about what's going on there. I'll be interested to see if they mention the suspension bridge themselves; they must be aware of the competition. I mustn't breathe anything of our involvement to them at the moment, but I'll keep a sharp ear open to discover what they know. All in all, this could turn out to be a very useful visit.'

'Quite so son' replies Edmund, 'Pass on my regards to the pair of them. I do remember meeting them some years ago when they ventured down this way. As I recall they were surveying to see if there was stone of any value beside the river around here.

154

But most of the land is too flat in these parts, seems they figured nothing could be extracted at a profit.'

'Well father', Maynard replies, 'I'm done with Clover. Are you sure there's nothing else I can do to help? If not I'll go back to the farmhouse and get something to fill my belly. And I must change my clothes too, for I can't meet George and Eddie dressed like this. I'll see to the saddling of Hermes myself today; I've ample time before setting off. Can I give Mary Ann an idea when you will be coming up to the house for your own breakfast?'

Edmund replies with a grunt that gives Thomas no idea whatsoever about his intentions. But that's not a surprise. So he fills a jug with milk from his own bucket and carries it up to the house where he knows it's going to be needed. And sure enough he finds Mary Ann in the kitchen, measuring out the porridge oats and awaiting his return.

'Just in time Thomas' she says, pouring the milk from his jug into a pan, 'I'll have this ready for you soon and you'll be well fortified for your ride to Conham. The weather's going to be warm today, I think you'll have a more comfortable journey than last time. But please, please promise me not to return too late; I don't want you to be attacked by highwaymen again.'

'Oh, Mary Ann, don't make it out worse than 'twas', says Maynard, 'Those scoundrels were not highwaymen. Not real highwaymen anyway – more like a pair of impetuous young lads. There's a surfeit of vagabonds hereabouts, I reckon the young ones pick up on their behaviour and try it out for themselves. With good fortune I'll be back here by mid afternoon; it's not all that far to the quarry. I'll have time to call in at the village, or in Bitton, or even Hanham if needs be. If there is anything you would like me to collect on my journey you need only tell me now.'

'Thank you Thomas my darling' she replies, 'But you're excused running any errands on my account today. There's really nothing I'm in need of. Just be certain to get yourself back here before it becomes dark.'

Promising faithfully to do just that, Maynard leaves to saddle the horse before returning to don suitable attire for the journey. Kissing Mary Ann goodbye he sets off on Hermes with hope rising in his heart.

The route he follows is, for the most part, the same as his ride into Bristol some six weeks ago. But Conham is considerably closer. Happily today there are only has four miles or so to travel.

There are two roads joining Bristol and Bath with the river running between them. The medieval market town of Keynsham sits on the lower road, midway between the cities and is probably the reason that particular thoroughfare has become the turnpike. The narrower upper road meanders through villages and suburbs. Nevertheless its surface is unusually good and it's still the most convenient way to travel to either city for Maynard.

This upper Bristol road runs across the end of the smallholding's rough track, which Thomas negotiates carefully, as ever. Out on the highway he gives his horse a longer leash and the gentle incline between bleak and windswept fields takes him shortly through the village of Bitton.

As a lad, when he and John Carey were exploring together, this was as far as they'd venture. Since then quite a few more cottages have been built here. Over the roofs of these dwellings, alongside the road, he can see the soaring spire of the magnificent parish church. Its graveyard evokes bitter sweet memories. It's there that he and John sometimes met in secret to smoke one of his dad's clay pipes, usually retching after the experience. It's there that Emily was christened. And it's there, not that long ago, his mother was laid to rest.

The creaking signboard of the White Hart Inn swings lazily in the breeze as he passes beneath it. A few people are already going about their daily business, the shops on the main road are being opened up to customers.

Very soon he's left the village behind. Fields now border both sides of the road, as he presses on towards Bristol. Trees become more abundant and a handful of farmhouses are within sight of the thoroughfare. He's climbing away from the level plain through which the river meanders. The road becomes steep, though the incline soon changes in his favour and stays that way until he reaches the bottom of Wilsbridge Hill. His route eventually winds into Hanham, past the Blue Bowl Inn, a hostelry that's reputed to have stood on this spot since Roman times. Just a little further on he swings Hermes down a track to the left, leaving the main thoroughfare, and following smaller, rougher paths to Conham Hill. This outcrop juts out over the river; the same River Avon that flows past his own stone-yard and joins Bristol to Bath with its wide and navigable waterway.

Here, where one might think the air would be clear, a miasma of acrid smoke hangs above the trees. A multitude of different industries have sprung up in this rural outskirt of the city. Copper smelting, going on in a small way for a hundred years, is now an intensive industry. And there are rich deposits of coal, some being mined, yet others still being prospected. Then there is the red stone that's prolific in this area, particularly along the banks of the river. A number of quarries profit immensely from these rich seams and they're all situated, cheek by jowl, on either side of the Avon. The largest is owned by the two brothers Maynard has come to meet. He turns off the main track and rides through a gap in the stone wall that marks the boundary of their property. A large painted signboard beside this entrance advertises the proprietors' names and the nature of their business.

157

Rider and horse have not trotted far before a dusty quarry-worker in workman's overalls steps into his path and waves Maynard to a stop.

'Hold hard Sir', he calls with an air of some authority, ' I'd be obliged if you would just tarry here a while. 'Tis purely a precaution you understand; there's a gang up ahead undertaking some dangerous work. We narrowly avoided an accident just afore Christmas see, cos some visitor was wandering abroad when we was splitting the stone. Since then Mr Edward has asked us specific to keep everybody clear of the face workings whenever there's any likelihood o' danger. However, you are welcome to observe Sir and watch what they're doing from here.'

About twenty yards away there's a gang of stone-getters, working above the rock face. They're standing, mostly in a line, close to the edge, which is just about level with the track where he's standing. Before them is a line of upright round iron bars that have been driven into holes drilled in the rock. The men strike each bar in turn with heavy sledge hammers as a foreman bawls numbers in sequence. The men are stripped to the waist and, despite the still chilly air, sweat is pouring down their backs.

The lower ends of the bars they're hammering are shaped like wedges. Each is being forced down between a pair of steel feathers, already pushed into its hole. With every blow the men are building up the stress along a line between the bars, where the stone should eventually cleave. There's a resonant ringing tone, like a bell, as each sledge makes contact. Suddenly the tones start to change, the tune from the bars becomes less resonant, as if a cracks have suddenly developed in the bells. The men step back, anxious not to be standing on rock that will fall away when the split is complete, but they continue their blows in turn, one after the other. Within a minute all hammering ceases and an eerie silence replaces the noise. Suddenly, an urgent warning shout. Followed immediately by the deep rumble of a gigantic stone mass, slipping down the face, breaking into massive pieces and sending a cloud of choking grey dust billowing into the air.

It's an impressive sight and, all of a sudden, Maynard realizes that he's not the only one to be an audience to this performance. About twenty yards away, almost hidden behind an oak tree, is a man of about his own age, smartly attired with straw hat and thick pebble glasses. He's only noticed this man because the fellow suddenly moves; and then darts across to the face that's just been cleaved as if it holds wonders that Maynard cannot see.

'All clear now then Sir', shouts the worker who halted Maynard's progress and politely waves him on. So he continues until he reaches a clearing in front of the quarry masters' office, where he tethers Hermes to the wall of the small building.

The office is a simple stone hut, tiled with black slate. It has just one door which stands ajar. Within, one of the two proprietors, George Strachan is seated on a wooden bench. Other than a deep window cill and a battered tin tool chest, there appears nowhere else a bottom might be rested. Before him is a wooden table strewn with paperwork, a variety of drills, plugs and feathers with slab splitters and the like leaning up against the walls. An un-stoked fire glows optimistically in a cast iron grate. A glance at the contents of the table reveals three open ledgers which, whilst extremely dusty, contain neatly written records of orders, shipments and other details of the establishment's commerce. Clearly this is the heart of the quarry operation, faithfully mirroring the dusty nature of its business.

'Heavens, do my eyes deceive me or is it really Thomas Maynard?' George utters as he catches sight of the mason, framed in the doorway. 'What a coincidence. Eddie mentioned your name only yesterday. He was wondering how you're faring now that chapel enterprise is winding up. Forsooth. I'm glad to see you again my friend, it's been too long. And Eddie will be pleased, when he gets back. I imagine you saw them breaking the Chapel Road face as you came through? Eddie's off at yet another face we're working further down river. But he'll not be long. So Thomas, are you well? Sit yourself down man, if you can find anywhere. What's afoot? What work have you got lined up now?'

The quarryman pulls a pipe from his tattered jacket and pushes the door shut to keep out the draught whilst he lights it with a spill from the fire.

'My situation's still a little uncertain George, but I've good reason to be optimistic' replies Maynard. 'I've been asked to tender for a nice little job close to Bath; if all turns out successful I'll need a fair quantity of your best Old Red and quite a bit of Pennant.'

The words are no sooner out of his mouth before he's regretting them. Why has he lied? There was no call to do so. He can't really understand why he's misled this man he likes and trusts; Hartnoll's insistence on secrecy must have wheedled into his unconscious.

'There's no-one Eddie and I like better that those in the market for goodly quantities of stone', jests George, 'but tell me more, what is this job? What sort of building is involved? What will you be using our stuff for?'

'Until the contract is safe in my hand, I'm genuinely not at liberty to tell you' replies Maynard, 'There's significant confidentiality surrounding the whole thing. But I can say that the Old Red will be facing stones, so I won't want them too thick. I'm looking for a lot of them though, five or six hundred square yards if all goes to plan.'

Strachan lets out a low whistle, 'Well Thomas, it sounds like you have fallen upon your feet, that's for sure. I congratulate you. When will you be requiring all this?'

'The client's specified the work to be completed in stages my friend. Over the next six months, all being well. The red you'll ship to my yard, in the largest batches that you can load onto your barge, the pennant goes straight to site.'

With a bang the shed door is thrown wide by Eddie Strachan, returning from his trip to the farthest quarry face. The newcomer bears an uncanny likeness to his elder brother - large, muscular, outrageously loud and good-humoured. Twins they are not, but many mistake them for such. The principal point of difference at the moment seems to be that Eddie is even dustier than George. Like his brother, Eddie greets Maynard with genuine surprise, though teasing him predictably in the process.

'Your business must be thriving, mister mason', he remarks, 'You look a ways too healthy to me. Or perhaps it's on account of that lovely wife of yours, feeding you up. How is she?'

'Mary Ann?', says Maynard, 'Is as beautiful as ever. But I'd no notion you'd even made her acquaintance.'

'Oh, yes Thomas my friend. Just after you set up at Swinton. Meself and two of the lads took our first delivery to your new yard. I'd come down myself particular like, to have a look at the place, since you had been telling us about it for weeks beforehand. That pretty wife o' yours brought out mugs of tea whilst my boys unloaded the cargo. Now, tell me man, what is it we can do for you?'

A jumble of words results as the other two reply at the same time. Eventually it's left to George to go over all the details of the previous conversation for Eddie's benefit.

'Hmmm, that's a prodigious weight of stone. Doesn't sound like any new building around Bath that I know of' Eddie observes, 'I'll be fascinated to know exactly what you've turned up here young Thomas. But it's not our business to pry into your affairs, I'm sure you'll tell us in good time. Certainly we can supply what you need, though it might require us to organise additional shifts, depending on the quantities you'll demand for any one shipment. We've more than sufficient stone already cleaved here, but the rate at which you say you'll consume it is ambitious. Are there still only four masons in your little band? If so, the pace you'll need to set will keep you all at it from dawn to dusk every day I reckon.'

'We're patiently waiting on a final answer from our client, so I'm hoping to confirm my order on you in about two or three weeks time' explains Maynard, 'But I do want you to be prepared. My prospective client won't tolerate any delays, he's been very definite about that. Once he gives the word, we'll all have to spring into action.'

'And now, there is another reason I've come to see you. Part of this job is delivering the finished pieces to site, of course. To win the work I've pared my costs to the bone. So ideally I'd like to take care of the transport myself and not incur huge charges from a haulier. So, I've got my fingers crossed. I'm hoping you might lend me one of your barges for a couple of months - for some sort of payment of course. Every time I come here I've noticed a vessel you never seem to use, tied up alongside your landing stage.

'Lord! No one has ever asked us for that sort of arrangement before. It's true my friend that we have the two boats, the Celeste and the Blanche. It's also true we only use Blanche although the other one is perfectly sound' says Eddie, 'However, I think George and myself will need to talk this over before we give you an answer.'

Looking at Maynard he motions, with a slight move of his head, towards the door. 'Don't want to be rude Thomas, but could you step outside and give us a bit of privacy? Then we can give your request some consideration.' Maynard takes the hint finds himself again in the bright sunlight with a flurry of activity all around him. A gang of around twenty men, leading horses and donkeys are moving gear from one worksite to another. Maynard is fascinated by the tools they carry, sledges ten times the weight of the splitting hammers he uses in his own workshop, blocks and tackle of prodigious dimensions. Across the clearing in front of the building a noisy steam engine spits and sprays boiling water into the air as its whirring flywheel comes up to speed.

So much weighs upon the brothers' answer that this wait seems to last an hour. In truth only a few minutes have elapsed when Eddie opens the door.

'Well my friend, George and I are agreed. We'll comply with your request. We're content to rent you our worthy vessel Celeste' he says, 'and we trust you'll think fifteen shillings a week a fair sum. However if you really do take all the stone you've been bragging about, we'll make allowance for half that fee when you return the boat. Sadly we can't provide you with a horse to pull her. As you know we have ten heavy horses here, but there's always more than enough work for them in the quarry, let alone pulling Blanche when we're making our own deliveries.'

'Eddie, I can't thank you enough my friend' replies Maynard, 'Securing the use of your barge was the biggest challenge for me; I think I can find a horse with the strength to pull it. In fact he's tied up right over there. Your offer is a blessed relief and I'm grateful to accept it. It's true we have a business arrangement, but I also count you both as good friends. I'm so pleased I decided to ask for your help. You've shifted a great weight off my shoulders.'

'As always Thomas, you're welcome' said Strachan, 'Now, come back into the shed before you think about returning. Brother George is a dark horse. He keeps a bottle of rum hidden beneath that table. He can be persuaded to open it on special occasions. Share a glass with us before you go.'

The quick drink Maynard anticipates turns out to last a considerable time. Having passed around the mugs, Eddie produces a packet of bread and cheese that his wife has provided for his lunch. Unwrapping it, he tears the bread apart and divides the meagre meal equally between the three of them.

'There was something I'd meant to tell you', says Maynard as he starts to eat, 'Did you know there's a strange fellow hanging about the quarry? Never seen the chap before and he doesn't look like one of yours. Dressed more like a clerk I should say. Mutton chop whiskers. And thick glasses.'

'Oh don't you worry about him', says Eddie, 'We know who he is. Came to ask us permission to hang about here. He's from London. Lyell he says his name is.'

'D'you know what he's up to? He seemed very interested in the quarry face.'

'He claims he's a geologist. A paleontologist is the word he used. Never heard of them myself. But he's interested in fossils. Says studying them will tell us how the land round here was formed by nature. That's why he wants to examine the face after every cleave. To see if there's any fossils exposed by the break.'

'Well, if you're happy with him hanging around, who am I to interfere? But he looked a bit odd to me Eddie.'

Their conversation turns naturally from this to some other subject and to the next; before they're aware an hour or more has elapsed.

Even so, it's only just gone two o'clock when Maynard trots out of the quarry, knowing he's plenty of time to reach Swinton in daylight, as promised. The ride back is easy and passes without incident until he's just cleared the boundaries of Bitton village. Suddenly his attention is caught by another horseman on the road ahead of him, too far away to identify clearly. He and the distant rider are making about the same pace. Maynard doesn't gain until the horse ahead stumbles and its rider slips to the ground, gripping the reins frantically and coming off in a very ungainly fashion. Clumsy though the incident appears, Maynard realizes, in all probability, it was a fairly skillful escape. The stumble he's witnessed was severe enough to have thrown the rider, who may well have avoided injury by a whisker. Kneeling now, the unseated horseman is examining the animal's fetlock and making no immediate attempt to remount. Thomas urges Hermes to a canter to catch up and offer help.

A real surprise awaits him as he gains ground on the figure he's been following. The unlucky person turns, alerted by the sound of his approach. A movement of the head reveals a profile he's seen before.

As he draws closer, his doubts are dispelled. The crouching rider to whose aid he's coming is no other than Lady Whitefield. Something so unexpected that it confounds Maynard's sense of intended gallantry. Instead of appearing confident and capable, he's self-conscious and tongue-tied. She, on the other hand, is composed as ever despite the trying circumstances and greets him cordially. There's nothing for it now, he must help her best he can whilst trying not to appear a fool.

'My lady, I saw the stumble from a distance. I'm so pleased you appear to be unhurt. But surely you're not alone, on the road without company? Where are the rest of your party?'

But the response is simply a knowing smile. 'You underestimate me Mr Maynard', she says, breaking into a gentle

165

laugh, 'I have no need for company. I'm more than able to fend for myself on a short ride around my own estate. Though I must admit the stone in that rut was more than I bargained for. And I'm concerned for poor Juno; I believe she may have torn a ligament in her foreleg.'

'Would you allow me to look for myself?' asks Maynard. He's known a long time now that his father's empathy with animals is something he shares and that he's reasonably competent in the stewardship of horses. Bending to one knee himself he runs the palm of his hand along the length of the injured limb, then coaxes the animal gently to walk a few paces on the reins. The horse seems calm but is reluctant to put any weight on its injured leg.

'I don't believe your mount has suffered any lasting damage my lady. There would be some swelling if it had. But she's definitely lame and may stay that way for a day or more. It would be unwise to ride her further; that might well exacerbate the injury. Let me accompany you back to your stables. You can ride Hermes here and I will lead Juno on her reins.'

'Mr Maynard, I thank you, but that would be an unwarranted imposition. Why, it's not far to the gates of the estate. I'm sure I'll be safe alone and I'm really quite content to make my own way.'

Her rebuff unsettles him. On one hand the prospect of leaving her would put an end the embarrassment he's feeling, the stress of trying to appear educated and sophisticated in her company. On the other it sits very badly with his natural chivalry. How would he feel if, once left to her to her own devices, she was attacked on the road? Mustering his courage he launches into a courageous response before he loses the nerve.

'Lady Sophia, there's no way I can countenance you returning by yourself' he blurts out, 'I'd never live with myself if you came to harm. The roads around here are not without danger as I discovered recently to my own cost. I beg you to accept my assistance. If we walk forwards slowly all will be well.'

She seems won over by this forceful argument and allows Maynard to help her onto his own horse, putting her foot in the step he forms with his linked fingers and placing her hand lightly on his shoulder. In such close proximity he can't avoid breathing the tantalising fragrance of her perfume. It unsettles him; a sensation entirely new to his experience. An involuntary frission tingles across his skin and he senses colour flushing in his cheeks. With some difficulty he manages to keep his head turned away until these feelings subside.

But after a while he knows he should look up and continue their conversation. If not he'll turn into some self-appointed stable-hand, simply leading her horse.

'Forgive me if I speak out of turn', he ventures, 'Surely it's uncommon for a lady of your station to be out riding alone?'

'I'm sure that's true Mr Maynard, and if I could only find a suitable companion I'd be delighted to venture out in company. But my husband, along with those of our guests who are still fit enough to sit on a horse, have ridden off to a shoot near Carrington. Such pursuits don't interest me. I cannot bear to witness birds falling from the air or a fox being pulled apart by the pack. I have tried – Heaven's knows I've tried - to play the part of the country gentlewoman – to follow the hunt and revel in their kills. But the very idea is abhorrent to me. However, my love of horses, indeed my passion for all manner of animals, is genuine. And that's why you have discovered me out here alone, enjoying the air, the countryside and the sheer pleasure of Juno's company.'

'But doesn't Sir James have fears for your safety, whenever you venture abroad like this?' asks Maynard.

'He did at first. But I think he quickly realized it was important for me to spend some solitary hours by myself. I've never come to any harm in the past, so it's an indulgence with which he has come to be content. Now, enough of me Mr Maynard, you must better acquaint me with your own adventures. I assume you've been on a journey yourself, so please tell me this interruption is not delaying some important engagement you should be attending.'

Her words bring Maynard back to earth with a jolt. During the last few minutes in her company all thoughts of normal life have flown from his mind. Things that had been of ultimate importance to him just a couple of hours previously seemed to be part of a distant world, unconnected to the present.

The dogged reticence about his affairs, that's up to now made him coy, dissolves in the company of Lady Sophia. He doesn't break any confidences, but he shares things a deal more frankly with her than he did with his friends at the quarry. He tells her about his new challenge, his visit this morning and the success he's had in securing the loan of a boat.

'So that leaves me with just one matter yet to be resolved', he concludes, 'I've got a barge with which to take our carved stones to the site downriver. And fortunately I've got a strong, healthy horse; indeed the very animal you're sitting on at the moment. And the first loads shouldn't be exceptionally heavy so he'll make easy work of it. But I've not got a harness or breast-collar. Without those the boat is not of much use. The journey being ten miles or so, it would be foolish to attempt it without the correct equipment. The best solution would be a plough harness with chains and a whippletree, but I've no idea who might be prepared to lend me tack like that.'

'What a coincidence Mr Maynard,' replies Lady Sophia, 'It may be you'll find the search easier than you anticipate. It's just possible one of my husband's eccentricities will prove the answer to your problem. I'm sure you know he gets very

168

involved in all the estate's business and regularly attends the fairs at Lansdown to keep abreast of prices being fetched for the animals. He's always returning with odd things he's picked up from the stalls, mostly it seems to me, on a whim. I'm sure he'd say that they're all items he knows the men will need one day, but more likely he's simply taken a fancy to them.'

'Whatever the case, I have a vague recollection he brought back a new plough harness not so long ago. There's a special room at the stables there where they keep equipment that's not in frequent use. If my memory turns out to be correct, you'll be welcome to borrow it for just as long as you need. After we've attended to the horses I'll get someone to search it out for you.'

The driveway up to the big house is lengthy and their walk with the hobbling horse takes a good twenty minutes. The stables and the parkland surrounding them are deserted. Every able bodied hand has been conscripted to the shoot as either beater or gun bearer, leaving Sophia and Maynard with no alternative but to look after of their own mounts.

Maynard gallantly insists that he will rub down Juno, but Sophia is equally adamant that she should shoulder her share of the burden. After all, she reminds him, the only reason he's here is on account of her foolish accident. But she does ask him to wait with the horses for a few minutes since her riding attire isn't the most suitable for the task at hand.

To while away the minutes, Maynard strolls around the stables, awaiting her return. It amazes him to see how the gentry live and he can't decide if he's envious of their pampered existence or not. Why, there must be thirty or forty loose-boxes here all lavishly equipped with freshly painted hay baskets, each one recently cleaned and strawed in readiness for the returning guns.

Memories of his early childhood and the near poverty of his parents have always driven him, starting with the

169

apprenticeship to his uncle. Some curious fear that his own little family might slip back into penury through some silly mistake on his part has constantly lurked in the recesses of his mind. Only in the last few months has this buried paranoia started to drift and make itself known less often. Through his own endeavours he's now confident he's created a relatively safe haven for them all.

But now, looking around these splendid buildings, not human dwellings but merely a shelter for dumb animals, the difference in fortunes between titled folk and his own kind becomes starkly clear in his mind. No matter how hard he struggles, nor for all the years in eternity, he will never acquire wealth on this scale. Is that such a terrible thing? Would he be content with the rigors that go hand in hand with all this affluence? To be obliged to entertain regularly, to dress formally each and every day, never again to enjoy the working companionship of real, genuine people like his fellow masons? Probably not. Perhaps his life is better than he gives it credit.

To his surprise, sooner than anticipated, Lady Sophia has returned, full of energy and with an energetic, purposeful frame of mind. She points to the brushes, blankets and pails; between them they make short work of cleaning and stabling Juno. She seems very efficient, now attired in a light day dress adorned with a print of grasses and ferns, somehow managing to keep it clean despite the dust covering her horse's coat.

Their task complete, there's still no sign of life other than themselves. 'Well Mr Maynard', she says, 'It looks as though finding that tack you need is something we must do for ourselves. Follow me and we'll find out if my memory has served me well.'

Three of the four stable blocks form a square around the yard consisting almost entirely of loose boxes. The fourth serves as accommodation for the stable hands, offices and storerooms. They enter this through a high central hallway that runs the length of the wing. To the left is a doorway leading into a corridor, off which a number of small storage chambers can be seen. Striding confidently to the very end of this passage, she opens the farthest door.

'This is where they keep superfluous tack and field equipment' she explains, 'I think there are spare items of practically everything we use. During busy times, like the harvest, any breakage costs us dearly if we have to wait on a repair or replacement. So Sir James is very keen on taking every precaution to ensure this doesn't happen. So perhaps I malign him by saying his strange purchases are simply a whim. If the harness is anywhere, this is where it will be.'

Maynard follows her into the room and realizes their search might take more than a few minutes. Unlike the rest of the building, almost uncomfortably neat and organized, the equipment here is higgledy-piggledy, in places several items are stacked on top of one another. 'You start at that end', Sophia tells him, 'and I'll look here'. Maynard doubts the propriety of being alone with her in this small room, but does what he is asked. What right has he to question her? After all, if the harness is discovered it will resolve such a major problem that any slight departure from social protocol will be more than justified in his own mind.

'Aha, I thought so', Sophia exclaims. Turning, Maynard sees her holding the sought-after article aloft with a triumphant smile on her lips. She hands him the collar and pulls out the chains which are beneath a saddle on a bench. 'Put it all over here', she says, 'I'll get one of the men to deliver it to you tomorrow.'

'Lady Sophia, I simply don't know how to thank you enough', he replies, standing and ready to follow her back to the loose boxes. But she makes no move to leave. Instead she steps forward, taking his hands in her own. She looks purposefully into his eyes, her own steady and unblinking.

Instinctively, Maynard feels uneasy. He knows this isn't be right, she shouldn't do this. Glancing over her shoulder he realizes, for the first time, that she has shut the door behind them. He should find some excuse to break free from her hold but he's powerless to do so. He struggles to find some suitable words, but cannot. What does he want to say? What should he say?

His dilemma is never resolved, for he's quickly overtaken by events. Suddenly she places the slender fingers of one hand on the back of his neck and pulls him urgently towards her. Her warm lips close over his and her left hand slides down to his waist, pressing their bodies together. The perfume he'd earlier found so intoxicating once again pervades his senses. Her kiss is passionate, exhilarating, but he knows this is all very wrong. He can't seem stop a violent passion stirring within himself but chivalry overrides and he pulls his head away from hers.

'Stop this, Lady Sophia, I beg you', he implores, struggling to find a breath, 'What's this all about? Are you trying to make a fool of me?'

'Not in the slightest Mr Stonemason', she replies coolly, 'Trust me. I'm truly in earnest. I admire you. You're a very handsome man. Ever since we first met, that night here at the stables, I've been having thoughts about you of which I know I should be ashamed. But they keep coming back; they spin around and around in my head.'

She pulls her soft body tighter against his; through her thin cotton dress he can feel every contour.

'But we can't do this', he protests lamely, 'It's shameful. What about your husband, what about Sir James?'

'Don't fret about him, he will never know', she replies, 'I do love him Mr Stonemason, but not in that way. Not in the way that I ache for you. And this is the only chance I'll ever get to quell my desire. Admit it to yourself, I know you want me. I can see it in your eyes, I can feel it, I can taste it.'

Again she pulls him towards her and presses her lips against his and he falls hopelessly under her spell. Somewhere, inside his head, he can hear a sober voice speaking. God, surely he must disentangle himself, musn't he? But how, without seeming cruel and heartless? What to do? No answer is obvious as his brain races to bring one to mind. Meanwhile Sophia's tongue is playing with his own and her hands are moving sensuously up and down his body. For pity's sakes, he must keep a clear head and fathom a way out of this.

Relentlessly she pulls him tighter, pressing herself against him. With a shock he realizes that thin cotton dress is the only garment she's wearing. He can feel every inch of her deliciously warm body close beneath it. Without his bidding, a surge of desire rushes over him. It is unquenchable. All notions of resisting her advances fly like straws cast in the wind. As she rubs herself sensuously against him, he abandons the unequal struggle to behave as he knows a true gentleman should.

Chapter 16

At much the same time that Maynard is meeting with the Strachans at Conham quarry, events of immeasurably greater importance are unfolding elsewhere. Over one hundred miles away, Sir Charles Wetherell is politely jostling with his fellow Tories, striving to stake out a place for his own substantial backside on the teeming benches of St Stephen's Chapel.

Elbows dig painfully into his ribs from all directions. In God's name, he's never seen this place as damnably packed in all the years he's been in office. The sweltering heat is already making him perspire. It's going to be unbearable in here before this session comes to an end. And the din, coming from Members on both sides of the chamber, is infernal. They're shouting at one another, across him and across the floor of the House. He'd expected an enthusiastic turn out for this debate, but never anything quite like this. With so many sweating bodies, pressed so closely together, the smell is rapidly becoming obnoxious. The unpleasant odours of his near neighbours hang pungent in the air around him. He flourishes a handkerchief, thoughtfully scented with lavender, and holds it close to his nose.

Wetherell is a senior man within his party, but not yet entitled to a seat on the front bench. His immediate neighbours turn out to be no more than nodding acquaintances. In any event they're engaged in furious conversations with colleagues several yards distant. They certainly have no time to speak with him. Wisely Wetherell decides not to add to the volume of noise but instead quietly looks around the Chapel. It will be interesting to note just who sees fit to be absent.

The faces on the Whig front bench are easiest to pick out - there's Althorp, Holland and Brougham sitting beside him; at the very end must be James Graham. Of his own Tory front bench, his view is far more restricted. He's behind them and crammed in too tightly to get a good view of everyone. The back of a few heads are however instantly recognisable; Peel, Crocker, Ashley and that irritating man, Goderich. Most of those characters he'd expect to be fiercely interested in this Bill, on both sides, have indeed turned out for its first reading.

He glances upwards. What other personages can he identify? Which notables have quit comfortable seats in nearby public houses to be present at this debate? The Singer's Gallery is quite literally heaving. Most appear to be ordinary citizens, drawn in by the promise of a lively afternoons' entertainment, or just possibly by their own zest for reform. But here and there are some well-known faces, faces he's seen before. William Cobbett, standing at the front, leaning precariously over the balustrade. Doubtless his Political Register will appear on the streets tomorrow, packed with half-truths and lies as usual. Further towards the back, unless he's much mistaken, is Francis Place, a man he recalls involved in a scandal with an actress last year, or maybe the year before. And there, next to him, that must be John Stuart Mill, the Benthamite.

Damn it all, this is crazy. There are so many bodies up there the whole structure is creaking. God protect us, let's hope the architects of this building knew their business or the whole thing might come down around our ears.

A huge glass candelabra is suspended from the central crossbeam of the vaulted ceiling and fills the hall with the light from a hundred jets of gas. Smaller wall lamps hang from brackets on the oak panelling of the galleries and add to this with their own illumination. Precious little daylight comes in through the tall windows. It's mid-morning but the sky is leaden without.

Grey, Prime Minister, enters to take his seat on the Whig front bench. Wetherell notes with no great surprise that Wellesley has decided to stay away. Grey's entrance is a cue to the assembled Members that the session will shortly commence.

The cacophony of noise dies slowly away as they all wait for the debate to begin.

The speaker, Charles Manners-Sutton, otherwise Viscount Canterbury, is already in his place. Occupying a high-backed chair at one end of the chamber, his eyes move around the assembled House with some trepidation. Keeping order is no easy responsibility, even when the benches are half-empty. Today will challenge his competence and he'll rely on many tricks acquired over the last ten years. He consults a thick sheaf of papers and, following a whispered conversation with the tellers, calls the House to order.

'The Member for the City of London', he barks, knowing that he's merely rung the bell on the first round of an exhausting parliamentary bout.

In response a distinguished gentleman rises, comparatively young, but someone who's already established himself as a veteran of the House. He's thin and diminutive but despite this summons up an abundance of energy. Wetherell glares at him across the floor with a mixture of contempt and mistrust, for he knows Lord John Russell is a formidable opponent and not an easy man to defeat.

In the lawyer's opinion Russell is wildly ambitious, bitter at being merely the runt of a noble family. True he's a Lord, but he's not a peer in his own right, which is why we find him here, in the Commons. However at thirty-nine he's recently become Paymaster of the Forces, a cabinet minister and now he's striving for yet more recognition and advancement. Perhaps the past disappointments of Wetherell's own career have coloured his views and prejudice him against the man. Whatever, he simply can't abide being lectured by the fellow, but that's precisely what's about to happen.

'Mr Speaker, Members of the House' Russell begins confidently, 'It is my honour to place before this House a Bill we

176

now introduce to amend the Representation of the people in England and Wales.'

'Whereas divers abuses have long prevailed in the choice of Representatives in the Commons House of Parliament', he begins, reading from his carefully prepared speech, only to be immediately interrupted by a cacophony of riotous objections.

'Interfering Whigs', a voice somewhere behind Wetherell pipes up, 'why can't they just leave things be. The Members of this House don't see 'owt wrong the way things are done at the moment.'

Resolutely ignoring such protests, Russell starts to lay out the background for his Bill, citing the great changes that have taken place across the country in recent times; the rapid expansion of manufacturing in cotton and wool, the growth of large cities that paradoxically have meagre representation in the chamber.

By contrast he cites those constituencies with just a handful of electors, some returning more than one Member of Parliament. Votes that can literally be purchased if the sum is sufficient, a travesty of democracy. And then he turns to the lack of representation given to the run of the mill citizen. The franchise being conferred on land-owners alone.

The Bill, he goes on, will widen that franchise to include citizens who pay rent. Extensive changes will be made to constituency boundaries, sweeping away those that fail to represent the general population fairly.

Much of what he's saying is drowned out by increasingly frequent, increasingly hostile interruptions. But he pushes on regardless, determined to finish. As he lists a hundred boroughs that will be replaced by new constituencies, the impact on their incumbents becomes starkly apparent. Howls of protest.

Struggles break out amongst the benches. The speaker is stretched to his limit to maintain some semblance of order.

The Member for Bewdley is particularly outraged, and understandably so. The pompous Whig has unjustly included his own constituency. He jumps to his feet and protests vigorously.

Hence Russell rises again to announce that he has some corrections. Bewdley will in fact remain unchanged, since it returns one Member and not two as he'd previously indicated. Certain suburbs will be joined to towns of which they form a part; Chatham and Stroud will be added to Rochester; Sculcoates to Hull; and Portsea to Portsmouth and so on. The right of suffrage will be extended to the whole parish of Halifax, which comprises 100,000 inhabitants, giving them the privilege of returning two Members. He declares there's nothing else to add to the statement he's already made and moves that the Bill be scheduled for a second reading, on the following Monday.

'He just can't do this, it's preposterous', Wetherell hears the indignant cry from a Tory colleague along the benches somewhere on his left, 'I've laid out good money for my seat and now these damned reformists want to abolish it completely. It's daylight robbery, plain and simple.'

But, nobody in the chamber can honestly claim to be surprised by the Bill's general tenor. Rumours and speculation have circulated for weeks, inside Westminster and also in the columns of the broadsheets. Everybody - parliamentary Members, pundits and ordinary citizens all expected some measures like these to attempt reform. It's simply the extent to which the Government intends to go that's causing the uproar. Not one part of the country will remain untouched; the Bill will impact upon everybody who has been listening.

The most vocal, boisterous objections to Russell's proposition have come from the Tory benches. But his proposals have stirred up dissent amongst the Whigs as well. They too will be affected, some in the same manner as the opposition. Members in each camp can be found on both sides.

Reform, to some degree, is probably inevitable. A bubbling cauldron of unrest has been hissing and spitting away for years. Wetherell counts the causes on the fingers of his hand. The Catholic Relief Act, the uprisings of unemployed, first in the textile industries then spreading round the country, the abolition of slavery across the Empire. Perhaps it's not surprising that those in power now feel threatened. To them it must seem the framework that shores up their authority is being pulled down around their ears. Personally he doesn't share these fears, because he's certain it will never come to pass. Of course, others have a more liberal agenda. They say the current situation is untenable in the long-term and taking no action means the population will eventually rise in frustration, much as it did in France. Fools.

With passion and anger largely spent, something like calm is restored. Onlookers up in the Singer's are drifting away. The sitting winds up with some tame discussion about the Scotch Reform Bill and the speaker sets a date for the second reading.

As the chapel clears, Wetherell sees Sir George Warrender pushing his way through the throng to catch up with him.

'Well, what are your thoughts Wetherell?' the man demands, clearly indignant and annoyed, 'I don't think my friends from Chatham and Portsea are going to be best pleased by what Russell had to say. In fact I reckon a good number of common folk might be incited to violence by the prospect of such a ridiculous thing coming to pass.'

'Calm yourself Warrender. This nonsense has a long way to go before it gets onto the statute book', the lawyer replies, 'If indeed it ever does. There are a lot of clever men who'll be keen to speak out against it. I can see several months of fiery debate, here and in the Lords. They will certainly not give it an easy passage. In my opinion it will die on the vine; it will never come into force. I'll wager it will eventually cause the downfall of Grey's government. And a damned good thing, if I may say so.'

Despite these brave words, Wetherell is not as confident as he makes out. He's resolved however that he'll go to any length and do everything in his power, legitimate or otherwise, to see this loathsome Bill defeated.

Chapter 17

Two o'clock in the morning and Maynard tosses restlessly in his bed. Sleep refuses to come. He looks across at Mary Ann dreaming peacefully, her faced picked out by moonlight that creeps around the curtains, and his head is a maelstrom. No matter how hard he tries to block them out, the events of that day, specifically those of the afternoon, keep leaping back unbidden into his mind. He's tried every which way to slip into some unconscious state where they'll trouble him no more. But all without success.

Only that morning, he recalls, he'd contemplated Mary Ann lying in this very same bed. He'd congratulated himself on his great fortune to have her as his wife. Now, just hours later, he has been outrageously unfaithful. Along with the guilt about what has taken place come countless fears and doubts. Surely it's inconceivable those turbulent events haven't marked him in some way? Or if not a mark, some alteration in his bearing, some change in his countenance that will betray him to Mary Ann?

It might be that his words, maybe the way he's kissed her goodnight, have already given her good reason to be suspicious. Can he keep up this pretence for ever? And what of Lady Sophia? Shamefully he admits to himself that he must have enjoyed it as much as she. But there's no doubt it was at her instigation. How long before she wants him to comfort her again? And what if Sir James should discover the truth? If she should let it slip, or simply decide to tell him? He's absolutely certain she has the nerve to do such a thing.

He had to admire how quickly her composure returned once their passion was quenched. How calmly she straightened out her dress and freshened her cheeks with a perfumed handkerchief. How she picked up the distant sounds of the returning guns and ushered him discretely away so they should'nt be discovered together. A very cool headed lady indeed, but equally one who threw caution to the wind in order to purge her lust. What in God's name will he do if she seeks him out again?

These troublesome thoughts circle around, like an endless whirlwind. Tumbling ever faster but getting nowhere. The more he thinks back, the more concerned he is. It seemed like things were happening by chance at the time. But that can't be so, he can see now she must have planned it. At the very least from the time he encountered her on the road. Maybe before that. Maybe the horse's lameness was engineered simply as a device to lure him to the stables. Could she really be that devious?

There was no doubt of her premeditation once they'd reached the estate. If not, why else did she reappear at the stables dressed as she was? It can only be that she intended the events to unfold just as they did.

And what of himself? He loved Mary Ann deeply before this event took place; he loves her still. He feels the same for her, despite everything that's happened. But how, and why, did he let this come to pass? It's true his defences were overwhelmed by carnal desires, perhaps that is understandable. But didn't he experience a wondrous thrill? From the clandestine nature of it all, from the beauty and allure of Lady Sophia, from the risk of discovery as they coupled earnestly in the tack room?

He resolves nothing, but still the memories flood back. He recalls leaving the stables with the harness, attempting to concoct some story in his mind, one that would explain away his late return to Mary Ann and Edmund. He stopped on the road somewhere, seeking out a trough in a field, and washed himself thoroughly to expunge any possible evidence of his infidelity. Then wrestling with himself all the way home, with his guilt, with his conscience, damning himself for his weakness.

The harder he tries to banish these thoughts, the faster they come back into his mind. Even now, at three o'clock, the same whirlwind rages within his head. He knows now he'll get no sleep tonight. His body wants to toss and turn, but he can't let it, for Mary Ann will wake and that mustn't happen. Talking to her just now would be a torture. What could he say? Is it possible he'd tell her? Will he ever be able to confess to her what he has done?

Thinking a drink might calm him, Maynard decides to fetch a glass of water from the kitchen. He slips out of bed, making as little noise as possible. Treading carefully across the boards, his whole being tense lest any sudden creaks might sound. As he passes the window, he eases apart the curtains, just sufficient to look at the still night outside. The whole world is black, silent and still. From this vantage he can see ripples on the Avon glittering in the moonlight, the sturdy beech trees on the far bank and the rolling fields stretching into an inky oblivion. And there, below is his own stone yard, the one thing he's worked so hard to establish. Could it be that his foolish recklessness today has put this all at risk?

He pauses for a few moments, staring at the scene. But in truth his attention is not focussed on the sight at all. He's looking through it, rather than at it. His mind is yet again elsewhere, wrestling with his guilt and his fears. However, a sudden motion in the stone-yard does register in the corner of his unseeing eye. Immediately his attention is alerted. Was that an animal, or something larger – a man perhaps – moving away from the sheds next to the dressing shop? He can't be sure, the shadows are just too dark. But no, wait, now there's no doubt. The figure is out of the shadows and into the moonlight. Yes, it's a man, walking confidently to the wall. He vaults skilfully over the capstones and strides away, without haste, along the tow-path in the direction of Bath.

What can this mean? Maybe the extortionists who've never bothered him before are now taking an interest in his business.

Or is this clandestine visitor linked somehow to his indiscretion with Lady Sophia? Perhaps it's she who's sent this mysterious visitor to investigate his humble domain?

Maynard treads the stairs carefully to the parlour. He pours himself the glass of water and sits pondering in a chair for ever. His mind's racing even more. There's no doubt about it now, he'll not sleep tonight.

Chapter 18

Morning arrives and yet again the low sun shines brightly on the smallholding. Maynard feels anything but sunny. He has to screw up his eyes when looking in its direction. He feels sick. His eyes are sore. There's a space in his head that seems to be stuffed with wool; his shoulders and neck are beset by a dull, persistent ache. Worse, after his absence from the yard on the previous day, there's a backlog of work to catch up. The hammering and ringing of his fellow masons' tools do no favours for the throbbing pain in his head.

For all that, he's reached a resolve. The shame and guilt of his infidelity can never be undone. But, however difficult, he must now keep his own counsel. For ever. Any admission of his infidelity can only hurt Mary Ann and she does not deserve that.

He must also avoid any possibility of coming into contact again with Lady Sophia. If, by chance, he should fail in this, he'll rebuff any approaches she might make. He can now only fervently hope that the affair will slip away into the passage of time and never come back to haunt him. He's going to start life again today, as if the events of yesterday never took place. And should they ever surface, he'll deal with that when it happens. He simply can't live in fear and dread and guilt for the rest of his life, nor will he allow this stupid mistake to harm his family, or his business.

These are brave pledges. Pledges that have been made by Maynard, to himself. Sincere, but known only to him. Now, despite any difficulties, he has to start living by them.

And so he's forced himself into the dressing shop, focussing on shaping the final capstones for the Zion chapel. Relying on the necessity for total concentration to banish all other thoughts from his mind. A careless slip at this point, with either point or claw, would mean the waste of hours of painstaking labour. Particles of stone and dust fill the air as he skilfully creates an image of the Virgin Mary from a rough block of basalt.

Sapped of energy and reluctant to engage in conversation with his fellows, he's succeeded up to now in avoiding their eyes. But it's all too obvious they're keen to talk with him. It's not long before Ben Gurney breaks their silence.

'Well Thomas' he starts, 'I imagine you'll soon be telling us what you know about this new job. After all, we'll be in it together and you can surely trust us. Lionel and I reckon you must know a good deal more than that fellow Hartnoll told us last week. But we were decidedly excited by the little he did let on, all three of us. It sounds like an important piece of work. But surely by now you can now give us some idea, in confidence, of what it's all about?'

'Ben, Lionel. You know I think of you as friends as well as being my workers. But please bear with me for a just little longer. Of course it's hurtful to be left out of a secret, especially when you're going to be involved. But trust me please. It's best that the fewest possible souls know exactly what's afoot. The damage that would result from injudicious disclosures would spell the end of it all for us. Be patient my friends, it is only two weeks more and then the details will be disclosed plainly to us all.'

Reluctantly his colleagues cease to pester. To their annoyance, they can sense his determination to hold tight to his intriguing secret. So the four continue to work alongside one other in a resentful silence, each bent over his own stone. Maynard knows this has created a distance, almost a distrust between them, which just adds to his feeling of frustration with life.

To his tired senses, time drags endlessly on through the day. Surely the sun is taking longer than usual to complete its passage across the sky? His hands go on with their work without, it seems, his mind playing any part in guiding them. At last the sun does set and the masons put away their tools. Exhausted, relieved there's finally a time to rest, Thomas returns to the farmhouse for the evening meal.

'My goodness Thomas, are you ailing? You don't look at all well to me my darling. Heavens, the shadows under your eyes', Mary Ann says as she sees at him properly, across the table, for the first time that day. 'Your face is quite grey and you seem to have lost your appetite.'

'Don't fuss my love', replies Maynard, trying to make light of her concern, 'It's true I've been a bit under the weather today, but it's nothing that should worry you. I'm sure I shall be just fine again tomorrow.' But these brave words only serve to conceal a resurgence of the guilt and fear within him. I simply cannot stay in the house this evening, he thinks. If I do, and Mary Ann continues to be attentive like this, I'll end up by telling her all.

As ever, she has put a delicious meal on the table before them, but the food sticks in his throat. His mouth is dry, he just doesn't feel hungry. But somehow he must clean his plate or her anxiety will be redoubled. So, mustering all his resolve, applying mind over matter, he succeeds eventually in swallowing everything, down to the last morsel.

'Mary Ann, that was, as ever, a delicious supper', he announces, 'but now I'm hoping you'll all forgive me if I rush out. I agreed to meet John Carey at the Old Boar tonight and he's not able to stay late. So, I'd really better start out now or he'll think me very rude.'

'Well, if you've promised, husband, I suppose you must', says his wife, 'Though you could have told me about beforehand and have come in earlier for our meal. I've made an apple pie and you'll go without if you rush away now. I'm not sure it's sensible either, you going out tonight when you're not well. Promise me you'll leave when John does and come straight back here.'

Some hours later Maynard returns, sober but having taken sufficient ale to give him courage and to attempt to eradicate those persistent thoughts from his mind. The excuse he gave about meeting John was, of course, a contrivance. God grant Mary Ann will never discover the lie through Betty. Upstairs, he falls clumsily into bed alongside her. The whole family must have retired some time before he got back. Thankfully sleep overcomes him almost immediately, relieving his mind of the demons that inhabit his imagination.

The following morning he awakes a new man. Rest, and the passage of time, is distancing him from his fears. From this day forward, as far as Maynard is concerned, life will return to normal. Save a concern that he might have been ailing, no one seems to have noticed anything untoward. And now, for him, the monotony and security of his daily routine becomes an important way of burying his indiscretion.

An old acquaintance in Bath, Abraham Robarts, has previously supplied him with granite for jobs he he'd carried out on Samuel's behalf. Later in the week Thomas rides off to meet him, hoping to negotiate advantageously, much as he did with the Strachan brothers. Their meeting is a long one since Robarts insists on hearing the entire history of Maynard's new venture before talking of business. But eventually they get around to grades and prices and all turns out satisfactory. Robarts agrees to deliver the stone himself to Maynard's yard.

At the end of that week, on Friday, Thomas takes Ben with him in the trap to the Zion chapel. Practically their last task is to help Locke's men set the final pieces in place. Elijah is there in person. This, at last, is the culmination of many months of effort for them all. He's determined to ensure everything is unquestionably in order before handing the finished building over to Hare.

'Well, I reckon our two little firms have done a sterling job here Thomas', he says, 'I imagine Mr Hare will be more than delighted with the result. God willing he makes his last payment without delay, for that new job won't occupy my men immediately. But your boys should be ready to go. Are you all set to start?'

'That I am', replies Maynard, 'I've made all the preparations I possibly can. We just have to wait now for the raw materials to arrive in Swinton.'

Several days follow where the four masons can't find sufficient work to occupy their time. So they set to tidying the yard, sharpening the tools, repairing hammers and mallets and building additional shelves to hold the tools that will now have to be crammed in one shed. A thick layer of dust is swept from the floor, roof tiles are replaced, gates, doors and walls attended to along with anything else that needs refurbishment. The little band set about these tasks with a shared sense of purpose and in anticipation of hearing more about their forthcoming assignment.

Wednesday the sixteenth of March comes and goes. Maynard is in a great state of agitation from morning to nightfall. He can't sit still, nor stay in one place for long, so great is the consequence of Brunel's design actually winning the competition.

'Whatever is the matter with you Thomas?' asks Mary Ann after they've finished their lunch, 'You're fidgeting. Do try to calm down. I'm sure everything's all right. All this worry and fretting won't change the outcome of events.'

'I'm sorry my love' he replies, 'I simply can't help myself. Up to now, the prospect of this bridge has given me hope in my heart. It's allowed me to have me confidence the future. It's only now the time's come, that I think about the other possibilities. What if another engineer's design is accepted instead of

Brunel's? What if Hartnoll's wrong after all? How can he be so confident? If that happens, you do realize we'll have no work at all. Worse, we'll have a yard full of stone we've no purpose for. Ben, Lionel and Peter would leave us because I couldn't afford to pay them. God, how did I get myself into this?'

'Thomas, stop it please. It's happened now. We made our decision and we did so for very good reasons. What's been done cannot be undone. Whatever the consequences of this, we'll all have to make the best of it, and I'm sure we shall. I'm certain your fears are groundless. Mr Hartnoll would not have come all the way here and talked to you and your men if he hadn't every confidence himself in the outcome. There is simply nothing you can do about this today, so just try to relax. However, tomorrow I think you should ride early into Bitton, after the mail coach has been through, and see if you can purchase a newspaper. Betty tells me the coach usually brings copies of the Bristol Mercury. It will be certain to announce the result of this competition. At least you'll then be relieved of this uncertainty, whether the news be good or bad.'

'You've got enough good sense for us both Mary Ann and more to spare. You're the cleverest wife a man could have', Thomas replies, 'That's excellent advice. I'll be sure to do just that, first thing in the morning.'

Accordingly, next day does find Maynard in Bitton making, for him, a most unusual purchase. He leafs through the pages of the Mercury until an article catches his eye. Bold headlines proclaim that Brunel's design has, as expected, been selected for the new bridge. Maynard is elated. It's only later, at home, when he reads through the entire article that he realises how closely they've courted disaster. Brunel, it appears, submitted four designs to the committee. But their deliberations didn't initially mark him out as the victor. They'd placed his preferred design in second place. Somehow Brunel got wind of this and stormed into the council building, demanding an audience with the committee. It was only his personal intervention and persuasion, or so the article had it, that turned their decision around, resulting in him being officially declared the winner.

Filled with relief, Maynard gallops home to tell his family the good news and to share it with his fellow masons. They're still in high spirits when, early that afternoon, horses are heard in the yard and Hartnoll arrives in a carriage with Locke following close behind, astride his own horse. Maynard hurries up the path and greets them like brothers. Locke has a smile spreading from ear to ear, even Hartnoll appears to be in unusual good humour.

'I see you already know our excellent news' remarks Hartnoll as he spies the newspaper, lying on the kitchen table. 'So much of what Locke and I have come to impart will be of little surprise to you. But the time for action has now arrived, so I must explain in greater detail what we must be accomplished over the next few weeks.'

'And can we now tell the men what this is all about?' asks Maynard, feeling a huge sense of relief, knowing a weight is about to be lifted from his shoulders, 'All this secrecy has put a strain on us. Say they can now be made privy to what I've committed them to?'

'Oh yes Mr Maynard and I suggest we address them just as we did before, in your workplace down by the river'.

And so for a second time the four masons and Locke find themselves places to sit, under the canopy of the dressing shop, eager to hear what Hartnoll has to say.

'Gentlemen, I am delighted to address you again' he begins, 'To provide some further details regarding my previous announcement and to dispel some of the mystery that was unavoidable at the time. Please remember that what I have to tell you, even now, is still secret and must be treated with the highest confidence. You must not tell anybody exactly what you are engaged upon, however I imagine by now Mr Maynard must have hinted that it concerns the construction of a suspension bridge over the Avon. You might know some of the history regarding the selection of the design, but if not suffice it to say that Mr Isambard Kingdom Brunel submitted his proposal which was approved yesterday by the municipal administration in Bristol. Mr Locke and Mr Maynard have now been engaged by us because we are anxious to proceed with the building works immediately.

The outcome of your endeavours will be a suspension bridge, hung between towers on either side of the Avon Gorge. One will be built at Leigh Woods, the other on the opposite bank at Clifton Down. This bridge will boast the longest span it's possible to support. The longest span for any suspension bridge in the entire world. Even so, such a span is not as long as the distance between the cliffs on either side of the gorge. So the supporting towers for this bridge will stand on abutments, built into the cliffs on either bank. These will effectively extend the cliff faces into the gorge and reduce the length of the deck needed to form the suspended section of the bridge.'

'Your first task gentlemen will be to build one of these abutments, the one on the Leigh Wood side. This will be the bigger of the two, by far, and that's why your two firms have been appointed to the job. It will be constructed principally from rubble-stone and brick, by Mr Locke and his men, but will be supported on a foundation of granite blocks that you will be responsible for. Locke is having the bricks fired not far from the site, I'll be relying on Maynard to ship in the rubble. As construction proceeds it will be faced in red sandstone ashlar, and that you will fashion, so that it presents an attractive aspect to people standing on the downs or voyaging down the river itself.'

'An official starting date has now been declared for work on this enterprise. There will be a ceremony on the 21st of June to lay the foundation stone, which will be on the Clifton side of the river. However, as I said before, we are committed to getting the structures on both banks built as soon as possible. There is a lot of work we can accomplish before June such that, once that day arrives, building can advance rapidly.'

'Firstly, the banks of the river at Leigh Woods will have to be cleared of trees and vegetation. A landing stage must be constructed. All materials will obviously be delivered by boat and lifted into place with crane and winch. That means erecting a number of derricks on ledges cut into the face. To establish a solid foundation for the abutment, two flights of steps will be cut into the bedrock of the cliff. Broad and deep. Onto these will be laid large granite foundation blocks that you men will be working on within the week. Brunel's plan has them fixed in place with mortar, but in addition with steel pins set in holes on the mating faces. Precise alignment of these foundation blocks is vital for a flat level surface upon which all further courses of brick and stone can subsequently be laid. The weight of this structure will be immense. The absolute integrity of these footings is imperative.'

'Mr Locke's men will commence clearance of the site this week. Within three weeks they will have started to cut those foundation steps. We will need one of you to work at the abutment site, starting quite soon, to help with the drilling and to record measurements so that granite blocks can be turned out with holes precisely aligned. The remainder of you will start work here almost immediately, checking for flaws in the stone, facing it off, creating the holes once the dimensions are communicated to you. By the time those are complete you will be ready to start on the facing blocks which you'll also help to fit once that stage of the job begins.'

'Until the 21st of June nearly all the stones you finish must be stored here, at this yard. Only the first course of granite blocks arc to be transported to the site, and those in secrecy. We don't want the world to know that building work has actually commenced. Indeed, no one should even guess it's

193

getting under way for another month. Mr Locke will carry out trial fittings and then conceal the blocks with brash alongside the derricks. Once we can openly show progress, it will be fast. For much of the work will already have been done. You, Mr Maynard, will arrange for regular and timely deliveries of stones by barge. These will be hoisted up the cliff and fixed in place by Mr Locke, assisted if necessary by your men. I do not expect Locke's crew to ever be idle for lack of materials.'

'Now, I'm sure you all understand this scheme is ambitious and requires great care in execution. You need to work very closely with Mr Locke and his men, which was a crucial reason for the selection of your firm. You have proven your ability to work well together in the past and I trust you will do so again. I wish you all good fortune in your endeavour and now will be happy to answer any questions you might wish to put to me.'

This speech is received without a single interjection or interruption from the men. Maynard had given his colleagues the very briefest of details before Hartnoll's arrival, so none are astonished by what he has to say. The masonry and building aspects of this undertaking are rudimentary, so they're not concerned about their ability to deliver what's required. Only the sheer quantities of material involved and the speed of construction raise questions in their minds, but not ones they want to expose to Hartnoll.

'Very well' he concludes, 'Maynard, I have a sheaf of drawings here, detailing the sizes and quantities of the foundation blocks. Those should enable you to order the right granite and get started. Meanwhile, in my carriage, I have a full set of documents and a case of fragile instruments that I wish to secure in that shed you've promised to let me use. Naturally I've brought my own padlocks, for my peace of mind. Locke and myself will be the only people to hold keys. I'm sure you understand. He may need access to the instruments when he visits you, which he certainly will do from time to time. Why don't we all walk up and collect these things, you can show us where your shed is situated.'

The crate Hartnoll's referred to is large and heavy and lies on the floor of his trap. It proves awkward to carry, requiring the combined strength of Locke and Maynard to shift it to the stone yard. The Corporation official extracts two solid brass padlocks and several wallets of drawings from under the bench seat and follows the others with this vital, but considerably lighter, burden. He satisfies himself as to the sturdiness of the shed; he and Locke test their keys to ensure they work the padlocks.

'Thank you again for your cooperation Maynard', he says, 'I'm confident everything is off to an excellent start. Your men are enthusiastic and I'm satisfied with the things you've put in place so far. Little remains apart for me to wish you good luck. I expect you to send me a report of progress by messenger every other day. And I may well visit myself on occasion. Now, I think I should take my leave. But Locke, you stay here and spend some time with Maynard, checking your schedules. It's vital nothing is left to chance.'

Locke stays on until early evening, deep in conversation with Maynard, documents strewn across the parlour table. Mary Ann chides them playfully, but concedes her plans to serve dinner will have to be shelved. Obligingly she produces cheese and pickles instead, which they eat from plates soon buried under drawings and papers. Maynard breaks open bottles of porter to toast their mutual success. At last, as darkness falls, the builder makes his own way home.

Chapter 19

With the prospect of endless employment fixed in the masons' minds, work commences apace. Spirits have never been higher. A contented atmosphere of purpose and resolve is palpable. Now the men are clear what's to be accomplished, now they have clear drawings to work from, nothing can divert them from the task. The first shipment of granite arrives by boat from Bath early the following week. With Hermes between the traces it's unloaded and the stones hauled on wooden sleds to a storage area beside the sheds. The delivery will later be shifted, piece by piece to the dressing shop, for each to be cut to size and shape.

Locke and Maynard have already agreed that a dovetail slot will be cut into the hidden face of each stone. A special lifting claw, a three-legged Lewis, will then be used to haul up and position each stone. The builder has never seen one of these before and is fascinated when Maynard demonstrates it to him. The claw's hinged jaws are expanded by turning a screw thread. They jamb against the sides of the slot holding the stone securely. With the claw attached to the end of the winching rope the, stones can be hoisted and accurately positioned.

The masons will carve the same size slot into the cladding stones. But in these it will serve an additional purpose. When Locke's team lay the brick courses, they'll set heavy iron brackets at regular distances into the mortar. When the cladding stones are fixed the slots will be aligned over the brackets and they'll simply slide down into place. Firmly held onto the structure with both mortar and iron. By fashioning identical slots into every piece, the lifting gear can be used continuously without needing to change the claw.

Their work on the chapel has given Maynard a pretty good idea of his men's particular talents. Of the three, Lionel Emden is by far the most experienced and self-assured. Maynard has little hesitation in singling him out for a special responsibility.

During the last week in April the two of them travel to the gorge in the trap. The last half mile has to be tackled on foot. It's no more than a rough single track path, recently hewn through the brambles, alongside the river, leading to the construction site itself. And there, a sight of perplexing disorder. Soil torn from the rock face, piled in heaps alongside the river. Timbers strewn carelessly against the bushes, barrows and tools hither and thither. Only progress on the landing stage looks up to scratch. But Locke seems happy enough. In his mind everything's going to plan. He greets them cheerfully and they set to without delay.

Throughout the day masons advise him on the construction of the sheerlegs, that will be used to lift their stones from the barge onto the landing stage, and also the winches that will subsequently hoist them half way up the cliff side. They survey the exposed rock and agree on the nature of the steps that will be cut there as a base for the foundation blocks. It's a demanding task and they work on until late in the afternoon.

With understandable misgivings Maynard sets off for Swinton with the sun low in the sky, leaving Emden to stay on at the site for the next three or four weeks. His task is to help cut the steps and record accurate measurements for the granite blocks and the positions of the holes required to locate them.

Maynard's also asked Lionel to make record, every day, of the times when the river's sufficiently deep alongside the landing stage to unload their barge. Due to the tidal range way out in the Bristol Channel, the water here almost vanishes at low tide. The mason's determined to be certain he can offload his cargo and then regain the safety of the floating harbour before there's any risk of grounding the Celeste. Lionel promises to send him this information by post as it's so critical to planning their trips with the barge.

After making some enquiries amongst his new workmates, Lionel takes lodgings in a street near the waterside at Hotwells. It seems very convenient. His journeys to and from work should be easy. That very evening he's discovered a lad with a rowing boat who'll be happy to ferry him across the river each day. And the rough path from there to the site will get easier as the brambles are trampled down by the workers going to and fro.

On the first morning it turns out to be a novel and exhilarating experience. The bustling sounds of early morning activity in the streets, the dense mist hanging over the water, all so unusual and different from his journey to work at Swinton. In the evening he retraces his steps, to be welcomed by the commotion of the city and the noises of the port as he nears the ferry post.

His landlord is a cheery tanner going by the name of Norcott. He and his family occupy a terraced house so narrow that Emden feels it must have been squeezed upwards by its neighbours on either side. On his second day he's introduced to the Norcott brood; the wife Catherine, four screaming children - Lionel never does manage to remember their names with any certainty - and Catherine's mother, the formidable Mrs Jane Jukes.

Shoe-horned into the roof space of the three story building, Lionel's room can best be described as tiny. It's comfortable enough in its own way, but comes with a few disadvantages. The younger Norcotts romp around banging and shouting, Mrs Norcott and Mrs Jukes frequently screaming in unison to silence them. Until the four of them are successfully put to bed, the noise in the house is unbearable. Even with the door to his own room firmly shut, Emden finds he can hardly think.

He's been working with Locke's team for several days before coming across a further issue with his billet. Summer seems to have appeared well before it's due, the sun has been blazing down on them all day. To a man they've been working stripped to the waist. When he returns to his low-ceiling garret the tiles, having been baked all day long, start releasing their warmth. It's twelve o'clock at night before the room cools down sufficiently for him to sleep.

What's more Norcott, a tanner, carries around with him a strong, unpleasant aroma. He's usually out 'til late, thank the Lord, but his obnoxious miasma seems to cling to the walls of the house. Clearly his family have become immune, but in this warm weather it makes Lionel feel vaguely noxious. All in all, despite Mrs Norcott's entreaties that he should eat downstairs with them, Lionel makes his excuses for being out of the house whenever possible.

To fill the time he's usually wandered into a nearby eatery or a public house for his evening meal. There are a dozen dotted around the streets nearby. Occasionally, when he's felt particularly energetic, he's ventured further into the city, seeking some variety in the fare on offer. He's not a man to court excitement as a rule, but he's unlikely to be in Bristol again. Why shouldn't he see a little of it while he has the opportunity?

And so, one evening in early May, he's entering an establishment, appropriately called The Rummer, not far from Corn Street in near the centre of the city. Turning down the rum in favour of porter, and having ordered a steak and oyster pie, he seeks out a corner table alongside the grimy bottle-glass windows. The sign outside boasts rooms and entertainment so he's pleasantly surprised to find it less crowded and quieter than he expected. Probably, being early evening, most of its regulars are still at work. Whatever the reason, he's delighted to sit alone and enjoy its peace. Some way off a group of men are talking, but they're hidden by one of the booths formed by high-backed settles. He can't see them and they don't seem to have noticed his presence.

Their conversation is animated and friendly, but carried out in lowered tones. A group of workmates he concludes. His attention's drawn by one voice in particular, which seems strangely familiar. Frustratingly, he just can't place it. He listens more keenly, willing himself to put a name to that voice, for he's certain he must know its owner. But as he concentrates, words and expressions that also ring bells float across his ear. These men, he's certain, must be in his own trade. Only they would be talking of levels, fillets, dressing faces and the like.

'Pie and mash sir, as you ordered, piping hot', a pot-boy interrupts Emden's musing as he puts the steaming plate on the table, along with a clattering knife and fork.

'Thank you son', Lionel replies curtly, waving the boy away, trying hard not to lose the thread of this disembodied conversation. And then it comes to him. That voice belongs to Richard Lambert. He's a stonemason himself. Lionel worked alongside him on a couple of occasions in Bath. He's tempted to walk around and introduce himself, but with a forkful of pie in his hand, he decides to bide his time.

The men's discussion continues and Lionel, with growing interest, strains every fibre to make out what's being said. Slowly it dawns that these men are also engaged in building suspension bridge footings, but on the Clifton side of the river.

'Here's to your health Padraic' says one 'As this will be our last day here for a while, we'll not be seeing you tomorrow.'

'To be sure, it's a shame' comes the reply, from a fellow with a distinctive Irish brogue, 'We could be pushing ahead with the job but I'm told that doing more than clearing the ground might create too much interest. There's far too many people coming to have a look at what's going on already. I'm under orders not to bring over any materials, even though they're all prepared and ready to come.'

'Who's been giving you your instructions?' asks Lambert, the man whose voice Lionel had recognised.

'Why that Gabriel Hartnoll, who else?   As far as I can make out he's in control of everything connected with this little enterprise.'

'Hmm, Hartnoll.' rejoins Lambert, 'That gentleman's a curious fellow and no mistake. I still can't fathom him out. He's very formal and business-like. Seems genuine enough on the face of it, but there's something about him that makes me uncomfortable. What's your opinion my friend?'

'Between you and me, I think he's got some game of his own in play' replies the Irishman, whom, from what had been said, Lionel assumes to be the builder, 'My brother's dealt with him in the past and he's not convinced of the fellow's integrity. Maybe Joe really knows something about the man, maybe it's all idle supposition. Meself, I prefer not to ask too many questions. Not of my brother, nor of Hartnoll. What I don't know can't hurt me. All I care is that this job will make us all a tidy sum of money. So, I'm happy to remain in ignorance and, despite your curiosity, I'd advise you to follow my lead.'

Emden slowly sups his ale and reconsiders making himself known to the men in the adjacent booth. He resolves however to mention what he's overheard to Maynard as soon as a suitable occasion arises.

Chapter 20

Maynard takes a minute to sit back and take in what's going on at the yard. The change in its routine is a surprise, even to him. Why, just a few weeks ago every stone they cut was treated almost like a character itself. When it came in as a rough-hewn block the mason assigned to shape it would size it up lovingly. Run his hands across the surface. Picture in his mind how he was going to transform this into the elegant profile shown on his drawing. In Maynard's trade there has always been some sort of curious empathy between man and material.

But the sheer volume of that material, now moving around the yard, has turned their skilled craft into nothing more than a routine. Several shipments of granite have arrived from Bath in the last two weeks. It's been roughly cut to shape and dressed, then stacked back in the yard ready for finishing and for the fixing holes to be bored. That can't be done until Emden's information comes through in the post. In the meantime the first boatload of Old Red has also turned up and the masons currently spend every day shaping one cladding slab after another in accordance with the directions left by Hartnoll. Every one identical to the one before.

There used to be space to move around. Rarely would the men get in one another's way. But now there are stacks everywhere he looks. Stone piled upon stone, held apart by rough wooden planks. Dust and chippings swept up three times a day by the apprentice. Did he realize this was how it would be, at the outset? Probably not. But it will be more than worth the inconvenience. Everyone will profit, if they just keep up the pace. He figures he should take all three of them down to the Old Boar one evening. The last thing he wants is any of them losing heart due to the monotony of the work.

~

News arrives from Locke, during the second week of May, that the landing stage at the gorge is complete. That the cutting into the cliff is well advanced. By the very same post Emden's first report comes through. The masons can now complete the first foundation stones precisely, following the dimensions in Emden's letter. These heavy blocks will interlock side to side and be anchored to the rock footings with steel bars fixed in molten lead. There's perceptible relief that at last they can get on something different. In less than a week they've polished off a dozen. Not long now before they must make their first shipment.

It's fifteen days since he left Emden at the gorge and Maynard decides to set out early for the quarry, with all the tackle he'll require to collect the barge. Since that fateful day in February, when he returned with the plough harness, the cursed object's been hanging on the wall of the stable. He'd covered it immediately with an old blanket. He'd have said for its protection, but in truth it's because just the sight of it would stirs up memories best forgotten. As time's gone by, they've eased themselves pretty much completely from his thoughts. Only now, when he lifts that blanket, does the confounded article shout back his indiscretion, conjuring up all the fears he had the very evening he placed it there.

God, he can't go through all this again, it's ridiculous. It's water under the bridge. Nothing's come of it. No one's mentioned a thing. But no matter how hard he tries to convince himself, a nagging doubt is hanging on. In the gloom of the stable he suddenly feels cold, alone, uncertain, and fretful.

Outside the sun is warm, the birds are singing, the rhythmic tapping of Edmund's hammer fills the air as he fixes a plank on the feed store door. Life continues as it always has, the daily routine of the farm and the men slaving away in the yard. Nothing's altered from yesterday and it will be just the same tomorrow. The familiarity revives his composure and yet again he pushes the haunting spectres to the back of his mind. With a deep breath he renews his resolution and sets out astride Hermes on the road to Conham.

The two brothers greet him warmly when he pokes his head through the door of their makeshift office. He senses that he's become a very important customer for them. The potential value of his business is something he hadn't given any real thought to until now, but it's clear it's not escaped the notice of the Strachans.

'You'll be here for the Celeste I dare say', says George, 'Wait a minute and have a natter with Eddie. I'll rustle up a couple of the men. They'll soon make it ship shape for you and get it roped up with your horse. I checked it over myself the other day and it seemed in good order to me. I'll tell one of them to go on to Swinton with you. Managing the locks can be a tricky business if you've never handled one of these vessels before.'

'That's mighty generous of you', Maynard replies, 'But how will your fellow get back here?'

'Don't you worry about that Thomas, the man's got legs and he'll just have to use them. He'll be pleased to do so I dare say. It's a sight less arduous than working here at the quarry.'

Maynard realizes it'll be increasingly difficult to keep his business secret from the brothers. He's acutely conscious he's already told them a barefaced lie about the location of the site. The warm welcome and spontaneous generosity they've given him today embarrasses him. So, when George gets back, he starts to sow some seeds about the real nature of the enterprise he's embarked upon. Remaining vague about exactly what's being constructed, he admits it's all located not far from the floating harbour, and not in Bath as he'd previously led them to believe.

Of course he expects his revelation to spark a barrage of questions and he's not disappointed. So he parries these with as much diplomacy as he can muster and again begs them to keep everything under their hats in case he's already said too much.

Finally their man turns up to report that the barge is made ready and, to Maynard's relief, the interrogation comes to an end. Together they walk down to the river with him to see him set out. With Strachan's man at the tiller, Maynard minding the ropes, the vessel starts its journey back. Blessed by the benefit of company, it's not a taxing trip. He tries to remember any peculiarities about their progress in case he should ever have to manage the journey single handed. The appearance of a cheerful lock keeper at Keynsham, who's happy to assist, gives him a deal of comfort. Whilst the lock's filling, the keeper explains the tariff he'll have to pay, at each lock, for the cargo he'll be carrying. He'd failed to account for that in his calculations. But it doesn't concern him too much and they continue. The tow path is firm and passable in most places, even through Cleeve Woods where the tree roots stretch right across to reach the water.

The journey passes without incident. It has taken Maynard and his helper just over four hours to reach Swinton. Overall he's very satisfied with his maiden voyage. His confidence in Hermes' ability to haul the first loads to their destination is has been vindicated. He calls the masons to come and inspect their new acquisition; then they all set to in earnest to finish off as many stones as possible before the daylight fails.

~

A week later it's Peter Austin who accompanies Maynard on a journey, on this occasion in the barge. Its open hold is loaded up with finished stones. It will be their first attempt at navigating to the gorge, and is therefore a considerable adventure. The difference made by the heavy cargo is immediately apparent. Near Bitton ferry, Maynard has to haul on the tow as they pass too close by another boat. Despite heaving with all his strength there's absolutely no change in the vessels' course and he ends up being dragged ignominiously through a patch of nettles. Controlling this leviathan obviously requires a lot more thinking ahead.

In addition to delivering their first set of blocks it's also their intention to pick up Lionel Emden. He's now done as much as is necessary on site and he's sorely missed back at the yard. Maynard has thought through every way of planning their journey but he can't see how to complete this first trip in less than three days. The outward leg, past the quarries, Troopers Hill, Netham Lock and along the new Feeder canal will take the best part of a day. So they'll make the basin of the floating harbour, but by then it will be too late go further.

That means they'll have to spend the night in the harbour itself. At least they can catch the early tide on the following day. As he promised, Emden's letter contained the times of recent tides along with all the other information. Maynard figures ten o'clock tomorrow will be perfect for what they need to get done. There will be sufficient water then for them to pass through the big lock gates and make the short distance downstream to Locke's mooring.

With any luck Locke's men will set to and unload the cargo quickly. That's vital as they must make it back to the harbour whilst the tide still holds. Sadly there will then be yet another night sleeping aboard the barge, followed by the journey home on the final morning.

He's heartened that it won't always be this difficult. In future he'll have the luxury of choosing on which day he sets out. If he picks them when there's an evening tide there's every chance of making the delivery late and getting home on the second day.

Everything really rests on the speed with which the builders can offload.

Their outward journey is accomplished without further problems. They get the hang of looking for trouble and taking early action to avoid collisions. By six in the evening they've made the port of Bristol and have moored up alongside the dock wall. Thoughtful as ever, Mary Ann insisted they take several old rugs and straw to use as pillows. They lay out their makeshift beds in the bottom of the hull immediately they've seen to Hermes. But the comfort will never measure up to the beds at home and Maynard decides a few bottles of ale might help them sleep. He's just sent Peter off with a handful of coins when two men from the Customs House stroll up to look over his vessel. This he's not expected, since their onward journey will only take them a mile from the port. But the officials politely explain that they have to take note of everything going through the port, the nature of the cargo, the purpose of the journey and the final destination.

It turns out to be a novel evening for them, sitting on the flags of the dockside, eating the meal that Mary Ann had stowed in the bow, enjoying their ale and playing a hand of cards. It's a most enjoyable diversion and their chattering reveals things about Austin's life that Maynard had never understood before. But the journey has tired them and as the light wanes they retire to their makeshift beds.

They both sleep fitfully for, in addition to the discomfort of the planking, noises of one sort or another go on throughout most of the night. Every so often there's an outburst of tuneless singing and when that dies away the creaking of planks from the ships moored alongside. Nevertheless a few hours are snatched and by mid-morning on the following day they've finally reached their destination at the site of the bridge.

Maynard's greatly impressed by the progress made Locke and his team in such a short space of time. It's obvious that he, like

207

Maynard, had been making considerable preparations prior to Hartnoll's instruction to start. The wooden members of the sheerlegs, hoists and landing stage were clearly fashioned in advance so that they could be rapidly assembled once the word was given. His team have already made paths, cleared steps and terraces and almost finished cutting into the rock face to form the footing surfaces that will underpin the massive structure. From a distance they can see the place is a hive of activity, men all over the site busy with shovels or sledgehammers.

The arrangement had been that Locke would be there to meet the two masons, but when they step off the barge he's nowhere to be seen. Instead they're met by his clerk of works. Maynard recognises the face instantly, but for a moment can't recall where they've met before. Then it comes to him it's Jeremiah Baker, Hare's supervisor from the chapel. He can hardly believe it. The fellow was a waste of time. Presumably he's quit Hare's employ to join Locke. But why would Locke give the man a job? He, too, knows the fellow's useless. Maybe he shouldn't ask, it's none of his business anyway.

Despite these thoughts, the mason's greeting is diplomatic. 'A pleasure to meet you again Jeremiah, why it must be four months now I reckon. I look forward to working with you again. You probably realize we're come collect my man Emden, in addition to bringing this boatload of stone for you. D'you know where I can find him?'

Baker returns his greeting and ushers them in the direction of a roughly hewn path leading up the side of the gorge.

'Is that Lionel, standing by the wooden hut?', Maynard asks Austin as they reach the upper terrace where a good deal of noisy rock-cutting is progress.

'I think you're right, replies Austin and hails Emden at the top of his voice.

'Thomas, Peter, what a sight for sore eyes. Am I pleased to see you', Emden bellows as he strides across to meet them. 'I've really enjoyed my stay in Bristol but I'll be delighted to get back to my own home and my own bed. The people I'm lodging with are friendly enough, in their way, but I really wouldn't want to be exiled out here much longer.'

Keen to return on the high tide, and with no other call on their time, the three masons help the gang of men assigned to offload their barge. The labour's heavy but between them all it's completed in good time, allowing an early departure back to the port.

Despite his earlier protestations, Emden actually spends a more comfortable night than his two friends, since he elects to sleep at his lodgings, rather than on the boat with them. He's had to return there in any event, to collect his belongings. The following morning he turns up early at the Celeste, in great good humour, ready to help his friends make the journey back to Swinton.

Maynard congratulates himself on the successful completion of their first delivery. The exercise has borne out that his calculations are correct, meaning that he can deliver all the foundation stones to the gorge himself once building officially commences. Reassured, he impatiently awaits the day of the official opening. For he's certain that once the ceremony had been performed Hartnoll's demand for progress will be insatiable.

His only concern now is the speed with which finished stones are being stacked up on the piece of ground next to his own landing stage. The masons have established a very efficient production routine and there are almost three weeks to go before the foundation stone is laid. They'll be lucky if they don't run out of space.

The day of the ceremony comes and goes. Maynard would dearly have liked to attend but Hartnoll had been most definite that neither he nor Locke should be present. No hint of their involvement should be apparent to anybody at this stage. In any case, a ticket was required to see and hear the speeches; the event was only open to those dignitaries who received a personal invitation.

The following day, Maynard decides again to ride into Bitton and purchase a copy of the Mercury. It's bound to have a report of the ceremony and he intends to keep both papers safely, for Emily. In the future she may treasure them as a reminder of the role her father played in this great engineering feat.

The periodical does indeed have an article about the ceremony on the front page. Leafing through, Maynard's surprised by just how many aspects of the bridge project have been reported upon. There's an article about Brunel, and his father, and their various achievements; another describing what the structure will look like when finished, complete with sketches of the bridge and the engineer himself.

As he scans each page for these articles he can't help but notice the numerous reports of crime. And the records of trials in and around Bristol. There's a full column listing the names of those felons committed for deportation. And two gory reports, complete with graphic sketches, of murderers who've been hanged this week in the city.

Another prominent article describes the progress of the Reform Bill through Parliament. It seems the Bill passed its second reading by just one vote, with a great many Members speaking against it, convinced that revolution will follow if it becomes law. The writer of this article is more sceptical about its chances when eventually it reaches the upper house. The Lords, he claims, are firmly wedded to the status quo and are almost certain to send it back. He describes the mayhem that might ensue if the Bill does get defeated in that august chamber. The country's more volatile than it's ever been, he goes on to explain, there's discontent everywhere, from the tin miners in Cornwall to the cotton millers in the north. Haven't last year's riots, stirred up by Captain Swing, been fair enough warning of the powder-keg this kingdom has become?

Maynard scans it all with interest, but gets no sense it has any bearing whatsoever on his own situation. Living on the edge of a village he never becomes involved in political debate, nor does he make any attempt to stay regularly acquainted with the news. Reading the Mercury this evening has provided him with more worldly information than he'd usually learn in a year. Of course he overhears discussions at the Old Boar and men like the Strachans sometimes pass comments that give him a sketchy knowledge, but has no opinions based on an understanding of the nation's affairs. Perhaps he's a fool. Perhaps he should be more curious, like his good friend John Carey.

The following day he's ready and eager to move ahead with the work. However rain and hail is suddenly lashing the countryside and the tow-path beside the river's now covered in slippery grass. Elsewhere it's quickly turned into a sea of oozing mud. The second delivery of foundation blocks will therefore be staying in Swinton for a few more days and the masons continue to dress yet another batch of cladding stones. There's so little space to move that storing the finished pieces is becoming dangerous. Maynard gets increasingly anxious to make the second delivery as soon as he can.

That evening, in a somewhat frustrated state of mind, he's at the kitchen table with his family taking their supper. Emily is opposite and he senses she's holding something on her knee beneath the table. Whatever it is, she keeps glancing at it when she thinks he's not looking.

'What's that you're hiding under the board Emily?' he demands, 'Your Mamma and I have told you before about bad table manners. For goodness sakes put it away, whatever it is, and pay full attention to your meal.'

'But It's only the newspaper you brought home yesterday pa' she replies 'you left it on your chair in the best room. I've been looking at it ever since I got back from school this afternoon.'

'Really? And just how much of it can you read my sweet?' Mollified somewhat by the thought of his daughter improving her skills, his approach towards her softens. He and Mary Ann have both done their best to instruct her and, since she was five, managed to have her attend the village school two days every week. He's quite determined she will benefit from a good education.

'I can read all the words in capital letters pa, and quite a lot of the smaller ones. But I have found a lovely picture too. Here, look. '

She pulls the folded paper onto the table and points out a large advertisement with a line drawing of a man on stilts surrounded by tents, horses, wild animals, sheep and cows and a crowd of jolly, smiling people.

'It says it's the Lansdown Fair pa. It looks really exciting. There will be a lion there, and a camel. I've never been to a fair. Can we go this year, please, please, please?'

Her entreaty takes Maynard completely by surprise. He's been to these local fairs regularly with his father, has occasionally seen some children there, but never considered it a suitable place for Emily, or even Mary Ann. Yes, there are attractions, sideshows, booths and games, but the real purpose of these events is for hiring labour and the buying and selling of animals. He'd also noticed a lot of lewd activity, thinly disguised prostitution and plenty of petty thieves eager to take advantage of people out to enjoy the day. He's always thought of Lansdown Fair as a place of work, never as entertainment. The advertisement Emily has found says it will take place in mid-July.

'I know it looks exciting my precious, but it's a rough and smelly gathering. It really wouldn't be a very nice place to take you'.

'Oh come on Thomas, why don't we all go, just for the day?' urges Mary Ann, who has been listening. 'I've never been to a fair myself and I'm sure I would enjoy it. There will be lots for all of us to see. Look, it says there will be a menagerie and a travelling theatre and fireworks in the evening. We never do anything like this. It would be a grand day out together and I'm sure we'll all have fun.'

'Mary Ann, I don't think it's wise. There are always ruffians at these events, I've seen them myself, and some of the sights are really not fit for a child like Emily. I know Edmund will want to be there and I'm happy to go along with him as usual. But I really think you and Emily should stay at home. Perhaps when she's a couple of years older it will be more suitable.'

'Nonsense Thomas, you're far too cautious, we'll be as safe as houses. You will be our brave protector in any case. I'm sure we'll come to no harm with you to look after us. Grandpapa will be there too, so we'll be doubly safe. Of course there are some shady activities at any fair but I'll make sure Emily doesn't see anything we wouldn't want her to. It will be a little holiday for all of us. You've been working far too hard recently; you deserve to put it out of your mind, if only for a day. Please husband, won't you agree to take us all in the trap? I shall be so delighted if you will.'

So, principally due to female coercion, the decision is made. The whole family agrees to attend the fair, which will be held over a week in the hills to the north of Bath. It will not be far for them to travel in the trap but Thomas makes it a condition they will start their return journey at five o'clock, no later.

On the following day the sun shines once again and a drying wind has sprung up from the west. Maynard's spirits recover. Very soon, he reckons, the tow path will be sound enough to make our second delivery.

Chapter 21

It's late afternoon before Hugo Wakelin reaches the vicarage. His arrival's noticed by all, but occasions little comment. Just whispers well out of his earshot. The shady nature of the activities carried by the occupants of this dilapidated building means it is best not to ask too many questions. Wakelin proffers no explanation of where he's been in the preceding days, in response to greetings he merely grunts.

Young, who had been impudently occupying the Captain's chair in front of the fire, boning a fox's tail with his knife, hears him enter and vacates the seat like a scalded cat. Wakelin sits himself down, pulls off his boots and silently contemplates the room, chewing on a well bitten cheroot.

The itch to quit the life he's leading has troubled him for weeks, urging him to act on some of the notions he's already roughed out in his mind. The wherewithal to pull off a string of respectable robberies is already in his hands ... they sit around him in various corners of the vicarage. Left to their own devices these brigands are simply a wanton, undisciplined rabble. But Wakelin's convinced he can inspire the fear and respect to weld them, for a brief spell at least, into an effective criminal gang.

But really valuable loot is generally easily identifiable loot. The means of turning such a haul into good money had been the one missing link in his scheme. Hence his lengthy absence from the vicarage. With a little help from an old acquaintance, one with whom he once shared a prison cell, a solution has at last been discovered. It requires a little trust however, from amongst his Kilbridge colleagues. With them, trust is a commodity almost impossible to come by. Nevertheless he prowls the vicarage for the remainder of the day. Engaging those felons he feels he can rely upon in hushed conversations. Persuading them to contact a number of others who are not there. By evening a handful of men are informed that Wakelin expects them, in the presbytery of the church, at midnight.

~

'Push that door together Saddler, everybody's arrived now. I've called you vagabonds here because I think I can rely on you. Rely on you to be sensible. Rely on you to carry out instructions. I don't want any of you proving me wrong, understood? And I almost didn't include you Saddler, because you're a fool and a hothead. You've shown that to me a number of times. But you are strong and you're sharp and I need your skill with horses. But no way can I tolerate a repeat of that scrap with Young – do you hear me boy? '

'And the rest of you. You're here because I've seen some shred of discipline in you and the stomach for a scrap. And because I reckon I can count you not to get cold feet, not to chicken out, not to squeal if, through bad luck, you're apprehended. You've probably guessed this is all about a job. A job that's too big for just one or two of you. A job that will mean all eight of us working together as a team. Now, are you with me? Or do any of you want out? If so, you can sling your hook right now.'

'What in your mind Captain? And what's the gain in it for me? Why all this talk about being nabbed?'

'Relax Bythorn. No one's going to collar us if we do this right. And the loot, I assure you, will be considerable. Pocketbooks, watches, jewellery, all the usual stuff. You'll get a chance to divide everything between you when we get back here. But this mark's going to be very different to our usual targets.

216

Quality gentlemen, quality. Heavy items. Items that are marked – gold plate, silver plate and the like. Stuff we'll never fence around these parts for anything like its true value. So, I've made arrangements to send it abroad. When it's sold there, you'll get a deal of money in your pockets.'

'What? You mean let it go, with nothing to show in return?' asks Bythorn

'There's the rub. There is no other way. If we sell it here it'll just end up melted down. This job will create a hue and cry and those valuables will be hunted for, count upon it. They'd be easily identified. Anything the local lads might fork out would be just a fraction of their worth. And there's always a risk a fence here might betray us, there'll be a reward offered for sure. No, it's safer and more profitable my way lads. You'll just have to trust me.'

'Where's the surety for us that you'll divvy up the proceeds, if indeed you ever get them Cap'n?' asks another 'If they're worth what you suggest, any man in his right mind would take off as soon as the money was in his pocket.'

'Well I don't suppose I'll ever convince you of that son', says Wakelin, 'But believe me, this will be no flash in the pan. I want more. Pull this job off properly, and there'll be others following behind. Those of you who do your bit will become rich men. No further need to risk your freedom robbing travellers on the road. But the mark I've chosen will test us to the limit men. I don't want anyone aboard who isn't prepared to take a life if it becomes necessary. So, one last time. How many of you are up for the game?'

There's a good deal of mumbling and cursing amongst them. But greed wins through in the end. One by one his seven associates pledge their allegiance to his scheme. Painstakingly, Wakelin starts to sketch out the part each will play in the ensuing robbery.

A half moon, mostly obscured by scudding cloud, casts its eerie light over Branwell Manor. The country seat of Sir Henry Belingfold, fifth baronet of Abson. An impressive three story house, built some fifty years ago, with tall windows and an ornamented balustrade stretching the entire length of its frontage.

Sir Henry leads all his visitors to understand that the Adam brothers were instrumental in its design. But he's an arrogant, pompous man and no one knows if this is true, or not. On every side of the house are attractive gardens, well set out and painstakingly tended, all in the middle of forty acres of rolling green parkland. The main drive is around four hundred yards long and meets, at the gates, with the London Road.

With those gates chained at night, two dogs on watch and several servants on hand in the house, the Belingfolds and their guests sleep soundly. Confident of their safety even in this remote and lawless countryside. The day has seen one of Belingfold's renowned shoots; the great and the good have all attended. Tonight every bedroom is occupied. No one turns down a Belingfold invitation. His shoots are famous throughout the county, not just for the abundance of game but also for the fine fare that's provided during and after the event.

It's half past three in the morning. All is silent save, for the occasional hoot of an owl. To the rear of the house, farthest from the London Road, the gardens give way to parkland which in turn merges into the surrounding fields. It's a long boundary and has no wall. Just a sturdy wooden fence behind a blackthorn hedge.

Since darkness fell three men have been labouring here. As quietly as possible, with saws, picks and axes, they've hewn down a section of the hedgerow and cut through two of the uprights that support the willow hurdles. It's not long before five accomplices arrive on horseback. The beasts are all healthy, powerful creatures, borrowed or stolen specifically for tonight's business. And three riderless mounts in tow, since every man will need a saddle before it's over.

The Captain has them all dismount and runs through his instructions yet again. With a bit of muscle applied to the fence, the separated willow hurdle crashes to the ground and two of the villains drag it to one side. Saddler and an older man, Perkins, are sent through on foot. They're dressed in dark clothing and have rubbed soot onto their hands and faces. Together the make a wide arc around the gardens to the outbuildings, using the cover of trees whenever they can.

The Captain's aware Saddler could carry out his instructions alone. But a wiser head with him won't go amiss, if only to temper his enthusiasm. And now the Captain, along with the others, stares intently into the darkness in the direction of the house.

Ten minutes elapse before a dull red glow can just be detected behind the stable block. As yet more minutes tick away it grows larger and more distinct, changing suddenly into a bright yellow light. Across the silent parkland the villains can hear the frightened whinnies of horses and dogs starting to bark. Then the distant shouts of Saddler and Perkins, running around the outside of the house yelling 'Fire! Fire! Run for your lives!' Followed by the sound of shattering glass and the men see lights starting to appear at the windows of the house, lanterns moving through the darkness as servants race to the stables.

'Now', instructs Wakelin, one foot in a stirrup, 'You all know what to do. Use violence only if necessary but, if you're in danger of being held, show no mercy. Let's get on with it.'

On his word the six men mount and gallop through the gap in the fence, across the parkland and gardens stretching to the rear of the house. Each carries two hemp sacks, joined at the throat with a leather strap. On they gallop until they reach an avenue of conifers bordering the flagged path running from the house to an ornamental lake. As they approach Saddler leaps out from behind one of the trees and seizes the traces of each horse as it's reined in. His face still smutted, his chest covered in blood.

'My God, he's killed some bastard already' exclaims Bythorn in a hoarse whisper.

'Steady Nathan' Saddler replies, 'The blood's not from a man. I lured the dogs with meat and then secured their silence with my knife, as we planned. One of them had a stout heart, stronger than I expected and it covered me in a gush of blood.'

The men, now dismounted, run up the path to the rear of the house and waste no time in breaking the window and shutters with steel mallets they have hooked onto their belts. Their blows make a lot of noise, but it goes unnoticed amongst the shouting and other commotion from the front of the house and down at the stables.

A long day of repetitive drilling by the Captain dictates what the men do next. They split into pairs. One climbs the back stairs to the upper chambers, plundering personal valuables left on nightstands and anything else they can find in the bedrooms. A second pair combs the dining room and withdrawing rooms, lifting plate and anything else that looks worthwhile, smashing cupboards and sideboards indiscriminately. The third takes the corridor to the estate office, to ransack it for the men's wages. When bodies impede them, they're swiftly bludgeoned to the floor. However, it's only a few occupants who interfere with the gang in the short time they are stuffing their sacks. Most guests have, by this time, fled their beds and rushed to the front of the house to see for themselves what's happening at the stables.

The gang's search for loot is swift and effective. Wakelin had been able to brief his associates beforehand with a rough but accurate description of the layout of the house. He's told them exactly where to look. It's as though he'd lived here himself. Each pair embarks on a purposeful rampage, pushing everything of value they find into their sacks, without breaking their stride. The Captain has given them a strict time limit, 'No heroics lads', he'd emphasised, 'And don't let your greedy eyes lead you to mess up the job. We're going to be mighty quick. In and out before anybody realizes we were there.'

So, as planned, within five minutes they've all returned to the orangery through which they gained entry. Wakelin ushers them out through the smashed shutters, urging speed. He pauses himself to scoop up a silver jug that one of them has dropped when a shout of 'Thieves!' is heard close behind. He turns to see a portly, whiskered gentleman, teeth out and attired in a full length nightshirt, rushing toward him with a fire iron grasped in his raised hand. Wakelin seizes a mallet, discarded after the door was broken, and flings it at the face of his assailant. It catches the old man on the chest and brings him gasping to his knees. Wakelin doesn't tarry to see how badly his victim's injured, in a trice he's outside the house and running like the devil with the others for the horses.

~

By dawn the band of brigands have made it back to the church and drag their sacks to the presbytery from which they'd planned the daring robbery. The challenge, for now, is to keep it all a secret from the villains at the vicarage who have not taken part. To a man, the gang is exhilarated and in a high good humour. There is delight and manly satisfaction in their success. Yes, there was danger, but there was real excitement

221

too and they've all returned safely. They invaded the impenetrable home of the gentry and escaped with a magnificent haul. Nothing could do more to stir feelings of pride and righteousness amongst this band of thieves.

With the contents of the sacks tipped out onto the floor, the loot is pawed over keenly. The estate office has sadly not yielded much ~ just a little money in a drawer, held there to settle with tradesmen. The estate wages, if indeed they'd been there, were either too well hidden or were safely secured. The bedchambers had proved much more generous. Sir Henry and his many guests had been predictable with their personal belongings - jewellery, money, watches and the like, when retiring. Most were found on tables beside the beds or in trinket boxes on the tops of chests. Then, a considerable haul of fine silver, taken from the ground floor rooms, all engraved with the Belingfold family crest. The two men charged with this part of the job had turned up so much they could not cram it all into the four sacks. Their escape had been impeded by the sheer weight of loot they had to lug from the house. Wisely Saddler and Perkins had stayed at their posts to help the others remount along with the haul.

Wakelin extracts all the items of negotiable value and gathers them into a pile, which he then divides equally between the men. For each man this alone amounts to a prize that's more than agreeable for just one night's work.

'Well boys, what's your verdict?' asks Wakelin, 'Did it not turn out exactly as I promised you?'

'I'll own I'm surprised' says Teeley, a dour-faced, normally taciturn villain, who had plundered along with Bythorn that night, 'To be honest I had this down as a daft scheme when you explained it to us last night. But in the end it did work like a dream, just as you say. Cap'n, I think you've proved we can pull off some really cracking jobs if we just work together.'

'That's so Teeley, you've hit the nail on the head man. Be minded lads, you've not seen all the spoils from this job yet, neither' replies Wakelin, 'When I have disposed of all this plate, we'll all be a darn sight richer, there's no doubt of that. So, now I have shown you what we can do together, are you ready to join me in the next enterprise?'

Every man in the room is a criminal in his own right and on his own account. Every man jack is selfish and wanton, each arrogantly convinced he's the master of his own destiny. Yet they all, through the night's adventure, have got a taste for working together and marking up a score more profitable than one of them could pull off alone. So they eagerly accede to Wakelin's offer. To a man they agree to join him if he can conjure up another snatch as brilliant as that at Branwell manor.

~

Sir Henry Belingfold stays long abed on the following morning. His chest throbs, it's painfully sore and he knows, once risen, he must face the sullen, unspoken approbation of his unfortunate guests. They've all suffered in one way or another, most robbed and some badly bludgeoned. None of this was Belingfold's fault but it all took place in his house. He'll be the man to take the blame for failing to protect his visitors.

Even once he's resolved to dress he does so in as dilatory a manner as possible. Eventually he takes a solitary breakfast in the dining room and reviews the carnage of the previous night. A large part of the stable block has been saved by some brave servants and his two sons who had moved speedily to douse it with water. But three of his treasured mares have perished in the smoke. Several others were led to safety and are now temporarily housed in a barn. Countless windows have been broken at the rear of the house and the orangery doors are hanging uselessly from their hinges. A large quantity of valuable items have been stolen, both from the family and from his guests. However, over one thousand pounds, located in a safety box placed in the cellar beneath the estate office, was fortunately never discovered by the burglars.

Shaken and angry, Sir Henry reflects that this robbery is an outrage upon every person of his class and position. If these villains can so easily invade the well secured privacy of Branwell, there is little to prevent them doing the same thing on other estates around the county. The assault on his person, and the damage to his reputation as a host, has left him seething with fury. He sends for the local constable and summons a servant to fetch his writing case. It's now high time the authorities are woken up and spurred into action against this wicked crew of villains.

Of course he'd heard about the Kilbridge Lane gang, their notoriety means few people haven't. But the name has meant nothing to him up to now. But he's convinced it was them, in his own house. One, at least, he got a good sight of and at very close quarters. Without doubt he'd recognise the scoundrel again. Those dark eyes and the long scar below his mouth would mean he's identifiable anywhere. Belingfold's more than confident he has friends in both Bristol and Bath who can be counted on to press his case with the judiciary in both cities. But first he must write to the editors of one or two newspapers, certainly the Times, because they have proved influential in the past. He guesses the local constable will be deferential, put on a good show of investigating the crime, but turn out useless as always. Far more positive action is essential to redress the mighty indignity that's been perpetrated on his person during the night.

Considering carefully what words will best achieve his aims, Belingfold picks up his pen.

224

Chapter 22

Just over the mason's yard wall grasshoppers are making enough noise to wake the dead. In the past ten days a profusion of colour has burst out along both banks of the river. A pungent aroma of wild garlic hangs in the air. Two wood pigeons are calling lazily to one another in trees across the water. High above a buzzard hangs motionless in the sky, silent, intent on the observation of some small creature in the field beside Maynard's enclosure.

For the Maynards, time has raced on apace. The very last week in June is suddenly upon them and the smallholding has been bathed in glorious sunshine for days. Summer, at last, has surely arrived. The spirits of the whole family are lifted by this glorious weather. For Thomas, his own exuberance is tempered by an endless succession of messages being received from Locke. Now the official opening ceremony's over he's determined to get on. How soon can the next shipment be made? When is Maynard setting out? The mason's replied that, given the good weather holds, it will be today, Monday 27th.

Working hard, and as a team, all four masons have loaded up the barge over the weekend. This advance preparation means that Maynard and Gurney, who's the chosen mate for this trip, are fit and ready to make an early start. Just as they're carrying the final baskets of food, drink and bedding on board, a horse can be heard arriving in the yard. Running up from the Celeste, to find out this might be, the mason encounters Locke, who's turned up with one of his workmen. He catches the builder in the act of dismounting from his stylish town gig.

'What's the devil's afoot Elijah?' Maynard enquires anxiously, 'By Jove, you must have set out early to reach Swinton by now. Surely you got my message that we're setting out today? Did you not trust me?'

'By no means' replies Locke, 'But the delays we've suffered, due to all that bad weather, has brought home to me just how vital it is your stone gets there on time. Without the materials to hand most of my men fall idle, and idle men means wasted money. My money! So, whilst I'm sure you've organised everything, including the weather, to a tee, I've resolved to accompany you there and see for myself how it all works. Two heads are better than one and I'd like to find out beforehand anything else that could possibly impede your deliveries. Besides, I'm confident I can be some help to you. And there's another more important matter. To fix those blocks you're delivering, my men will need the drawings and the levelling instrument currently stowed away in your shed. I've got the key here. I'd be obliged if you'd help me carry them aboard. Then we can all set out without my interruption causing any further delay!'

'If that's your wish Elijah, I'm happy. You'll be a welcome addition to our crew and no mistake. But I trust you know what that entails? Depending on the tides, the journey up and back will take two or three days. Gurney and I are planning sleep on board; it saves us the unnecessary expense of an inn. We take along straw and blankets and use the canvas covers stowed on board to keep us warm and comfortable. What will you do overnight?'

'That's a good point Thomas, I hadn't thought of that. Could I trouble you to rustle up bedding for me? I shall only be staying with the boat until we reach the bridge. Look, let me go call my man. He can help me with the instrument case whilst you get the blanket, after that he'll drive my trap back to Bristol.' So saying he turns and bellows for his employee. Maynard seeks out Mary Ann, pleading additional provisions for his uninvited shipmate. He's not surprised to find this leaves her somewhat short tempered.

Finally, about an hour later than intended, the Celeste is under weigh. More bedding, victuals and the instrument case
226

have all been taken aboard. Locke harnesses up the horse and the slow journey commences. For Maynard it now holds little novelty; he's spent more than enough monotonous days in the company of this vessel. But for Locke and Gurney it's a new experience and one they're enjoying to the full. After months of sweating away, day by day in the yard, this river trip feels like a holiday to Gurney.

Each man takes an hour's shift leading Hermes along the path, one of the others takes the tiller and the third keeps a lookout. The latter also lends a hand to the lock keepers when they open the sluices and gates to let the vessel pass through. By now Hermes has become used to the plough harness and its blinkers. At times, when the tow-path is wide and unobstructed, he can safely be left to walk unaccompanied. The weight of their cargo on this occasion is considerably increased. Maynard begins to wonder if he really does need to find a shire horse since Hermes appears to be making fairly light work of it. The river's flow, he realizes, gives the beast some considerable assistance on the loaded outward journey and when they return, against the current, the barge is always empty.

Locke's unexpected arrival and the flurry of activity that ensued means they've had no chance to talk about progress at the site since Maynard had last been there. So, as soon as Locke hands over the tiller to Gurney, he leaps over the side of the barge to join Maynard who is taking his turn at Hermes' head.

'Everybody's much impressed with the workmanship of the stones we've put in place so far' Locke remarks, 'They've all aligned perfectly with the steps in the cliff. The holes for the iron pins have matched to a tee, so our progress has been rapid. We're pouring the molten lead around them once they're in place. That's made the whole assembly as solid as a rock.'

'Because we got ahead with much of the work before we were officially supposed to have started, I've have made significant

227

progress on my side of the river. I climbed up into Leigh Woods and saw from there that Hartnoll's engaged one of my rivals on the Clifton side. An Irishman, he is. I've come across him occasionally in the past. His firm uses around twice as many men as mine, but since they couldn't do a thing until the foundation stone had been laid, the progress he's made lags well behind ours. I'm also fortunate that the face of the bedrock where we're working is firm and cuts well. We can proceed with confidence. If that rock had been crumbling and fragile, it would all be a very different matter.'

'I'm delighted you're content with what we've done so far' replies Maynard, 'And I'll admit, luck's been on my side in that. The quality of quarry stone provided to us, the granite, the pennant and the red sandstone have been remarkably good so far. Our skills in cutting and shaping will always produce a fine result with sound material, but no man can ever make poor quality stone good. One of the most valuable things my uncle taught me was where and how to root out dependable raw materials. It's all a matter of getting to know the men who mine them.'

'And thank God you're confident we'll get the abutment finished in time, because that's vital to our chances of winning further work from the Corporation. How you think we stand, my friend? When d'you think contracts for the towers and the deck will be awarded. Has Hartnoll let slip any further information?'

'Curiously, apart from regular exchanges of correspondence by messenger, Hartnoll and I only seem to meet up when we both visit you at Swinton. But I do know, now the foundation ceremony is passed, their committee has published a list of those firms engaged for the work, including yours and mine. I'm sure, provided the standard of craftsmanship continues to be satisfactory for the next three months, we'll be engaged to build the tower on our side of the river. Hartnoll did send a message to say he's getting formal contracts for the current stage drawn up at the moment'

228

'Good. That's a relief. All this secrecy and uncertainty around payments has made me deuced nervous over the last few weeks. Any arrangement set out on paper will greatly ease my mind.'

'Once we complete all this work, you'll be a man of considerable standing' says Locke, 'I imagine prospective clients will flock to your door; your reputation will go before you. What will you do then? You should really be located within the city you know, either Bristol or Bath. Not out in Swinton, it's too remote for most clients to find you easily. Have you ever considered moving? I'd seriously advise it. It's the most sensible way for your business to progress.'

Actually Maynard has given no thought this possibility, preferring to focus his mind on achieving the task at hand. On reflection he can see that Locke's well intended suggestions are entirely sensible. He knows that Mary Ann, Emily and he would fare well in the city, but surely such a move would distress his father. To shift yet again, and leave him alone at the smallholding, thrown back onto his own resources; well it frankly can't be countenanced. And it's really not a decision he needs to reach this morning, so steers the conversation onto other topics. They meander on, talking, until the tow-path becomes too narrow to walk side by side.

At around two o'clock in the afternoon they draw alongside the wharf that forms part of Strachan's quarry. Maynard insists they tie up, so that he can introduce Locke to Eddie and George, provided he's lucky enough to locate them. Leaving Gurney to mind the barge and eat his lunch, Maynard and Locke go in search of the quarrymen, carrying their own victuals in a sack on the mason's shoulder.

They find them inside the stone building that Maynard has visited so many times before. Eddie, with considerable ingenuity, manages to clear spaces for them to sit and the brothers are delighted to share Maynard's bread and cheese, covered with Mary Ann's pickle. He's enormously relieved,

229

finally, to admit to them in detail exactly what he and Locke are up to. When the story's recounted, George emits a low whistle.

'Well, it's a rum way to organise such a huge undertaking' he says, 'But of course I'm delighted you got the work, even with such a cat and mouse arrangement. It's turned out excellent business for us both, I don't mind admitting. But the way you were engaged does sound fishy to me. I'd counsel you both to find out a bit more about who you are dealing in that administration. I've seen these sort of arrangements go awry in the past. It only needs for your man to fall out of favour and it could go wrong all of a sudden.'

'I think you're being over cautious there George. I'm confident our part in this business is secure', retorts Locke, who sounds somewhat affronted by the well-meant advice, 'We'll soon have contracts for the work and our sponsor is firmly established and highly regarded. I think you may leave it to me to ensure we're all in a safe position.'

'No offence meant Sir, I trust you've read it correctly' replies George, 'It's odd though. On my life I can't understand why we need a bridge to reach Somerset. Not just there anyway. It's not as though there's anything apart from green fields worth visiting on the other side.'

'Who are we to say George?', counters his brother. 'We're mere mortals and lack the intelligence of our betters. If they've gone to the lengths of passing an act of Parliament to get this bridge built, it must surely have a good use for somebody.'

'And when do you get to meet the man?' asks Eddie

'You have the advantage of me', retorts Maynard, 'Who exactly do you mean?'

'Why, this Brunel chap of course. His father's got a fearsome reputation. I imagine he'll want to inspect the progress of his brainchild.'

'That's a really good point', replies Locke, 'Nobody's made any mention of the engineer since we were set to work.'

'Quite likely he's overseas somewhere', suggests George, 'These fellows get everywhere in the world nowadays. You're bound to bump into him sometime soon, I'm sure.'

Lunch complete, Eddie takes Maynard and Locke on a tour of the quarry to show them where their stone is being cut and to demonstrate some of the advanced methods they employ, including a horse-drawn tramway used to carry blocks from the banker benches to the wharf. Locke's deeply impressed with the visit and they return to the Celeste, resuming their slow progress down river in the direction of Bristol.

It's late in the afternoon when they finally make harbour and tie up, yet again, alongside the high stone wall. This is all old hat now for Maynard and he walks Hermes off to the stables, located within the harbour buildings, so that he can be fed and rested for the night. The stable lad there is a boy of few words but, having met him before, Maynard realizes he's kind and gentle with the horses. Hermes is such a critical part of his plans at the moment it's reassuring to know that he'll be well cared for in his absence.

It stays light now till about nine o'clock in the evening and the three men sit on the quayside, idly observing the constant flurry of activity around them. Ships that have just arrived on the tide are being hastily tied up alongside, others are being unloaded by derrick and by a stream of dockers carrying cases and barrels on their shoulders down the gangplanks. Locke smokes small black cigars and the little group plays whist with a pack of cards Mary Ann thoughtfully put into the food basket.

That night Maynard is all for eating at a local tavern and even offers to stand supper for his two travelling companions. But Locke, usually the most outgoing and gregarious of men, will have none of it, insisting they stay with the barge for security.

'But it's just full of stone Elijah' Maynard protests, 'Nobody would want to steal it from us, nor for that matter can I see how they could possibly manage it.'

'That may be so' retorts Locke, 'But it's still vital to our building work and, with all this delay, it's important we leave nothing to chance. We can't afford to have any of these blocks lost or vandalised. Besides, we have my drawings which are too cumbersome to take to an inn and that levelling equipment which extremely valuable and impossible to replace if it were stolen.'

The strength of Locke's argument and the vehemence of his resolve eventually persuade the others. So Gurney's sent off to the inn and eventually returns with a flagon of ale which they set about, along with Mary Ann's lovingly prepared cold supper, on the boat.

They all drink more than their usual ration, sleep extremely soundly and are inconveniently awakened by the shouts and noises from nearby vessels getting ready to catch the early morning tide. Maynard's head is thick and he is stiff from lying in an uncomfortable position on the hard boards of the hull. He has little inclination to jump to and prepare for departure. However there is no choice if the unloading is to be accomplished in time at the bridge site, so he hastens off to collect Hermes from the stable and pay his dues.

Returning he finds the barge has been made shipshape by his companions and is ready to cast off. As he harnesses Hermes and checks the knots in the pulling ropes, the two customs men who he'd met on his last trip with the barge arrive at the quayside next to the Celeste. They're breathless. They've been having a busy time of it, checking out so many vessels intending to depart. Maynard looks around and sees there are others in similar uniforms on the deck of a middling size topsail schooner berthed close by.

'Good morning to you gentlemen. Please don't cast off just yet. We'd like to come aboard to take a look around. Which one of you in charge of this vessel? We need to take a few details about your voyage. '

'I'm responsible for this boat sir. My name is Thomas Maynard. I'm a mason from Bitton near Bath and we're transporting this finished stone not far downriver.'

'Ah yes. We met a few weeks back did we not?', the official says, licking the end of his pencil, 'Could you give me a more comprehensive description of your cargo and also its destination?'

'It's all much the same as my previous journey through this port. Just dressed stone; forty granite foundation blocks and thirty facing stones, plus a few tools. As you can see it's a much larger load than last time. We'll be sailing it just a mile from here, up the Avon, as we did before.'

'Is that so? I assume then that you are engaged in the construction of that new suspension bridge we've all heard so much of recently?'

'You're not mistaken, Sir. My friend Mr Locke here is building the structure you may have seen from the river bank. I supply the facings that render it elegant and attractive. We shall haul this stone to the bank below the foundations on the Somerset side, unload it and return empty through the port in about six hours from now.'

'Well, I doubt you'll have anything here that we'll be interested in', the customs man says. Nevertheless he and his colleague cast a practised eye over the cargo in the barge. 'No, everything seems to be in order. You may pass into the lock Mr Maynard and we'll see you on the way back later on.'

233

Luck is with them. The size of their vessel means they've been allocated an early turn leaving port. Gurney, Locke and Maynard, with the help of Hermes, manoeuvre their vessel into the vast lock, the harbour facing gates of which are open to let them enter. Then they have to wait whilst the schooner, which had been moored behind them, takes its place alongside. This vessel, with its high sided hull and handsome rigging, completely dwarfs the Celeste, throwing a shadow over them as it draws abreast.

With much creaking, the huge wooden gates are closed by a small army of men and boys pushing and cursing in unison. The lock keeper uses his large iron key to open the paddles and let the level of water in the lock drop to the level of the rising tide in the Avon, which is being forced inland by the Bristol Channel, some eight miles distant.

The schooner and the heavily laden barge descend slowly together as the water flows out of the lock. Maynard shivers as the hull of the schooner and the wall of the lock cut out much of the sun's light and all of its warmth. The sound of dripping water and the creaking from wood and rope echo around the dank chamber whose walls are coated in green slime below the water line. As the barge sinks ever lower, Maynard muses on the wonder of the floating harbour, which now allows ocean going ships to be unloaded efficiently and conveniently, rather than being beached when the tide goes out. It was only built about ten years ago, a miraculous feat at the time. Without it all this, heavy stone would have to be transported by horse and cart, talking many more far longer journeys to accomplish the same result.

Finally the water levels equalise and the lock gates creak slowly open on the other side. They wait until the schooner is away, catching a light breeze which takes it slowly downriver. Then they make a start themselves. Locke, who has been sitting motionless on the crate since they cast off, suddenly stands up and stretches happily in the sunlight.

'It's good to be alive on a morning like this Thomas' he declares, 'and we're nearly there. In excellent time to get this lot stacked on our landing stage and you ready to return.'

Maynard decides last night's ale must have found its mark with Locke and that the sunshine and breeze is finally reviving him. Up to now he's been decidedly preoccupied, but suddenly he's cheerful and boisterous, back on his usual form.

Rounding the bend beyond the lock, the builder's moorings come into view in the distance. Maynard's relieved to see that a new and more robust derrick has been constructed to hoist goods out of vessels and onto the riverbank. Like its predecessor, it's operated entirely by hand, but this new machine can be raised or lowered and also rotated. It will be far faster to unload using this than the old sheerlegs that still stands alongside. As they pass, they observe another temporary wharf on the Clifton bank, apparently erected by Locke's competitor for a similar purpose. Construction there is mostly at the top of the gorge. Maynard can hear all the noise of men building but discovers he can't see any activity from the boat, no matter how he cranes his neck.

They moor at the staging and Locke's men spring to action, unloading the vessel of all its cargo. Locke insists the crate is raised to building level first so that his foreman can check the alignment of a foundation course that had already been laid.

'We'll get this done first Thomas' he remarks, 'When we have you can take the instruments and the drawings back with you in the crate. I don't want to leave them here any longer than I must. They're valuable items. And it's essential they're available at the stone-yard, in case we need to check the parts turned out by your men. Now, follow me and watch your step; we have to climb that footpath my boys have recently made in the side of the gorge. It's still pretty slippery. But I'd like to show you what we've achieved since you were last here. I trust you'll be impressed.'

Without any doubt, Maynard judges the progress made reflects to Locke's enthusiasm. The short round iron bars, intended to key the foundation course to the bedrock are, at this very moment, being set into holes and set with molten lead. Bricks, stone and rubble not immediately required are stacked, awaiting use, on a broad shelf cut into the cliff which also serves as the builders' general work platform. Saw horses, mortar mixing boards and fires for the lead occupy every spare piece of ground. Wooden scaffolding has been erected to make bricklaying easier. The men seem to be a well-disciplined bunch and Locke's new foreman, who came over so ineffective at the chapel, appears to have a firm hand on his team.

'Truly, I'm amazed' says Maynard, 'I had no idea just how immense this structure would seem, close up.'

'Oh yes. It's no wonder the city were keen for us to start as soon as they could. This abutment will be over one hundred feet in height when it is finished. Only then can construction of the actual suspension tower commence. On our side of the river that tower will be supported entirely by the abutment we're building here. It's the only way Brunel could keep the span to a safe length.'

'I know I'm shipping you a prodigious amount of material' Maynard remarks, 'And I can see you've got stacks of bricks and a deal of rough stones, but it doesn't look sufficient to create such an immense platform for the tower.'

'Ah, that's where the cunning of Mr Brunel comes in. You've assumed this structure will be solid stone and brick, haven't you? But you are mistaken. The drawings Hartnoll gave me call for a number of huge voids within the construction, some at least thirty five feet tall. The structure won't be solid throughout, most of it will be just fresh air.'

Maynard's fascinated by Locke's insight into this curious design and would really like to hear more about it. But he's conscious that he and Gurney cannot stay much longer. It's imperative they get back to the harbour before the tide falls too low. Consequently they bid their farewells and navigate the empty barge back through the port. The evenings are now light until a late hour, they manage to pass through Netham lock before tying up for the night. Maynard makes sure Hermes is fed, watered and comfortable on the tow path for the night before retiring himself.

Whilst waiting for sleep to overtake him he ponders Locke's insistence on continually lugging around the measuring tools and drawings. For Locke instructed him, before their departure today, that they'll now have to follow the same procedure on every trip. He maintains the equipment might someday be needed to check the surfaces of blocks cut at the yard. But having observed the levelling instrument being employed on site, with its tripods, sights, chains and mirrors, Maynard cannot quite see how or why. Nevertheless, Locke was adamant. He also maintained that his own presence on this journey had been decidedly necessary and that he'd be sending one of his own men to accompany the masons each time they made another delivery. Without coming to any conclusion about the extravagance of this plan, Maynard finally drifts into sleep.

Chapter 23

The early-morning sluggishness, usually habitual in Emily, has miraculously vanished. On any other day she'd still be resolutely snuggled under her blankets. Today she's out of bed by six o'clock and bouncing into her parents' bedroom, eager to disturb their slumbers. Already excited beyond the point at which she can contain herself, her chattering about the day ahead tumbles like a waterfall. Mary Ann and Thomas get no peace until they're up and dressed and preparing an early breakfast. Edmund has risen especially early himself to milk the cows. Emily rushes to find him in the barn, badgering him too, until he gives up the unequal struggle and returns to the house to eat with them. Thomas is concerned as his father seems to have lost his appetite, but he puts it down to nervousness at the prospect of making his pay off.

Of course the cause of all Emily's excitement is Lansdown fair. Every day over the past week, on occasion several times a day, she's asked yet again exactly when they'd be going. Now the great day has finally arrived and she's brimming over with the excitement in store. Maynard proposes they set off at ten o'clock, once he and Edmund have attended to all the regular daily tasks at the farm that need be taken care of. It's not easy to concentrate on these with a little shadow pestering him at every turn. Fortunately he's already asked Lionel to take charge of the masonry shop, since he'll be unable to give that any attention until tomorrow morning.

Mary Ann fills a wicker basket with meat patties and other tasty morsels to sustain them and they all climb up onto the trap, with Hermes between its shafts. Family outings are all too infrequent. Even Thomas's spirits rise at the thought.

Edmund would have gone to this fair in any event. Through an unspoken arrangement he turns up every year to part with the ransom money that ensures his stock stay safe. Thomas accompanies him whenever he can, out of a sense of filial duty. Or, if he's really honest with himself, a feeling of guilt that he can't free his old father from this wicked exploitation. Not that he's ever attempted to interfere with Edmund making his clandestine remittance; he's just conscious how close his father physically comes to the felons that are leeching on him. A desperate need, to be there to lend some support or at least show that he cares, is lodged in his conscience. Consequently, when Emily insisted they all visit the fair, it didn't alter his plans significantly. It just means he'll have to keep his wits well about him, to look after her and Mary Ann as well as his dad.

The journey to Lansdown is little more than a gentle trot; it takes no more than twenty minutes and passes uneventfully. At the top of the hill, several fields have been marked off with white posts and flags. As they get closer to these they find themselves amongst a colourful procession of vehicles and people on foot, all converging on the event. Signs direct them to a field set aside for carts and traps, all set up with tethering rails and posts. Unhooking the traces, Thomas leads Hermes out from between the shafts and finds a place to tie him up in the shade of a chestnut tree. The family walk off together, in the direction of the tents, the music and the noise of the crowds. The high clouds that had cast a grey pall earlier that morning have now all been blown away by a westerly wind. The sun is shining down on them and it looks as if it's set to be warm for the rest of the day.

Every year the fair grows bigger, every year it's louder and more boisterous. Maynard has always been undecided about the event. For sure it provides wonderful amusement for those seeking it, but at the same time there's a sinister and threatening atmosphere lurking not far beneath the gaiety. Jostling crowds already surround some of the stalls, hawkers are shouting in the pathways, people are walking and running in all directions. Amongst them is a juggler dressed in green and red. They pause as Emily watches his whirling clubs with wide eyes.

'Hey! Watch where you're going lad' Maynard bellows at a lanky youth who brushes against him and knocks him off-balance in the process. But the boy is gone immediately, swallowed up by the crowd in seconds. 'God damn it', thinks Thomas, 'I've probably been robbed already'. He frantically checks his pockets to see what might have been lifted from him in the encounter. But nothing's gone, it was obviously an innocent mistake. Nevertheless, he'd been caught this way before and the incident prompts him to be more alert for this sort of danger.

'Please don't get separated from us father' he implores in a hushed voice, 'I'd like to go along with you this time, when they come for your money'. But this is going to be difficult since Emily, who is dancing ahead, will insist they get involved in all sorts of distractions, whilst the gang's go-between might approach Edmund at any time. Nevertheless Maynard has promised himself that this year he will at least attempt to identify the felons responsible. Suppose he succeeds? What then? Perhaps some idea will come to him about what he might do to put an end to his father's blackmail.

As expected, Emily pulls them this way and that. Several sideshow attractions catch her eye, firstly bobbing for apples, then trying the bran-tub. On every occasion she wheedles more coins from Maynards' pocket. Surrounding them on all sides are canvas tents, in the main a natural buff colour but some are gaily dyed in reds, blues and yellows. Notices pinned to the flaps, or on boards beside them, announce what goods or entertainment they have to offer, but others are mysteriously anonymous, having no signs at all. Unseemly characters keep entering and leaving these from time to time, something that doesn't escape Maynard's notice. He keeps an eye out for them and carefully steering the family to avoid them with a wide berth.

A deep trumpeting noise can suddenly be heard above the general clamour. Emily's face is full of wonder.

'Daddy! What's that?'

'I can't be certain but I think it must be an elephant, little one. By the sound of that call it must be right at the other end of the fairground.'

'Well come along, hurry up. We must get there quickly', she retorts, dragging on both her parents' hands.

But they've only moved on a hundred yards when the tents on the right of the path give way to a roped-off oval on the grass. In the centre horses and riders are wheeling around, feet stamping, some rearing up in anticipation. They snort and whinny, the grooms trying desperately to bring them into a line. There's a tangible sense of excitement amongst the crowd, starting to press up against the rope. It's clear that a race is about to begin.

As if by magic, all thoughts of the elephant vanish from Emily's mind. She's always loved Hermes and that's encouraged a fascination with horses in general. She squirms between the onlookers to the front of the crowd as the excitement builds.

A man with an outrageous moustache and a bright yellow waistcoat stands on a stout wooden box. He holds his flag to the ground, waiting for all the riders to line up with their mounts. As his arm comes up, Maynard senses someone behind him, trying to attract his attention.

'Want to make a profitable wager Dad?' a skinny lad of about sixteen and reaching only to Maynard's shoulder asks him with an unabashed cheek, 'Point out any horse and I'll make you a fair bet. If yours should win, you can count on getting back twice your stake.'

'Not for me lad' replies Maynard, but Emily has overheard this exchange and implores him to bet on a roan she's already decided to be the finest horse in the ring. So he good-heartedly parts with two pennies, wondering if he will ever see the lad again, let alone his money. The flag falls, Mary Ann and Emily are both pressed against the rope, cheering on the roan at the tops of their voices. With the noise and excitement at a peak, another lad, taller but of similar build to the bookies' runner, taps Edmund on the shoulder and unclasps a fist held under Edmund's chin. Between his fingers is a white china thimble, decorated with a spray of red roses.

'My masters respectfully request your donation of two shillings and sixpence, as customary, sir', he breathes into Edmund's ear. His demand is a ritual that occurs every year; the thimble merely a token that was taken from the smallholding years ago, during one of the visits from mysterious strangers. It serves as a sign from Edmund's persecutors that the unknown youth is acting as their agent. Edmund, expecting this approach at some point, already has the money in his fist. He thrusts it into the youth's hand, on top of the thimble and curses none too quietly.

'You and your bloody friends, you're nothing but vile bloodsuckers. Why, you must have had twenty pounds out of me over the years'.

Immediately the coins are safe between his fingers, the lad is away, disappearing into the crowd like a shadow. But Maynard is alert. He's been waiting for this, one eye open for exactly this sort of approach. He's ready, on this occasion, to memorise the face and clothes of the go-between and sets off quickly in pursuit, knowing he'll recognise the lad again if he sees him.

Making no attempt to push through the throng directly after his quarry, he skirts around the side of the crowd to its rear and loiters in the shade of a tent flap close to the main pathway. Keeping very still, he keenly observes the flow of fairgoers passing by. What seems like an age passes, but his patience is eventually rewarded. The same lanky lad is coming towards him, not running now, but sauntering nonchalantly and heading in the direction of a small tent pitched at the very edge of this sea of conveniently anonymous temporary shelters.

Taking a wide arc, using the cover of neighbouring canvas structures, Maynard eventually reaches the rear of the tent which he saw the lad enter. Kneeling as though to tie his shoe, his eyes roam across the canvas wall for any opportunity that might allow him a glance inside. To his surprise, he is in luck. There's a very small tear about two feet from the bottom. He risks prising apart the edges of this rip with his fingertips in order to peer inside. It's a peculiar vantage point, especially as he has to lie on the grass to make use of it. But it does give him a glimpse, if by no means a complete view, of the interior.

He can see a number of rough looking fellows. They're all standing, most more than a little unsteady, clearly in drink. By craning his neck to glimpse the faces, he identifies one of them as the go-between, the lad with Edmund's money. The boy is passing the coins to a ruffian of singular appearance with a scar on his cheek that runs right down under the lower lip. Words are exchanged between the two. Maynard strains to make them out, but they're drowned by loud, raucous laughter coming from the others.

Maynard would like to see more, but there are at least six people inside the tent; one of them might spot him stretching the tear at any time. He eases his fingers out gently, to avoid the possibility of being discovered, but not before a whiff of acrid tobacco, one that he recognises very clearly, has reached his nose. His observation has lasted only a few seconds and he's reasonably confident none of the tent's occupants are aware of it. He, on the other hand, has a very clear image of the scar-faced brigand fixed in his mind. He looks around behind him, checking that nobody had spotted his eavesdropping, then stands up slowly and walks away as casually as he is able. He strives to appear relaxed but inside every fibre of his being is trembling.

Reaching the safety of the main path, he returns as quickly as he can to the spot where he left his family. By now the race and all its excitement is over, the crowd that had been watching largely dispersed. From a distance he spies Mary Ann's lace bonnet, which she's was proud to put on for this special occasion.

'Did I win that wager you encouraged me to make?' he asks Emily as he reaches them.

'No, the poor roan started way out in front, but it pulled up before it reached the finishing tape. It was limping dreadfully, I think it picked up a stone or something like that' she replies, 'But papa you should have been here to see for yourself. It wasn't fair to sneak off when we weren't looking. We are all supposed to be enjoying the fair together. Where have you been?'

'I'm truly sorry Emily, it was wrong of me to slip away like that. But I saw somebody I know and had to catch him to talk about my masonry business. I promise you it was important, otherwise I'd not have been so thoughtless.'

'All right papa, we will forgive you on just this one occasion' she replies, placated, 'but only if you promise to stay with us from now on.'

So saying she strides off ahead, arm in arm with her mother, leaving Edmund and Thomas chuckling.

'Bless me, she's growing up quickly' observes Edmund, 'I reckon in time she's be as formidable as my beloved Ada.'

The four continue walking until they are well away from the crowds and the tents, and find a dry, clean patch of grass that will serve for their picnic. Mary Ann unpacks the basket, handing out slices of cold ham pie; along with these she's brought four apples from the orchard at the farm. The little meal should be sufficient to take the edge off their appetites until they get back to Swinton later in the day.

'Well, this is a rare treat for us all,' she exclaims, 'And very pleasant it is too. I'm sure this is the most enjoyable day I've had for months and we've only been here a couple of hours. There's lots more to do and several parts of the fair we haven't even seen yet. Thomas, to think you tried to stop us from coming, you should be ashamed of yourself. How could you deny Emily the fun she's had this morning? Why, I believe we should try to do this every year, especially if the sunshine is as glorious as it is today.'

Thomas has to admit that they are all having a marvellous time and that no harm had befallen them so far, despite of his natural aversion to the crowds and seamier sideshows. Naturally he doesn't tell them what occurred whilst they were watching the race, preferring that the remainder of the day should be devoted to unsullied enjoyment.

'I should like to stroll over and visit the cattle and the horse sales now' says Edmund, once they've eaten everything in Mary Ann's basket, 'They're on the far side of the fairground, beyond the saddlers' tents. If we are all intent on staying together, will you all come with me?'

Once there, they spend an hour or more walking between the wooden pens that corral the animals, Edmund examining the shine on their coats and general condition, standing around the crowded sale ring to get a view of the prices such beasts are commanding. Maynard guesses Edmund's trying to get an idea of the value of his own herd and is using this visit as a means to that end. Emily eventually grows impatient and fractious, so Mary Ann takes her off to in search of the elephant that can still be heard above the crowd now and again. They make an agreement to meet up at the toffee-apple stall in an hour or so.

'Is he considering a sale or a purchase?' Thomas thinks to himself, as he watches his father intently following the progress of an auction. 'Does he want to sell up his little herd or does he have a hankering to expand it? If this bridge job turns out as I expect, I might well be able to help him buy some more stock.' He makes a silent promise to himself to discretely ask Edmund about his plans for the smallholding's future when he can next bring it up in casual conversation.

Turning away from his father he walks the few steps to look at an impressive display of new ploughshares. His attention has been diverted for just a minute or so when he hears a low groan. He turns to see his dad bent over and clutching his side. Immediately he rushes to help.

'What's happened? Where are you hurting?' he enquires.

Surprisingly, Edmund manages to stand straight almost immediately and dismissively brushes off his son's solicitations.

'There's nothing wrong, lad, nothing at all. Just a bit of indigestion I reckon. Happens to me now and again, but it passes off pretty quickly. Let's just carry on.'

'Are you sure?', asks Maynard, 'You're quite certain you wouldn't rather set off home now?'

'Nonsense Thomas, I'll be fine. And there's a collection of young bullocks over there that I specifically want to get a look at.'

And so their tour of the livestock continues. But eventually Edmund admits that he's seen enough cows and horses, though this is the part of their day that he's clearly enjoyed the most. To round off their outing they meet up with the women folk and make one last visit to the sideshows that so engrossed Emily when they arrived.

They spend yet more pennies as she takes turns at the various diversions. A woman selling linnets in tiny wicker cages approaches their daughter and shows her a bird that sings beautifully. Tears flow copiously when Thomas and Mary Ann bluntly refuse to purchase this tiny imprisoned handful of feathers. So finally, at a stall they all agree must be the very last of the day, Emily tries to pitch three wooden rings over iron pegs sticking out of the ground.

Maynard is shouting fatherly encouragement, when his eye is drawn to a pair deep in conversation, some forty yards off at the end of a narrow alleyway of canvas between two rows of tents. One of the two is facing in his direction. Even at this distance he recognises the scar-faced rogue he'd spotted earlier through the slit in the tent. The man with whom he is earnestly exchanging words has his back to Thomas, but his outline is vaguely familiar. Thomas starts edging cautiously towards them between the tents, stepping carefully over guy ropes to avoid making any sound. Within a few seconds however the pair have stepped out of his view. When he eventually reaches the point where they had been standing, there's not a soul to be seen.

Chapter 24

Days pass before Emily can be persuaded to stop talking about their adventures at the fair. In quieter moments of contemplation, Maynard ponders deeply on the experience. But he doesn't say a word. Not even to Edmund, for he knows how jumpy his father would get if he suspected Thomas planned any action to tackle the blackmail. There are other things too, from that afternoon, of which he can still make no sense. So Maynard puts them to one side and sets to the work in hand.

The screw is beginning to turn. Recently Hartnoll has been steadily increasing the pressure on both himself and Locke. Messages arrive once or twice a week urging him to improve the rate of production and frequency of deliveries; moreover demanding he make regular written reports on progress, which he naturally has to take into Bitton each week and put on the stage bound for Bristol.

Locke had been persuaded to take on thirty more men at the gorge and the abutment is fast beginning to take a shape that's visible from the edge of the Downs. Maynard rides into Bath with Emden to seek his uncle Samuel's advice. The stone-yard will need two more skilled masons if they're to keep pace with the production demanded by Hartnoll and his superiors in Bristol. Emden and Gurney had been excellent recruits, but they were the only good men Maynard knew personally from his time in Bath, the only ones he'd trust to work for him.

Fortunately, with his wider experience and as a respected member of the guild in Bath, Samuel has half a dozen suggestions about men they might approach. He's able to say where many of them can be found. An arduous day ensues, with Thomas and Lionel seeking out each man Samuel has identified and trying to convince him to join their endeavour. Every fellow they approach is enthused by the prospect of working on such a well-known project, but they're all a bit nervous about the risk they might be taking. Particularly with the need to remove themselves to Swinton. Money however is no longer a problem; the Corporation's early stipends adequately covered Maynard's expenses and a formal contract is now in place. Regular monthly payments mean that he's well able to offer any new recruits decent remuneration.

Eventually the pair come to an agreement with two men who are persuaded by Emden's assurances and who are able to commence work almost immediately. Leaving them with suggestions about families who might provide lodgings in Swinton, Maynard and Emden return to the village themselves. There can be no let up in their efforts. They'll both need to start early next morning to make up for the time consumed by their recruiting venture.

'There's something I've been meaning to tell you Thomas', Emden remarks as they're sat together on the bench seat of the trap, 'It may be of no consequence but I overheard a very interesting conversation with a builder working on the Clifton side of the bridge.'

'O'Dwyer isn't it?', replies Maynard, 'An Irish chap? Locke seems to have an idea about him. He mentioned the fellow when Gurney and I made the last delivery. How in heaven's name did you come across him Lionel?'

'I didn't exactly meet him, but I'm certain it must be the same person. The man I overheard was definitely Irish. It was in an ale house in Bristol whilst I was working at the gorge. By chance the group of men he was with happened to be drinking in the same inn as me.'

'So, what caught your attention that you've remembered it all this time and think I should know about it?'

249

'There was a lot of banter, the way men always talk in our business', replied Emden, 'It was just that, in fact, that put me onto them being in the same trade as ourselves. But the tone of the Irishman sounded more serious. I got a distinct impression he thinks Hartnoll is not the most honest of men. Unfortunately he didn't say more before he left.'

'Well, thank you Lionel, my friend. You were quite right to tell me. Mr Hartnoll's conduct has raised some questions in my own mind, ever since I first met him. But all our business arrangements with his office are perfectly above board now. I suggest you keep this information to yourself, but I'll keep my eyes open in case there's any truth in it.'

~

With the business of employing additional masons taken care of, the punishing working schedule continues relentlessly at the stone-yard. But now it's even more hectic. More men, more stone. They have to spend time extending the walled-off area to cope with the volume of material being stored.

The little smallholding is welcoming more visitors than it has for years, with messengers appearing frequently on horseback, two more masons turning up for work each day and a build-up of activity on the river. More raw stone is being shipped in from the Strachan's quarry and, almost as regularly, more voyages made back to Bristol with finished pieces. Maynard realizes that he's losing valuable time by seeing to all this transport himself and that he now can quite reasonably charge the city for it to be carried out professionally. He talks to Edmund about hiring an established haulier for the job as soon as possible.

To help his son, who is now working every day from dawn to dusk, the old man rides Hermes into Bath and finds a company that can ship the stone from Swinton to Bristol. This is a relief, although Thomas knows it won't resolve all his delivery issues. It's quite difficult, with five men now cutting stone, to predict exactly when the next barge load will be ready to go. But the pressure to deliver finished pieces, as soon as they're available, is becoming more intense. Consequently he contracts the haulier for one shipment every three weeks; he'll supplement these, whenever necessary, with trips himself using Hermes pulling the Strachans' barge as before. With this arrangement he can meet the ridiculous demands that Hartnoll and Locke are putting upon him.

The weeks pass quickly with so much to be accomplished. The remainder of July and much of August come and go. It's a glorious summer but the masons can do no more than enjoy the warmth it brings. And, of course, the uplifting view across the river, the sight and sounds of birds and insects, whenever they can be heard above the ringing of the chisels. To a man they're working every hour that the long summer days allow.

Gradually Maynard's family begin to notice the stress he's suffering from this punishing schedule. Mary Ann starts taking his lunch to the stone-yard so that he doesn't have to walk back in the middle of the day. Emily reads to him in the evenings, since he now regularly throws himself into his chair after supper and shuts his eyes, much like his own dad.

As the September evenings start to draw in, Maynard takes stock of his situation. He knows in his heart they're all working far too hard and that it's doing none of them much good. He needs a break and he realises that he hasn't seen John Carey for months. So he asks Emily to run over with a message suggesting that they meet at the Boar later. Just the one evening, relaxing over a drink or two. The outing might make a lot of difference to his frame of mind.

When he eventually lifts the latch on the inn door Carey has already established himself in the snug. A full tankard of ale for

Thomas sits in front of him, alongside his own, by now half empty.

'My, it's good to see you again' says John, 'I thought you'ld been transported to Australia. Whatever have you been up to over these past three months?'

'You might well ask John, it's a fair enough question. I can't recall myself if I've ever told you what's happened. I guess Swinton's gossip mill must have given you a clue or two by now though. Truth is we somehow landed ourselves a huge job. Splendid news for my little business but it seems to have swallowed us all up completely since it started in earnest'

'Well, congratulations my friend. I allus said you'd do well in life. You've never looked back since that day you walked off to Bath. I've often wished you'd taken me along with you.'

'There's a chance your faith in me is justified John. This job has turned out to be quite important, quite prestigious. I suppose you know we're involved with the new bridge to be built over the river at Clifton?'

'In a way, friend. I've read the articles about it in the newspapers Old Silas keeps on the bar. The rumours are that you have some part in its construction?'

'Indeed we do John. The boys and me have been contracted to finish all the stones that will clad a huge pillar being built to support one of the towers. But the bloody work's nearly done for us. I've just taken on two more men, but there's still more to do than we can all keep on top of.'

By heaven, isn't that wonderful though?', Carey interjects, 'Sounds like as you'll be a rich man when it's done.'

'Perhaps, perhaps. I'm not counting my chickens yet. But please can put all that aside John? When I suggested we meet I hoped to put work completely out of my mind for an hour or two. No one is as good as you are at diverting me. That's always been the case, since we were lads. Now, I know you bury your nose in that newspaper every time you visit this hostelry. Why don't you tell me what else has been going on in the world since we last met? Take my mind off stone cutting for a while?'

'Where to start Thomas? Remember that fellow who was set on, round the turn of the year? About the same time you and your dad had your own little scrape with the footpads?'

'How could I forget John, it shook me up and no mistake. And I really thought it might have done for the old man.'

Well friend, if it was the lot from Kilbridge Lane, as we suspected, that was just the start. Whoever it is, it's turning into a wave of criminality. And the capers they're up to are becoming more brazen by the month. But I'm sure you've already heard something about it.

'No, I've not. The lads and me seem to be hermits lately. Nobody tells us anything.'

'Well, from what's in the papers, the gang has set its sights on bigger things recently. Three or four country houses have been turned over, all under the cover of darkness. Out and out shameless raids involving arson and violence, not just a broken window. Silver and stuff, in substantial quantity, has been seized from right under the noses of the gentry. The reports say the thieves are better organised than they've ever been and probably have some intelligence about the properties they're targeting. Some of the victims have been injured, though none mortally as yet.'

'And these scum are meeting precious little resistance, I'll wager.'

'Probably not. But my guess is that they've gone too far now. The class of gentry they're robbing don't take such things lying down. They have influential friends. I've seen a bunch of indignant letters in the papers, even the Times, demanding that something's done about it. There's a lot of pressure being put on the authorities to end this for once and for all. And things are being done as a result. Vehicles that might be carrying stolen goods are frequently searched at the toll gates and on the roads into Bristol and Bath. Apparently customs men have stepped up their inspections at the ports, since it's almost certain the thieves' hauls is finding its way out of the country.'

'So, as pretty much every man in the county knows very well where they're holed out, why don't the authorities just come to Kilbridge Lane and take them John?'

'I reckon that's likely to happen sometime soon Thomas, I really do. They've robbed too many powerful men for the authorities to prevaricate for much longer. But the broadsheets say they're trying to gather sufficient evidence to sweep up all the conspirators at once. This crimes have taken on the pattern of a well organised plot, not just the work of a few petty criminals. If they come to snatch the perpetrators at Kilbridge, I guess there's a risk the ringleaders might scarper or somehow evade the law. I imagine the authorities are playing a very careful hand.'

'By God John, I'm stunned at how much I miss, holed up at the stone-yard. But look here; I've improved myself in some small measure. I've now purchased the grand total of two newspapers in my life, though I've got to admit, simply to read about the suspension bridge. Nevertheless, I did study the last one from cover to cover. It was full of articles about voting reform. What's that all about? The whole thing really confuses me, I can tell you.'

'Oh that! A lot of fuss about nothing, if you ask me. But the papers are full of it. If you believe what they say, the ordinary man might get the vote, but it'll never happen for us Thomas; leastways not for me. No, it means nothing to us. I'm sure Members of Parliament and the like think this new Bill thing is terribly important. And the broadsheets seem to be stirring up the populace to violence as though it will be dreadful for them if the Bill doesn't get through.'

'And will it John?'

'God knows. In Parliament they have to have these things called readings and a whole bunch of votes before the Bill becomes an Act. It seems the House of Commons passed it by a very small margin just recently, so it's a tight call. The Bristol Recorder, he spoke against it apparently. Provoked a lot of anger in the city. But next month the House of Lords have to vote and the papers are pretty sure they'll throw it out. Blood on the streets, across the land if that happens, so the reporters have it.'

'Nonsense. I'm sure the editors exaggerate that sort of thing just to sell their papers.'

'Maybe you're too confident. It's not just the newspapers Thomas. Betty's got relatives living near the docks and they're convinced the discontent is real in those areas where people are living on top of one another. Poor conditions just create a tinderbox. There's a lot of bad feeling to do with low wages and unemployment. They can see agitators at work, stirring up the resentment for their own ends. They seem to have latched onto the Reform Bill as an excuse to cook up some sort of revolution. If the Bill doesn't get passed by the House of Lords there might be a good chance of violence breaking out.'

'My God, you almost make me feel glad I'm cloistered like a monk in my stone-yard. There's more trouble in the world outside than I'd know how to deal with. Most of it is beyond my comprehension. It's worrying though, especially if people are likely to be hurt. Thank heavens we'll not be affected by it out here. God willing it won't interfere with my business; that would be disaster.'

255

Despite the sombre tone of their conversation, Thomas is enjoying himself for the first time in weeks. John's company has ousted all thoughts of work from his mind. The change of scene, being here with his friend, enjoying the comfort of the inn, is decidedly pleasing. He promises himself not to let such a long interval pass before they do it again.

'I can't believe you've no other news to share', prompts John, 'You can't possibly have been locked up at the yard since we last met; there must be some adventure or gossip with which you can amuse me whilst there's still ale to be drunk.'

Thomas reflects wryly how avidly he could hold John's attention were he to recount his adventure with Lady Sophia. But he knows also he could never do such a thing. It's bad enough keeping this secret alone, but if John were to know, he'd never sleep easy. However there are a couple of nuggets he can share. Why, he's become an accomplished barge captain, he's sailed his craft to the gorge and the whole family's visited Lansdown fair. These are all stories certain to entertain his friend. So he hands over the coins for more drinks and tells him about the family day out, the bustle, the noise, the horse race and the cheeky lad taking bets.

'There's something else I could tell you John, but you'ld have to keep it to yourself' he continues. Unused to the ale he's become animated and confident. Somewhere, deep down, he knows he's about to disclose a secret that he has no need to share. For good or bad the drink has loosened his tongue.

'I saw my father passing his shakedown payment to a runner at the fair. Fortunately, he was a peculiar looking lad. With some difficulty I followed and spotted the same fellow later on. Eventually I tracked him down to a tent near the grain-merchants. By good fortune I was able to peep inside and there were about six of the ruffians who were obviously collecting in their money. The Kilbridge Lane gang I'd bet my life. I got a good look at one of them; the fellow who seemed to be in charge. Wicked looking cove, with a scar on his chin.'

'Thomas, for God's sake lower your voice' breathes John, 'You may have come within a whisker of great danger. And if you let all this be heard abroad, you'll be in greater danger yet. I'm almost certain the man you're describing to me is the one the gang call the Captain. Their leader, if such a band of criminals can be said to have one. But for my sake and your own, stop talking about this here in the inn, or anywhere else where you could be overheard. Now, forget it ever occurred and tell me more about your expeditions on the barge.'

In describing the adventures to his oldest friend, Maynard again finds the relaxation he'd been seeking. With the easy atmosphere and the strong ale he becomes more and more mellow. In fact he can't be sure he's hearing everything that John's saying.

But something his friend says seizes his attention and within a second he's a sober as ever.

'I'm sorry John', he says, not certain he heard correctly, 'I missed that, what were you telling me?'

'How happy our old employer must be. Old man Whitefield I mean. Why, I was up at the house last week taking the washing back for Betty. There was Lady Sophia on the drive, stroking the muzzle of that horse of hers. Why, I'll be damned if she's not with child.'

Chapter 25

The joyous ringing of hammers and billows of dust fill the summer air. The sun still beats down relentlessly most days and all six masons can regularly be found working stripped to the waist. Perspiration runs down Maynard's back as, along with the others, he slaves away to achieve the number of finished pieces that are daily demanded by Locke and Hartnoll.

It's punishing, repetitive work. He's still feeling the stress of the many of responsibilities weighing on his shoulders. Nevertheless he counts his good fortune. It's a regular employment and, God willing, one that will improve the fortunes of them all beyond anything they might have initially dreamt.

So not one slackens his pace, not one of them complains. They've settled into a regular routine and share the work seamlessly, like a well-oiled machine. All this encourages Maynard no end. For the first time he really believes they will succeed. Even more exciting is the message received just yesterday from Locke. Apparently Brunel himself will be visiting the construction site during the week. Probably tomorrow, if not almost certainly on Wednesday. Exuberant with the opportunity of meeting such a great engineer in person, Maynard is determined to ride over as soon as possible.

On this particular morning, early in September, their carrier's boat has just moored up to collect the next consignment of freight. Maynard summons his men to down tools and help load the vessel. They've only set to for a minute when Mary Ann appears with a worried look on her face. Thomas breaks off and walks over to see what she wants.

'It's Edmund', she explains, breathless through running down from the farmhouse. 'He was working in the yard as usual. Just now. Stacking the barrels of apples we'd picked yesterday from the orchard. I had glanced at him through the kitchen window. He just seemed to collapse without warning. It all happened in front of my eyes Thomas. One minute he was standing there, lifting the last barrel, the next he was on the ground, clutching his stomach and groaning horribly.'

'Oh my dear God. I think I've seen this happen before, Mary Ann', replies her husband, 'Some weeks ago, a similar turn, when we were milking. But he was sitting then, he didn't fall down. Just gripped himself, and held his breath. He assured me it was no more than indigestion. It didn't last more than a couple of minutes.'

'Well, I reckon it's more serious that that now Thomas. The poor old chap found it almost impossible to get to his feet. Even with me helping him. I've put him into his bed and told him he must remain there for the rest of the day.'

'Well done my love. That's for the best I'm sure', the mason replies, 'Perhaps he'll feel better after a rest. You've caught me at a difficult time. Do you think I need to come and attend to him myself immediately, or can I finish up this loading first?'

'You continue husband. I don't believe you could do much more at the moment. I'm sorry to have interrupted you. It was just the shock that prompted me to run down and let you know. He probably just needs rest and a little food. I'll get back and make sure he's comfortable.'

With this she turns away and walks back up the meadow to nurse her father-in-law.

As the morning wears on, the sun becomes ever hotter. They finish loading the cargo and the boatman pushes off from the bank. Wiping the sweat from his brow Maynard sees threshers in the field across the river, hard at work, bringing in the harvest. A cloud of fine brown dust hangs over them as they sweep away with their scythes, young boys walking behind, forking up the severed stalks and heaving them onto a cart.

Maynard goes over in his mind what he might say to Brunel when they meet. A few months ago the notion that he'd ever come face to face with a man of such stature would have seemed fanciful. Now the meeting is imminent he struggles to decide how he can acquit himself to advantage in such eminent company. But he can't ponder too long as there's yet another stack of facing stones to tackle, something that occupies all six of them for the rest of the day.

The harvesters continues into early evening as both they and the masons work on to make the most of the late summers' evening.

And thus it's nearing nine o'clock when Maynard trudges wearily back to the farmhouse, having almost forgotten his conversation this morning with Mary Ann. However, one look at her face, as he opens the kitchen door, tells him all is not well.

'How's father?', he asks needlessly, with more than a little trepidation about her reply.

'I'm really worried Thomas', replies his wife. It's obvious she's holding back tears. 'The poor man has eaten nothing since I came down to see you. He says he's feeling better but I can see he's still in constant pain.'

'Well, we'll leave him be tonight and see how he is in the morning', declares Maynard, 'He did get over it before. If there's no improvement by breakfast, I'll go straightway and fetch the physician. I know father wouldn't want me to do so tonight. He'd shout me down, I have no doubt.'

'It's a confounded nuisance though', he muses, 'I was determined to ride over and meet our famous engineer. Most likely this will be my only chance. Locke says he sets out for

France at the weekend. I do hope this doesn't throw my plans out completely.'

'Well, see how he is tomorrow', she replies. 'Come and have your dinner husband. You've not eaten all day, you must be starved by now.'

~

The following day breaks with no change in the weather. The whole family rises early as glorious sunshine streams in through the windows. Thomas picks up a trug and strolls out to collect the eggs. As he kneels beside the hen-house a mournful bellowing from their small herd puzzles him. Usually, by now, Edmund would have milked them; they'd be quiet and peaceful.

Edmund! My God! How stupid to forget. The poor old man's unwell. So of course he's not been up to follow his normal routine. Oh well, it won't be difficult to take care of the beasts now, before he starts at the stone yard.

But first he'd better see how his dad is; coax him to take a little breakfast perhaps. And make the decision if he should call for the doctor. Unless he's really well enough to get out of bed, Maynard will be firm. Insist that the doctor comes; to give an opinion at least. Having made this resolution he picks out half a dozen eggs and returns to the house.

Taking the stairs two at a time he rapidly reaches his father's bedroom. The old man's still beneath the coverlet with his back turned to his son. Maynard shakes him by the shoulder, urging him to wake. There's no response. Something about the way the shoulder moves beneath his hand precipitates a sick sensation in the pit of his stomach. Gently he eases the inert invalid onto his back and lays a palm on his wrinkled forehead.

261

Edmund's eyes are open but his waxy flesh is stone cold.

Chapter 26

A heavy grey coach rolls out of London and swings onto the Bristol turnpike, throwing up clouds of dust and grit from the Macadam road. A private carriage, provided from the palace stables, it has been especially adapted, and to a purpose. Outwardly, at a glance, it might be mistaken for a stage. Closer inspection would reveal features not common in such conveyances. Pulled by four strong horses, two drivers sit atop facing forwards. Behind them are two armed footmen, each with a musket, facing to the rear. Blinds and bars are visible at the windows. The shell itself conceals thick iron strips as reinforcement. Robust safety locks are built into the doors. Security was clearly the watchword when all these modifications were made at the royal stables and its smithy. Dragoons, deployed as outriders on fast mounts, ride one ahead and one to the rear of the vehicle. Nothing less than a platoon of soldiers stands a chance of interfering with this little procession.

That of course was the intention; the intent of King William IV of England, Ireland and Hanover. For the passengers travelling in this coach are his honoured guests. Whilst they remain within his realm he feels a bounden duty to protect them. In any way at his disposal. Providing them with a sturdy coach and an armed escort, whilst they travel to visit their cousin in Wales, is the very least he can do.

'Who exactly is this relative of yours we shall stay with tonight my dear?'

This sudden enquiry, spoken in guttural German, breaks the silence. The tone is petulant and comes from the lips of a haughty lady. The man she's addressing sighs silently. Why has she taken so little notice of the details he must have explained six times already?

'Not a relative Helga. A good friend of my second cousin, Nicholas, and a wealthy landowner. His name is Whitefield, Sir James Whitefield.'

'Well husband, I hope we get there soon. It is far too hot in this frightful contraption. I feel like a common prisoner, locked up in a cell. Yvette, pass me my fan. I don't know how long I can bear this torture.'

Within the vehicle sit Johann Count von Winneburg, his lady the Countess Helga and her precocious French maid, Yvette. For the last three days this party have been guests at St James Palace, the official London residence of the King. Now they're making the long and tedious journey to Newport to pay the promised visit to the Count's cousin.

As close relatives to the Prussian royal family, it was no surprise the Winneburgs finally received an invitation to attend on the new English monarch and be formally presented. Only the Count was privy to clandestine efforts that had gone into ensuring it arrived when it did.

And this simple summons had proved a godsend to the plans laid out by his prince. On the pretext that he would be in England soon, the Count had corresponded quite naturally with Ernst Friedrich Herbert, arousing no suspicions whatever as far as he was able to determine.

Yesterday, having politely stomached an English breakfast, the Count and his lady had gone their separate ways. She, maid in tow, set out on a string of genteel visits. Many of her old acquaintances are now resident within the city walls and it was her determination to call upon the two most well connected. Once that duty was behind her she intended to embark on a furious circuit of the finest dressmakers in Regent Street. Her extravagant purchases would later create no small consternation for Yvette, who is charged with packing all these additional garments safely in the trunks.

Von Winneburg had left the dining room in far more leisurely style. He also had an appointment, but required no coach to attend it. For his was to take place within the very palace in which he stood. He'd no desire for people here to be aware of this appointment and had foreseen the possible difficulties weeks ago. Asking for directions to the Chancery would have to be avoided at all costs. Cunningly, in his several letters to Herbert, he'd repeatedly stressed his love of choral music. It was natural therefore, in his final communication, to suggest the two of them meet up at the Chapel Royal. Herbert would be able to show him around the magnificent building and the fine Beyer organ, recently brought over from Nümberg. Why, they might even be lucky enough to find the choir practicing whilst they were there.

As it turned out, there was not a chorister to be seen, but his ruse ensured none of King William's household had taken any real interest in whom he was meeting. Their introduction over, and suitable appreciation of the chapel complete, Herbert was happy to lead him through many corridors and staircases to the suite of rooms comprising the Chancery.

'Take a seat Count', implored his host, indicating a comfortable chaise-longue with a sweep of his arm, 'Or should I call you cousin? Whatever, do let me offer you a sherry wine. It's one of the delightful British habits I've acquired. I find it a very acceptable drink at this time in the morning.'

'There are about a fifteen of us working here', he continued, 'all but one of us native Hanovarians. Oh, and some English clerks, runners and the like, of course'. Our work is often quite mundane. I have monthly meetings with the Privy Council and occasionally get an audience with the King himself, but I'll admit I sometimes wonder if we are really necessary. I have a lot of involvement with policy, but very little influence. It wasn't always like this. In the time of George the Second Hanover itself was governed from here. But, as you know, our world is always changing. Changing far too quickly in my opinion.'

'You are so right', von Winneburg had replied, 'A new order seems to be establishing itself across Europe. It seems to be a little slower in some countries, especially our own German states, but it's certainly coming. Why, Friedrich Wilhelm has seen this himself. He is, perhaps, the most farsighted of the monarchs in our new Confederation. He sees nothing to be gained through distrust between Prussia and England. You might be the very person to help us bring this to an end.'

'It's obvious to me Ernst that you are an extremely clear sighted person. I'm sure your views would interest Friedrich. When I return to Prussia, let me attempt to convince him of this. If I'm successful, he'll consent to grant you an audience. Would you be happy to visit us in Charlottenburg if I succeed?'

'I should be honoured Count. That is a most generous suggestion. I'd dearly like to visit Prussia again and I'm sure my wife would be delighted. It would have to be at the start of the coming New Year however, for my responsibilities here tie me down all too frequently at the moment.'

'They sound more significant than your modest description. Whatever can they be to keep you so busy?' asked the Count, with a well feigned ignorance, casually refilling his host's glass from the decanter that sat between them.

Their conversation continued for an hour or more. With each sip Herbert became increasingly talkative, even putting on the bureau a number of the documents he'd referred to in connection with his Chancery responsibilities. The Count listened intently, feigning a mild disinterest and a convincing confusion about what he was being told. Belgium had been mentioned on a number of occasions and the progress of negotiations was not difficult to ascertain.

So, with a minimum of disingenuity, the Count had learned everything he'd hoped to discover about the political situation in England. Moreover he'd won the confidence of Ernst Herbert and laid the foundations for further help from the envoy. He left, after several more glasses of sherry, expressing great bonhomie to his host, a carefully purloined paper now tucked discretely inside his jacket.

The formal presentation to King William and Princess Adelaide of Saxe-Meinigen, the monarch's German wife, had taken place that very evening. It was a glittering and sumptuous evening banquet, with a ball to follow that continued into the small hours. William was anxious to swell his popularity before his coronation, expected to take place that September. So around one hundred and fifty royals, nobles and other notables, had been invited to the affair taking place in the reception rooms and grand dining room of Buckingham Palace.

Von Winneburg is well aware of his wife's shortcomings. As he thought, most of what he'd told her about their trip to England passed in through one noble ear and out of the other. But the one thing she didn't fail to pick up was that she'd be meeting the Queen of England. One of her own countrywomen. Not to mention royals and noblemen from every corner of Europe.

It would be an insult to her hosts if she didn't arrive looking as stately as she was able, of that she'd been convinced. She'd have to wear the priceless rope of pearls and the diamond tiara that had been bestowed upon her personally by Friedrich Wilhelm the Third. Appearing in such finery wasn't a matter of personal pride or vanity. Certainly not. It was her bounden duty to represent Prussia properly and demonstrate the nation's prosperity and fine taste to the world.

The Count had expressed a deal of agitation when she'd informed him of this decision. He shirked from the responsibility of looking after items of such value when travelling in a foreign country. A country he knew none too well. But the Countess was adamant. In truth, it was difficult to argue with the case she made, so he reluctantly complied. This didn't however prevent him from worrying. Or from having a confidential word with one of the king's equerries after the banquet. It was as a result of that conversation that the trio are now travelling in the king's special coach.

Their journey continues for several hours without hindrance, blighted only by the stuffiness of their cabin and frequent complaints from the countess. Their one stop is at Marlborough, to change horses and take some light refreshment at a coaching inn. When all's been made ready to travel again they resume on the turnpike to Bath, turning away outside the city to follow the smaller thoroughfare to Bitton.

As the heavy coach rumbles along the rougher surface, the dragoons and footmen redouble their concentration. They're aware they've now entered more dangerous terrain. Their principle responsibility is to protect the occupants of the coach. They've been briefed about this road. They've been told robberies and attacks can take place several times each month. Only when the horses reach the gateposts of the Whitefield estate do they relax a little; the coach turns and progresses slowly up the drive to the expansive semi-circular sweep of gravel in front of the big house.

From an upstairs window, Lady Sophia observes their approach with anticipation and breathes a deep sigh of relief. At last, if only for evening, she will enjoy some vibrant company. People of consequence who can regale her with stories of what's happening in London, and indeed other capitals around Europe. She hopes fervently that the Countess speaks good English. How seldom have such opportunities presented themselves since she married Sir James? Already attired in her finest evening gown she descends the grand curving staircase, ready to greet her guests.

From further afield another pair of eyes follow the coach as it disgorges its occupants, as the luggage is unloaded and as the vehicle is finally drawn away to the coach house. They belong to a new hand on the estate, a stable lad who commenced employ with Whitefield's establishment just two months ago. He's dressed considerably more smartly than is usual for him, his speech and his manners are also remarkably improved. The transformation is so marked that his friends at the vicarage might easily pass him by without recognition. The eyes belong to none other than Dick Saddler.

~

Just one lamp is visible through the window of an upper room at the vicarage. Strickland's stolen timepiece shows seven o'clock in the evening. Wakelin's hand-picked associates are assembled to prepare themselves for the enterprise at hand. Once again they have borrowed, begged or stolen the very fittest horses they can muster and, on this occasion, Wakelin arrives to hand out four muskets in varying condition. He entrusts these to the men he feels will be most likely to discharge them in anger. In his own belt, tucked alongside the knife, is the flintlock he'd confiscated from Saddler and Young.

'Right my handsome boys' he hisses, in a half-whisper, 'Our side of the job takes place in daylight, tomorrow morning. It'll be the most dangerous we've yet attempted but, believe me, the prize more than compensates for the danger.

I know several of you distrusted my scheme to sell our booty in France – you thought I would run off with it I'm certain. Well, I hope you're convinced now. You've all got good money in your pockets as a consequence. It's the proof in the pudding my lads.

I'll be getting you out of your beds in the dead of night because there's a long way to ride. It's vital we're in position and ready for the game if my plan's to succeed. We must have concealed ourselves before dawn breaks. That means setting off in at three o'clock to be certain we arrive in darkness.

I want to make sure now that each of you understands the part you will play. This robbery's not straightforward; it's going to require meticulous timing. And, make no mistake, there will be danger. We'll certainly be facing armed men, but take heart - we're armed ourselves. We hold the element of surprise and I'm not expecting any of you to hang around and fight. No. We'll have our adversaries well marked, we'll be in and out before they come to their senses. They'll not be expecting us. But if anything does go awry, don't hesitate. Use your muskets to good effect and then scarper as fast as you can.

Now, before I take each of you through your part, I need to know you're up for this. You've heard the risks in my scheme. Is there anyone amongst us who's suddenly developed cold feet? Anyone too yellow to pull this off?'

Murmurs start up, and whispered mutterings, but no one pipes up in response to his provocation.

'Remember men, the escapades we have pulled off together in the last few weeks will look tame compared to this one. I've been planning this job for weeks and it must be run like clockwork. Now my boys, are there any questions?'

'There are indeed Captain', pipes up Bythorn, 'Are we going to be torching our mark again?'

'I truly hope so' replies Wakelin, 'But probably not in the way you're thinking Bythorn. Now, gather round and I'll explain exactly how it's all going to play out.'

~

270

With the last of the horses rubbed down and stabled, the loose boxes freshly strawed, hay in the racks and water in the troughs, Dick Saddler finally comes free from his duties. Breaking with the habit of previous evenings, when he's gathered with the other lads to eat and play cards, Saddler retires quietly to his cramped garret in the loft of the stable block. It's small and uncomfortable, just a hutch in truth, under the eaves of the tiled roof. A straw mattress, a pitcher of water, a chamber pot and a half-height door that must be entered at a crawl. But fortunately he's its only occupant and that means he has privacy. The youth lays on the prickly horse-hair mattress, if only to rest his body for a few hours. He's going to be very busy tonight and he certainly won't get any sleep.

Darkness falls, but lights still shine brightly from the big house and the noise within carries on unabated. The signs of activity continue for three hours or more. Music, dancing, the sound of laughter. Obviously some sort of congenial entertainment is underway. It eventually breaks up around midnight, with two parties of gentlefolk leaving noisily in their coaches. Then the lights in the house are slowly extinguished, one by one, and silence falls over the estate. Saddler allows another thirty minutes to pass before he silently eases himself from his quarters and carefully, quietly, descends the wooden ladder that takes him to ground level.

Some days ago he discovered a tack room at the end of the long stables corridor that the estate staff rarely visit. It seemed to be a store for surplus equipment and here, for this very reason, Saddler has already secreted a small collection of equipment he'll be needing tonight. In the unlikely event it was discovered, no-one would guess it ought not to be there.

He selects first a wide wooden plank with a hole drilled at one end, a rope, a sharp spade and a large pail. Carrying them through the stable block with infinite care, so as not to disturb the horses or his fellow stable lads upstairs, he slips out into the night.

271

Keeping close to bushes and trees he creeps slowly away from the buildings until he's at the top of the main drive. He selects a point where rhododendron bushes push out close to the edge of the gravel driveway. The bushes give him a degree of cover, despite that hardly being necessary. But their presence will be essential on the morrow, because he'll need to hide himself close by. Slowly, as quietly as he can, he scrapes a line of gravel from the drive and places it carefully into the pail. Then equally patiently, waiting some seconds between each thrust of his spade, he digs into the compacted rubble and soil forming the drive itself. With painstaking precision he excavates a small channel running at right angles to the drive and stretching halfway across.

Every spade-full of soil is thrown well out of sight into the bowels of the bush. Progress proves surprisingly slow, but he continues relentlessly until the depression is ten inches wide and seven or eight inches deep. Then he ties one end of the rope to his plank, places the plank into the top of the channel and straightens the rope so that it is snaking off into the bushes. With great care he spreads the gravel from his pail over the plank to conceal it completely.

Pleased with his efforts, he stands back to check out what he's achieved. He's made a pretty deep hole in the drive, but it's well hidden and will remain so whilst that plank stays in place. The moonlight falling on his work convinces him it won't be noticed. Finally he breaks off some branches from the rear of an adjacent bush to ensure he'll be able to squeeze into the foliage and easily locate the free end of the rope. The first part of his night's work is complete, but he'll have to wash his hands before starting on the next.

As he swills his fingers in a trough, he runs over Wakelin's instructions in his mind. Hour after hour had been spent at the vicarage, learning and practising; the Captain not satisfied until he could carry out every one of his tasks in total darkness.

He returns stealthily to the tack room. Beneath an old horse blanket is another nest of items that he's secreted, one by one, over the last few days. Each being left for him, as agreed, under the gorse alongside the ice-house. Some will be troublesome to carry without making a disturbance, but they all have to be taken to the coach house. To avoid any accidents he makes three trips.

In his pocket, his own roll of housebreaking tools. Everything else supplied by Wakelin.

The coach house has a pair of tall double doors opening out onto a spur of the driveway, firmly bolted and chained. Halfway along a side wall is a much smaller door, secured with a hasp and padlock, the usual entry for drivers and other workers on the estate. It's here that Saddler has brought his equipment, it's here where the value of two weeks patient preparation will be proven or otherwise.

One by one, over previous days, Saddler has removed each screw from the hasp, filed off most of its thread, then replaced it within a plug of beeswax such that, to all appearances, it is secure. Each screw took him about five minutes which was the longest interval he could risk to be sure of no discovery. He'd perspired copiously on every occasion; this was the most nerve-racking aspect of his commission by far. The blacksmith or a footman would only have had to come around the corner for the entire scheme to have been exposed. So care and patience had been essential and it had taken four days to complete.

But now, faced with the apparently impenetrable door, entry to the coach house proves child's play. Saddler removes the frame plate screws that are not covered by the hasp and then just tugs hard on the padlock. The doctored screws pull free from their holes and the door swings noiselessly open.

Entry gained, he takes in all the items he's just lugged up from the tack room and stacks them next to the coach which had brought the Prussian Count and his party. With genuine relief he discovers its doors have been left unlocked. Inside, he uses his screwdrivers to remove the kick boards beneath the seats. Working quickly, he brushes neatsfoot oil onto all the hidden surfaces of the cavities he's exposed beneath the seat pads. Wakelin told him he'd chosen this oil because it is odourless, but makes a damned good blaze once ignited.

A noise, from somewhere behind an adjacent coach, stops him dead. He freezes, brush in hand, blood draining from his face with fear. No, he can't be apprehended. Not after he's got so far. Like a statue he stays inert for a full two minutes. There's no recurrence. It must simply have been a rat, or the crack of drying wood.

Confidence returns and he lifts in four oil-lamps that Wakelin has specially adapted. Each has a low reservoir and a wick that burns with an open flame. Just a very shallow glass chimney protects the flame from draughts. In place of a shade there's a thin vertical metal rod, affixed stoutly to the base. Brazed to the top of the rod is a metal cup. It looks like the scoop of a miniature shovel. Saddler carefully places a small cotton bag, filled with gunpowder and sealed with a long drawstring, into each cup. He ties the strings to a loop, fashioned at the top of the rod. The primed devices then are pushed gently in the four corners beneath the seats of the carriage.

These four adapted oil lamps are the lynch pin of Wakelin's scheme to plunder the armoured coach, even though it will be securely locked and moving at speed. Once they are alight, nothing untoward will happen until the coach moves. Even then, the jerks created by coupling up the horses or rolling over a roadway should not dislodge the little bags due to the shape of the cups. But once the coach is subject to a significant sideways lurch, the bags will slide from their cups and fall to the extent the strings allow. This will leave them dangling directly over the flames. Wakelin's calculated that so long as just one of the lamps stays alight, the movement of the coach will cause this to happen at some point in the journey. He and his associates intend to be ready to take advantage. But his scheme is that Saddler's other preparations result in control of exactly when this inferno will commence.

On hands and knees, working by the dim light of a conventional oil lamp, Saddler puts a screw though a hole in the base of each lamp and secures it to the floor of the coach. Then he packs the space around them with crumpled sheets of newspaper sprinkled with neatsfoot oil and a little gunpowder. Into the top of panels he removed he cuts some small ventilation holes with a saw from his housebreaking kit. These are so small and inaccessible, they'll not be spotted by casual inspection.

Finally he sits back on the floor of the coach to wait for dawn and for the routine of household activity to start up once more. There's a chorus of birdsong and the muffled sounds of doors and shutters being reopened to the world.

Choosing his moment to be as late as possible, but still with safe margin to avoid discovery, Saddler ignites all four lamps. Wakelin's entrusted him with a small packet of lucifers and a striking pad. These wooden sticks still seem like some sort of magic to him, even though he's now practised with them time and again. A month ago he never realized they existed and still can't believe they so easily make fire. Nevertheless he uses them expertly to ignite each wick, taking great care to quickly extinguish the lucifer once it has served its purpose.

He gently replaces the kick-boards, not screwing them tight, so as to guarantee a passage to the air that will keep the lamps burning. Ensuring he's left no evidence of his presence inside the coach, or the coach house, he creeps away, replacing the screws in the side door frame as best he can. With luck his interference won't be discovered until he's long gone. Barring some extremely vigilant coachman, it might be days before his tampering will be come to light. He returns warily to his garret in the stable block.

Just a little later, pretending to his fellow grooms and stable lads that he, like they, has just left his bed, Saddler commences his normal daily chores. His stomach is churning with apprehension and one eye continually wanders, almost of its own volition, to the big house. Wakelin has told him the Prussian party will be leaving early to continue their journey to Wales, but he has no idea precisely when that might be. At seven thirty however he's told to walk one of the four greys up to the coach house and help to put the animal in its traces. Thirty minutes later he can see the Count's vehicle, now made ready for its journey, drawn up before the steps at the front of the house. Footmen bring out the luggage, including a large metal trunk, and secure this onto the rear of the coach. 'That trunk. That's probably where the jewellery will be' Saddler breathes to himself, 'either in there or on the person of the lady herself, I'll wager my life upon it.'

Later still, a number of well-dressed persons appear under the stone canopy at the front doors. He can see curtseying and handshakes, it looks as though farewells are being exchanged, words of gratitude no doubt being heaped upon the hosts. Saddler acts immediately.

'I've been told to give the trap a run to check it's in good order and then take it up to the house' he tells the stable lad he works alongside as a rule, 'I'll be coming back just as soon as that's done.' He leaps onto the driving seat of the trap, which he'd harnessed and made ready half an hour beforehand. He drives it in a wide arc around the grounds, out of sight to the rear of the bushes where he was working on the previous night and secures the horse to a firm bough. Wriggling inside the bush, he quickly locates the end of his rope.

Patience, concentration, alacrity. These are the watchwords drummed into his head, time and again, by Wakelin. The three critical elements in the success of their scheme. The Captain spent many hours sitting alongside Saddler at the vicarage, going over and over what he's expected to do. A night without sleep's not the best preparation for putting his planning into practice, but Saddler's a young man and won't let this deprivation impair his work.

The parting ritual at the door of the big house seems to take forever. Saddler stares harder and harder, almost believing he might will the coach to move. But still it stands, immobile. Was there sufficient oil in those lamps for the flames to still be alive?

When he's all but given up hope, he sees the footmen climb up to take their places on the roof of the coach and its wheels start to turn. His body tenses. Here it comes, slowly around the sweeping gravel frontage, onto the drive leading down to the highway. Picking up speed a little as it straightens out. Saddler eyes are now set fixedly on the point on the drive where he's buried his plank. He opens his shoulders, grips the rope, draws a deep breath and tenses every muscle in his body. The coach comes on, gathering pace. He sees the hooves of the leading pair cross his plank, then the pair behind. With all the strength and urgency he can muster he heaves on the rope like a man possessed. The plank flies up into the air, gravel scattering in all directions as he hauls it back into the bushes. The leading wheel of the coach nearest to Saddler bounces hard in the trench he's dug, immediately the rear wheel follows suit. The driver lets out a curse and grabs a rail to steady himself. All Saddler can do now is to wait and watch. What are the chances this madcap plan will succeed?

For fifty yards the coach progresses without any sign of mishap and Saddler's heart sinks. But, just when he thinks all is lost, the muffled sounds of an incensed guttural voice can be heard screaming from within the vehicle.

'Stop! Stop! Stop the coach. We are on fire in here! Stop or we shall all die.'

Alerted by the desperate cries of his passengers, the coachman swiftly reins in his team and comes to a rapid halt.

The footmen jump from the roof to open the doors and Count, Countess and her maid leap to the ground, heedless of waiting for steps to be lowered. By now they are all choking, and for good reason. Smoke is billowing out in great clouds behind them, tongues of flame are starting to lick through cracks in the bodywork of the carriage.

'It is an inferno' shouts the countess. 'The whole thing will be destroyed. Quick, save my jewellery. Get the trunk untied you fools, before the flames reach it.'

As the two footmen, braving the flames which are now rapidly engulfing the whole coach, tear the trunk from its leather straps, a trap arrives at speed from the direction of the house and draws up alongside.

'Quickly' shouts its driver, 'Get everyone aboard, the luggage too. I'll drive you all back to the safety of the house!'

With some alacrity the nobleman and his entourage are handed up onto the trap and the trunk slid onto its floor. The two dragoons, still mounted and some way from either end of the blazing coach, look on, not quite knowing what they should be doing to give protection. As soon as the trunk is on the trap, Saddler cracks his whip and sets off at pace towards the house, across the smooth parkland beside the drive. But the trap travels only twenty yards before he wheels it around in a half circle and sets off again at frantic speed towards the gates to the estate.

At this the footmen, still standing beside the blaze, level their rifles. But they cannot fire for fear of injuring their master. The two dragoons spur their mounts and give chase. As the trap speeds down the drive it meets a company of horsemen galloping equally fast towards it, muskets drawn. But this posse has no intention of stopping the trap, instead it's intent on incapacitating the pursuers. Behind him Saddler can hear volleys of gunshots, but he pays no heed. Wakelin's voice is loud inside his head, "Your only notion now is to get clean away". At the gateposts of the estate he's forced to slow.

'Stop this contraption immediately. I insist you return us to the house', bawls the indignant Count. The last few minutes have shocked him to the very backbone and he's only just forming the notion this trap driver must be part of a conspiracy against him. Taking advantage of the drop in speed he manages to find his feet and pitches himself forward. Abandoning all caution, he attacks Saddler from behind with his bare hands. He'll break the young turkey's neck, you can count on that.

With Saddler wrestling to free himself, he's unable to control the horse and the trap comes to an untidy rest between the gateposts. The attention of the two petrified ladies is consumed by the violent struggle taking place before them. Unobserved, a lithe figure leaps onto the rear of the trap in a single bound. Alerted by the impact of his landing, the Countess turns. Standing with one foot on her trunk is a tall, vicious looking man with long black ringlets and a long red scar across his chin. In his hand is a flintlock. She lets out a piercing scream, but to no avail. As she does so he levels his weapon and discharges it, at point blank range, directly into her husband's back.

Chapter 27

It's mid-October, a chilly wind blows, the days are drawing in. Heavy clouds threaten rain and hang above the city like a shroud, obscuring light, pointing up the cold and dreary aspects of all those miserable streets that are homes to the poor. Braziers burn here and there where men are working outside, but most have the good sense to stay indoors if they're able.

An individual with every intention of remaining on the streets, whatever the weather, is striding purposefully along the Malago Road in Bedminster. He cuts an unusual figure, strangely out of keeping with the run-down surroundings. About him the houses are shabby, their inhabitants poorly dressed, sapped of energy and enthusiasm. The well attired stranger however reflects none of these things. His acquaintances in these parts assume he's in his mid-twenties, though probably none of them have any idea of his true age. Let alone any real knowledge of his life or his background. He's of middling height, fresh faced, fair haired and fired with demonstrable purpose and vigour. It's clear to any who listen that he's been well educated; he's an articulate and convincing speaker. Even when he finds just a handful of people to converse with, he always seems to end up at the centre, holding court and proclaiming his persuasive arguments with confidence and certainty.

One might assume also that he's affluent, or no stranger to affluence in the recent past. For his clothes are quality, though worn and dusty from too much service in these grubbier parts of the city. This resolute fellow is one Daniel Latham, a young man bursting with fresh ideas, a young man of zeal and vision.

The assumptions mentioned would all be correct. He does indeed hail from a well to do family, living in the affluent parish of Clifton, not far from the city. At twenty three years old he should by now be earning his own living. But he's never managed to hold down a position for more than a few weeks. Despite this his father continues to stump up an annual allowance that gives him free rein to pursue his various interests.

Blessed with a talent for rubbing along with people of every social class, Daniel has many, many acquaintances. But sadly few true friends. If indeed any. For the last few months his reforming spirit has drawn him here, to the seamier parts of Bristol; St Phillips, Lawford Gate, Totterdown, Bedminster and the like. Here he's acquired a host of new comrades, mostly meanly paid or unemployed. Whilst all these people know him and admire the principles he stands for, they would be amazed to learn about another group of men he often converses with in the genteel houses of Clifton village.

These other acquaintances are upstanding gentlemen, most of whom live in Bristol, but some joining the meetings from outside the city altogether. They are without exception affluent, liberal individuals of excellent education and high ideals. All are successful and respected in their own field of endeavour, whether professors at the Merchant Venturer's school or busy shopkeepers. One or two are industrialists who've been responsible for the growing wealth of the city. They meet monthly, usually in one another's houses, to discuss advances in science and engineering, but often also debate the social impact of such changes. They all are widely read, predominantly of a good age and most with flourishing business of their own. No topic is considered outside the scope of their debate, whether politics, religion, medicine, the empire or the human condition.

But for his father, the lad would never have encountered this elite, high-minded assembly. A meeting had taken place at Latham's house; Daniel had helped with cloaks and refreshment. He dallied, unnoticed, listening intently as the discussion began. Fired by the heat of the debate he suddenly spoke out himself, horrifying his father. But he did so with conviction, with passion and with ideas that caught the imagination. His social transgression was overlooked and invitations to future meetings had followed.

'It's good to have some fresh young blood amongst us', a white-haired timber merchant named Barker had said to him, by means of an introduction during a break in proceedings. 'I sometimes feel that we're full of good ideas in our little group, but too established and frankly too comfortable to make them come to anything.'

'But all the gentlemen here are influential and wealthy people', replied Daniel, 'Surely if anybody has the power to change things, it must be you?'

'You might think so, young man. We've all got enough experience of life now to see things on a much broader canvas. But most of us are hampered by our interests. We all advocate change, we recognise the need, we know it's inevitable. But we're not comfortable with any change so radical that it threatens what we've each built up.'

'I'm not sure I follow you', replied Latham, 'Is there an example you can use, to help me understand?'

'Not amongst our group, just at the moment. But I can think of a situation an old friend of mine in Birmingham finds himself in which illustrates of my point perfectly. I'm sure you're aware that railways are now being constructed in the north of the country?'

'Why yes, of course'

'And tell me young man, now Birmingham has become so heavily industrial, how much commercial freight do you think is moved every week from Birmingham to London?'

'I've really no idea', replied Latham, 'A thousand tons a year maybe?'

'You're not even close. It's nearer one thousand tons a week', replied Barker, 'One thousand tons a week and it's all transported on the canals. My friend is owner of a company that transports freight this way. He has thirty canal boats in his business and pays one hundred men who continually make the journey back and forward. Now, he needs no convincing about the advantages of a railway system, but if a line should be laid between London and Birmingham, his business will disappear overnight. We happen to know Mr Robert Stephenson has been recently engaged to draw up plans for just such a line. So, my friend understands in his heart that he should be supporting the railway venture, but he's actually fighting it every inch of the way. And sometimes the gentlemen here come up against similar paradoxes of their own. We all know what's right, but it's sometimes impossible to reconcile that with our own interests.'

In the first months of Latham's informal membership, the meetings of this quiet and private debating society considered many matters. Slavery, the adoption of new machinery, discontent amongst the agricultural workforce, violence in the manufacturing towns, Catholic emancipation and many other causes of the current social unrest. The discussions sometimes lasted long into the night because none of these strands were entirely unconnected. It always came back to the well-being and contentedness of the working class. Every issue had some effect on the attitude of the masses to the ruling elite. After each debate concluded most philosophically closed this book and put it out of mind until it was opened again at the next meeting. For the majority the discussions were a purely intellectual pursuit. Not so for Daniel. Suddenly his eyes were opened to the injustices being perpetrated on the poor. Moreover, remedies were easy to envisage. He rapidly developed a determination to translate thought into action.

For nearly a year he's been laying the foundations of a scheme that exists only inside his head. Walking the streets. Striking up conversations with strangers. In beer houses, in inns, catching them as they leave church, reaching out to them whenever they will stop to listen. He takes the flowery prose of the intellectual debates in Clifton and translates it into the language of the working man, a language he's slowly learnt to understand. He's started to convince these people that they're not getting what they deserve, that the ruling classes are selling them short, that change is absolutely essential for their happiness.

As his tireless, self-imposed missionary work has progressed, small groups of working men have started to take him seriously and show some respect. They've arranged small meetings where he's recounted his story to their workmates and friends. And so his influence has blossomed within this unlikely cluster of acquaintances, the underprivileged poor of Bristol.

Tireless involvement and compelling speeches have steadily established credibility for Daniel's ideas amongst these simple folk. More indeed than he could ever have hoped. He's become accepted, trusted. One or two have even turned to him for advice. But he's suddenly realized they're now looking to him for more than just that. It's struck him, with some dismay, that he's standing on the end of a plank; and a plank ironically that he's placed there all by himself.

In hindsight he was a fool not to have seen it coming. For months he's been stirring them up, convincing them they're badly done by, rousing them to take some action to bring about a change. And he's been successful, perhaps too successful. His words have not fallen on deaf ears. The mood of these people is becoming increasingly resentful, increasingly expectant. They're keen to act, eager to strike the first blow, but they've no idea of when or where or why. What's more natural than to look to Daniel to supply the answers, to organise a protest for them?

So far his thinking's gone no further than convincing them of the need to act. He's given not a moments consideration as to how, let alone that he might become the driving force. The men

284

he deals with here are simple, pleasant, reasonable folk in the main. But one or two cause a chill to run down the back of his neck. Taciturn, hard-faced individuals. Tolerable when they agree with you but short tempered and violent if they don't. He's never worked up the courage to enquire as to their employment, but can hazard it's not legitimate. And a couple of these characters, who've never shown him the respect afforded by the others, have recently offered the bluntest suggestions. Suggestions that might be confused with threats. They expect him to get some action started and to do so pretty damn soon. That much is crystal clear.

Since the summer, a recurring topic at the Clifton meetings has been the Reform Bill. It's kept coming up because strong feelings are roused by the arguments for and against. The good men are mostly liberal in their philosophy and see the Bill as logical and just, sure to improve lot of the ordinary citizen. They're consequently appalled that their own city Recorder, Wetherell, spoke so vehemently against it in the Commons debate. Most are grudgingly content that parliamentary representation within their own city and its surrounding boroughs should change. After all, the port of Bristol is now a major contributor to the economy, with huge importance to trade in commodities such as tea, wool and sugar. The group's support for the Bill is thus almost unanimous, despite the recent rejection in Parliament dampening hopes of it coming to pass. All this discussion has not been lost on the youngest member.

And in a moment of inspiration it comes to him that this is the answer to his dilemma. Here's a cause any reasonable man's bound to embrace. An attempt to right the injustices heaped on the heads of his own motley rabble. They'll jump at the chance to make their feelings known, once he's explained to them what those are! That should be simple. Then all that's required is careful organisation and a little gentle persuasion.

That's why Latham is pounding the streets on this gloomy October afternoon. He's seeking out the men he can count on to join the protest he's got in mind. When the Bill was thrown out by the House of Lords earlier in the month, there was a real avalanche of public outrage. And the newspapers had put all the blame on twenty one bishops, all casting their votes against. But for the intervention of these cynical churchmen, all would have been well.

And through his father Daniel's learned that one of these noble priests, the Bishop of Bath and Wells, is shortly to visit Bedminster. Here, on the twenty fourth of the month, to consecrate the new Church of Christ. Latham had handbills printed up immediately. Everybody he can muster must get there, to protest volubly and leave the Bishop in no doubt they're outraged. There's a bundle of bills to hand out in his satchel, a dozen men to chase up before darkness falls.

Hours later, tired and weary, he's satisfied the Bishop will be getting a very warm reception when he arrives. The walk back to his father's house, for that's where he still lives, seems to last a lifetime. He's exhausted. He bathes, changes his clothes, then throws himself into a comfortable chair. The withdrawing room's like a sanctuary, so different to the miserable places he's been visiting today. He picks up his father's newspaper. There must be some recent news about the Bill that can be turned to his advantage. But the publication seems to be filled with articles covering a far more gory event. There on the first page:

'MURDER AND HIGHWAY ROBBERY

An honoured Prussian nobleman, Johann Count von Winneburg, visiting this country to meet the King, was murdered yesterday at Bitton. He fell victim to a daring and successful highway robbery. Two dragoons, assigned to his party to give protection, were badly injured by gunshot wounds. von Winneburg's Countess and her maid were abducted for a period but luckily escaped without injury. The travelling party had been

286

guests at the estate of Sir James Whitefield near Bitton. Their coach was attacked by a vicious gang of horsemen as it left the grounds.

The Chronicle believes those responsible for this horrible deed are the infamous Kilbridge Lane Gang, known to have been perpetrating ever more daring crimes over recent months. If so this will be their most audacious outrage yet, relying upon both arson and murder.

Amongst the property stolen is jewelry of incalculable value, including a pearl necklace and a diamond tiara which are irreplaceable. A reward of £1,500 has been offered by the countess against the return of her property and the apprehension of the dastardly felon who took her husband's life. A witness described him as tall, lithe and muscular, with long black curls, a scarred chin and a criminal appearance.'

Even in these violent times, Latham is shocked by the report lying in his lap. Let's hope this scum will soon be caught and hanged. He continues to scan the newspaper for useful articles about the Reform Bill.

Chapter 28

Maynard's last evening at the Boar with Carey had bucked his spirits when he was at a really low ebb. At the beginning he's been downright miserable, by the end of the night he was a different man. So they'd resolved the meetings must be more regular events and between them they'd fixed another date. Over a month has passed and that day has come around. An awful lot of water has flowed under the bridge on the meantime.

Yet again he craves the company of his friend. There are things he can share with the man that he'd find awkward with Mary Ann. The guilt about his father, for one. Why he'd done practically nothing even though he knew the old man was ill. The work, meeting Brunel, it has obstructed his judgement. He can't get the feelings out of his mind. But explaining it to John might help a little. And then there are a raft of things where John's advice would be very useful.

So he sets off to walk to the inn with much on his mind. Besides, the whole neighbourhood's still buzzing with the awful event up at the big house. He knows John will be keen to discuss that. Probably tell him exactly what went on, blow by blow.

Even Maynard's hermit-like existence couldn't prevent him from hearing every specific already; all scrupulously accurate as far as those relaying the information were concerned. Details had slowly seeped out into every corner of the village. First gossip spread by those who'd been on the estate when it happened. Then by others who embellished these stories and finally friends who just recounted what was written in the newspapers. If only half of it was true, the mason is still concerned.

Nobody in the village doubts that the guilty men are the Kilbridge Lane Gang. What worries Maynard is the prospect of getting personally involved. He suspects he has information that might help, but it's of frighteningly little substance. Merely that he recognises the man described as the murderer and saw him briefly, face to face at the Lansdown fair. And that he might have seen him there again, for just a second, talking with another individual he thinks, but only thinks, he also recognised. A man, who at the time, was standing a considerable distance away with his back turned. On the other hand, the things he doesn't know are substantial. He has no idea where to find this murderer, he doesn't know where the jewellery might be stashed; even if the murderer was found he could only identify him as the man who had probably taken his father's ransom money.

He realizes this deliberation is getting him nowhere. He's confused. Perhaps he should do something, but he's not really sure what that is. His indecision's not unlike the torment following his indiscretion with Lady Sophia. An impossible problem circling around and around. But this time it's different. On this occasion he'll be able to confide in John and ask for his advice. Well, didn't he almost tell him the whole story of the episode at the fair last time they met? John had been right then of course. The ale had loosened his tongue. There was a risk he'd speak far too loudly for their safety. But tonight he can seek John's counsel in a whisper, once he's sure they are alone in the snug, or better still on the road as they walk back together.

Maynard arrives first on this occasion and loses no time in buying the ales. He's handing his money over to Silas when John comes through the door. Before long they've found comfortable seats in the parlour at the back of the building. A fire roars in the stone hearth, green wood spitting violently and showering sparks onto the surrounding flags.

289

'Thanks for turning out John. I can't tell you how good it is to see you. Your company was such a tonic last time; life had all but done me in. That evening was like an elixir. It buoyed up my spirits; I was twice the man the next day and back on my usual form. I'd forgotten how important it is to spend some time with your friends.'

'God, don't thank me Thomas. I enjoyed the evening too, believe me. And I want to say how sorry I am about your father. He was such a game old fellow. It really distressed me to see how downcast you all were at the funeral.'

'I can't put it out of my mind', his friend replies, 'If I hadn't been so tied up in my work. If only I'd been less tardy in calling for the doctor.'

'Stop it Thomas. You take it too hard. You can't blame yourself. Anyone would have done the same as you. It was clearly his time and not in your power to alter. Now, try to put it out of your mind for God's sake. Accept that what's happened is not of your making.'

Maynard's surprised by the conviction of John's retort and doesn't know quite what to say. But he feels encouraged nevertheless.

'Let's talk about things that don't distress you Thomas. If I remember rightly, last time, you wanted to hear all the news. Well, there's been a murder on our own doorstep since then. There can't be a chance in heaven that you don't know all about that!'

'I really can't credit what I've been told' says Maynard, 'Every report speaks of an outrageous, brazen attack. Whoever did it must have known those foreign nobles were travelling with articles of immense value. And they must have had some inside assistance to stop an armoured and guarded coach.'

'Oh, you're correct there my friend. I've got mates working on the estate. Apparently a stable lad went missing immediately after the attack took place. He stole the trap that was used to make off with the passengers and their luggage. It was discovered sometime later, floating in the Avon near Moore. Not a soul can be found who saw how it got there. The horse is still undiscovered and so is the trunk.'

'What about the passengers? No two stories seem to agree on what happened to them.'

'The foreign nobleman was shot dead, in cold blood, a ball between his shoulder blades. The lady and her maid were bundled into the road and left stranded outside the gates of the estate. The trap took off immediately but the pursuers never got near it. The gates had been pulled together and chained by the time they reached them. The other assailants, all on horseback, fled across open country to the north. With the two dragoons wounded, there was no one else saddled up to give chase. I'm told it was all over in minutes, everybody taken completely by surprise.'

'And there's a reward of £1,500 for delivering up the jewels and the murderer they say.'

'That's so Thomas, though there's little chance it will ever be claimed. What's certain is that the thieves' haul is useless to them in England. A hue and cry's afoot, more extensive than anything I've ever seen. There are dragoons and city guards from Bristol all over the place. Descriptions of the jewellery have been circulated and they're looking everywhere. Even the mail coach gets searched, every day on the road. The only hope the thieves have to profit from this robbery is to get the goods out of the country and I can't see how they'll manage that.'

'John, nothing changes, whatever matter we discuss. You're always know far more than me. But I need your advice about something that might be very relevant to this robbery. You just stopped me blurting it out last time, but I really must share it with you tonight. If it's really risky to speak here, can we chew it over as we walk home?'

'Surely, if that's what you want, friend. But no more of it now. I know it seems as if we're alone here, but you never can be sure. I fancy another glass of ale before we leave, how about yourself?'

'An excellent suggestion. And whilst we get it down you can tell me some of the more humdrum news, just as you did last time.'

'All right' replies John, 'Well, there's been trouble all over the place connected to that Reform Bill I was telling you about. Riots in Manchester, Nottingham and the like. And now, so they say, even in Bristol.'

'Good Lord man, what's happened there?' asks Thomas

'Seems the Bishop of Bath and Wells came up special to Bedminster yesterday. To consecrate a church that's been built there recently. No, not your Zion chapel Thomas. I don't think he's responsible for that one! When this cleric arrived there was an angry mob outside the church and he couldn't enter for half an hour or more. Eventually the constables were summoned and they made a way for him, though the crowd was acting more peacefully by then. But not long after that violence broke out. Stones were thrown and no end of windows smashed. They say it was stirred up by a young troublemaker, egging on the crowd. Despite all that they say the Bishop carried out his ceremony and left unharmed.'

'Good' says Thomas, 'That Reform Bill, sounds sensible to me. I hope it does get passed. But there's enough violence already with the murderers around here. We shouldn't let it happen to innocent folk as well.'

'A pious hope my friend. I reckon we'll be seeing more trouble yet' replies John. 'The bishop was attacked because he stands for the government, the ruling classes. And a lot of people are sorely angered by them just now. The rumour is there'll be even bigger trouble when Wetherell comes back to Bristol, to open the Assizes at the end of the month.'

'What's the reason for that John?' asks Maynard

'Because he's seen as a real traitor to the city. As Official Recorder, he's supposed to be one of our own, there to represent us. Yet it was he who spoke out most vehemently against the Bill in Parliament. He's to blame, in a large part, for the time it's taking. And now lots of citizens are up in arms. It seems certain they'll give him a rough old reception.'

'In that case he needs to listen to them. But Heaven forbid it becomes violent. Well, I seem to have finished my beer. Are you ready to pull on your coat John, amble homewards and allow me to unburden my troubles?'

John falls in with him and they stroll out side by side. Maynard waits only until he's sure it's safe to speak before sketching out the situation and his dilemma.

'You might not credit it, but I read a newspaper occasionally now, old friend. And I've seen the description of the rogue for whose capture that reward is been offered. I know who it is John. He's the very man I saw through that slit in the canvas at Lansdown. The fellow who seems to hold the strings in the extortion of my poor dead father, and most likely several of our neighbours too. And I might have a notion about one of his associates, though if I'm correct it worries me even more. What should I do John? I can't figure out what would be for the best. Should I go to the authorities or not?'

He doesn't have to wait long for his friend's advice, which is categorical.

'If you value your life Thomas, and the happiness of your family, listen to me carefully. Forget this ever happened. Do nothing. Absolutely nothing at all.'

Chapter 29

Daniel Latham wakes late the following morning. It takes time and determination before he succeeds in dragging himself out of bed. He's most unaccustomed to strong liquor. A single glass of sherry, taken with his high minded friends, is the usual limit of his imbibing. But yesterday had been different altogether. Some of the troublemakers who'd protested with him outside the church on Monday had insisted he join them at the Miners Rest. The trouble at the church was being acclaimed as a huge success. Around forty men and women had heeded his call and Latham had certainly spurred them into action. The flags had been strewn with broken glass and the Bishop had been jostled roughly despite the constables' presence. Articles referring to the event as a riot appeared in newspapers the following day. Overnight, Latham had become a hero. Men whom he'd never even seen before bought him ale. As the afternoon wore on, he discovered his glass was never empty. Toasts, lewd encouragements and endless re-tellings of memorable deeds that day filled the room.

Towards evening, the Miners Arms welcomed yet more who'd heard about the protest and Daniel's capacity to think clearly diminished rapidly. The bar room became noisier and nosier, but the gist of the conversations were rapidly turning from recollections to resolution. The mob had proved to themselves that they could forcibly make their point. What they did on Monday had fired their spirits. But if they could achieve that much, with so little preparation, what more could they do if only they were properly organized? Surely, here was an opportunity to fix on something that would make the toffee nosed bastards really sit up and take notice. And they put this idea their reluctant leader, Daniel, as he sat in the bar, struggling to hear or think clearly and starting to agonize about the consequences.

Very quickly it all became too much for him. He desperately needed to escape from the bar, and from the people who were trying to pin him down every side. In order to leave with honour he was compelled to promise them he'd return tomorrow with a plan. With his offer accepted, he stumbled outside and made his way unsteadily home, yearning only of crawling into his bed as soon as possible.

Now finally up and amongst the living, he sluices his head under the pump. It doesn't cure the dull ache behind his eyes. The cold water's restorative effect is only temporary so he seeks out food and some hot coffee, hoping for further improvement. He desperately needs a clear head to think things through. Gratifying though it is to have become the peoples' champion, the leader in their struggle for social justice, it's regrettable they also expect him to spearhead the fight going forward. It would have posed a problem for him without the headache, for he can't think of a tangible cause to rally the men behind. Sitting distractedly at the table he idly flicks over the pages of a newspaper. His eyes fall on an article reporting the aftermath of his demonstration in Bedminster. It's been reported as a determined attempt at insurrection. Latham, if the justices only knew his name, would probably be in custody by now. My God. All he'd really done was to hand out pamphlets and bawl encouragement to his fellows, wasn't it?

But, reaching to the bottom of the article, he finds a sentence or two that suddenly gives him fresh hope:

'The strident citizens of Bristol have made their views very clear. The manner in which they chose to protest has left your correspondent with trepidation and concern. If the sight of a Bishop can give rise this much anger, what might they do when Wetherell arrives on 29th. The Chronicle will be present at the opening of the Assizes and will bring you a full report.'

Latham reads the last sentences over and over. Yet again, here, in the newspaper, lies an answer to the scrape he's got himself into. A scrape that makes his spine go cold. All he needs to do is to turn this reporter's prophesy into reality. With the number of people who turned out previously, now champing at the bit for more action, rustling up a good crowd to give the Recorder a boisterous welcome should be easy.

With fresh hope in his heart and a head that's now clearing rapidly, Latham strikes out for Bedminster. He should reach the Miner's Arms by lunchtime, just as he promised. On the long walk he mulls over how he might stamp his mark as their leader and champion. Now that he's reconciled to this unsolicited role, he's determined to carry it through, and without interference. He concludes he must appear strong and fearless, advocating an aggressive, pre-emptive campaign.

As expected, the bar at the inn is like a bear-pit; no voice can carry far above the din. Every soul in the place is shouting, especially those who are already intoxicated. Daniel beats a pewter tankard on the wooden table and then climbs onto it. The noise gradually abates.

'Friends', he begins, 'I don't need to convince you - we made a damned good show of our contempt for those bloody Bishops at the church on Monday. I know most of you were there, doing your bit for our cause. It was a magnificent demonstration. You should be proud. But so far it's made not a jot difference to getting that Reform Bill through Parliament. If we're to achieve that, we've must strike much harder. The next protest has to be one the authorities will find impossible to ignore. Are you all with me?'

A roar of approval goes up and Latham knows he's judged his audience well.

'We'll not rest until the Bill is passed' he continues, 'Until then we must fight like wild animals to make our voice heard. And I know of an opportunity to do that. One we mustn't squander. The Recorder of Bristol, who's a Member of

Parliament himself, a fellow named Wetherell; he'll be arriving in the city on Saturday. He'll be in a coach, coming from London. This scummy lawyer's been a traitorous opponent to our cause. Whenever he arrives, I want all of us to be waiting for him. He's spoken vehemently against the Bill in the House of Commons. We must open his eyes boys. We must make him see how wrong he's been, and that we, the people, won't tolerate his high-handed attitude.'

'What are we to do if the coach doesn't stop?' cries one of the drinkers, 'It's no bloody use to just shout at a coach. It will be there and gone in minutes.'

'You're right. Just shouting won't be sufficient this time lads. We've got to frustrate his passage, stop his vehicle if we're able and throw stones through the windows at the very least. Let's attempt to bring his journey to an early end and have him out of that carriage. See what he thinks about conversing with us face to face' replies Latham, 'But if we can't manage that, don't give up my friends, don't any of you stand still. Chase the bastard. Chase him every inch of the way until he reaches his destination. Then for certain we can confront him in person. Spare no efforts, heed no restraint. Be bold. We must make Wetherell see the sense in our argument. This is the best chance we've got.'

'Now, friends, remember this well. You must all be there on Saturday. Every man must be present, we'll tolerate no excuses. But here's another charge, equally important. Go back to the people you live and work amongst. Encourage everybody you know to join us. Anybody who will spare you a few minutes of their time to listen. Make sure they all come with you on Saturday. Let's make our voice as loud as it can be.'

Another roar of appreciation erupts and the meeting gives way to the determined consumption of yet more ale.

Chapter 30

Locke is riding as hard as his large, rarely exercised frame will permit. His breath comes in short painful gasps. Under normal circumstances he'd have hired a messenger, not come all this way himself. But today there's an urgency. One that doesn't allow time to wait on a reply, nor tolerate any evasion in the answer. Dispensing with the trap for the sake of speed, he's riding his damndest in the saddle. For the first time in years. And it's taken a desperate toll on his over indulged constitution.

His singular object is to find Maynard. Things have changed. It's vital another load of stones is dispatched to the gorge without delay. Finally, the ride having completely spent his strength, he arrives breathless and sweating at the smallholding. Trotting up to the farmhouse, he slides gratefully out of the stirrups and tethers the animal to a post.

The yard's deserted so he hollers out hopefully. Not a sound. Nothing stirs. But eventually a little girl hesitantly emerges from the barn where animal feed and the like is usually stored,

'Good afternoon Mr Locke Sir', Emily greets the visitor tentatively, 'My ma's away down to the masons. You look very hot Sir. Are you all right?'

For several seconds, Locke is incapable of a reply. Cramp has finally caught him below the ribcage, robbing him of speech. Bent forward, his right hand grasping the nearest wall for support, he struggles to catch his breath and a semblance of composure.

'Why no little girl', he finally replies, 'I'm just a bit puffed. But I do need to talk with your daddy as soon as I can. I'll walk over to find him.' The rhythmic chipping of the stonemasons' tools can be heard in the distance and he strides off towards the noise.

'Well, I'm sure you will soon Mr Locke', the girl shouts after him, 'He's not gone far, but you won't find him at the stone-yard. He rode Hermes to the smithy because he's thrown a shoe. But that was just after lunch, so he should be back in a few minutes. Why don't you come into the parlour and wait? My mummy will be here soon too.'

Locke accepts the offer with good grace; there's little else he can do. He perches himself on the chair pulled forward by Emily, but fidgets constantly. Mary Ann does indeed soon return and offers him all manner of tempting refreshments, but he declines every morsel. He just broods in a fretful silence, wringing his hands and glancing frequently at the clock   When Thomas finally steps through the door the relief around the room is palpable. Locke leaps up from the chair to greet him.

'Thomas, thank God you're back. Believe me I'm sorry to arrive unannounced like this. But I need your help and there's no time to lose. Things aren't looking good in Bristol and some action is called for to make sure it doesn't grind us to a halt. But first I must explain and we can figure out what's to be done.'

'My God, Elijah, I've never seen you so worried. Let's go out into the yard. It's quiet there and we can talk over this problem, whatever it may be. Let's not burden Mary Ann and Emily with our troubles.'

Outside, the mason insists that they take a seat. There's a rough bench some steps from the door. No sooner than his bottom has touched it, Locke launches into his tale of woe.

'There's serious unrest in Bristol Thomas' he begins, 'It blew up yesterday. And those who understand these things expect it to get even worse over the next few days. People whose judgement I trust are sorely afraid it might bring commerce to a stop if the authorities fail to stamp it out.'

'Yes, I heard something about this. I'm aware that trouble's in the air. But surely that hasn't induced you to ride all the way out here?'

'Thomas, I don't think you quite understand. I've got forty five men on site now. The walls of the abutment are fifty feet above the footings, but there's another sixty to go. They're getting through the stocks there at a rate of knots. I can't allow a stoppage. It would lose us a small fortune. If these disturbances in the city stop delivery of the stones, we'll be in the mire.'

'So what's the best thing we can do Elijah??'

'Let's just get every stone that's already cut onto your barge. And any that are nearly finished. If necessary your men can finish them off on site. We'll set off for the gorge immediately. I'm trusting, even if there is trouble, that it will die down after a few days. Than we can get back to normal. But if we don't act now, there will be a shortage of material for my boys.'

'We can do that Elijah. But even with the bankered stone it probably only comes to a three quarters load.'

'That will be enough Thomas. In truth it's much better than I hoped. Now, when can we set out?'

'Steady on Elijah, steady. Let's say I get my men to down tools now and rallied around to help. It will take us the remainder of today just to load the Celeste. If we get everything else prepared tonight, we can set off at first light. But what about you? I'd offer you a bed for the night, but we've got a scullery maid living in since dad died and there's not a berth to spare!'

'Don't worry about me Thomas. I passed an inn in Swinton on the way over. I'll be surprised if they don't have a room I can take. When we've finished the loading I'll ride down there and fix up my accommodation for the night.'

The following day, a Saturday, blesses them with encouraging weather for their unexpected journey. With six men working like navvies the previous afternoon, the ready cargo was stashed far faster than Maynard imagined. The little team then bent to, knocking out as many more stones as they could before darkness fell, carrying each one on board as it was completed. And now, as they cast off, the hold is almost full. Locke, up long before the others, has been chiding them to leave since dawn. With equal vigour he's been double checking everything else, the provisions, the bedding and the measuring instruments that habitually accompany them on every trip.

By now, Allot, the haulier that Edmund engaged for them, makes four out of every five deliveries. But that still leaves Maynard and his men doing a good many trips. It's almost second nature for Hermes and it's safe to leave the blinkers off on the easy stretches of tow path. At a push one man could probably now manage the journey alone, but Maynard's not unhappy to have Locke with him. Especially if they do run into some trouble.

They've got no more than twenty yards away from the landing stage, Locke walking Hermes and Maynard at the tiller, when Mary Ann can be heard running along to the tow-path to catch up with them.

'Hold on a moment', she cries, 'A boy's just arrived from the big house with a message for Thomas'

'Did he say what it concerns Mary Ann?' Maynard shouts back, whilst Locke struggles to haul back the tow line.

'It's sent by Lady Sophia. It's here', she replies, 'It says there's no urgency, but she and Sir James would like you to attend on them as soon as it's convenient for you to get there.'

Within him, her husband's blood runs cold. A handful of reasons for receiving this summons flash through his mind. John did say some time back that he guessed she's with child. Surely it can't be anything to do with that? But what if their assignation in the stables is indeed the reason for her present condition? What if Sir James has somehow managed to wrest the truth from her? God, it doesn't bear thinking about.

The man's mind and body are in turmoil. He looks down and his hands are shaking. But he can't let Locke and Mary Ann see that this simple message has affected him the way it has.

'I'll attend to her request just as soon as I possibly can', he answers, trying to stop the quaver in his voice, 'But Locke and I can't delay our departure now. Please give the boy a reply to take back, my love. Inform them that I'll be absent for a few days, but they have my word I'll call at the estate just as soon as I return.'

So they resume their progress and Maynard is lost in contemplation. Perhaps he half expected something like this would happen. He'd just about convinced himself that all danger was past. That Sophia had put him, and their guilty secret, behind her. What is it now then? Perhaps Sir James has nothing at all to do with the message. Perhaps she still desires his attentions and this is a contrivance to tempt him yet again. What would he do is she offered herself to him again? My God, can he extract himself from this knot? What if he shuns her and she goads him with the threat of exposure?

His reverie is broken by Locke, walking close on the path, and it doesn't ease his concern.

'Hey, Thomas, isn't that Lady Sophia the young wife of old Whitefield? I'm sure I read something about her in the Mercury last week' he cries, 'How does a humble fellow like you get honoured with a request to attend the gentry?'

'It's a long story my friend. Fifteen years or so ago, my father was in Whitefield's employ', blusters Maynard, his mind racing to think up a satisfactory explanation and, at the same time, a way of changing the subject, 'Through that, I've occasionally had reason to call upon them. And Whitfield recently loaned me that plough harness that's around Hermes shoulders. I'd guess her request concerns its return. They probably they need it back. But, let's not worry about such matters Elijah. Hell man, you seem to know a lot about me, but you've never shared your own history. Tell me how you came to be a builder.'

'It all came about by accident really' replies Locke, jumping aboard as the boat passes a shaky wooden pier, 'My family was poor and my schooling was threadbare. But my parents were tolerably literate and encouraged me as much as they could. Perversely I showed no interest in anything. I had a complete lack of a resolve to follow any particular line. So at fifteen I became apprenticed, for no particular reason, to a carpenter. Once the ties with my family were loosened a bit I became wrapped up in the confusion of youth. I'm sure you remember what that was like. I got into quite a few scrapes over the years I was apprenticed. Built myself a shaky reputation. Towards the end my parents suggested pretty forcibly that I should join the army. They'd helped me to repay a lot of debts I'd built up, so I didn't really have a choice. I complied. I guess they believed discipline in the ranks would do me a power of good.'

'And did it?' asks Maynard

'In part' replies Locke, 'Immediately I'd taken the King's shilling I was posted to Gibraltar on a troop ship. Walking down the gangplank I thought I was on a building site. The military docks were undergoing massive reinforcement, and the garrison buildings into the bargain. I guess my error was simply to show overmuch interest. Of course I was still wet behind the ears. Must have let my mouth run. Some bright young officer rumbled that I had experience and set me to work as a carpenter, instead of as a soldier. O' course that didn't excuse me the military training; still had to do drills and parades and the like. But my real service was four years fortifying the garrison.'

'And my skills slowly grew from simple carpentry to general building. I must say, t'was a great life. The weather was agreeable in the main, the work handsomely paid and I made a couple of firm friendships. I didn't return to England for all those years. But I did eventually yearn to come home. I packed up there, returned to Blighty and set up on my own account. A business that's flourished quite well, in its own small way. Then you and I started the Zion Chapel and you know the rest.'

'But you can't have started with much money in your pocket. Or did you somehow get free a discharge from the army? I was always told that soldiers in the ranks have to buy themselves out of their service'

'I suppose you might call it a lucky break Thomas. For it can't be denied it was a break', replies Locke, 'A severe fracture of my leg. The right one, as it happens. I was just in the wrong place when a pile of bricks toppled and fell. The ligaments around this knee were torn. I was deemed unfit for active service. Happy to say the leg's almost completely mended now, as you can see. But they discharged me with a pension in compensation.'

'Now Thomas, that's more than enough of me. I'm keen to work out how long it'll take us to finish that abutment. Can you say how many more weeks you need to cut all the facing stones?'

Not long ago Maynard had contrived to change the topic of conversation. He gets an intuitive feeling that Locke's now trying to do the same thing himself. There's something not quite right in the way he's told his story. Maybe there are parts that he'd rather Maynard doesn't learn. The end of his army career might be one of these, but Maynard's not about to pry. Perhaps there's some embarrassment there he'd rather not expose.

Striving to move the conversation onto more comfortable ground, the mason talks about the progress his team's made and sketches out what they still need to accomplish. In the past he's covered many aspects of their job with Locke, but much of the masonry work still seems to be a closed book as far as he's concerned.

'Finishing any cladding can be achieved a number of ways', Maynard explains, trying to interest the builder and keep the conversation alive, 'Brunel's drawings call for a clawed surface, but he could just as well have specified them to be axed or batted.'

'What difference would that have made?' Locke enquires.

'A lot comes down to cost', says Maynard, 'The finer the plane of the surface, the more work we must put into it. Then there are the chisels. Different surface, different chisels. Naturally they all have to be frequently sharpened. The more sharpening that's involved, the more expensive the stones.'

'It also alters the appearance of a structure, especially from a distance. The shadows cast across a clawed surface make its colour seem lighter or darker, depending on the position of the sun.'

Maynard's effort pays off. With the conversation steered away from personal issues, Locke becomes more affable and relaxed. Their parley quickly drifts into a technical discussion between craftsmen and time passes quickly during their trek to the first lock.

As it comes into view, Maynard chuckles inwardly. Since Locke's last passed this way there's been a change of keeper. From his experience so far he guesses his friend will be amused.

The new Keynsham lock keeper is a diminutive, shrivelled man in his late sixties. His weather beaten face, lined from brow to chin, lacks room to accommodate any further wrinkles. He makes certain his bald pate's kept permanently warm with a filthy woollen hat pulled down tightly over his ears. On the several journeys Maynard's now made through his lock, he's never seen the man bare headed. He's convinced the keeper must sleep in it. Whenever the weather has been clement, he's found the man sitting beside the iron railings surrounding his cottage, looking uncomfortably erect on an upright wooden chair.

But what's amazed Maynard is the contrast between this man and his wife. Inexplicably, for they're both taciturn individuals, she's always sits him alongside, knitting. A woman of double his girth, she's positively wedged into her low rocking chair, ensconced in a mass of plump pillows crammed around her ample frame. Head, shoulders and arms completely muffled in a thick woollen shawl, only her hands visible, moving like a well-oiled machine to form the stitches.

Maynard's never heard the couple converse. An endless silence seems to hang between them, broken only by the clicking of her needles and the keeper sucking on his briar pipe. They're always monosyllabic, even when dealing with the boatmen wanting to use the lock. Today, however, everything seems to have changed. Unbidden, they both greet Maynard and Locke with a hearty 'good day'. It's obvious they're desperate to tell the newcomers something.

'Glad to see ee Mr Maynard,' says the man, whom Thomas had met several times by now. He has no idea of the lock-keepers name, but clearly his own has got around, probably through gossip from further up river, 'Have ee heard, there's been some furious activity hereabouts of recent.'

'Do you mean constables and the like?' asks Maynard, guessing that he must be referring to the hunt for the highway robbers of that John had been so excited about at the inn.

'Aye, that's it. Two constables from Bristol there were, and with them half a dozen city watchmen. They descended three or four days back, like a pack of eager dogs. Searched right through the cottage, they did, though I told them any vagabonds would get short measure here. They stayed for a couple of days, local mind you, and poked around in all the boats going through my lock. They must have twigged it was a waste of their effort, for they packed it in after a time. But I hear they're calling at dwellings all along the Bath road now though, asking searching questions about strangers and the like.'

'Well, I hope they'll have success' retorts Maynard, 'The villainy in these parts has bothered me for years, but now it's turned to daylight robbery and murder, we could do with the authorities stamping it out for good. To have a murderer abroad who's happy to shoot another man in the back, that's enough to worry us all.'

He fishes a sixpence out of his pocket for the man, since he's keen that the Celeste passes quickly through the lock. The unkempt keeper takes the hint, thanks him for his generosity and picks up the heavy steel key from the grass beside his chair.

~

Three hours later the two men are going through another lock at Netham. This is the last before Bristol and the gateway into the Feeder Canal. The Feeder is a straight stretch of water around a mile in length, built twenty years back to allow boats to move from the floating harbour to the river Avon. It was dug

308

because the river, which flows in parallel to the canal from here, is tidal. As they've made their steady progress, several workmen on the banks, including two Conham quarrymen, have passed the time of day. They all tell the same story. There's intense activity everywhere. It's obvious a serious manhunt for the highwaymen is under way. Locke is very interested in the details they're picking up and seems to be pondering the news deeply.

They've got about halfway along the canal when they're forced to tie up for a couple of minutes. Hermes has been showing signs of discomfort for a hundred yards or more. And it's obvious, when Maynard investigates, what the problem is. A strap on the harness is broken, giving rise to a rubbing sore on the animal's shoulder. As Maynard makes the best repair he can Locke swings himself over the side of the boat to exchange a few words.

'Thomas, my friend, I've been thinking about my men at the gorge. When this cargo of stone eventually arrives, there's not a lot of room around the landing stage to unload it. A delay could mean the boat's left high and dry by the tide. Much better if I go on ahead now and get them to clear some space before the stone arrives.'

'The canal's dead straight now and the tow path is excellent; I'm confident you can manage the journey from here alone. I think it would be best for me to leave you, pick up a horse at an inn on the road and get to the site as fast as I can. With luck I can get the men started before it starts to grow dark.'

From the way he speaks, it's clear that Locke's made up his mind and won't brook any argument. So, with little more than this brief explanation, Locke shakes Maynard's hand, collects his belongings and strides rapidly away down the tow-path in the direction of Bristol.

'I'll see you tomorrow then Thomas' he shouts.

309

For a moment Maynard continues to refasten the harness, his mind furiously pondering this sudden turn of events. Something doesn't add up. Without untying the barge, he climbs back aboard. He needs a little time to think.

Various happenings over recent months start to piece themselves together in his mind. The mysterious nocturnal visitor in the stone-yard. The insistence of Locke and Hartnoll that he provide a secure shed to which only they had the keys. The routine that ensued of always taking that crate to and from the gorge. The Irish builders' distrust of Hartnoll. The distant figure he'd seen at the fair. The man he couldn't make out clearly but whom might well have been red headed. As these recollections float around in his mind, a possible explanation that makes sense of them all starts to gel in his mind.

With a pounding heart he searches behind the wooden doors at the prow. Yes, here it is. A small bag of tools, stashed away in case of emergency. He's looked at it before and he's sure it contains a sturdy screwdriver. He's right. Its blade is a little blunted but it will serve his purpose nevertheless. Checking that there are no onlookers, Maynard removes the screws holding the top of the instrument crate in place. He tugs at the lid, but it refuses to shift.

A closer inspection of the lid reveals four very small keyholes, one in the centre of each side. Anybody wanting to open this crate needs a key as well as a screwdriver. Taking a deep breath, Maynard jams the blade of the screwdriver beneath one end prises with all his strength. There's no going back now. If he's wrong, what he's about to do will plainly mark him out as a thief.

The screwdriver bends without making any impression. He looks for a better tool. Sure enough there's a small jemmy at the bottom of the bag. This time he hears the screws that secure the locks tearing out of the wood as he levers against the lid. Finally, with a resounding crack, it comes away, giving him a sight of its contents. The complicated levelling and measuring devices are certainly there, neatly tied for safety to wooden supports that hold them in place. He takes out each in turn, placing it carefully on the stack of cladding stones beside him. For a ghastly moment it seems there's nothing else to be found. But then, under one of the supports, he glimpses the corner of an oilskin rag.

A little more effort with the now bent screwdriver allows him to break through a panel within the crate itself. What he's glimpsed turns out to be a folded package and he pulls it out into the sunlight.

Unrolling the oilskin he reveals a white silk bag, drawn at the neck with a string. With trembling hands Maynard loosens the knot and peers inside. Thank God, he wasn't mistaken. There, protected in sheepskin, lay the items that he immediately recognises from Carey's description at the inn. A handsome pearl necklace and a glittering diamond tiara. There can't be any doubt. It's the haul from the murderous robbery at the Whitefield estate.

Chapter 31

The chariot bearing Charles Wetherell to Bristol, on this the twenty ninth of October, makes reasonable speed as far as Brislington. It's drawn by four greys and is already well protected, both driver and guard carrying a brace of pistols with a blunderbuss propped against the seat rail for good measure. But rumours of trouble have spread speedily over the previous day, so two burly watchmen, armed with nightsticks, board at Brislington to reinforce the others. Sitting at the rear of the vehicle, they make an intimidating sight, which is precisely to the purpose.

As the coach draws closer to the city the number of people gathered alongside the road has been growing. This was to be expected, but it's the sheer numbers of onlookers now that astonishes Wetherell and his colleagues as they peer out between the brocade curtains. Clearly they're not all simply individuals going about their lawful business. Shouts and catcalls are heard at regular intervals and the mood of a group of men standing in the path of the coach is starting to take an ugly turn.

Progress is brought to a snail's pace as the road becomes completely congested with bodies. A glance at the crowd, uncouth ill-dressed boys and men with obviously no gainful employment, confirms that the baser elements of vice-ridden St Philips and Lawford Gate have been marshaled onto the streets. Here and there a number of women, mostly of ill repute, mingle with the men. Occasionally the odd smartly dressed workers can be seen, men that might be considered capable of a legitimate protest against Wetherell. But, in the main, the profanity, the violent language, the mood of the throng, all suggest the deliberate recruitment and encouragement of a mob.

After the Lords rejected the Bill, newspapers had been printed with black margins to proclaim their displeasure in the outcome of the vote. This sense of indignation had been spread abroad, by word of mouth, to those who could not read. Many residents of Bristol, mostly of working class, but also some of the most respected citizens, had announced their contempt for the high-handed manner in which Wetherell had opposed the motion. Feelings were running high, something that had not gone unnoticed at the Mansion House. Officers there, particularly the Sherriff, had started to make early preparations for unrest.

This morning, genuinely concerned for the Recorder's safety, he'd organised for fifty special constables to be sworn in. Each was armed with a short stout staff and he had them assembled at the Exchange, along with a far greater number of regular constables and some of his own officers. This combined force, now three hundred strong, then marched to the city boundary near the Blue Bowl tavern at Totterdown, led by the Sheriff's own carriage.

It's half past ten in the morning when they meet up with Wetherell's party, which has now come to an unplanned standstill. The city militia are deployed strategically to protect the two vehicles and a hurried conference ensues. As a result, Wetherell and his travelling companions are transferred to the Sheriff's coach. They subsequently proceeded, under escort of the constables who use their staves with enthusiasm to clear the road of all who attempt to block the way. The sheriff's coach is deliberately attended with much ceremony, preceded by trumpeters and officers with favours in their caps. But this show of pomp and force merely enrages the angry mob, thwarted in its aim of engaging the Recorder directly. Surrounding and following the entourage, they become ever more violent in both speech and action. Making slow progress the jostling procession comes to a narrowing of the road.

It's at precisely this point that Latham and his followers have been waiting impatiently since nine o'clock. Determined the magistrate will not slip past early and avoid their censure. A few had gone forward and manfully attempted to mob him as he transferred between the two vehicles, but the sheer number of constables had kept them at bay.

'Stop that damned coach if you can', Latham shouts to his acolytes, 'This is our chance to have Wetherell out. Let's see how well he can explain his outrageous opinions standing in the roadway.'

A young, slightly built lad of around eighteen is loitering behind a gaggle of women. Latham recognizes him at first glance. The boy had demonstrated enthusiasm and daring during the protest at the church. He crouches suddenly and Latham sees he's brought a broom handle along with him. In a flash he launches his body through a sea of ankles and forces the broom handle between the spokes of a carriage wheel. But his brave effort is in vain. Dragged to the footboards it snaps like a twig. Before any damage is done he's hauled away by officers, the offending handle removed along with him.

'Bravo. Well done', screams Latham as the young man's taken roughly into custody, 'Now come on lads, that was a brave try and I want to see more like it. If we can't stop this pompous toff now, let's follow him to his destination and lay hands on him whenever the coach stops. Stick by me all of you. We're going to find there'll be others of a like mind to help us by the time that happens.'

The progress of a cortege would seem speedy compared to that of the Sheriff's carriage. The rowdy, untidy procession passes a string of inns and beer-houses along the way. The noise brings out yet more rough fellows, who fall in with them, swelling the tumultuous cries of approbation. Some understand the reason for all this commotion, others just go along with the throng, eager to be part of anything disorderly. By the time it nears the centre of the city the crowd is a good two thousand strong, many of them have already consumed a full day's measure of ale.

To a man the constables have been briefed to protect the Recorder. They all stay close and none are following the mob at its tail. Were they doing so, they might notice a number of purposeful individuals carrying pick axes, hammers and hatchets, all stolen that very day from nearby factories. Interestingly, these men are sober and, whilst they appear to be part of the crowd, they're not mobbing the coach, nor are they making a commotion. Well wrapped in long coats to conceal their tools, they have other ideas in mind.

Finally, at noon, the Guildhall is reached. Latham's plan is foiled. Rotten fruit and vegetables fly, but Wetherell and his companions are safely ushered inside, under the protection of a double line of constables. The hall is packed with people, all of a like mind as those without, the atmosphere now growing steadily thicker with hostility and anger.

The opening ceremony commences. As is perennially the case, with the reading of the royal Charter. In previous years, during this event, the audience had always been respectful and silent. Today that's not the case. Barely a sentence is completed without some threat being shouted from the public benches, or a blood-curdling whistle, or a curse of admonishment. Attempting to bring the ceremony to a swift conclusion, Serjeant Ludlow, the Bristol town clerk, makes some provocative remarks about reform, which spark off a general outbreak of commotion within the hall. Wetherell, his patience now tried to the limit, attempts to take control. He threatens to commit anyone who further disturbs the court. Special constables move in amongst the throng to pick out and arrest offenders. Finally the court is adjourned, with the crowd now raised to a pitch of unconcealed anger and Wetherell is escorted to Quay Street where the Mayor's state carriage is waiting to convey him onwards to the Mansion House.

315

Forcing its way through the crowd, the coach at last turns into Queen Square and draws up before the steps of that grand building. The crowd, now sensing they'll be denied their opportunity to confront Wetherell directly, begin throwing stones and breaking into a deafening clamour of abuse and whistling. The constables wheel to form an avenue, again two deep on either side, providing Wetherell with a safe passage to the doors, which are thrown open just as he approaches. He briskly climbs the step and his protectors breathe a premature sigh of relief. They've held the line, their charge has been safely delivered. There are dragoons they can call on at Cattle Market if the mob doesn't settle now. For them, the danger they'd sensed seems to have passed. If they only knew that, less than a thirty paces distant, the real trouble is just at that moment being set in motion.

The silent, sober men have squeezed through the crowd surrounding the Mansion House. Their hammers and picks begin to swing at the base of the railings running along the frontage of the building. As these are torn roughly from their footings, unarmed members of the mob seize the uprights as makeshift weapons. Dozens of the rioters then start to beat on the shutters, the windows and the doors facing onto the square. Walls and pavings are attacked with sledgehammers and broken up to provide suitably sized blocks as missiles.

Within five minutes of the first blow striking, the building is subjected to a serious siege. The constables and watchmen detailed to man the portico can see the situation rapidly getting out of control. Serjeants responsible for the building's security are taken by surprise and struggle to decide what orders they should give to their men. Some of the special constables are zealous and eager to demonstrate their courage. They charge the crowd and pull out the rowdier individuals, whom they then drag into the Mansion House to beat viciously with staves. But this merely serves to incense the crowd further. Appalled by this summary injustice, and they rush the building as one to rescue their unfortunate colleagues.

'To the back', comes a shout. Those who understand this instruction push through to the rear of the great edifice, where the doors are less secure and less well guarded. There they also discover sticks to arm themselves and faggots, suitable for starting a fire, stacked against a wall. A couple of them, armed with crowbars, succeed in gaining entrance through doors and windows.

As the wood of the door jambs and window casements can be heard splitting, an up to now unspoken panic starts to show itself within. None of the city's executive wants to appear weak and flustered in front of his colleagues, however all of them are aware that what's going on is beyond any experience they've witnessed in the past. To a man, an icy chill runs through their veins.

Suddenly, to the crowd's amazement, the Mayor himself appears at the top of the steps. Arrayed in his ceremonial robes and tricorn hat he calls upon the mob to desist and return to their homes. The answer is a fusillade of well-aimed stones, one of which narrowly misses his head. He retreats rapidly and sends out an unfortunate constable to stand in his place and read the riot act. This is the last recourse of civil control and the mayor prays it will have the desired effect. Little does he know that it will have to be read out again twice today before order is restored. With jeers and whistles, the crowd fall upon the constables who beat a hasty retreat, leaving the Mansion House doors unprotected.

Dignitaries are rapidly fleeing to the upper floors to escape the wrath of a growing number of invaders. Within minutes, all kinds of chattels are being flung onto the streets through the smashed or opened windows. Tables, chairs, earthenware pots, parts of the splendid chandeliers from the entrance vestibule, all come flying into the square. As the rioters warm to their task beds and bedding descend through the air from the upper floors. Wetherell's travelling portmanteau comes crashing down onto a lamppost where it dangles dangerously on a cross beam. His clothes and papers follow, a blizzard of loose leaves fluttering slowly to the ground. The rout of the Recorder is complete.

Down in the cellars, oblivious to the commotion above, the cellar master and potboy are checking through their stock. By the light of a lantern they move from rack to rack, chalking numbers onto a slate. It's deep below the surface, there are no windows and they remain ignorant of the carnage nearby. The trap door above them being wrenched from its hinges is the first clue they have to the unfolding events.

'What in God's name is happening?', the old man asks, 'You stay here lad. Give me that light and I'll go take a look.'

Left in the gloom the boy senses that something is very wrong. He can just make out his master, half way up the flight of steps, being suddenly bundled unceremoniously backward by a gaggle of descending bodies. The old man loses his footing and tumbles awkwardly down the remaining stairs. His lantern shatters and goes out. The boy can see nothing now but a sudden silence falls where the cellar-master's body has come to rest.

'Shit, I think we've killed the old bugger', says one of the group, having now stopped themselves halfway down the flight. 'Bring us a lamp. We'll need to move him out of the road in any event.'

It takes some time for the lamp to be found, so the boy takes his opportunity to crawl quietly under one of the dusty racks. It sounds as though the men have already taken plenty to drink and he doesn't relish engaging in a discussion with them. No, he'll see if he can remain undiscovered until they've done whatever it is they intend to do and leave.

At last lamps are brought down and a great deal of clumsy lifting, pushing and shoving ensues. The cellar master's heavy corpse is dumped beside the very rack under which the boy hides. In the gloom he can make out the man's face. He reaches out to touch it with a finger, quickly withdrawing it, covered in sticky warm blood.

Satisfied with having restored order in the cellar the rioters get down to business in earnest. Despite their drunkenness they manage to find empty sacks and boxes which they fill with one hundred bottles of the finest wine. A great many of these are opened and consumed as soon as they get to the top of the steps, some are carried away from the rear of the building by the more sober conspirators.

Meanwhile, the first attempt to burn down the building is in progress and is only arrested by the arrival of a platoon of Dragoons who, after much resistance, restore some semblance of order and eject the mob into the streets. In places the fighting is furious and, in the endeavor to protect both the Mansion House and the Council House from further attack, two of the protesters die savagely at the hands of the soldiers.

Unaware that help was on its way, Sir Charles had fled to a small room at the very top of the building. With no idea of what to do next, but in fear of his life, he opens a narrow lattice window and squeezes himself out. He finds he's on a ledge, high above the square, no more than a foot in width. As he looks down, nausea overwhelms him and he fights back the desire to vomit. It's sheer drop with nothing to break his fall, should he do so. There, fifty feet beneath him is the angry mob, baying noisily for his blood. Fortunately not one of them bothers to look up in his direction. With heart in his mouth he slowly shuffles his feet, back to the wall, until he reaches the end of the building. Here, to his immense relief he discovers that he is able to step onto the flat roof of the adjoining property.

319

Finding it's now possible to move from one building to the next across the flat roofs, he gingerly navigates from one to another. He has no idea where he is, he simply wants to find a way to escape this dreadful situation. Finally he discovers an unlocked door in a small projecting brick canopy. Descending several flights of stairs he finds himself in the hayloft of empty stables, where at last he's able to hide and regain some composure.

It's a full ten minutes before he's truly satisfied that he's in no immediate danger. A vertical wooden ladder leads down to the loose boxes. There he ransacks the cupboards, desperate to find anything that might make his escape easier. In one, by an unbelievable stroke of luck, he finds a postilion's uniform which might just fit him.

Without a second's hesitation, Wetherell exchanges this for his own clothes, which he rolls up and hides beneath the straw. He's then able to emerge into the street without being recognised. To forestall any suspicion he mingles briefly with the crowd before slouching away at a leisurely pace. Every fibre in his being tells him to run, but he knows he must quell his fear and adopt a pedestrian amble in the direction of College Green.

The Recorder still has many friends he can call upon in Bristol and they don't let him down. By a little after midnight he has been safely conveyed to Newport. At this point the Mansion House cellars have been almost completely emptied. The pot boy has somehow escaped in the confusion. The liberated alcohol has been freely distributed to refresh the mob, eager for more action on the following day. Although few would credit it now, before twenty four more hours have passed, almost all of the buildings in this battle-scarred square will have been completely destroyed by fire.

Chapter 32

An hour passes before Maynard is ready to move the Celeste on towards the floating harbour. Single handed, the short journey turns out to be more tedious and take longer than he expected. The prolonged break, occasioned by Locke's decision to depart, had given Hermes the impression that his day's work was over. So when Maynard chides him, from his position at the tiller, Hermes will walk for a while, then dawdle again and search out a clump of interesting grass to pull at. Much exertion, enticement and goading has to be put to the cause of keeping him moving forward at a steady pace. In the end it's early evening before the vessel finally arrives in port.

The quayside is teeming with people, far more than Maynard has ever previously seen here at dusk. He can see they're all animated, gathered into small groups, talking eagerly and exchanging news with one another. There's a mood of tension and excitement hanging, like a cloud, in the air. He ties up alongside the quay wall and unhitches Hermes to get him safely stabled for the night. Before he's a chance to move away the two friendly customs men, who have visited him many times before, appear beside the boat.

'Good evening sir, I assume this is another shipment of stone for the bridge?' one of the men enquires.

'Yes, indeed' replies Maynard, 'I've committed to get it there early tomorrow morning.'

'I hope you're prepared for disappointment sir. You'll be extremely lucky if you succeed' comes the response, 'There's been dreadful rioting in the centre of the city today. It has yet to abate and the authorities are fearful it will continue tomorrow. The port is open to traffic entering and leaving at the moment, but my conjecture is that it will be closed by dawn. Now sir, if we might have your cooperation, we have new orders to search every vessel very closely, regardless of its destination. I know you are only going to the site of the new bridge, but we shall nevertheless now have to make a thorough inspection of your barge and every part of its cargo.'

With this explanation the senior man leaps aboard, followed by his companion. Maynard has now been through the docks on several occasions and these inspections have previously consisted of no more than a glance at the cargo, which is clearly comprised of stone blocks and nothing more. On this occasion the efforts of the two men are far more industrious. They look in every corner, under and between the stacks of stone, lest there should be any place of concealment. They then turn their attention to the covered area built into the prow.

'Open these doors for us if you please?' they instruct Maynard and, with a good grace, he obliges. The men rifle through the contents of the small space within, determined to carry out a thorough inspection. Finding nothing of interest they turn to the only other interesting item on the barge.

'What do you carry in this crate?' the senior of the two enquires, 'I've often wondered. It seems exceptionally well secured.'

'Intentionally so, I believe. It contains the delicate measuring and levelling instruments they use to ensure the sides of the abutment are correctly aligned' replies Maynard, 'They're valuable items and in consequence they must be carefully protected, especially when loaded alongside heavy stones such as these.'

'Well sir, I'm afraid I must ask you to open this crate for us also' replies the man, 'The top appears to be screwed on. I imagine you have some tools you can use to open it, so we can have a look inside?'

Maynard produces the same screwdriver he used just a couple of hours earlier and removes the lid once again. He lifts it away for the men, who proceeded to remove and examine its contents. True to Maynard's reply, they discover it contains simply the measuring instruments he had spoken about and nothing more.

'Well, I've never seen devices like this before sir, but I don't think any of them would interest my superiors', he pronounces, 'Now I just need full details of yourself and your journey for my records sir. I seem to recall that you're Mr Maynard. Am I correct?'

'That's my name yes. Thomas Maynard, a master mason from Swinton.' As requested, Thomas provides information to the men about his intended onward voyage. Seemingly satisfied, they eventually gather up their effects ready to move onto inspect another vessel, now drawn up aft of the Celeste.

'Many thanks for your forbearance Mr Maynard. These new instructions have caused us a lot more work. Quite a few seafarers kick up a fuss when we have to carry them through. It's a pleasant change when people such as yourself cooperate in such a friendly manner.'

'I'm more than happy to assist you' replies Maynard, 'But you could tell me a bit more about these riots. What in the devil's name has been happening in the city today? How could anything happening there be serious enough to mean the harbour must be closed?'

'There's been the most calamitous rioting since noon Mr Maynard, mostly in Queen Square. The mob's main target was seemingly the Mansion House. By all accounts they were trying to confront Recorder Wetherell. A group of the more cunning trouble makers have been here, at the docks, attempting to steal cargo and tools from the boats to attack the constables and soldiers. Some of the vessels have now been anchored away from the quayside to make access more difficult. We shall follow orders, but our expectation is that the harbour will be closed up, battened down and guarded tonight by a force of constables, whilst others in the city continue their attempts to quell the riots.'

'That's truly astounding' exclaims Maynard, 'Has there been any trouble yet around Hotwells?'

'Not as far as we've been told', replies the senior officer, 'But then there's nothing in that area to attract the mob, nothing I know of that they might want to attack. Why, have you got business there yourself?'

'No, but up to now I had intended to spend tonight aboard my barge. From what you say, I might reconsider. For my own safety and comfort I think I'll incur the expense of a room at a tavern. Tomorrow, if the lock gates are opened, I'll be bound for the gorge, so I might well move the barge so that it's ready to depart, then rest myself at a convenient hostelry, where it will be quiet and peaceful.'

'Sounds like a capital idea to me Mr Maynard. Now we must get on. There's been a sizeable increase in traffic and we've been ordered to inspect every vessel before nightfall.'

True to his word, Maynard moves the Celeste further down the quay and then leads Hermes off to the stable, where he pays for a stall together with hay and water. He removes the harness, covers Hermes with a blanket and leaves him in the care of the stable lad who he's encountered there before. It's a comfort to know the horse will be well looked after. It's a long walk back to the boat to collect his possessions and a longer walk still to Hotwells. Then he has to scour the streets for an inn that looks tolerable with a room he can afford. He tries a number before coming to the Mangrove tavern, which has a pleasant bar and can provide both food and accommodation. The room the landlord shows him is cramped, but in truth he has little need for space.

Maynard spends the best part of that evening in the bar. A fire is blazing in the grate, not far from the table he'd taken when he ordered his meal. He congratulates himself on the decision to stay here, even though it will involve an expense he'd not intended to incur. The boat will be really cold on an October night and the air outside is already damp. He's ruminating on the strange circumstances that have brought him here this Saturday evening, when a stranger, a much older man sat at an adjacent table, bids him a greeting in a cheery manner.

'Good evening to you sir' Maynard replies, 'May I enquire whom I'm addressing?'

'My name's Robin Burges my friend, a long-time resident of Hotwells. But I live alone and often come down to here on Saturdays for my evening meal. I thought, as we both seem to be without company, that you might welcome some small talk.'

'Why indeed Mr Burges, I'm delighted to make your acquaintance. I'm Thomas Maynard. I have a small masonry business down at Swinton, near Bath. I'm often in Bristol, but I've been truly amazed by the events that I've heard about here today. It's mainly due to the prospect of trouble at the docks that I've decided to stay at this inn. Have you come across any of this commotion yourself?'

'Why yes Thomas, if I may call you that. I work in an office in the heart of the city. Coming home today was a decidedly frightening experience for me. It seems that ordinary folk, who would otherwise go about their business peaceably, have suddenly become completely lawless and run wild. I was forced to take to narrow streets to avoid the throng.'

'I understand the protest is all on account of the House of Lords rejecting the Reform Bill?'

325

'That is what has been publicly pronounced as the cause Mr Maynard. That's what the newspapers have been stirring up for days now. And they say there have been protests of a similar nature in other parts of the country. But what I've seen today was truly extreme violence, not just a protest that has got out of hand. It was a riot. I am sure there must be more behind it than just frustration about the Bill.'

'I'm not quite sure I understand your meaning, Mr Burges?'

'Why sir, the mob are far more incensed than any vote taken in London should warrant. For most of them, the proposals contained within the Bill that's been rejected are of little significance. Their circumstances will not be changed, whether its provisions are implemented or not. However for some reason they're sufficiently riled up to loot, to destroy and to set buildings on fire. Why some have even become bold enough to injure and kill. I believe the majority have been put up to this by agitators who may have a more questionable motive altogether.'

'And what motive might that be Mr Burges?'

'I fear it may be to incite a more general insurrection against the government. There are people in this city who would happily see life as we know it turned upside down, if it helps them gain their ends. In short I think they aim to provoke a revolution, just as the French Revolution came about, some thirty years ago.'

'Well, that's a plausible theory Mr Burges, and I can only fervently hope you're mistaken. I've heard there's long been trouble festering amongst hands in the manufactories and men working on the land. And now its apparently come to a head. But surely most of our citizens are wiser than that? Our nation wouldn't really tolerate a revolution of the sort you're suggesting, would it?'

'Sadly there we'll have to differ Thomas. From what I saw today, standing well back from the trouble but able to observe it all, I'm convinced a mob like that, once roused, can be encouraged to do almost anything. But let's not argue, particularly as we've only just met. We should move onto other less contentious topics. Tell me what brings you to Bristol tonight?'

Believing that he can trust this man Maynard proceeds to relate his part in the building of the great suspension bridge and describes the journeys he's undertaken with the Celeste. His companion shows a great interest in his story and listens intently. When Maynard's tale has been told, he is able to give the mason some highly pertinent information.

'Strangely enough my position is with one of the private companies that has invested in your suspension bridge' he says, 'and I imagine therefore that telling you this would be much frowned upon by my employers. But I can see you are an honest man and I'd feel very guilty were you to suffer through too much candour on my part. So, here is something of which you should be aware. The sheer magnitude of these riots has completely shaken confidence in the commercial institutions of Bristol today. There were questions being asked this afternoon, by senior people at my office, about the security of their investment should the authorities fail to contain this trouble quickly. When I left the centre of Bristol this evening, there were no signs of any such containment. I know my employers. They are not individuals who are prepared to run great risks. I would have some serious doubts myself about the continuation of this project unless all is peaceful in the morning.'

Maynard's deeply shocked at receiving this confidence. For months he has been looking out for pitfalls that might threaten his success, but never conceived of anything like this. He says nothing in reply, although there is a great deal that he might have said and asked. A sudden end to this work would be disastrous for his business and he'd need an alternative plan

327

immediately. He can't be certain how well informed this casual acquaintance may be, so what has been divulged merely serves to worry Maynard since he cannot qualify its credulity. Nevertheless, Burges' conjecture makes a lot of sense in light of the events that are unfolding. Maynard has no need, and no wish, to appear discourteous and so he remains at Burges' table for some long time discussing topics of lesser consequence. But he retires to bed sober and with time in hand to think through the various courses that now may be open to him.

What, in God's name is he doing here anyway, marooned in the lodging room of a Bristol tavern on Saturday night? Why, tomorrow he would normally be taking Mary Ann and Emily to church. After that he'd be enjoying the rest of the day at leisure. Instead he'll now be wrestling single-handedly with the barge and meanwhile worrying himself to a thread that his perseverance is to no purpose. How the devil has he come to this? Who is responsible for this unwanted complication in his life?

Locke. Locke is at the root of this. All of it. The more he thinks it through, the more certain he becomes. It was Locke who had insisted their trip was made today and the reasons he gave seem pretty thin. It was Locke who abandoned him before they reached the floating harbour. Again, the grounds he gave for doing so don't bear up to any close inspection. Why then?

Because the man knows only too well about the contents of the instruments case, of that he is convinced. So, in some way, he surely must have a hand in them being placed there. He's always suspected Locke of holding a certain disregard for the law but, for God's sakes, the man is surely never a highway robber. So, by what strange circumstances has he come by the booty from that murderous attack? And why, if indeed he's done so, and if he is an honest man at heart, has he not handed it over to the authorities? How is it, flying in the face of everything that Maynard believes about him, is he now trying to smuggle it through the port?

Maynard casts his mind back for any events that have seemed unnatural or unusual during his friendship with Locke. On reflection there are several. The first meeting with Hartnoll and the cloak of secrecy over the entire affair. That seemed odd at the time. Now, in hindsight, it seems deeply suspicious. That curious insistence on having sole access to the shed at the stone-yard. The regular and arguably unnecessary transportation of the crate. The strange meeting he glimpsed through the tents at Lansdown fair. The agitation that Locke experienced, but tried hard not to show, as they travelled along the river today hearing news of the hunt that was in progress.

An answer to all these odd events starts to assemble itself in the mason's mind. He eventually drifts into sleep having finally come to an important decision.

Chapter 33

Maynard strides along the footpath in the gorge. The site of the abutment finally comes into view. As far as he can tell it's deserted. It's just shy of ten o'clock on Sunday morning and not a sound can be heard, certainly nobody is working here. The arrangement with Locke had been that he should arrive in the Celeste around about now. Well, there would be nobody on hand to unload it for him as they'd arranged. So, Locke had lied through his teeth. He's not surprised. Despite all that, if the mason's correct about Locke's interest in the crate's contents, he's bound to be here somewhere, anxious to get his hands on it.

A furtive look around the stacks of materials shows there's no one at the level of the landing stage. But that doesn't mean the upper terrace, where all the building work is currently in progress, is also unoccupied. He hopes to have the element of surprise, but it's impossible to be confident. It's possible he's already been spotted by unseen eyes.

Moving as quietly as he's able, he slides his body along the cleaved face of the gorge in order to reach the steps. This should keep him out of the view of anyone above, unless they're directly above him, on the very edge of the terrace.

He takes the steps slowly to reach the shelf, hewn from the rock. Still no sign of life. Perhaps the man's not here after all. Half completed walls, swathed in wooden scaffolding rise above him. But there are large gaps between the planking and it's obvious the platforms are empty. The saw horses, barrels and stacks of timber aren't sufficient to conceal Maynard's partner. Only the wooden hut, erected to store the tools and drawings, remains. The mason approaches with care; the hasp is hanging free.

With a shove from his boot he thrusts the door open and steps inside. The construction is windowless and the change from bright sunlight to deep gloom renders him sightless for a second or two. And then, in the corner, sitting on an upturned tea-chest and slumped over the rough tabletop, he spies Locke. A half empty gin bottle in his hand. The disturbance made by his entrance is enough to stir the man.

'Ah, Thomas', says the builder, his words a little slurred from drink, 'Thank the Lord you've arrived. I feared the port would be closed and our cargo stuck there for days. I'd intended to watch out for you on the river, but I had other problems to worry over.'

'Is that so? And where, my friend, are the fellows you promised me would be here to unload the barge?'

'Somewhere in the city, as far as I can make out', the builder answers, 'The majority of them seem to have been talked into joining the riots that started yesterday. The rest are probably too frit to turn out. From the reports I've heard, I'd be surprised if they're not all blind drunk by now.'

'You seem to have been taking that course yourself, Elijah!'

'Oh this? No. Just a shot of Dutch courage Thomas. The consequence of all this has weighed heavily. I felt I needed a drink. But never mind. You're here now and that's all that matters. We can't unload the stone by ourselves, but we can at least make a start with the other bits and pieces.'

'What other bits and pieces?'

'Why, the crate for example. We can at least carry that up here to the hut so that it's safely locked away.'

'It's not there, Elijah. The barge is not there. It's confined, as you feared, in the port. Nothing is allowed in, nothing's allowed out. It will all be stuck there until this trouble has run its course.'

The blood drains from the builder's face. He's as white as a sheet. For a moment he can think of nothing to say as he wills his fuddled brain to think of some plan.

'Well, let's both walk back there together. We can ..... '

'And what could we do, partner? Guards have been placed everywhere to protect it from incursion. There's nothing on that boat that we could remove from the port. We'd be apprehended immediately.'

'But Thomas, you must think of something. There must be a way.'

'So what is it you're after Elijah? What's aboard my barge that's so important we should walk back to find it? As far as I know, all that's there is a few tons of best Conham Old Red sandstone.'

The builder's eyes narrow. Despite the effects of the gin he can sense that Maynard's cleverly taunting him, that his secret is not a secret any longer.

'Damn you Thomas! You know something don't you! You know there's more aboard that boat than just a heap of stones.'

'Yes I do my friend. And oddly, all because of you. If you'd not deserted me yesterday, I'd never have had the opportunity to look inside your precious instrument crate. Indeed, I don't think I'd have had any reason to. Even less connect its concealed contents with you. It was only my sensing your apparent nervousness about the manhunt that led me to investigate.'

'So, mason, what have you discovered? What is it you think you know?'

'I know the haul from that robbery in Swinton was stowed in a secret compartment within the crate. I found the little sheepskin bag you'd boxed in. I figured the articles must have come into your possession, though God knows how. And I'm sure you were using my barge as a way of getting your loot past the customs men. What really goads me is how long you have been taking me for a dupe?'

His partner slumps back over the table top and groans.

'Damn, Thomas. It's true. I've shamelessly abused your trust. I had no choice, but any apology would just rub salt into the wound. I know you too well. You would never forgive me in any event. And I know your honesty means I'm as good as done for. But if you've moved the valuables, where are they now? Are they still on the barge? Are they likely to be discovered?'

'Calm yourself man. They're out of harms' way.'

'Where? Where? I have to lay hands on them, it's a matter of my life.'

'It's not that easy, they're within the port as you guessed.'

The builder's frayed nerves can take no more. This damned mason seems to be bringing him hope and then dashing it away in an instant. He seizes his partner by the collars and shakes him till his head's striking the planking of the hut. There are tears in his eyes.

'For God's sake man, stop playing with me. That jewelry isn't mine. I had nothing to do with the robbery. But I have promised to get it to a schooner bound for France and if it gets discovered first I might just as well cut my own throat. The man I'm doing it for hasn't a merciful bone in his body.'

He reaches behind to his belt and pulls an ugly knife which he holds to Maynard's throat.

'It pains me to threaten you Thomas, but I really haven't a choice. I need you to tell me where the goods are now. If you won't I'm as good as dead and you may as well join me.'

Maynard is trembling from head to foot. The knife is pressing against his Adam's apple and Locke's gin-soaked breath is hot in his face. His mouth is dry as parchment but he gets out the words he's known since yesterday that he'd need to utter.

'Don't be a fool Locke. If you murder me you'll never see that little bag again and you know it. And don't take me for a fool either. I despise your complicity in this crime, but equally I need to look after myself. Without you the work on this bridge will cease and that I cannot afford. It will probably will do so anyway tomorrow, despite us both. In which case I'll need funds. So, for all that it may stick in my crop, I need you and now you need me. Put down the knife and let me go. There's just a chance we might both come out of this with something.'

With a resigned grunt the builder pushes Maynard down onto the tea chest he'd been occupying himself, standing between the mason and freedom. He sheaths his weapon and demands an explanation of what's to be done.

'Why in God's name are they in the port anyway?', he implores, 'That was a bloody daft thing to do when you must have known the danger involved.'

'Because the notion they might be there only came to me when I was tying the boat up', replies Maynard, 'The sight of that customs shed just across the quay crystallized the whole thing in my mind. I was petrified, in case my guess was correct. It was then I broke into your precious instrument crate and all became clear.'

'It put me into a panic. My first thought was to conceal the find so that the customs men wouldn't discover them. Other than throwing them overboard, there seemed to be nowhere. Then I looked at Hermes. His nosebag. It came to me in an instant and I thrust your package in, along with his oats.'

'So that's where they are now?', asks Locke hollowly, 'Very likely being eaten by some old nag?'

'They would be if a better idea hadn't struck me as I walked the horse to the stables', retorts Maynard. Naturally I had to go past the customs shed and it was locked. The men were busy, every one on inspection duty around the place. I saw the roof tiles sloping down immediately above a heavy oak lintel. They've constructed that building to withstand pretty much anything. I looked about me and was certain I was unobserved. So I slipped the package from the nosebag, eased up one of the tiles and slid your precious bag underneath, on top of that lintel. With the tile back in place no-one will ever know it's there.'

'For God's sakes man. So, the thing that's vital to my very life is now within arms' reach of a dozen customs men? Is that it?'

'Yes. That's exactly it, Locke.'

'Well you must be stupid Maynard. What possessed you to put it there, of all places?'

'The stable lad's no fool', replies the mason, 'If I'd left it in the nosebag you could count on him finding it before daybreak. And there was no certainty I'd get a chance to stash it somewhere else in the stables. However idiotic it appears to you, it's probably in the safest place I was likely to find. Why the customs men did come aboard the moment I returned, whence they turned the Celeste, and indeed that crate, inside out.'

'And think about it man. Let's say those customs men are scouring the port high and low at this moment. The very last place they'll look is within their own office. Our only challenge is that we can't leave it there long. At some point they almost certainly will discover its presence, if only by accident.'

'Oh, Maynard, accept my apologies. Clearly you're a man of genius', responds Locke in a heavily sarcastic tone, 'Now, with their door doubtless locked tight and the whole port under close guard, how the devil d'you suggest we actually get my valuables back?' demands Locke.

'Well, there's no way we'll manage it alone. We'd need a deal of assistance.' replies Maynard, 'However, I reckon the criminals you've been mixing with must be more than up to the job. Our best chance will be tonight. During the hours of darkness there are few men abroad within the harbor compound. But it's not completely deserted, so we can't rule out encountering resistance. And unless we're very lucky, at some point we shall almost certainly be discovered. The key is for us is stealth. To lay hands on those valuables before we're discovered and then fight our way out if necessary. We need strong fellows who know how to handle themselves, but fellows capable of making a noiseless entry into the port. Now tell me Locke, d'you think you could find such a band of men I in the next couple of hours?'

The audacity of Maynard's suggestion takes Locke by surprise. It sounds crazy, he instinctively wants no part of it. But it quickly comes home to him that there is no better plan. His mind races to calculate how quickly he can ride to Kilbridge Lane and rustle up Wakelin along with some of his associates. He's no doubt it's possible to get there and back by nightfall. So the builder replies with a nod and a grunt of assent.

'Excellent. The harbour is surrounded on land by stone walls. The only entry open during nightfall is the Cumberland Road Gate, which is strongly guarded. However, I reckon we can slip in on the water, by way of the Feeder canal. There's no guard there; harbor master expects to be aware of vessels coming and going, since they're easily seen. I'm convinced we can enter unobserved in a small rowing boat, if we are stealthy about it.'

'But what then Maynard? If the shed door is locked, it'll take us time to break in. And we're bound to make a deal of noise, even if we're not seen. For a certainty we'll be discovered before we find the bag.'

'Remember Elijah that I know exactly where that bag is' replies Maynard, 'It will be quite unnecessary to break down the door. We simply remove the roof tiles at precisely the place where the bag is resting. It should take only a second or so and, if skillfully done, we'll not disturb the peace. With a bit of luck, and some vigilant look-outs, I reckon we can pull this off without anyone spotting us.'

'Let's assume we get that far' replies Locke, 'How do we then escape from the port with our booty?'

'That's where the need for some strong-arms to help us becomes essential. My plan is to get the bag away in the same rowing boat we'll use to get in. As long as that makes it beyond the harbour walls, the bag's as good as ours. We'll have horses on the bank, ready to fly as soon as the boat heaves to. But I just don't believe we won't have raised a hue and cry by that time.'

'It would take too long to get our men safely and silently down ladders into a rocking rowing boat. No, they'll just have to dive in and swim and that will kick up a commotion. Someone will try to stop us, pursue in other boats or the like. We need as many bruisers as you can muster, men who are not afraid to use violence, to keep them off our tail. And some muskets. Once they've dealt with any pursuers, they can run the short distance to the horses and escape by the same route we came.'

'But what if we're discovered inside port? A hue and cry is sure to be raised. The constables and watchmen outside could easily reach our horses before we do ourselves', says Locke.

'You forget Elijah. The destruction being wrought all over Bristol yesterday is still going on. More rioting is probably afoot as we stand here talking. It won't have died out by tonight if I'm any judge. Most of the constables will be in the city attempting to keep the peace. Those on guard at the gates won't be eager to leave their posts. They'll have more fear for their own lives than to risk a confrontation away from the safety of the port.'

'That's why tonight is our only chance to succeed in this. So we must grasp it Elijah, grasp it or kiss goodbye to a fortune. Time for you to do your bit, recruiting the help we need. But before you do, I think you owe me an explanation. God knows man, I could be in jail now if I'd not discovered your little surprise before the authorities came across it, which they surely would have done.'

'How the devil did you come to be involved in all this? I've not forgotten that that jewelry is linked to a capital crime. So we both risk a death sentence death if we're captured. I need to be sure of you now, and that your friends are well able to protect me from such a fate.'

'Well, it looks like we're in this together now Thomas, so I'll explain. But briefly. Cast your mind back to our first meeting with Hartnoll. I could tell then, by your expression, that you sensed something was awry. Remember, we'd worked together then for many months now; I could read your face quite well. You were puzzled by how we'd suddenly got involved in the suspension bridge project, in such as unusual manner.'

'Your instincts weren't letting you down Thomas. You were right to be suspicious. I'd told you that Hartnoll was just an acquaintance of mine from the trade. But I lied. My wife and his are sisters. Through their relationship he and I became firm friends. We soon found his position and influence could be turned to our mutual advantage.'

'I knew it', exclaims Maynard, 'I sensed from the very first conversation we had that there was something not right about the whole enterprise. But I could never put my finger on what that was. It certainly never passed through my mind that the two of you were in cahoots.'

'Thomas, there was no reason you should know. Far better that remained my secret. Why, you were doing very well out of the arrangement, and so was I. And it turned into an almost legitimate contract in the end. No risk or danger for either of us. The only risk, which was almost nonexistent, was that some other party might suspect what Hartnoll and I were up to.'

'Well, that certainly explains my first impression', says Maynard, 'But it doesn't explain how you've come to be mixed up with murderers and thieves.'

'And nor would I have been, left to my own devices', Locke retorts, 'You can't think it's my wish to be in this mess my friend, let alone to have dragged you into it. But I ended up with no choice but to go along. Otherwise I'd have brought penury and disgrace down on us both.'

'Things were going remarkably well. Our little deception had paid off handsomely. Hartnoll and I were very careful about being seen together. We visited one another's homes as infrequently as we could. But one evening I had to go and see him. He'd drafted our proper contracts and asked me to look through them first. He'd make a mistake with the date we started – something that might have raised eyebrows had the document been presented.'

So, I had to reach him quickly, to prevent him taking the document to his superiors. On the walk back home I sensed that I was being followed. God knows how, I never saw anyone on that occasion. Old army training dies hard I suppose. I just had this feeling.'

'Well, it happened again, on a number of occasions. By around the fourth time I was certain. There's a barber shop on the road I was taking, I've known the old chap who owns it for years. So I ducked inside and out through the back faster than you could say knife. Down the corner of the terrace and there he was, standing beneath the pole, as large as life and twice as ugly.'

'Who?', demands Maynard, 'Who in God's name are you talking about?'

'An old dog called Wakelin. A man I served with in Gibraltar. He'd already messed up my life there. Persuaded me to join his little scheme selling army provisions, bricks and the like, to the locals. It worked for a bit and we made a precious shilling or two. But our little enterprise was discovered. He was given a prison term and cashiered. I was suspected, but they couldn't find any evidence to prove my involvement. Nevertheless they found an excuse to cashier me and that's how I came back to England eventually, to start my own business.'

'Of course Wakelin always bore me a grudge. Probably because I hadn't stepped forwards to take the blame alongside him. Hugo bloody Wakelin. I thought I'd never see the man again.'

'I suppose he threatened to expose you unless you did something for him?' asks Maynard.

'Perhaps that was his original intention' replies Locke, 'But he is very thorough. Not only had he followed me for some time, he'd also been following my wife. He'd met her when we were army colleagues. It just happened he was on her trail when she met up with her sister, who of course lives at Hartnoll's grand house. Well, he'd already seen me at the same place myself. I guess it can't have taken him long to start putting two and two together. Doubtless he did a lot more digging after which it appears he worked out the whole thing. And devised a scheme to profit from his knowledge. He is a rogue for sure, one of the very worst I've rubbed shoulders with, but I can't deny he's a cunning and resourceful fellow.'

340

'When did he approach you?' asks Maynard, 'What was he asking for?'

'Sometime in March. When he was good and ready. He knocked at my door late one night. When I saw him stood there, on my own threshold, I felt sick to the pit of my guts. It takes a lot to make me afraid Thomas. I sent my wife to bed and asked him inside. He laid out for me the conspiracy I shared with Hartnoll. His guesswork had been excellent. He expected my cooperation. If I denied him, or failed to deliver the assistance he demanded, he would expose us. He also threatened to harm my wife and Hartnoll's wife, if ever we should cross him. If I found a way to help, I'd get half his cut.'

'What was it that this rogue asked of you?'

'You'll not know it, but you'll have heard of this Hugo Wakelin before. He's more often known as the 'Captain' and he's the leader of your notorious Kilbridge Lane gang. They hide up somewhere in your neck of the woods. He masterminds their robberies, arranges to fence the ill-gotten gains picked up during their exploits and generally keeps them in order.'

He simply told me he'd have a number of packages that must be put on a schooner leaving Bristol each month, bound for France. My end of the bargain was simply to get them to our building site at the bridge.'

'But why involve me and my barge in all this?' asked Thomas, 'Why risk carrying his contraband through the harbour?'

'Wakelin realized that the crimes he had in mind would raise a hue and cry. The loot would have to be exported; any sane body would realize that. So all craft leaving the harbour would be inspected before they departed, but close inspection would only fall on those with foreign destinations. An old tub full of stones was hardly likely to register with the authorities. Who, for heaven's sake would trouble to go smuggling in a horse-drawn canal boat?'

'He knew though that the gorge was likely to be watched from time to time. The possibility of transferring goods from a small craft to a seagoing vessel is probably something the authorities are on the lookout for. But our landing stage, down below us here; that's a different matter. There's continual activity going on, men are always working along it, or close by. We have no access from the top of the gorge, so no one would believe that anything of value could be here to be passed over. All we had to do was ensure the schooner passed close enough by the stage and sling the contraband aboard. And that's the way it left the country, completely undetected.'

'So, my regular deliveries of stone were a godsend?'

'Well that's true. But something that was an even bigger godsend was the measuring equipment. If a close inspection of the barge had been made, it would almost certainly defray any suspicion. I even think you might have got away with it yesterday Thomas. Face it man, nobody knows what to expect to find in there. It's all very scientific stuff – nothing the ordinary man can figure out for himself. They'd probably have thought the bag contained spare lenses or the like and never bothered to open it.'

'And was your brother-in-law aware of all this?'

'Of course. I had to let Hartnoll know what had happened. He and his wife are in as much danger as me. He too saw no alternative but to comply with Wakelin's demands. Strangely it was Hartnoll who first came up with the idea of using your deliveries as our cover. Kilbridge Lane is not that far from Swinton, so it was easy for Wakelin and his gang to secrete anything that needed to be transported inside the crate in your shed. We simply had another key made and gave it to him. He could visit your yard in the middle of the night and safely stow his booty. No-one else had to be involved. Your property is so remote, there was almost no chance of discovery. The transport would then take place and only yourself and your colleagues had any part in it. Since you knew nothing of the contraband in your care, you'd all behave as innocent as lambs. I came along on that first trip just to ensure there was nothing we had left to chance. To be sure, had the goods been discovered, it would have been you, and you alone, who would have taken the blame. But you would have no explanation for its presence. Nothing could lead back to Hartnoll and myself. The treachery is inexcusable certainly, but it was also unavoidable.'

'Damn you Locke. A fine friend you've turned out to be. If I had any real sense I'd quit now and have no further truck with you. I'm only offering to help you now because I'm determined to share your split of the profit. I believe I'm going to need that money. There are some heavy bills outstanding to my account. I met a fellow from one of the private investment companies at the inn last night. He was quite certain they'd be pulling out. I think our goose is cooked.'

'Sadly I've heard the same story from other sources Thomas. You're right, it will give us both a real headache. But now, there's not a moment more to lose. If I'm to get help, I must be away. Can I trust you to find a rowing boat and have it waiting for us with muffled oars? There is a footbridge on the Feeder at Saint Philips not far from where I left you. Be ready for us there at ten o'clock tonight. Trust me. I shall arrive with all the assistance we need.'

With this Locke leaves Maynard to fulfill his side of the bargain.

Chapter 34

Long before Maynard sets out from his room at the Mangrove on Sunday morning, Daniel Latham has been rudely awakened. Emerging all too soon from a deep reviving sleep he's initially confused regards his whereabouts. Yet again his head is fuddled by drink, but not to the same extent as after the session at the inn with his rowdy disciples.

The events of yesterday begin to come together in his mind. He had met with his associates early, at the Miners Arms; they had then walked by a circuitous route, gathering others as they went, and proceeded to Totterdown where they knew Wetherell's coach would enter the city.

With Latham responsible for the organisation and urging-on, his ever swelling group followed the coach into Bristol, heckling Wetherell all the way. They met up with others whom he didn't know, at Totterdown and at many other points along the route. All seemed equally intent on expressing outrage as they were themselves. Latham considered that he'd made a good job of organising his party, but unknown to him, others had been agitating across the city in a similar manner.

Violence had ensued at the Guildhall and the Mansion House. This was regrettable. Not something that Latham had planned, but wasn't it the only way to make their feelings plain to Wetherell? Some of the blows that his men had struck were admittedly vicious. But they were only reacting to the violence shown by the special constables who showed no mercy when wielding their own bludgeons. The day had passed, the intensity of the attacks had grown. More and more forays were made on the Mansion House and the Council House, until eventually the Dragoons arrived to disperse them. He had achieved everything he hoped to achieve and for him the protest was over. By that time it was very late and Latham gratefully accepted an offer from one of his protesters, Davy Cooke, to sleep on the floor of his lodgings at this run-down terrace in St Philips.

Indeed it's Davy Cooke's own foot now stirring him from his slumbers.

'Rouse yourself Daniel, it's dawn. We must get some food inside us and then find the others. There's unfinished work to attend to.'

'What do you mean Davy? We did what was necessary yesterday, and very thoroughly in my opinion. Wetherell had certainly quit the Mansion House by midnight. Why I'd be willing to wager we've run him out of Bristol entirely.'

'Were you drunk or deaf when the party broke up last night Daniel? Everybody agreed we should gather again at Queen Square as soon as it was light. There's a lot more to do before we can be sure the message is well and truly delivered.'

'So, what else d'you think we should attempt, now that Wetherell's gone?' asks Latham

'Come, come now young Daniel, you're our leader, you've got all the clever ideas. That's a decision for you. Whatever it is, it must be in plain view and shocking, outrageous. We've got to send an unmistakeable message to the bastards in power. God man, there must be a thousand opportunities for us to do that.'

Arriving eventually at the appointed corner of Queen Square, Latham and Cooke find everybody else in the same frame of mind. The Dragoons, so numerous yesterday, are nowhere to be seen. Word has it there are just a handful of officials still in residence, including the mayor and the sheriff. Sturdy barricades have been erected in front of the Mansion House, to protect it from further incursion. Smashed and empty bottles litter the square and the streets, alongside the wreckage of furnishings hurled out of the buildings.

Most of Latham's new found friends are baying for action. He senses he'll lose them unless he shows some direction. So boldly he attempts to re-assert his authority.

'Men', he starts, raising his voice as much as he can without aggravating that dull pain in his head, 'We all did a fine job yesterday. They say that Wetherell has fled. I think it's time now to demand an audience with the mayor. I'm sure I just saw him inside the building.'

'Bollocks' a voice pipes up from behind him, 'Let's break down the doors, there might still be things worth taking. Let's get inside.'

'Yes, break in, break in!', the cry is enthusiastically picked up by others and together they rush forwards, leaving Latham looking on, powerless.

With so many hands bent to the task, the flimsy barriers are easily torn down by Latham's associates. Immediately, a repeat of the previous day's events ensues. The mob gain entry to the rooms on the lower floors and begin ransacking them methodically. Others rediscover the wine cellars and bring up everything that wasn't plundered on the previous day. Cases of wine are brought out into the square and bottles passed from hand to hand. It's not long before the whole mob has drunk itself insensible and incapable of any rational thought. Again the Dragoons arrive but prove ineffective at restoring any sort of order. Sheer numbers overwhelm them and no orders are given to fire their muskets. By half past ten they have retreated to their barracks, chased off by the jeering crowd.

In the square an innocent bill-sticker turns up, visibly shaking with fear of that the mob might take against him. Bravely following instructions he pastes up some hastily printed bills, in places they can be plainly seen by the crowd. They read

'Council-House, Oct 30ᵗʰ 1831. Sir Charles Wetherell left Bristol at 12 o'clock last night'

'The Riot Act has been read three times. All Persons found Tumultuously Assembling are guilty of Capital Felony. By order of the Mayor.'

By now the mob is so intoxicated that they treat these notices, along with the unfortunate bill-sticker, as a great amusement. Shrieking with derision, they take his kettle, empty its paste and jam it over his head. Up goes a hearty roar of laughter. Then they rip up the notices and scatter them across the square.

Following this incidental amusement, the business of the day starts in earnest. Surging drunkenly from Queen Square, urged on now by a ruffian Latham has never seen before, the mob quickly converges on the Bridewell. This is the city's central lock up with an entrance secured by large iron gates. Breaking into a nearby smithy the men seize hammers and crowbars and use these to tear the gates from their hinges, finally hurling them into the river. They threaten the keeper and he relinquishes the keys to his cells. The triumphant mob promptly liberates all the prisoners within. As a finale to their successful work they set the building well alight.

From this point on the rioters cannot be stopped, despite the dragoons once again being summoned and turning out in an attempt to quell the mayhem. Having rendered the Bridewell an inferno, the crowd move on to the New Gaol on the Cut, then to Gloucestershire County Prison at Lawford's Gate, the Bishop's Palace and finally the Toll House. At every stop they repeat their reign of terror and destruction, ransacking, looting and burning. By eight o'clock in the evening, the sky over the city is aglow with the light from the fires, still raging at a dozen or more public buildings.

And as if this excess was merely a rehearsal, or a prelude to the main event, the crowd returns yet again to Queen Square to finish off what they started the previous day. Again they enter the Mansion House and, after ensuring there's nothing more of value to be taken, they set a goodly fire in the kitchen. Within minutes the entire building is engulfed in flames. Fire either spreads to, or is started independently in most of the other buildings on the square. The Council House, the Customs House, the Excise offices and many more all fall to the mercy of the flames. The entire Square becomes an immense inferno, its light dwarfing everything that was seen earlier in the evening.

The destruction that Latham, and others of his persuasion, have instigated is now complete.

Latham stands rooted to the middle of the square. Less intoxicated than his friends he suddenly feels alone, numb and pricked by conscience. For today, in truth, he'd lost his leadership after the first ten minutes. After that he had to simply follow the mob. A lot of things they'd done sat very unhappily with him. But every time he'd tried to stop the destruction, he was shouted down, vilified or ignored.

Despite that, it was clearly his own enthusiasm, his energy and powers of persuasion that set the whole train in motion.

He looks upon what his well-intended work has led to with absolute horror.

Chapter 35

Maynard slides quietly onto the cross plank of a rowing boat tied up next to the lock keeper's cottage at Netham. Stealthily he slips the mooring rope from its ring and uses a single oar to push himself silently away from the building. The stolen boat drifts agonisingly slowly into the middle of the canal. It's half past nine of the evening, there's no moon to speak of and he's confident there's little chance his felony will have been observed.

Now, plying both oars with extreme care, to ensure he makes no splash on the water's surface, he propels the small craft towards the west. Ten minutes of strenuous effort bring him to the stone and wooden footbridge that crosses the canal. Here he ties up again, quite certain now that no eyes are upon him. Withdrawing both oars from the water, he wraps each in turn with sheets he's brought from Locke's shed. These he secures tightly with string, tied off in strong knots. The sheets will muffle the oars and give this craft an excellent chance of entering the floating harbour unheard and unobserved. Looking at the sky over Bristol, ablaze with the light from numerous fires, he imagines that precaution is probably unnecessary. If anyone is loitering on the quayside they'll probably be looking at the sky too, contemplating their fine city being swallowed in the conflagration.

A long and anxious wait follows for Maynard. The temperature has fallen sharply and he shivers inside the thin shirt on his back. His heavy coat would just get in the way; he consequently left it at the gorge.

Much depends on the next hour or so. If Locke brings the men that he expects, Maynard will be rubbing shoulders with a bunch of vicious killers. But he's certain the plan he so hastily conceived for tonight's escapade is the best possible. More so that it stands a reasonable chance of success. But, of its very nature, it means he'll be placed in danger from every side. Without doubt from the Kilbridge Lane gang. Probably from the authorities at the port and more than likely from the hangman himself. This is the most nerve racking half hour he's ever spent in his life. His mind is racing and he can't sit still. If, heaven forbid, Locke fails to show up with his murderous associates, all will be lost. That bag of valuables will never be retrieved and his own future will be in ruins.

His fears prove groundless. The retrieval of the loot's clearly more vital for Locke than it is for Maynard himself. The distant sound of hooves pounding on grass floats into his ears and, minutes later, six horsemen canter up, bringing their mounts to a halt by the bridge. The surrounding countryside is low and flat; Maynard can make out each brigand, their faces eerily lit by the glow from the fires in the city. To a man they're a villainous looking crew. Each of them has a pistol or flintlock pushed into his belt. Maynard immediately recognises the fellow bringing up the rear as scar-face, the Captain of the gang.

'You' says the Captain, in a low voice, but clearly directed at Maynard, 'Row that bloody boat further down river. We'll trot alongside until we see a suitable spot nearer the harbour to come aboard.'

The unusual group embarks upon its parallel procession, neither the horses nor the boat making any discernible sound. Slowly they progress until they're a hundred yards short of the harbour entrance, where securing rings start to appear on the tow-path. Halfway along this stretch is a small copse of trees under which their horses might easily be hidden.

The brigands dismount, crouching in a circle on their haunches so that Wakelin can quietly give them their orders. From his seat in the rowing boat, Maynard can just make out the plan unfolding.

'Pearce. You will stay here with the horses. Don't stray from this spot for any reason, on pain of death. Once we return, you'll assist the others to mount. Then and only then will you flee yourself. Don't let the animals make any sound and, if by any chance anyone should pass by, then deal with him. There's only one way to do that and I don't need to tell you how. Dead men tell no tales. Do you understand? You're to take no risks.'

'The rest of you will come in the boat with me. We'll take Locke and Locke's matey there also. It's going to be bloody crowded, so each of you must sit stock still. If any of you capsize that boat, I shall personally slit your throat. You – Maynard or whatever your damned name is – can you hear me? – you will put up your hand when we're near to the customs shed on the quayside. Fenton, it's your job to secure with the boat to the nearest ladder and stay with it. The rest of us will climb carefully, and quietly, onto the quayside. I'll be going first to make a reconnaissance before leading you lot across open ground to the building. Every one of you must be your own look-out. Be sure you cover that ground singly, one at a time. Locke will be bringing along the crow bar.'

'When we reach the door of the building Locke's mason-friend here will indicate the place where the tiles must be removed. Locke will then prise them off as quietly as he can. Rigby, you will take each one and lay it carefully on the ground.'

Once the bag is recovered, I'll be running to the boat to throw it to Fenton. Fenton, this is your most important task. You have to catch that bag. If it falls into the water you're a dead man, on my life. And then Fenton, you just row back to this point as if your life depends on it. The rest of us, we shall all run like buggery for the apron wall, dive into the canal and swim out to the tow-path.

We'll meet together here, as fast as we can, and pick up our horses from Pearce. Fenton will hand the bag to me. Then we all ride as fast as we can across the common and back to our

351

original meeting point. Is that all crystal clear? Does everybody understand?'

There's a muffled murmur of consent, then Wakelin's voice can be heard again.

'You. Mason. Get out of that boat. Get yourself over here.'

'This is the telling moment', thinks Maynard to himself, 'Do they trust me? Or is he suspicious? My God, these could be the last few minutes of my life. 'But realizing there's no possibility of argument, he complies.

'Locke, I need your help here. You assure me this man will help us, but I've never seen him before. Unfortunately it seems we need him. Mark my word, that doesn't mean I'm going to trust the fellow. Take this piece of rope. Bind his wrists tightly in front of him and gag him securely. We'll have to take him in the boat, but we'll release his bonds only so he can climb the ladder. But for the remainder, he's to be treated as a prisoner. Now, Maynard, you'll do exactly as I tell you. If you don't, I'll be testing out the keenness of this blade on your neck.'

With that Locke seizes Maynard's hands and secures his wrists with the length of rope. Two dirty handkerchiefs are thrust into his mouth and he's tightly gagged. Maynard struggles and fights, even though he'd not intended to; the taste of the gag is disgusting and he's convinced, for a moment, that he's truly suffocating. But they soon get him pacified and calm; two of the gang lift him bodily and sit him in the boat. The others climb aboard to join him. Every board of the little craft creaks in protest, it's grossly overloaded and in dire danger of capsizing. Two of the men take an oar each and row painstakingly slowly towards the gap in the harbour walls. Locke has one of his massive hands firmly around the rope tying Maynard's wrists.

Sitting low in the water and under the lee of the high quayside, Maynard can only guess when they're getting close to the customs shed. He espies the Minerva, moored up at the far side and recalls looking over at it the previous day. And there's the rusty iron ladder, attached to the wall and running down into the water. He pushes his hands against Locke's grip to indicate they've arrived. Locke understands and touches each rower on his shoulder. The boat slows comes to rest, the prow groaning quietly as the lapping of the water rubs it up and down against the ladder. Fenton ties up and holds the ladder tightly with both hands to steady the craft whilst the Captain disembarks. Locke unties Maynard's wrist and they all prepare to climb up after Wakelin.

Reaching the top of the ladder Wakelin peers cautiously over the edge of the quay. He can make out the customs shed, but two men are standing directly in line of their intended approach. Shit. There's a muted conversation going on between them, but the words are indistinct. On and on it goes. They've not noticed Wakelin's presence. For five minutes everything seems to hang suspended, as though frozen in time. Two men on the ladder, arms aching; four in the boat, wondering why nothing is happening. From them not a movement, not a sound, save the gentle groaning of wood on metal. At some point one of the two engaged in conversation pricks up his ear and turned his head in their direction. But his colleague clearly says something to divert his interest and he quickly turns away again. At last their interminable discourse comes to an end and the two stroll off in opposite directions.

Once Wakelin judges they are well out of sight, he clambers up onto the quayside. The others follow silently, staying low and spreading out. At Wakelin's signal, they run, one at a time, to the customs building. Locke re-secures Maynard's wrists and the two follow on behind, the mason jerked forward by the rope

With the others casting their eyes and ears around in every direction to detect danger, Locke, Maynard and Wakelin

353

approach the door of the shed. Locke now has the back of Maynards' collar gripped in his huge fist. As Wakelin looks impatiently into his eyes, Maynard raises his arms to indicate a tile in the roof. As quietly as he can, Locke levers off a handful of tiles, one by one. The glow from the fires in the city is sufficient to show up a white bag thrust some way into the void above the lintel. With a suppressed sigh of relief Wakelin thrusts his hand inside to retrieve the loot.

The eerie silence is rent by an ear-piercing scream.

Chapter 36

For a second or two the group stand frozen, looking helplessly at one another, trying to figure out what has happened. Their confusion's dispelled as Wakelin, face white with pain, struggles desperately to withdraw his arm. Only the Captain himself heard the click of the gin trap's spring, which none of them had glimpsed, placed there to frustrate recovery.

The bag had been laid, like a piece of meat, over the tray of the trap. The jaws had snapped fast around the Captain's wrist. Blood is still spurting from the wounds inflicted by its razor-sharp teeth. The more he pulls at his arm, the more he bleeds, the more he screams. But there's no escape, the trap is chained to the lintel. As if suspended by iron fetters he's held there, his howls of pain momentarily pinning the others to the spot.

At that moment he door of the customs shed opens inwards and several constables spring out, armed with cudgels and blunderbusses. Immediately all but Maynard and Wakelin take flight, running back towards the quayside to escape. Shots ring out. Two of the men fall heavily by the edge. Locke somehow avoids injury and leaps into the boat. But in such haste it's impossible. He fails to land cleanly and the little craft overturns, leaving Fenton and himself helplessly flailing in the water. With pistols and blunderbusses trained upon them, they're forced to climb, drenched and defeated, out of the dock.

Two of the constables disarm Wakelin, shackle his good arm and release his other wrist from the trap. Up to now he has been screaming constantly in agony; as the jaws of the trap are unsprung he faints clean away. By the time he regains consciousness, he and his fellow villains are chained together in a cart, destined for the one lock-up in Bristol that escaped the destruction wrought that day by the rioters.

As the horses' hooves start to trot across the flagstones he regains sufficient strength to hurl foul abuse at Maynard.

'Damn you to hell, you scum, you shit, you bastard. You've crossed me for the last time Maynard, you foul dog. I shall haunt you for this, be certain of it. Live your life in fear, mason. I'll haunt you to your grave and beyond.'

With the Bridewell in ruins and the city gaols still in flames, Wakelin and his gang are taken off to a lock up in Clifton. Their journey is punctuated by a fusillade of shouting and banging on the sides of the prison-wagon in which they're carried away. A vain hope runs amongst them that their wagon might be intercepted by a mob who'll manage to release them. But it's too late at night and too far from any rioting still going on. Those troublemakers who have not been arrested, and who are not insensible with drink, are all standing around Queen Square, watching the greater part of it burn to the ground.

Unwittingly, the Kilbridge Lane villains had actually done Maynard a good turn by trussing him up. The ropes and the gag made it easy for the constables to identify him, sparing him from the violence inflicted on the rest. As the prison wagon clatters out of sight Serjeant Cuthbert, in charge of the constables, returns to the customs shed. Immediately recognising Maynard he frees his wrists and removes the foul tasting rags.

'Well, I must congratulate you Maynard. A job well done. And it all went off pretty much exactly as you suggested. The felons we've taken into custody are all well known to us. We've been trying to track a couple of them down for years. I can tell you now, they're the nub of the Kilbridge Lane gang. It'll be a miracle if they don't all hang. Tonight's little episode will be a considerable feather in my cap and you deserve my hearty thanks for it.'

'I'm well pleased it turned out the way it did', replies Maynard, 'But it was a harrowing experience. And I suspect I'd have been in trouble myself if the criminals hadn't turned up to reclaim their loot. You would have expected me to account for it and I could see in your eyes that my story didn't entirely convince you.'

'Well, you reasoned that out pretty smartly, Maynard. I reckoned your story was pretty far-fetched when you came to me this afternoon. It was only when you took me to the hollow pillar in that footbridge on the Feeder, and showed me the bag you'd hidden, that I started to give it credence. The fact that you've managed to bring those rogues within our grasp is an enormous credit to you. It does a deal to substantiate your version of events. We aim to take Hartnoll shortly and question him alone; I trust his answers will verify the unwitting part you've played in the movement of these goods. He'll have no notion yet of what's occurred here tonight.'

'I hope his answers do clear my name Serjeant. It's decidedly uncomfortable having this cloud of suspicion hovering over me. Despite practically shaking with fear, I was quietly amused when the gang met me by the bridge. If Wakelin had only known that his booty had been secreted there just a few hours previous. I'm sure he would have murdered me on the spot.'

'Quite so, Mr Maynard. Now, despite the fact that I'm almost certain of your innocence, I regret I must treat you as a prisoner for the time being. You'll have to accompany me to our police station at Clifton, where we'll be asking you a lot more questions. But I'll not send you in a prison-wagon, you may ride along unshackled with me. And I'll not be placing you in the cells near to Wakelin and his men. I imagine you would be a dead man if they could get their hands on you.'

Cuthbert is true to his word, but the relentless questioning goes on and on throughout the entire night. Every detail of Maynard's story is queried and checked and queried again. Then it's all written down and read back to him. Between interviews, Maynard's held in a locked room, but at no point is he confined in a cell. At about two o'clock in the morning he hears, through the door of this room, the sounds of outraged protest as Hartnoll is brought in for questioning. Through the wall it's clear the city official is as pompous and indignant as he could possibly be.

By the time Maynard is finally released, the sun is well up. He's completely exhausted by yesterday's adventure and by sheer lack of sleep. But he's also exhilarated. The constables have accepted the fact that he had no part in the crimes, that he was duped by Locke into transporting the loot. His information alone has led to the recovery of the jewellery and to the arrest of the principle perpetrators of the hideous crime at Swinton. Once Wakelin and his associates have been convicted, he's sure to receive the £1,500 reward that's been offered.

The constables are content to let him go, but offer him no transport to his home. He's simply released and walks out through the door, breathing deeply of the fresh air outside. The constables' building is on the main street passing through Clifton village. All around him life continues, oblivious to his own adventures and only vaguely aware of the drama that's been taking place but a few miles away in the heart of the city. Stall holders are yelling out inducements to purchase their wares, people, horses, dogs and carriages are passing up and down the thoroughfare. It all feels so normal Maynard even wonders, for a moment, if the last few days might have been a dream.

He's dog tired and his mind has been jaded by the stress of what's he's been through. He really can't be bothered to collect the Celeste today. He'll leave that in the harbour and get it later in the week. But finding his horse has to be a priority. Without Hermes, the journey back will be impossible for him. So, unwillingly, he has to revisit the floating dock. Thankfully the walls and fortifications have held up to a band of rioters who'd attempted to destroy them. And there is his horse, well fed and well rested.

Astride the animal's back, facing the long ride home and ravenously hungry, he yet again fantasises that the events of the last few days have been entirely imagined.

But he knows for a certainty they weren't. And, with equal certainty, that repercussions will follow. With Locke and Hartnoll on trial, the bridge work will dry up immediately. The money he's recently spent on materials almost certainly will never be repaid. There might be some stone at the site he can to bring back to Swinton, unless it's impounded. And what about his workmates? It's too big a problem to contemplate the way he's feeling just now. But he's sure it'll turn out the same for everybody else, O'Dwyer and the rest, unless he's greatly misinformed. The Serjeant had given him further news about private investment being cancelled as he came to return Maynard's meagre possessions.

In the long run the whole escapade might be good for business. Eventually his name, his trade, his reputation, will be known far and wide. He'll be infamous, especially when the men come to trial. Newspaper reports are be sure to publicise every detail. And the feverish riots in Bristol have clearly left much of the city derelict. That means there'll be an enormous amount of work for which masons will be needed. Who better to bid for those jobs than his own little team? When people connect his name with the heroic deeds they've read about, he could see a lot of business coming his way.

But all that will take a time and before then he could be destitute. He slips out of the saddle painfully at Netham. There's something in the coal bunker at the lock keeper's cottage that he mustn't forget.

On the road again, his tired mind slips back over that last nine months. So much has happened, it seems more like a lifetime than a little under a year. The work on the bridge was a constant worry, but it gave him great hope and satisfaction. A joyful experience and many new friendships. But for winning the job he would never have had come under Lady Sophia's spell. There's something else he's forgotten. The message that arrived just before he left. Is their escapade consigned to history for ever, or is its consequence waiting to confront him as soon as he gets back?

And his poor old father. Was his dedication to the bridge in responsible for the old man's early demise? Should he blame himself? He'll never know.

And the conspiracy in which he'd become caught up. His own part in discovering the plot and bringing the criminals into the arms of the law. His family, and his own men, none of them have any idea about this at all.

'How the devil will I explain all this to them?' he ponders, 'I've got no idea where to start.'

In his reverie, through his tiredness, Hermes has been making the last stage of their journey without his help. Habit and instinct have led him unerringly home. Maynard looks up to find they're nearing the farmyard. He hears a joyful shout and sees Emily running in his direction.

Chapter 38

As the empty dishes are whisked quietly away by a maid, the butler places a port decanter, equally silently, on the table. The room is expensively furnished but still reflects the simple, homely tastes of its new mistress.

Along with her young daughter she retires, leaving the head of the household alone to enjoy his own company. Pushing back his chair, against a resisting pile of thick carpet, he takes a long sip and closes his eyes. He's mentioned it to no one, but today is an anniversary. What a lot has come to pass in the intervening year.

He proved to be correct of course, from the start. The riots completely destroyed the confidence of shareholders in the suspension bridge endeavor. Within a week they'd all announced that any funds they could recover were being immediately withdrawn. Of course, one day it's almost certain to start up again and then .... who knows? But for the time being there's no money in it, it's of little interest to him.

And, as he suspected, it took months for other work of any substance to pick up again. There were insurances to sort out, court hearings to take place, planning committees to be dealt with before a lot of the rebuilding in the city could commence.

But for his foresight and his application, his own business, as he knew it then, would have foundered very shortly thereafter. There was little in his coffers to pay the men he'd invested so much in and trained up to a standard of workmanship that was capable of winning contracts like the chapel and the bridge. Without pay the men would definitely have quit. Why, their real homes weren't even in Swinton; they were paying rent in a village where no other occupation could have been found for them.

Ironically, the mason was due a sizeable reward for his part in apprehending the thieves. But that would only be paid out after a trial successfully convicted them. Which might be some time and couldn't be taken as a certainty.

His only hope had been the document. At first he had no idea what it might be. There was just a feeling in his gut that it had to be important. Thank goodness he'd done what he had.

The most extraordinary thing was that he came across it in the first place. If he'd not put his hand back into the hidden compartment, when he'd discovered the white silk bag, it might still be there today. He'd drawn it out carefully, so as not to tear it on the splinters of wood. A thin wad of vellum, folded in four. But there was a seal somewhere inside, he could feel it. There was no time to investigate then. But because of the seal, and for that reason alone, he'd held onto it rather than throw it into the canal.

Days later, when the euphoria of his adventures had subsided, when the endless questions from his family and friends had started to die away, he'd taken a closer look. It was an official document of sorts, that was for sure. And the text, very neatly drawn up, was partly in English, partly in German. The English section of it was small, it only provided a clue to the whole being some sort of a peace treaty. But what seemed to be in no doubt was the mark on the seal. William IV. The king of England. Whatever this was, it was clearly important. Not an article that ought to be in the hands of an unemployed mason.

His next move had been inspired. He copied out the German words as neatly as he could. It took time and patience, for he was determined to undertake this task secretly, in their bedroom. He didn't want either Mary Ann or Emily to get wind of what he was up to until he was more certain about what it all meant. Having made his copy he journeyed to Bath. One of his oldest clients, he remembered, a man he both liked and trusted, was a fluent German speaker. Handing over his careful transcript he begged the man for a translation.

Some awkward explanations became necessary once the English version of the text was read out by his client. Maynard couldn't pretend that the words had been taken from a newspaper, or had come to him in a vision. So he had to confess that he'd had sight the original and beg the friend to keep his own council until Maynard had dealt honestly with the matter. For it content was unmistakable. A peace treaty between England, France and Hanover, guaranteeing the protection of Belgium.

Back in Swinton, Maynard yet again poured over the original vellum covenant. With an eyeglass he used for examining fine tracery carving he carefully studied the signatures. One of the witnesses to the deed, he noticed, was Ernst Friedrich Herbert, Envoy, Chancery of Hanover.

It was time to take his uncle into his confidence, to ask yet again for his help. This he had done. Somehow, to this day the mason knows not how, his uncle's confidants negotiated a way to get a message to Herr Herbert in London. The next Maynard knew a splendid coach rattled into the farmyard, where it looked outrageously out of place. The three men who descended from it were however in deadly earnest. Once they had satisfied themselves that they'd found the person they sought, Maynard was bundled away immediately and driven to the capital at speed.

No one spoke throughout the journey. Maynard sat in comfort, he was occasionally offered brandy from a flask, and at one point tasty morsels. He felt he'd been kidnapped, but he wasn't being treated as a prisoner. When the conveyance halted to change horses the blinds were drawn and the occupants remained within. Was he a guest or was he a hostage? He had no idea. Treated like a gentleman but with no control over where he was bound.

At St James' palace he was escorted rapidly through a back entrance, opening into the coach-house. Using servant's corridors and narrow stairways his little party eventually emerged into a palatial hall and the doorway to an impressive office. With the greatest of respect he was ushered inside and announced.

There had been just one man within. Herbert himself. The interview had been preemptory. Half a dozen questions that he answered as honestly as he was able. He produced the treaty and handed it over. The envoy tried to hide his emotion, but the mason could tell he was shaking with relief. A small paper package was handed to Maynard in return. He was instructed, most emphatically, to erase the entire incident from his memory. He journeyed back to Swinton in the same manner that he'd been taken.

Up in their bedroom, when the coach had left the yard, when he'd explained things to his wife as well as he could, Maynard tore the wrapping from the package he'd been given. There, in notes, was the sum of one thousand pounds. His mouth had gone dry, his heart pounded. This he'd certainly never expected. But his instinct and his persistence had clearly not been in vain.

From that point onward a fresh confidence had sprung up within him. The weight on his shoulders slipped away. He'd continued to pay his men despite the fact that work was thin. He'd had them carry out a proper repair job at the church, just to stop their hands from becoming idle. The curate, Betts had been overjoyed, having only to purchase the materials required.

Enquiries from prospective customers had started to pick up after a couple of months and the masons were off here and there, taking on a few small jobs. Then there was a long period when Maynard had to attend the assizes in Bristol, almost on a daily basis, giving evidence at the trials of Hartnoll, Locke and the Kilbridge Road felons. The proceedings became infamous, such were the intrigues of murder, contraband and corruption within the city authorities.

At the end they had all been executed, at a mass hanging at the New Gaol. Maynard had agonized for days over whether to go or not. Finally he decided he couldn't bear to see their suffering, despite the cruel manner in which they'd treated him. The sight of men he's met with and dined with, dangling helplessly from the end of a rope, that would likely haunt his dreams for years to come.

He read about it however in the newspapers, which he now bought every day. Reports of Hartnoll's end were the most vivid. His acquaintances within the Corporation were unable, despite valiant efforts, to obtain him a reprieve. And when he finally met the drop his death was an agonizing sight, as he was slowly throttled by the noose.

Maynard was unsurprised that his own name appeared in many of the reports he read. Others were reading them too. Almost immediately people were anxious to engage his business, as much for the prurient curiosity of meeting him as any reputation he's established as a craftsman.

In consequence his enterprise had grown rapidly, at far too fast a pace for him to competently hold onto its reins. So sensibly he and his uncle Samuel combined their two concerns and shared the responsibility of looking after both between them. The Maynards took possession of a splendid town house in Bath, purchased with the reward money won for Wakelin's apprehension. It's the very same house in which Maynard now sits, reminiscing.

Rather than abandon the small holding in Swinton, Maynard offered the accommodation to John Carey who, in return, makes a small business for Maynard from the sheep, the cows and a couple of fields put out to barley.

The mason's fame and a new respect for his business abilities have made it far easier for him to move in circles that were closed to him before. It doesn't seem out of place for him to call occasionally at the Whitefield estate, and he does. And the new baby has been proudly shown to him by Lady Sophia. Could she really be Emily's half-sister? He guesses he'll never know, for he cannot decipher the ambiguous glances Sophia throws in his direction when they meet.

And as for his infidelity, he's certain now he will never tell Mary Ann. He's left it far too late and it would be of no good consequence for either of them.

Smiling ruefully to himself he pours another glass of port.

26148456R00206

Printed in Great Britain
by Amazon